P9-APT-053

The Undiscovered Country

by

Jay and Audrey Walz

DUELL, SLOAN AND PEARCE
New York

First Edition

Library of Congress Catalog Card Number 58-6764

MANUFACTURED IN THE UNITED STATES OF AMERICA

VAN REES PRESS • NEW YORK

All the persons in this book once lived. Many have numerous descendants. The two principals, however, have none in direct line, although at least one latter-day Elisha Kent Kane, named for his collateral ancestor, achieved distinction, as have many members of that gifted family.

There is no confusing the Elisha Kane in these pages with any other. He was the first great American Arctic explorer, and one of the last universal men—physician, scientist, explorer, artist, and a writer of enormous influence who never thought himself a writer. A sea was named for him; he died a national hero so beloved that his funeral train made a progress almost as impressive as Lincoln's; yet few Americans today have ever heard of him.

More of them, in fact, know of the Fox Sisters, the "Original Spirit Rapping Phenomena" whose Hydesville home was removed to Lily Dale, a spiritualist center in Chautauqua County, New York, where it stands a shrine for modern spiritists. Whatever the truth about those enigmatic little girls, their extraordinary talents are on record. The sisters were able, while still children, to persuade many of the country's best minds—literary giants, doctors, jurists, a few churchmen, some scientists, and many members of Congress—to take the rappings seriously. Others bitterly rejected the knockers, on grounds as ridiculous to modern skeptics as the Fox Sisters' claims. The sisters' powers, whatever their nature, failed them in their tragically afflicted later years. They became sad caricatures of their younger selves.

We have not tried to prove ourselves wise after the fact, but simply show the Foxes as they appeared to their contemporaries.

CONTENTS

FOLLOWING DARKNESS

THE VOYAGES

AT ANCHOR

Following Darkness

1. THE ENCOUNTER

THE LITTLE MAN IN THE BIG CARVED BED STIRRED AND CAME SLOWLY awake. In the numbing gray of early dawn his first thought was that old Sir John was dead. In full day, he could put down that fear, but whenever he woke before morning, the pallid half-light, Death's own air, weakened his resistance and convinced him that Sir John Franklin was dead. Not from cold, starvation, or scurvy, but dead of the polar night.

Dr. Elisha Kane denied it publicly, but in this secret light he acknowledged that the whole grinding labor of preparing for another expedition in search of Franklin might be a waste of himself and time, and Elisha Kane had little time. If only he were sure a handful of Franklin's men had survived, with what vigor he could drive himself to his endless tasks! Over the rescue of a half-dozen lost Englishmen, the public would shout itself hoarse, and fame be more surely his than if he discovered his Open Sea. His remote, beautiful, but theoretical sea.

He slid back into sleep to escape the nagging fear that they were all dead, the crews of both Sir John's ships, so suitably named *Erebus* and *Terror*. Out of Erebus, place of nether darkness, he dreamed he saw the Britons plodding, in a long, wavering line under a parahelion of four suns that made a blazing cross in the lifeless sky. One of the sailors stopped and with lips too stiff to speak looked full at the dreamer.

Kane shrieked at him above a wind that did not blow. "Are you alive or dead? Tell me, man, tell me!"

The cracked and bloody lips parted but without a sound, the sailor swayed and fell, and the men plodding on behind passed by as if the prone man were not there. Elisha came full awake.

"There's your answer!" he whispered to the ceiling. Then, sitting up, he rubbed at his numbed legs. His nightmares must be due to faulty circulation. Damn his inadequate heart!

At breakfast he read again the notice in last night's paper, "Miss Margaretta Fox"—only the elder of the notorious Fox Sisters was in town, it appeared—"will hold receptions at Webb's Union Hotel for all persons wishing to investigate spiritual manifestations." The archpriestess of the new cult performed twice daily, mornings and afternoons. In India, in Egypt, he had investigated "manifestations" stranger far than the ridiculous rappings that had made these Fox females the lionesses of the hour. He must compare their charade to some he had witnessed.

What he asked of this wonder-working witch was very little. Let her summon up one phantom from the horde of dead seamen, if Franklin's crews were really lost; better yet, summon up old Sir John himself. *His* rap should shatter the table. So he was on Arch Street, walking toward Webb's, when Mrs. Patterson recognized his quick, bold step.

"Elisha!"

At her hail the little doctor swung in midstride toward the carriage, with a warm smile of greeting for his cousin. The smile did not, she noticed, banish from his eyes the "eagle" look that was no fancy of hers. Others commented on it and young women in their circle shied from Elisha because of it. Intensity could be frightening.

"Cousin Pat." He took her hand and held it. "A bright day, and now that I've seen you, even brighter."

With her, he lost the timidity some mistook for coldness, never suspecting mortal shyness in a young man with such an exotic past and good Philadelphia connections; in a heroic young man who had been nearly to the North Pole.

"I haven't seen you for weeks! You're looking better." Not so fine-drawn as usual, she thought.

"The book is done! I am no longer chained to a desk." He flung out hands freed of invisible shackles.

What had begun as a report on the First Grinnell Expedition in search of the lost Sir John Franklin had grown into a book.

"No one made you write it, Lish," she said.

"And I'm no writer," he agreed. "If, however, I can make people feel the Arctic's fascination, that will help in raising funds for my own expedition. I need more money, Helen."

He yearned for the chilly North as for his homeland. Some lines of Longfellow's reminded her of Ly: "A youth who bore mid snow and ice, A banner with a strange device—"

"And more time than I have. We should sail next April but probably won't." He sounded like a small boy for whom Christmas has been postponed.

Really he was absurdly young for thirty-two, the oldest, but to her the youngest, of the four Kane brothers. The imperial and mustaches he affected didn't conceal his youthfulness. The years had little changed the wayward, stubborn boy she had, as a bride, been drawn to instantly. Lish had as quickly trusted her, showing her some of his most secret "scientific collections." For all his colorful life since, he remained that boy, still a scientist, still small. But none of the Kanes was really tall. They took after the Judge, even Willie, in every other respect a Lieper. But Willie was dead.

Their smiling encounter had made her forget it though Ly wore full mourning, her aunt's coachman had crepe on his hat, and she was on her way in the Kanes' carriage to Willie's future resting place.

Nodding toward the coachman and the bays, she explained, "I'm going with your mother to Laurel Hill again." Aunt Jeannie hovered over the workmen, trying to hurry completion of the Kanes' mausoleum so Willie could rest there.

She couldn't understand it, but then she was quite out of sympathy with the present morbid taste for elaborate funeral trappings. Black crepe draping houses from roof to cellar, funerals grown into monstrous parades, quiet, moss-grown burying grounds into congeries of statuary, she liked none of it. It repelled her that Laurel Hill had become a showplace, displayed to visitors. Knowing Aunt Jeannie's impeccable taste, that Egyptian monstrosity of a vault was totally unexpected.

So had been Willie's death, in the heat of last August, with Ly beside him, Willie, the youngest. "Only a boy," she said, to Ly now, "and never sick. When you were the one we did not think would live."

He let her hand drop, closed his own into a fist, and looked at it. "I do cling to life, don't I?"

"No, you defy Death. That's another thing."

It all began when he was stricken, at seventeen, with rheumatic fever. Judge Kane had brought his first born all the way from Virginia on a litter, nearly dead, but refusing to die. He had spent months in bed, listening to his own noisy heartbeat, his boyish face as grim as a pugilist's.

"Winning that fight was such a triumph," her husband said once, "that Ly has deliberately challenged Death ever since."

"Again and again," she complained aloud.

They had believed him dead or dying so many times, not of his heart trouble, of nothing so commonplace, but of war wounds in Mexico, yellow fever in China, Gold Coast fever in Africa, scurvy in the Arctic. No wonder Aunt Jeannie felt need of a house for her dead. "It's cruel to your mother!"

A passer-by gave Ly a reproving stare. Heavens, she was making a public scene. "I don't mean to scold," she apologized, "but I do wish Sir John Franklin had stayed home with his noble Penelope, so our Elisha could do the same."

Her ladyship! Majestically sending other men to her husband's icy fate.

The coachman shook his head at Ly as if to say, "Ain't that a woman for you!" To men, Ly was a hero.

But did any of them really believe Franklin and his men alive after six—or was it seven now?—Arctic winters? The current morbidity was probably behind the persistent search for men surely dead!

"Cousin Pat," Elisha protested, smiling, "I have no Penelope!"

"More's the pity. A sweet little wife might keep you here."

"A pocket-sized enchantress for little Dr. Kane." He laughed at her. He made a joke of his height, but he also, she thought, enjoyed being a bigger hero than taller men.

"None of your Lady Jane Franklin's, nagging her aging Ulysses into that fatal voyage. Your papa says she did; that they led a cat-and-dog life before he sailed."

"Father's own domestic life is hardly tranquil."

"Why, Elisha, your mother couldn't have a more devoted husband!"

"Nor his children a more Roman father. I was thinking of Tom."

"Oh, Tom!" she said impatiently. His brother, Tom, was given to emotional spasms. First it was the Mormons. Hearing of their miseries on their trek west, he had gone to suffer with them, and got as far as the Iowa country before a nervous affliction sent him home again. Now it was runaway slaves he wept over. He was prominent in Abolitionist councils. The judge had never interfered until Tom went too far.

"Ly, it was outrageous of him to set up an underground railroad station at Rensselaer! On your father's land and your father a Federal judge! Of course Uncle John had to commit Tom." Fortunately the Appellate Court let him out.

"Father did what he felt he must, so did Tom. So do I, though all our courses may be hard on Mother; and on any woman who marries into our difficult if devoted family."

"Several I could name would risk it!" Actually, there was no risk with John. He was so correct, he was really a rather dull young man. And Patterson, her husband's namesake, was so handsome he was quite a catch. "Tom, with all his faults," she said, "will be married by next year. Miss Wood and Bessie have that all arranged."

"Bessie will see to it," Ly agreed. "My artful sister has, however, never tried to make a match for me, knowing half my nights I fall asleep wondering if I'll see morning."

"Bessie thinks no one good enough for the family's genius." She spoke sharply. "You've seen the daylight come for fifteen years, and if you only lived quietly, you could be sure of many more."

He shook his head. "Believe me, Helen, a quiet life would be the death of me."

"All we do is disagree, and on such a nice morning! Let me drop you where you're going."

He backed away abruptly. "No, no, I need the walk. For exercise."

Exercise had been the Judge's unorthodox remedy for his invalid son from the beginning; exercise Ly's excuse ever since for his dangerous life. Why so vehement about it today? Perhaps he didn't want her to know his destination. How odd! He was always frank. Perhaps it wasn't the book that had kept him away for weeks, but a woman, some undesirable or married woman. Someone she knew?

The idea embarrassing her, she quickly said, "Of course, Elisha."

When the carriage had pulled away, she could not resist looking back to spy out his direction. What detestable curiosity! He was turning into a building just west of Third Street. Into that new hotel, Webb's Union Hotel. Their friends stayed at the Girard House.

Why in the world, Ly wondered irritably, hadn't he told Cousin Helen where he was going and offered to take her another time?

The Fox Sisters' séances were quite the rage, and in New York the best people, as they liked to fancy themselves, attended.

Naturally, he wanted to see for himself how this one of the notorious sisters contrived to fool the credulous, as well as some who should have been harder to fool. He was not surprised that the Swedenborgians were taken in by such nonsense, or the phrenologists, or Greeley, Robert Owen, and the other faddists; but that normally sharp, hard-headed men should babble of the witches' power—Helen would hardly suspect him of joining their ranks, a scientist of some standing—

His step faltered. It was his own not his cousin's suspicions that he feared! He was here, almost at Webb's, because of his dream. Dr. Kane, walking complex of inconsistencies, wanted to know what that Englishman had been trying to say, and hoped this Fox woman could tell him.

For your unscientific sins, he commanded himself, do penance by exposing these rappers. Don't fail as you did with that old Hindu.

The old fakir who had given him the cashmere robe he had pulled on this morning, that old man had known more about Elisha Kent Kane from distant Philadelphia than Dr. Kane could rationally explain. He had thought when he read of Dr. Braid's researches that hypnosis might have played its part. Neurohypnosis, Braid called the deep, unconscious sleep that Mesmer long ago seemed to have induced, though Benjamin Franklin, who investigated the Paris doctor thoroughly, had pronounced him a fraud. But it was absurd to associate in any way these upstate New York farm women with his scholarly Hindu, with Mesmer of Paris or Braid of Manchester. The women's trickery would be crude, whichever of them happened to be performing in Philadelphia.

The hotel clerk directed him, with a smirk, to the "Bridal Suite," the very place for Miss Fox, Bride of Endor, gaunt hag with hair like a fox's brush. When he opened the door, he thought the room was empty.

Then he saw a young girl, a child really, reading by the window, the delicate oval of her face framed by dark hair drawn into a low knot. Her dowdy dress was the blue of gentians, and the fringed shadows her long, dark lashes cast on her velvet cheek reminded him again of gentians, the minute ones that nestled in the Arctic moss, the entire plant not as big as his thumbnail, the minuscule flower-lets intensely blue. What a pretty child she was! He had stumbled into the wrong room. As he began to back out, she raised her head. Her eyes were the color of her dress.

Instead of apologizing, he asked, "What are you reading?"

She held up the book to show its title. It was a French grammar. "The verbs are very confusing."

At the sound of voices, a stout old woman came to the door of the inner chamber. "Can we help you?" The child's nurse; Juliet's nurse, too, she could have played.

"I beg your pardon, madam. I have made some mistake. Can you direct me to the rooms where the spirit rapper holds forth?"

"This here's the place," the old one said. "Have a chair."

2. DREAM CHILD

SMILING, he seated himself at the big round table covered to the floor with a velvet cloth that concealed any mechanism the unseen priestess might employ.

At Luxor, he had scrambled into the very lap of Memnon, the famed statue of antiquity that spoke, when struck by the dawn's first rays, in a clamorous, brazen voice. The all-powerful and all-knowing Egyptian priests had undoubtedly secreted within the idol the device which produced its utterance. Terror of them as well as the magnitude of the colossus discouraged the skeptical. Indeed, the mystery had yet to be explained. It was hidden in the knees or the lofty base, Ly believed, and searching for it he had marooned himself on a difficult ledge until his dragoman hauled him down.

In Philadelphia, the investigator was balked not by priestly powers nor weight of stone, but by ordinary politeness. He could not rudely lift that velvet skirt.

The old woman surprised him by her clairvoyance. "Go ahead and look. Just an ordinary table, see?" She pushed back the cloth unceremoniously. "Only extra heavy, so when it starts jerking and dancing, people know it ain't done by human hands."

Nodding, he pushed the cloth aside and underneath discovered nothing but a massive table with a heavy base. There might be a lever beneath that pedestal, but he could see no handle for working it. He took hold of the table's edge and heaved up the ponderous piece. But he was none the wiser, since he could not, while lifting, also examine the pedestal and the carpet beneath it.

"Stronger'n you look," the woman said. "I seen big men couldn't do that. Same time, you appear sickly. Sorrowing," she nodded, "over your loss."

He wore mourning. She was not again reading his mind from his expression. To prevent his dropping further clues, he would not this morning so much as think of Willie. Besides, it was of Franklin's fate that he wished some sign from the unseen sibyl when she appeared.

"Your wife, I reckon, and young, too. Seems a pity when the young go. But they're happier in the spheres of light. When people find that out through the rappings, they're right comforted. Ain't easy for my daughters to give receptions day after day, but it's their mission, my oldest says—that's Mrs. Fish. The spirits ordered it. At first, Fox and I was agin our girls being a public show. But the spirits wouldn't leave us be, so I give in." She breathed a mighty sigh.

So this was Mrs. Fox. Whatever mischief her brood conspired, this chatty old woman could not be in the cabal.

Blandly she read his mind again. Perhaps she really was a sorceress. "When we first come to New York City, Mr. Greeley, he says we should get five dollars off each visitor. But Mrs. Fish told him the spirits ordered my daughters to bring this revelation to rich and poor alike. So we don't ask no more'n a dollar."

Was Mrs. Fish's decision based on noble generosity or the shrewd realization that the poor are more numerous than the rich?

"Will the—a—reception begin soon?" He put down a dollar.

"Usually we wait for a circle." He thought at first she meant a "sphere of light" in her phrase, hovering over the table, but then realized that "circle" in her jargon meant enough customers around the big table to make the receipts worth the rapper's while.

"Nice mornings not many come, and today's right nice. Yesterday was real gloomy, and they crowded in. Better chance of a manifestation that way. Just one spirit you can't expect my daughter to reach for sure," she said, preparing him for disappointment.

He would have liked to answer, "But I may have a small navy of the dead trying to reach me, a hundred and fifty British seamen." That might rouse the child by the window into giving him another glimpse of those blue eyes. She had not, during this entire colloquy, paid any attention to them. Who was she? Mrs. Fish's daughter here as an apprentice in the family trade? She should be in school.

"But I guess she kin try. Put your book by, Maggie, and see if the spirits can help this gentleman."

Disobediently keeping book in hand, the girl rose with sweet grace and, eyes demurely cast down, settled herself beside him. Surreptitiously she continued to study those confusing verbs, not half so confusing to her as her identity to him. She could not be, but clearly was, the notorious Miss Margaretta Fox.

He had opened his mouth to protest this exploitation of a girl of tender age, delicate as the shadowy blue vein in her temple, when the room resounded with a thunderous rapping.

"Goodness, that's a strong signal! Some spirit sure wants you. Put your hands palms down on the table and ask away. Three raps is yes, silence is no."

He spread his hands on the red velvet and thought he felt the table tremble faintly. Then he knew it was himself quivering in schoolboyish excitement because Miss Fox had laid her small white hand alongside his. Their little finger tips just touched.

"Used to be a circle held hands, but some ladies criticized us, so now we just make contact," Mrs. Fox explained.

He felt cheated at not being able to grasp those slender fingers, and angry that any man might, for a dollar, once have enjoyed that liberty. Some men must have come night after night to hold that little hand, or worse, to press her foot under the table. But no, he saw she kept her feet clear of the velvet folds.

He was rapped to attention, the sounds emanating from the wall that partitioned off the inner room. This was not even clever. A confederate behind scenes obviously tapped with a muffled mallet.

"You thinking of someone in particular?"

"No." He would give the conspirators no help.

"Have to use the alphabet cards, I reckon." The old one gave him a reproachful glance. "Takes so much longer."

"I have time." His smile vanished when a roll of raps protested this.

Mrs. Fox took a pack of lettered cards and spread them before the child beside him. They were in no order. There must be some system for signaling. Watching slyly, he saw the little priestess's lips move as her hand floated from card to card. But reading those sweet lips, he realized she was conjugating verbs, while her mother laboriously wrote down the letters the Unseen chose!

"Franklin again," Mrs. Fox announced with a sigh. "In Philadelphia, he's the one we git every time. This new way of communicating is more important than the telegraph, he says—" She was interrupted by a barrage and frowned. "You ain't Benjamin Franklin?" she asked the ceiling.

The spirit was not content to let silence say nay. He entered into a noisy protest and hurriedly Mrs. Fox let him spell out his name. "J-O-H-N F-R-A-N-K-L-I-N. Never head of no John. The old gentleman had a son named William. He told us his troubles with that boy. But no John."

Her credulity made her an invaluable dupe. It was plain someone had recognized the Dr. Kane who lately lectured on the First Grinnell Expedition in search of the lost Sir John Franklin. Here in Philadelphia, in an effort to raise money for a second expedition. Where was the peephole? There was none. Instead, a mirror was so placed in the inner chamber that it reflected his face and probably his whole person when he came in the door.

While the old woman rambled on, the rapper had apparently slipped out the suite's back door and around to the front, which vibrated with a new series of raps. The rapper must be visible to the clerk at the desk, who, for a tip, must keep visitors away during the performance.

Miss Margaretta shivered suddenly. Drawing her hand away from his, she clutched her bare little neck. "Mama, I feel cold!"

This stock line, suitable at any time for indicating the "chill of death" in the room, was nicely apropos today when the spirit purported to be a famed polar explorer. But his "presence" would not please their only customer, a man dedicated to his firm conviction that Franklin was *not* dead. They should have heard Dr. Kane lecture!

How deep was his blue-eyed charmer in this deceit? He was unwilling to conjecture until, with a wise, wicked glance out of the corners of her long eyes, she said, "Cold as an iceberg!"

In body and face she was a lovely child, but that glance was a woman's. A woman whom they had already begun to corrupt. He wanted to take her hand in his, to lead her away from her shoddy existence. She should be freed of this moral squalor and schooled in the noble courses of a gentlewoman. But not too rigidly. He had never been so attracted to Philadelphia's proper young misses as he was to this childish Circe.

Her sly, sidewise glance flicked him again as she slowly laid one hand again beside his while with the other she helped the "spirit" to spell out his message.

Only by the greatest control did he keep himself from catching both her hands in his, from kissing her delicately turned wrists, not hidden as they should be by undersleeves of finest lace. What had come over him? Was there indeed some mesmerism here?

The good woman who was Miss Fox's mother declared fretfully, "All this here Franklin will say is 'Lost! Lost!' Like a lost soul. Makes me uneasy to get that kind. Put me in mind of that nasty reverend in Rochester denouncing my girls for witches. He said the rappings was done by their familiars, meaning demons or lost souls."

The Rochester reverend was not wrong, he decided, as the little witch lowered eyelids like camellia petals to become again a demure schoolgirl. How old was she? The bones that cupped the hollow at the base of her throat were as childish and as bare as her wrists. But she moved with expert grace, and her deportment, if a little affected, was well bred. She had not yet learned to dress her neck and arms, but otherwise, she appeared gentle and modest. He must send her undersleeves with a matching collar to hide that enticing hollow from any oaf who, by paying a dollar, could feast his eyes on Elisha Kane's discovery.

How startled Cousin Patterson would be when she learned where her little doctor had found a small enchantress!

Mrs. Fox thought their elegant gentleman caller was took with some kind of spell. Hearing the raps the first time affected some that way. She could see he was, for all that chin whisker like the French emperor's, a real young man. That was certain. What this rapper was trying to tell him, though, she couldn't for her life make out.

"Does K. C. B. mean anything to you, mister?" she asked him.

"Knight Commander of the Bath."

"What?"

He repeated the mysterious phrase. Maybe it was something to do with the Masons, but where did the bath come in? "I took them for his initials, but he puts them *after* his name."

"Sir John Franklin, K. C. B., is quite correct. The Queen gave him the Order of the Bath."

"Queen Victoria?" Her mouth fell open. "I wouldn't of thought she'd speak of bathing before a gentleman!"

Elisha laughed. *"Honi soit qui mal y pense,"* and thinking to trap the over-clever rapper in the hall, making a fool of this good matron, Ly on quick, light feet jerked open the door. There was no one there. The raps now came from the floor behind his feet, produced, he supposed, by a resonating device. But the problem no longer interested him. He wanted to concentrate entirely on Miss Margaretta's future. What could be done about it? What could *he* do about it? He picked up his coat.

"You going now?"

"I'm afraid I must. But I'll return another day, if I may."

"Glad to have you, Mister—"

He would not entertain either the unseen accomplice or that sweet, deceitful Maggie by giving his name. They obviously knew it. *"Au revoir,"* he told the earnest French student. She conceded him a half-smile in parting, a dimple flickering in one cheek.

In the lobby, however, he made, for science's sake, an attempt to probe. To the clerk he said mendaciously, "The Fox ladies I never met before, but I'm an old friend of Mr. Fish. Is he in?"

"No Fish staying here."

"He allowed the ladies to travel to Philadelphia *alone?"* His disapproval was not entirely feigned. He disliked that child's boarding the cars unescorted, changing to the steamboat at Camden or Taconey, being jostled in omnibuses.

"They ain't alone," the clerk smirked, "with all those spirits on tap." It was a standing joke of his. "Quartet of rowdies was asking smart-aleck questions the other evening, and Mrs. Fox come for help."

Leaving her daughter alone in the bear pit, Ly thought angrily.

"When I went to toss them out"—the clerk drew himself up until he towered a half a head over his listener—"darned if a book didn't fly across the room and hit one bruiser smack in the face! Left so plain a mark you could almost read the title."

"Miss Fox threw a book at him!"

"Not her. It come from where nobody was. Scared those bullies out fast. Miss Fox is used to books flying. Told me her sister sometimes can't sit quiet of an evening because the books on the table by her keep tumbling into her lap. That's Miss Kate. Her Odic Force is powerful. She may join them later, and then we'll have the two Original Spirit Rapping Phenomenons here together."

The clerk sounded like a lecturer in Barnum's Museum. "Odic Force" indeed! Elisha, irritated, plunged out of the hotel.

Walking at a furious pace, he gave vent to the angriest suspicions of Miss Maggie Fox, only to stop at the first flower shop to order a bouquet sent her. There he saw her face in every flower, smelled her fragrance in the moist air, and hardly knew whether he paid the tradesman.

The one flower she was truly like was a camellia, not to be breathed upon lest her velvety bloom shrivel. He must urge her mother to transplant her out of the dirt of notoriety. The woman had expressed some discontent with her daughter's way of life. Perhaps he could play upon this feeling. There was also the shrewd Mrs. Fish who would probably be unwilling to turn Miss Fox loose. Her young loveliness undoubtedly accounted for the family's peculiar success.

The difficulties in any situation only whetted his determination, and Miss Margaretta, he was determined, should be transported to a better life. "Why?" he suddenly asked himself.

Why? His mind slowly cleared and gave him a cold, preposterous answer.

Against all sense he had pitched into love; fallen at first sight like a stage lover, not the scientist he presumed himself. Miss Fox was the daughter of ignorant parents. She was a girl of small schooling but infinite guile, the creature of an older sister.

The very fact proved her pliability. Away from evil influences, she could be molded into the stuff of his dreams. While he was in the Arctic, her education could begin, her course of study planned not by her family but by him. He would return to just such a wife as he wanted, not an affected Philadelphia miss. If he did not return—she would lose nothing by the arrangement, but in time make a better match than she could now expect. By so much, such a plan was altruistic.

Her world would sniff suspiciously at his motives. His world would scorn her for a little charlatan. Until the thing was accomplished it must be kept secret, but he would need a few confidants. His cousin Patterson he had always loved and trusted. She was the very one to supervise Miss Fox during his absence.

He was developing his plan at his usual headlong speed when his mind and feet came to an abrupt halt. He had no idea whatever of Miss Fox's attitude toward Dr. Elisha Kent Kane. Beyond one sidelong glance, she had scarcely noticed him.

That night no haggard seaman haunted his dreams, but a schoolgirl, sweet and sly at once, whom he guided through a garden maze.

He awoke filled with the simple purpose of seeing her, and attended the Foxes' afternoon séance accompanied by some of his more frivolous friends. They found it a lark and the little priestess charming. Her gentle manner strengthened his resolve to lift her from the muck.

As he was leaving, he said in a grave undertone, "This is no life for you, my child."

She really looked at him then. "I hate it," she whispered.

"Will you drive out with me tomorrow, with my cousin's wife for a chaperone?"

"If my mother lets me." She frowned. "But I don't know your name."

He did not believe that. He had received another message today from Franklin. "I'm afraid you're an artful little fraud!"

She only laughed and swung gracefully away.

The next morning he made an early call on Mrs. Patterson, giving her an amusing account of the séances. "The little rapper, Miss Fox, is only a child, who reminded me of Willie."

"Is she so boyish? Another Rosalind?" So that's why he had gone into Webb's, to see the famous rapper!

"Not at all. Her pallor heightened the resemblance. She looks very fragile, and no wonder, shut up all day without exercise."

She laughed at his naïveté. "Very few women exercise, Elisha! I never walk myself. But perhaps we could take her for a drive. This afternoon, if you'd like. Would she enjoy that?"

"How thoughtful of you, Cousin. I'll send a note around at once." Elated at the success of his maneuver, he fairly dashed it off and did not see the look Mrs. Patterson gave his bent head. Men were so transparent. And her "thoughtfulness" was curiosity again. She wanted very much to meet the notorious girl who had attracted, to what degree she was not yet sure, the family's genius.

3. HONOR BOUND

MAGGIE FOX, the soft oval of her face framed in a modest bonnet, came out of the hotel just as they drew up. She must have been on eager watch. That pleased Ly, though he must tell her a lady waited in her suite for her escort. Until she entered finishing school, he would have to instruct her in such niceties.

Her wrap, while neat and new, had a faintly countrified air that suited her innocence, and it delighted him to the point of actual pain to see three of his rosebuds pinned to her collar, nestling at the curve of her chin.

His cousin found Miss Fox not so much a lovely child as an enigmatic if very young woman with remarkable eyes and a flawless complexion. She displayed an intriguing variety of moods and manners. After some initial timidity she was soon as coolly composed as any matron, only to become in an instant a wide-eyed schoolgirl.

Seeing the close-packed steamboats, merchantmen, and packets along the riverfront, she said, "If I were a man, I'd travel, too, Dr. Kane, but not to the Pole. I hate the cold. Where we used to live the snow came early and stayed late. I'd go to warm countries." She turned her face up to the thin autumn sun, her eyes half-closed, like a kitten's.

Elisha made them open wide over tales of his own travels in hot lands. In India, he had visited the caverned temples of Elephanta, journeyed by palanquin to Ellorah and Dowlatabad. (He did not tell her that perched high in his slow, swaying conveyance he had become as seasick as he always was on shipboard.) He had crossed the Ghauts in all their lushness at Kandalah, and in Ceylon he had hunted tigers.

"You killed a tiger!" Delight and wonder chimed in her voice.

With the help of officers from the British garrison, Ly insisted modestly. He tried to make her see, as he did in memory's eye, the tawny flash of the beast against jungle greenery, and his own pride and revulsion when his shot brought majesty low.

"But he might have killed you!" She shivered a little.

It was not so easily justified, Ly explained. The tiger had not stalked them where they picnicked in a summer palace among the hills or took their nooning under taliput palms. They pursued him!

From the girl's expression, she might have been Desdemona listening to Othello. Mrs. Patterson had never known Ly so eloquent. His reserved politeness to the prettiest usually exasperated her.

The feeble sun was vanquished now by clouds that threatened the first snow of winter. The air gave a moist tingle of warning. "Turn back, Elisha. Miss Fox does not like snow, and I myself do not consider an open carriage the place to enjoy it."

The first flurry brushed them before they reached Arch Street. To Ly's delight, several crystals bedewed Maggie's rosebuds. He had never seen anything so lovely, except Maggie's own face with flakes caught momentarily in her dark lashes and spangling cheeks like damask. Impulsively, he pressed Maggie's hand to his pounding heart.

Its thudding frightened her. "It's beating so! Are you all right, Dr. Kane?"

"Never better!"

At his excited laugh, the girl quickly recovered herself and withdrew her hand with, Mrs. Patterson thought, almost *professional* composure. At the hotel, she was quite the woman of the world as she alighted, made her thanks, and tripped beside Ly into Webb's.

He came out, his eyes so deeply anxious that Mrs. Patterson said at once, "She's very sweet with extraordinary eyes. But so young—" And oddly poised.

"Some say sixteen, but she's probably younger. It might be worth one's while to wait for her to grow up. Educating her, meanwhile, for a better life."

Then his jaw tightened, sharp lines showed on either side of his nose. He was considering how much time he had to waste in waiting. "You may drop as from a pistol shot," the Judge had warned his son from the beginning.

Impulsively Mrs. Patterson patted Ly's hand. What happiness he could snatch she felt him entitled to enjoy. But how would Aunt Jeannie and the Judge take their son's interest in the lovely little knocker? The Judge himself had championed more than one oddity: that musician with one eye and one wig, both fiery; the cockney artist whose productions filled Rensselaer; General Jackson, for that matter. Nevertheless, it might be wise for Elisha to put off presenting Miss Fox to his parents. That bridge he ought not cross at his usual breakneck speed.

With a tired sigh he said, "If it doesn't go against your conscience, Helen, don't say anything to Mother. Just yet."

She was enormously relieved. "Heavens, Ly, you're a man and entitled to keep your own counsel." He might not do it well, he was so used to being frank with his parents.

"Miss Fox's notoriety is bound to distress them," he said a little stiffly, being distressed himself. "Since there's no telling if this will come to anything, there's no point in upsetting them. Not in Mother's present state. Did you know she refuses ever again to live at Rensselaer because Willie died there?"

This was startling news.

"They may build a small house at Willie's Fern Rock of happier memory. Remember our little picnics there?" He could see Maggie in that magical glade, with fern fronds in her hair while she leaned, enigmatic as a Da Vinci madonna, against the big mossy stone.

The Kanes were too intense altogether. Mrs. Patterson was grateful that her husband showed little of the family's violence of feeling.

With that very Kane intensity, Ly said, "I can't cope with Mother right now!"

"I know, dear."

"Instead—I must convince Miss Fox of my love; persuade her parents to consent to her education; work out plans for her schooling. In an impossibly short time. It would be hopeless if I didn't know that her mother and Maggie, too, dislike her present life."

"Then why does she follow it?"

"They are dominated by a strong-willed older sister."

It was a tangle of wills. Elisha would have to best not only Miss Fox's sister but also his own parents someday.

"Did I tell you Miss Fox is trying to teach herself French? Give her a smattering of languages and literature, singing lessons, and piano enough to play her own accompaniments, and she could pass anywhere for a lady!"

"Yes, I think she could."

"Find a school for her, Cousin Pat! If I inquire, it might cause talk."

It might, indeed.

"In time, everyone will forget she was a knocker. Time! Do you realize how little I have? We sail next spring and there's everything to be done. Tomorrow I'll start prodding Mrs. Fox. The day after I must go to Baltimore to give a paper at the Maryland Institute. The day after that—"

"Can't someone read your paper for you?"

"No." He smiled with sudden impishness. "I intend to do it myself to such effect that I'll raise money there for the expedition. As I also hope to do in New York next month. And there's more money to come from my lectures. Did you know I'm to exhibit this live Arctic explorer you see before you? People will pay to hear him! Congressmen will hear him without paying—out of their own pockets. I want an appropriation out of those gentlemen and to get it, I'll have to go to Washington frequently. Whenever will I find time to woo Maggie?"

"Give up the expedition," she urged him. "Stay here and pursue happiness!"

He looked down at her with over-bright eyes. "For the first time I'm tempted. But I've pledged myself both to Lady Franklin and Mr. Grinnell, and as a navy officer I'm detached on that special duty. In ways I can't evade I'm honor bound. But help me to happiness on my return! You're my only hope."

"I promise, Elisha, to do all I can." How strangely willing she was to defy the family! Perhaps because she was related not by blood but by marriage. "Now I'm honor bound, too."

At her words, he kissed both her cheeks, and laughing with a kind of helpless merriment, said, "My falling in love at this juncture is the most lunatic thing I ever did. But this adventure you approve. Aren't you surprised at yourself?"

At herself, yes; at Ly, no. Inevitably, for him falling in love would be another adventure, possibly dangerous, even disastrous, quite unlike the average young man's fancying a not-impossible maiden. Aunt Jeannie should have expected something like this, but Mrs. Patterson doubted she did.

4. THE PEDDLER KNOCKS

WHEN he called at Webb's the next afternoon, Maggie, to his disappointment, was out. "To rap for a lady who's had a death in the family. Some regards our receptions as public entertainments they can't attend in first mourning."

The woman's standing was such he could not object. If such a woman were serious about the rappings, his own mother might next ask for a séance. He loathed the thought.

He's a broody one, Mrs. Fox decided, but he kind of appealed to her. Young, too, for a well-to-do and famous man like Mag said he was. "I'm real sorry you missed her."

Not as sorry as he. Next day he must lecture in Baltimore, and not until Saturday could he see Miss Fox. "When, with your permission," he bowed gravely, "I should like again to take your daughter driving."

"Glad to have you." Her full face beamed at his deference. "Maggie lives too tied down, I always tell Mrs. Fish, for a girl. Didn't know you was a lecturer, too. When my young ones first appeared in public, the committee called it a lecture or else an exhibition."

He winced from the designation which put Maggie in company with a mummified "mermaid" or General Tom Thumb. Only as an afterthought did Mrs. Fox's "too," amuse him. Since he, too, would be performing before audiences curious to see a man who had escaped the polar "maw of jagged ice and ravening snows," who was he to fret at Maggie's situation?

It was simply that he wished his dear child to be everything he was not; never to do as he did, but as he fondly bade her.

He turned earnestly on Mrs. Fox. "You're a good, loving mother. Why did you allow your innocent daughter to become involved in this business?"

He did get such a piercing bright look in his eyes at times. Like the finger of the Lord probing her conscience.

"You just think of Maggie," she said defensively. "I have her and Kate, besides, to worry me. Worried me from the first, I can tell you! Like I said in that statement I swore, it was our misfortune to live in that house at that time."

Not their doing, but the dead peddler's. She must make him see plain what happened in that house at Hydesville, with more misery in it than room. She had trouble aplenty in her life, but never such frightening trouble as came that terrible March.

She never did like Hydesville. Hydesville wasn't any sort of town, only a scattering of houses at a crossroads. But Fox said the land there was good and David lived near, so she agreed. No woman ever had a better son than David. December they moved to the common little wooden house that cramped the four of them. Fox promised he'd build a bigger place when he got round to it but he never had a chance. So she never had a true home, because that peddler wouldn't stay in his grave!

"When was this, Mrs. Fox?"

"December, 1847, we moved there." Question and answer were no more than ripples in the flow of her talk. Children, *babies,* the girls was, plodding through the snow to school, the end to their schooling coming sooner'n they knew. The house had two parlors and fronted south. More she couldn't say for it.

The first months wasn't bad. Fox wasn't drinking, he'd stopped as he swore to, but not drinking made him irritable.

"Never saw a more contrary man. Wouldn't believe his own ears, Fox wouldn't. If he heard same thing as you, he'd declare he heard different."

But he was teetotal. That much she won by living apart from him all those years. "That's why my two youngest is so much younger than my oldest. For once I had all my children round except Leah—Mrs. Fish. She was teaching piano at Rochester. About Fish, the less said the better. Left my Leah when she was only fifteen."

So much for the "Mr. Fish" he had conjured up as Maggie's confederate. How was the thing worked?

From the beginning she had been afraid. March had been wild

and stormy, snow on the ground, and more coming. That night the wind died down, and it was so still she heard the girls' first call.

She went into them, sitting bolt up in bed, eyes like saucers. "Mama, don't you hear it? Listen!"

Seemed like a faint tapping in the wall, but it had to be outside, a tree brushing the house, or a vine rattling. She opened the window and leaned out, knowing there was no tree near and no vine on the bare wood siding of the house. She shut the window, then, and listened again. Faint and regular the taps came, like a prisoner signaling in his cell. Frightened, she hollered for Fox.

Cross at their breaking his sleep, he said it was field mice. "Now you girls quiet down."

Easier said than done, but she finally dropped off. The girls said it kept up all night. Maggie drowsed in school next day and was beat on the knuckles for it, poor child.

The following night the raps woke her all the way in the next room. In their bed, the girls clung together, the covers over their heads. When she put her hand on the bedstead the raps jarred it. But they seemed to come from everywhere, the walls, the floor, the ceiling, where she stood in the dark, yelling for Fox.

"What in tarnation?"

"That's field mice! Tell me a mouse can hammer like that?"

"I do believe you've hit on it," he says. "Shoemaker over the way's working late again."

"Pounding so hard he jars *this* house."

"Have to complain about it," Fox declared. He never did.

It was Maggie ran over next morning and back again breathless. "It's not the shoemaker, Mama. Folks staying in from the cold don't wear out shoe leather, he says. Mama, what *is* it?"

"Little did I know," she said heavily, months and years later, to the handsome young doctor listening quietly. With no warning she burst into tears, ashamed she could not stop, blubbering into his big clean handkerchief. "Times I can't help myself."

"Now, now, it can't have been that bad."

"Worse," she said, and blew her nose.

She must make him understand how worrisome that everlasting tapping was. Night after night she and the girls waited for it to begin, prayed for it to stop. The children grew peaked from being awake all hours, Maggie showing it more than Kate, who was by nature skinny. She never saw a little girl with bigger shadows under her eyes than her Margaretta. Her own rest was so broken she was half-sick.

If Maggie had victimized her devoted mother, Elisha decided coldly, she was a vixen he must put out of mind.

That worst day of all, though, she had felt better in her mind. Friday, it was, last day of March. She made Fox move the children's bed into their room. Just doing something about the noises kind of cheered her. She'd bar the door and stuff rags around to shut out the tapping. David come by and she hoped he'd stay the night. But it was making to storm again and he thought he'd best get home.

About the noises he said, "Now, Mama, don't go complaining to the neighbors. Don't make anything out of it. Because when you find out the cause, it'll be some natural thing."

"Not a ghost?" she whispered. She'd never hinted that to the children, and Fox would have pooh-poohed it.

"Heck, no, Ma! I never saw or heard a ghost."

No more had she. She didn't really believe in haunts. It was that Lucretia Pulver's talk made her wonder. When Lucretia was hired girl in this very house, she'd heard something. Leastways, she said so.

But she'd take her own son's word it was a natural thing. That night, she had turned in at dusk, set in her mind to sleep, the little girls giggling at being in Ma and Pa's room. Fox was still up, fooling around in the kitchen like always. A slower man she never knew.

She was just drifting off, thinking she was giving in to weakness leaving the lamp on, when a drum roll of raps on the wall by her head made her eyes fly open. No! No! Not tonight!

"Have pity on us, Lord! I am so tired," she said aloud.

The girls were used to the raps now, so they weren't afraid. They laid there trying to imitate the sound by snapping their fingers, but it wasn't anything like. This rapping was dull thuds that shook the table beside her. The lamp wavered, and shadows leaped on the wall.

"Lord, have mercy!" she prayed silently.

Katie, who couldn't snap her fingers good as Maggie, tired of trying. Instead, she said in a shrill little voice, "Mr. Splitfoot, do as I do," and clapped her hands three times.

Right back at her came three raps. They died away into a frightening silence. Mrs. Fox couldn't so much as hear the children breathing. Holding their breaths like her at the notion of the devil himself in there with them.

Maggie wouldn't let her baby sister outdo her. "Now do as *I* do," and struck her hands silently together four times. Her hands were still palm to palm on the last soundless clap when four raps sounded.

"Oh, Mother," she whispered, "it can see as well as hear us!"

5. BURY HIM DEEP

KATIE had tried to comfort her. "Don't you be afraid, Mama." She climbed out of bed and put her thin little arms around her mother. "Tomorrow is April Fools' Day and somebody is fooling us."

But poor little Katie was small help in this trouble. Mrs. Fox had bellowed for Fox loud enough to wake the dead, only it was the dead waking them; or the Devil.

It seemed an age before he come. "Now what?"

"A creature not of this world is making those raps. He answered Katie just now."

"He really did, Pa. Listen!" She lifted her wren-brown head and spoke into space. "Rap once for no, twice for yes. Is somebody there?"

Whatever it was answered with two sharp raps.

"Will you for the Saviour's sake leave my poor family in peace?" she herself had pled, begging a boon of the Unseen. "You don't *see* anything, do you, Katie?" she had whispered.

Katie shook her head, frowning, and leaned forward to listen. The door shook with a single violent rap.

Fox protested, "Here now!" and went to see if the panel was cracked. Not a mark on it. "Don't know as I rightly know what to make of that." For the first time he seemed bothered.

Katie asked the empty air, "Is there something you want us to do?" Back came a barrage of raps, sounding so loud from every corner of the room that Fox thought the house would fall.

"Don't do that!" He shook Katie's shoulder roughly.

"Leave her be! She's only trying to find out what's tormenting us."

Maggie had the coverlet pulled up to her chin to hide her young breasts from the invisible stranger. She squirmed over on her own side to let Katie get back into bed.

"Are you really Mr. Splitfoot?" their baby inquired timidly, not giggling this time. The rapper firmly said "No."

"Could be lying if it is the Devil," Fox warned them.

That brought on such hammering her husband shut right up, and the children flung the covers over their heads again.

"We're getting nowhere," she had said, and sat down heavily on the edge of the bed. "Let me do the asking."

She found out who he was, she told Dr. Kane. "A man murdered in that house and buried right in their cellar. He had come to the door with his pack. A peddler but mighty prosperous, by his telling, murdered for the money on him, five hundred dollars. He was stretching it, don't you reckon?"

The entire story put a greater strain on his credulity than that sum on a peddler's purse, Elisha thought. But the woman appeared to believe all had happened exactly as she said. He was himself without a ready-made explanation of these occurrences, having discarded while she talked first one and then another hypothesis.

The little girls could not have used, in plain sight of their parents, some simple trick, such as bouncing an apple on a string. Since they were unable to snap their fingers, he found it difficult to believe they could snap with *expertise* less easily controlled joints. They might have rigged some sort of mechanical noisemaker in their room. As a boy he had devised maddening gadgets. But the Fox cubs' contrivance should have been exposed when their bed was dismantled and moved.

While Mrs. Fox rambled, his own mind darted about a house he had never seen. The jarring movement of the children's bedstead caught his attention. A noisemaker could be concealed in a squat fat bedpost, but the necessary carpentry would be beyond two small girls. Their married brother David, would he have helped torment his trusting mother? But when—and where, for that matter—could he have worked secretly in such small quarters?

Traces of Ly's old rheumatic fever rasped his nerves and pulling at this petty but insoluble problem increased his tension. He should give it up. Admit they were all in the deception, including this open-faced farm wife, who must, in fact, be an artful actress. Looking at her while she talked mournfully on, he could more readily believe her a simple gull than a trickster.

"I told Fox," she continued, "we come there too recent to know the truth about the folks that lived there before. Mrs. Redfield, now, she's been here a spell and she's a candid woman. 'If my husband fetches in a neighbor,' I asked the ghost, 'will you rap for her?' 'Yes,' he raps, 'yes, yes.' Clouds of witnesses he wanted. Well, he got 'em."

Mrs. Redfield, a real hearty person, had come in laughing, certain it was an April Fools' joke, too. Her face sobered when she saw the little girls, pale and red-eyed. "What's going on here? Can't make head nor tail of your pa's story."

They had all babbled at once, Katie bawling like a baby in the midst of it, until Mrs. Redfield said sternly, "Quiet! You girls let your ma talk."

As sensibly as she could, Mrs. Fox told the abuse they had endured. To demonstrate, Katie asked a couple of questions and the raps were loud in answer. That made Mrs. Redfield a little nervy herself, but she kept trying to laugh it off.

"I'll give your ghost a test. Mr. Splitfoot," she had copied Katie's name for him. "What's my real age?"

When he made her older than anyone would have thought, Mrs. Redfield said, "My own husband don't know it but the rapper's right. May be true about his being murdered. I want Charlie to hear."

That brought on such a thunder of raps, she had said, "I don't know how you folks can live here!" and hurried out.

She brought back not just Charlie Redfield but all the neighbors she could round up. Mrs. Fox was ashamed there wasn't chairs enough. Good thing they didn't everybody come in. The uneasy ones hung around outside. People fishing in the creek heard something strange was up, and they came running over, too. By now the girls were shoved into a corner, while Fox, as man of the house, took over. He asked the first question and when the rapper answered, a burst of talk broke out. Couldn't hear herself think.

They shushed while Fox helped the peddler tell about his murder again. The dead man gave more facts this time. They had sent their hired girl away for the night—was that Lucretia Pulver?—and cut his throat while he slept. He left a widow and five children.

"Pitiful!" Mrs. Redfield said.

"Who had done it?" They named people who had lived in the house and got a single rap every time. By now they worked it out with the ghost it would be less confusing if three raps was "yes" and one was "no." All the while everybody was trying not to look at William Duesler who lived there a spell with his father.

Will finally got the courage to ask, "Did my father or I ever—injure you?" He just couldn't say "murder you." Almost choked on the words as it was. A pin dropping would have made a clatter while they waited for the answer. None came. Not a rap.

"What does that mean?"

Will shook his head dumbly. Clearing his throat, he said, "Father and I never hurt anyone. Anybody remember who else has lived here? Before the Bells?"

At the name an uproar of rapping rattled the room.

"The Bells! Did we forget them? Hard-faced people."

Maybe their Hydesville neighbors hadn't cottoned to the Bells, but their friends and relatives other places were up in arms at the story, soon spread far and wide, that the Bells were murderers.

"I never knew them," Mrs. Fox told the doctor, "and never had no cause to do them hurt. It was the peddler accused them, not us, but a gang of their friends came after us at David's farm once. Wanted to burn my girls alive."

An infuriated mob of natives had attacked Ly and his companions in the Philippines after his descent into the volcano. Their god dwelt there and they considered his act sacrilegious. So he knew the horror of facing a bestial, blood-lusting mob. That two small girls should have suffered such an experience appalled him.

"Mrs. Fox," he said sternly, "you should have taken those children away from there. That first night."

"I did! They was both sickening from excitement, so Mrs. Redfield and me wrapped them in quilts and carried them to her house. I didn't go back, neither, until the noises stopped."

Ah. "They stopped when you and the girls left?"

"Not then. I heard after, Charlie Redfield went down cellar to find where the peddler was buried— It was in the written statements they all swore to."

One by one the women had gone fearfully home, their menfolk staying on to get to the bottom of this. "If we locate the body, that'll settle it," Charlie Redfield said. He and the rapper agreed between them the rapper would signify the exact place, and Charlie had picked up a candle and started down. Duesler would call from upstairs whether Redfield was getting hot or cold as he moved, stooping, around the musty little earthen cellar.

"A braver man than I am," Will Duesler acknowledged.

At intervals Duesler would ask the peddler, "Is he getting near?" or "Anywheres close?" or "That the place?" and get only silence for an answer.

Once Fox said, "Maybe he's gone" and was reproved with a roll of raps.

"Is he there yet?" Duesler was patient and kept on asking.

"Must be inching around down there." Fox stirred restlessly. "Taking so long you'd think that cellar was almighty big."

"Sh-ush!"

"There?"

"YES-YES-YES."

"Char-lie! You got it! Don't move!"

They all tumbled down the narrow ladder into the basement where Redfield stood staring uneasily at the ground under his feet. Carefully they staked out the spot. They would dig in the morning, not a man of them feeling up to it then. Too dead beat.

"What about Fox here? Can't leave him alone."

"We can bed him down at our house."

"No. I gotta look after my property." That dead peddler might knock the place down unless John Fox stood guard.

The bravest and most curious of them, Redfield, kept him company. "The Fox girls is in my bed anyways."

Early next day the men had commenced to dig. They spent hours at it, while a few silent observers, backed as far away as possible, jumped whenever spade hit buried stick or stone.

"Put him down pretty deep," Redfield said, straightening the crick out of his back.

Overhead the house itself lay wrapped in silence. The dead man, satisfied by their investigation, never knocked once all the time the men dug, the spadefuls of earth falling with rhythmic thuds. Nothing yet. Nothing. Nothing now but–

–water.

"Drat!" Their spades slopped up mud.

"Been a wet season." More mud. The sides of the grave they had dug began to fall in. "No use, boys."

Moving slowly with disappointment, they scraped their spades clean and went home. That night, with the house crowded, the rapping began.

"With none of you there?" the Doctor asked her.

"Only Fox. Madder'n hops he was, Redfield said, when the racket started up. John never did like the gawping crowds."

The one constant factor at Hydesville had been Fox himself, Fox the apparently skeptical, Fox the unconvinced grumbler. For purposes of dispelling suspicion, of compelling conviction, the role was cleverly chosen, Ly decided.

"Next day, Sunday," Mrs. Fox talked on, "folks come from miles around, more'n three hundred. Fox said we was getting to be a holy show. Came stamping over to fuss at me like it was my fault. The whole of Sunday the peddler didn't rap, some saying on the Lord's Day the Devil was powerless. Those that went away let down at not hearing nothing started the witchcraft story, it's my opinion, to have something to talk about. Sunday night David and his wife slept in the house nice as you please."

Because Fox wasn't there, Ly noted. His child was the dupe of the one person she should naturally obey, her father. Dear, obedient little Maggie!

"Monday seemed safe to move back, and my heart filled up that afternoon when I heard Katie singing away. You don't rightly know how sweet peace is till it's gone. That Monday was the last real peace I've known. Because Tuesday the peddler started up again."

"And Fox was at last"—at long and shrewd last—"convinced?"

"Not him. Told you he was contrary. He waited for a dry spell and then down he went to dig again. When he didn't find no body, he said whatever caused the rappings, he had no proof it was a ghost, and until he got proof, he'd have no truck with rapping. Wouldn't come to Rochester or New York neither, not Fox."

A rational man whom he had maligned, Ly conceded, and bowed apology to the absent Fox.

"An unnatural father!" Mrs. Fox denounced her husband.

Who might, Elisha thought hopefully, prove his ally.

6. FOX IN ERMINE

"MANY PEOPLE," Dr. Kane told her sternly, "would call you an unnatural mother in exposing two young, innocent—" This was unfair. Not Maggie's innocence but her precocious coquetry had attracted him— "girls to the lewdities of any rowdy. Worse is the morbid effect of constant association with the bereaved. How can your daughters flower into happy womanhood in the dank air of the tomb?"

"I was against it in the beginning, like I told you."

"You should be against it now. Make up to them for all that your weakness has cost them. Send them back to school!"

"Mr. Greeley's been at me about Kate, wants her educated."

"What of Maggie?"

"Reckon he thinks she's pretty enough to marry without much schooling. Kate's not so cute, but such a good girl. Mr. Cooper said she was a plain saint who eased his last days."

"Fenimore Cooper?" The truculent, tough-minded man whose books had provided the heroes of Ly's boyhood could not be a follower of these knockers!

But he was. Mrs. Fox, nodding, said, "Come from Cooperstown, with no airs about him. Allus liked Mr. Cooper."

"Miss Maggie must be schooled, too," Ly said firmly, "if she is ever to break completely free of this mesh the little bird is caught in. She must enter some good female academy."

"About that, I don't know, Doctor." Leah'd be against it. Without both the Fox Sisters rapping, they couldn't hardly stay in New York where Leah liked the life. Course, the less Leah liked the idee, the more Maggie would, the two of them everlastingly trying to spite the other.

"When I return from Baltimore," he continued, "I'll bring my cousin, Mrs. Patterson, to call. You'll find her just the person to advise you on a school for Miss Margaretta." He would demonstrate the respectability of his plan to this simple woman by immediately bringing a member of his family into it.

"Real kind of you, Doctor." She twisted his handkerchief uneasily. Ladies' academies cost money and Mag wouldn't be earning none there. "Truth is we can't afford to do more than send her back to her pa to go to country school, and she's kind of old now for fifth grade."

"No, no! She can skip that drudgery. She needs only a little polishing in the social graces, a smattering of lady's learning. As for the cost, my purse is yours."

"Gracious sakes!" Mr. Greeley said he'd pay for educating Kate, but Mr. Greeley was always turning out his pockets to help people. A famous man, but kind of a farmer she felt at home with. So his fussing about Kate hadn't surprised her. But imagine this young doctor wanting to do the same for Maggie. Some people had more money than sense. In Maggie's case, it would be money wasted. Mag wasn't one to apply herself.

"I am not being philanthropic." Elisha held her attention with his most compelling glance. "Say nothing to Miss Fox—"

"I shouldn't?"

"Not yet. But I wish her trained to take her place in society as my wife."

"Your wife!" Knocked her breath out, that did. Dr. Kane's father was a judge, Maggie said, and their carriage elegant. First day, Mrs. Fox had noticed the fur collar on his coat. Leah would have thought him a rich young man up to no good and here he was asking right off for Maggie's hand.

The depth of feeling in his eyes made her fretful. Maggie didn't seem the sort he needed. He looked kind of an invalid, and Mag wasn't inclined to kindness. She mimicked people that cried at the séances, "the snifflers and the bawlers." But she was young. A body has to endure considerable to learn pity. "Just a child!" she complained.

"A sleeping princess whom I want to waken to life." With kisses on that dear, deceitful little mouth! "There's a passion latent in her that must respond to a love as ardent as mine."

"Passion?" She shied from the word. Been little in her own life, not that she wasn't thankful in a way. "Just a child," she repeated dully.

"Has she indicated any interest in me at all?"

She'd come back yesterday smiling like a cat with its fill of cream, admiring, when she took off her bonnet, her own strawberries-and-cream little face in the mirror.

"His heart pounds when he's near me." She posed her head dreamily. "Isn't he handsome, Ma? Not too tall either." She had whirled around the room in the embrace of an imaginary partner.

"Watch yourself, Miss."

"Oh, Mama, don't be like Leah, always spoiling my fun. Because she's jealous, that's what. While we're away from her," the artful puss wheedled, "let's be happy! You want me to, don't you?"

"Flattered at a handsome grownup paying her attention," Mrs. Fox answered. Rich, too, as she couldn't say.

"I don't know much about women," he confessed, laughing, "but that's a beginning surely."

She hadn't meant to encourage him, only to say out of kindness what he wanted to hear.

Before Maggie returned from her rapping, more flowers arrived, creamy white ones, and next morning a fancy box, tied in wide white satin ribbon. It was addressed to Mrs. Fox, together with a note asking permission to present this trifle to her daughter.

Maggie was so excited she was all thumbs untying it, freeing it of fold on fold of tissue paper. "Ma! It's beautiful!"

The "trifle" was an ermine tippet, no whiter than Margaretta's skin, its spots no darker than her hair. For a man who didn't know much about women, Dr. Kane knew what became them.

Maggie whispered, "It's so beautiful I can't believe it's mine."

"You can't take such an expensive gift off a man you barely met, Maggie. Ain't proper."

"Don't be like Leah!" Maggie wailed. "I'll die if I have to give it back. Tell her it's a castoff from the lady I visited today. I'll wear and wear it so it won't look new." Lovingly she stroked its silkiness.

"Quick to lie, ain't you, Miss?

Maggie wasn't listening, but posing again at the mirror. "I never in my life had anything so fine." Her sigh was purest satisfaction. It would take a sterner—and better—mother than her, Mrs. Fox decided, to forbid the poor child such happiness.

To the members of the Maryland Institute, the slight young man many knew so well spoke with his usual magnetism. A few older men felt Kane was almost too fluent for a scientist, but there was no denying he was sound; for his age, remarkably so.

"We have now followed around its entire circuit the circumpolar ice bounding an imperfect circle six thousand miles in circumference. If it were solid, it would constitute an area one third larger than the continent of Europe. But theory suggests this great surface is not continuous. It is a ring surrounding an area of open water, the Iceless Sea. Although generally recognized to exist, I must admit the Open Sea has not yet been established by exploration, but by the well-elaborated inductions of Sabine, Berghaus, and by our own accomplished American hydrographer, Lieutenant Maury, by the observations of Wrangell and Penny and still more lately of Captain Inglefield—"

The first reports of Inglefield's findings had been garbled and he was sick with disappointment, sure the Englishman had reached his Iceless Sea. Only this week he had learned Inglefield did not come close enough to claim discovery. He must sail as soon as feasible next spring, returning to fame and love who had abandoned hope of either.

"—although strongly confirmatory, were limited to a range of vision in no instance exceeding fifty miles, and were subject to all the deceptions of distance."

Compounded by the Arctic's innate fantasy, with light refraction creating on this coast an illusory Thebes, along that a shimmering but forever ruined Rome. Its midnight suns not one but many as if to compensate by trickery for the soul-destroying months of darkness. Did its attraction for him lie in its shifting strangeness, its infinite deceits, much as Maggie, that sweet fraud, excited him more than any honest girl?

"The North Polar Ocean is a great mediterranean—"

They would go to Italy on their honeymoon. He must stop this wandering. But he was not yet accustomed to being in love.

"—draining the northern slopes of three continents, its river systems exceeding those of the Atlantic. . . . With such sources of supply, this surcharged basin must have an outlet."

Not Behring's Straits, nor the sea between Greenland and Norway, as he systematically surveyed it for them, but—

"—Baffin's Bay, and the Hudson and Greenland seas. It is by these avenues that the enormous masses of floating ice, with the deeply immersed bergs and the still deeper belt of colder water, are conveyed outward. Underlying the Gulf Stream, whose waters it is estimated to equal in volume, the vast submerged icy river flows southward to the Caribbean. The United States Coast Survey has, as the Society is aware, developed and confirmed the previously broached idea of a compensating system of polar and tropical currents. The isotherms of Lieutenant Maury point clearly to this conclusion, while the intercommunication of whales between the Atlantic and Pacific proves directly the two oceans are united."

He could give the arguments for the existence of this sea in his sleep; had delivered this lecture more than once in his dreams. He must refer now to Petermann's theory of a movable pole of cold—

"—a movement clearly referable to the summer land currents with their freight of polar ice."

So much for theory. Now for concrete evidences.

"Rain on Christmas Day north of the pole of cold . . . coarse grass and crucifers at latitude 70° . . . in West Lapland barley growing at the same latitude . . ."

White overhead—

"The eider duck, with the brent goose, seen by us in Wellington Channel, the loon and the little auk pass in great flights far to the north, all swimmers that find their food only in open water."

—and under the sea—

"—the whale and the narwhal with its horn like a unicorn's, the seal and that strange marine pachyderm, the tusky walrus, pass in schools toward the Pole. I have seen the white whale moving northward for four successive days through a sea of broken ice.

"So with the quadrupeds of this region. The polar bear ranges farther to the north than we have yet reached; and this informs us there are creatures there upon which this powerful beast must prey. The ruminating animals, whose food is vegetation, obey the same instinct for northern travel. Reindeer have come down in herds to make a 'moving forest of antlers.'

"Before passing from this branch of my subject I must mention that the polar drift ice comes first from the north. The thaw of the ice plain does not commence in our so-called warmer south, but closer to the Pole than we have yet penetrated—"

On the shore of his undiscovered ocean. A creature flitted across the radiant landscape that suddenly possessed his mind. Hummocked ice was twisted into faery forms and captive bergs glittered in the sun. On the ice the lithe little beast skipped and frolicked like a cub. The winter attire of an Eskimo woman made her appear round as a little bear, but her hip-high boots, her pantalets, and parka were not coarse, stinking sealskin. Clothed all in ermine was his little pet, and her eyes were brighter than an Arctic fox's.

He had been, he realized, silent for some seconds. Sweat beaded his forehead at this lapse, which his audience took for a scholarly pause before advancing on another phase of his argument.

"To penetrate this icy annulus, to make the northwest passage to the Pole has been an age-old dream—"

Maggie must not distract him so completely again.

"The question of access to this open sea is now brought before us, not as a problem for scientific inquiry, but as a philanthropic effort appealing to the sympathies of the whole civilized world—the rescue of Sir John Franklin and his men. The British squadron under Sir Edward Belcher presently in the Arctic may do everything; but I am far from sanguine as to their success.

"It is to announce another plan of search that I am before you. . . ."

7. THE PROPOSAL

ELISHA tramped the January slush of Arch Street waiting for Maggie to raise the parlor shades as a signal that this evening's special séance was over and her party of dupes was leaving. But who was he to scorn them? They were comfortable indoors while he moped in the cold and wet, since he could not risk being seen again at the séances.

Their atmosphere stifled him. His deceit of his dear family made him cringe. Yet he lied to his loved ones and had endured the "spirits" day after day for the sight of Maggie's face. Small white hands motionless on the table before her, head bent, she would glance across at him with guileless eyes while she contrived more deviltry! Besides the infernal rappings, the spirits now rang bells and played musical instruments, though Maggie vowed she couldn't read a note.

He no longer attempted, even idly, to discover the mechanics of her performance, but he could not help noting how eagerly her victims provided the facts she needed, and then how awed they were when the "spirits" confirmed what the living had said. It would have been laughable had it not, all too often, been tragic.

A shabby couple in makeshift mourning would inquire timidly if anyone on "the other side" wanted them. They would be told, "Your child is here." Safe assumption: Who had not, with medical science in its present ineffective state, lost at least one child? (He had almost as little faith in his own profession as in Maggie's.) The mourners would respond excitedly to this news, the father exclaiming, "Son!" the mother, "My little one."

By such simple means his wicked Maggie learned all she needed. More than once he had caught an odd, triumphant gleam in her gentian eyes before they were quickly shuttered. He shrank from that look, the worse for being quite unconscious.

When her guests were slack-jawed gullibilities asking to be pleasurably scared, then he could see her trade had its amusing aspects, and he would write her joking comments or else little love notes folded to appear questions for the "spirits." But more often his disgust at the way she preyed on her poor victims made him send her sharp words of reproof. Once he had put into poor doggerel his repugnance.

Weary! Weary is the life
By cold deceit oppressed.

Large, slow tears had rolled from under her smooth eyelids when she read it. But the next afternoon she laughingly nicknamed him "Preacher," because "You are forever sermonizing, Ly."

The window shades stayed obstinately drawn.

Neither by coaxing nor questioning could he draw from her any admission of fraud. Wide-eyed, she insisted it was the "spirits" who rapped or jingled or strummed. Once she had actually gone so far as to urge him to give up his expedition. "You know Sir John is dead, Ly. He told you so that first day. You remember!"

"Maggie!" He had gripped her shoulders so hard she whimpered.

"You're hurting me!"

"Never try to play on *my* credulity. Whatever excuse I give the world for coming here, that must be understood."

Sullenly she lowered her eyes, her little face shut against him. When he left, she still sulked. But the next day she had teased him on the subject. While her mother dozed in the big chair, Maggie tiptoed over to curl up, soft and relaxed as a little cat, in his lap.

"I like your nose, Ly"—she traced its length with a playful finger which he caught and kissed—"even when you look down it at me for believing in the rappings, when you really have more superstitions than me."

"Than I," he corrected absently.

"—than I, Preacher dear. That day in the cemetery—"

That wretchedly unsatisfactory day—

The two blind eyes that were the windows of Maggie's hotel parlor looked at him. He was chilled through. As a doctor he knew this wait in the sloppy cold would aggravate his inflamed joints. But he must see Maggie before he left for New York. She and her mother might rejoin her sisters there before he returned without his hearing from her. It was he who did all the writing, all the planning, all the loving. How had he got himself into this abject state?

There was no escaping it. He learned that when he went to New York to give before the American Geographical Society the same lecture he had delivered in Baltimore. Since Mr. Grinnell was the Society's first president, its invitation could not be declined. It was also time he spent a few days with his generous friend, Grinnell, whom he had been neglecting disgracefully. In New York, he found himself abnormally restless. First every hour, then every minute without Maggie became a torment.

His yearning prompted him to take a party of friends to one of Kate's "receptions," thinking she would remind him at least a little of his love. Kate, however, was nothing like her: a tall, awkward child, her plain countenance lighted by large gray eyes that showed a mystic's inward gaze, her light brown hair in long braids to her waist.

Her performance, too, had been as surprising. The spirits rapped out Greek and Latin tags beyond his own meager learning. Medical Latin, the jargon of his profession, he knew, but not Horace or Anacreon. Where, then, had this child— New York gossiped that Kate, when she had rapped in Greeley's house for Jenny Lind, answered sensibly questions the singer put in Swedish. How, in heaven's name?

Now in his wintry pacing he turned so sharply that the slush spattered his trousers leg. He slapped it off with a handkerchief and, straightening, thought he saw someone tug at last at the near blind. But no, it had simply wavered before a barrage of raps.

Kate had put her hand in his. "If you are a friend of Mama's and Maggie's, Dr. Kane, you must be mine, too." She radiated simple goodness, and was worth a dozen of his sweet cheat, Maggie.

But it was Maggie he had proposed to that day on the way to the cemetery. That was settled. Not his own father, not Leah Fish herself, could prevent it. The rest of the Fox family he had misjudged, but about Mrs. Fish he had been right. Full-busted, high-colored with an empty smile and hard eyes, to her their "mission" meant money and public attention. What her mother had written about him had aroused her mean suspicions.

Smiling her mechanical smile, she had said, "My sister's life and yours, Dr. Kane, are poles apart." Her smile broadened at her stupid joke and then vanished. "I trust you are not distracting Margaretta from her duty."

He bowed stiffly. "I have little time to distract anyone, Mrs.—ah—Fish, since I am busy preparing for my expedition to the Arctic next spring, in search of Sir John Franklin."

She raised heavy brows. "Of his remains, you mean? He spoke to you from the spirit world, I believe."

"You may believe it, madam, but I do not."

"Then why do you attend my sister's receptions for persons honestly seeking enlightenment?"

Young Grinnell was with his party and stood in earshot. Had Maggie's lover wished, he was in no position to tell this woman the true reason. It annoyed him, too, that Mrs. Fish's height forced him to look up to her.

"As a scientist, with a doctor's knowledge of anatomy," he said sharply, "I am trying to determine how the rappings are produced."

Maggie had told him Mrs. Fish was infuriated when a committee of doctors reported that the girls snapped the bones of their feet to produce the knocks. "So the spirits to protect us began ringing bells, too," Maggie had declared.

The woman's stare hardened. "I *thought* you were only amusing yourself."

He left New York that night in a fever of anxiety. He must reach Maggie and make his intentions clear before Mrs. Fish charged him with admitting he only entertained himself at Webb's.

The next afternoon, saying Mrs. Patterson had asked to be picked up later, he got Maggie alone in a closed carriage and began instantly to propose, though he seemed never to get to the point.

"You know you have been a godsend to me, my own lovely child, taking Willie's place in my heart. I cannot bear to see your delicacy every day outraged in your present tawdry existence."

"It *is* tiresome, Lish." Sighing, she leaned her head on his shoulder.

"Dearest pet, let me take you away from all this, efface the very memory of your miserable past!"

Under his chin, her head nodded happy agreement.

"My cousin will select an academy for you, where you can be educated to take your place in a different sphere—not a ridiculous sphere of light, but a sphere of life and love. Would you like that?"

"Yes, Ly." She rested contentedly against him.

"When you are thus changed, Maggie, I shall be proud to make you my wife," he said solemnly, twisting around to look into her dreaming eyes.

"Yes, Ly," she answered too passively, too easily.

"Don't answer me now, my darling. Make no promise until you understand how sacred, how binding it must be. Plighting your troth is a solemn surrender of yourself, heart, soul, and life to another. Forever, Maggie."

In his case "forever" might not be so very long. He drew a deep breath and continued more calmly. "You must not engage yourself to be my wife unless you can sacrifice for me all other hopes and dreams."

"But I can, Ly. I do, I swear."

Words would never rouse her. He pulled her to him and with despairing ardor rubbed his rough beard against her velvet cheek, and pushed her bonnet back to kiss her forehead, her eyelids, and, last, her childish little mouth.

"Goodness, Ly, I'll look a sight for Mrs. Patterson." Composedly she straightened herself, tucking her hair neatly under her bonnet, smoothing her ruffled tippet.

"Oh, Maggie! Maggie!" He buried his face in his hands to hide from her the hopelessness in it.

She put her hand on his bowed head. "Whatever is the matter? Ain't we engaged?"

They were indeed, and the carriage, it appeared, had been standing some minutes before Mrs. Patterson's door.

That tactful creature noted his distrait air, but said not a word beyond her usual friendly greeting. She did protest, however, when he directed Francis to Laurel Hill.

"Can't we celebrate your return to us more cheerfully?"

"Miss Fox has never seen the Kane mausoleum," he answered absently. If he could not yet take his betrothed to his family's house, then the family's tomb must substitute. Maggie must put foot today on some part of her future estate.

At the entrance to Laurel Hill Maggie did not see a little step in the path. She stumbled and would have fallen had he not been quick to catch her.

"I would not for the world have had that happen," he had told her somberly. "It's a bad omen. Like a bride's tripping on the threshold of her new home."

"Don't be so superstitious, Lish," Maggie chided. "Isn't he silly?" She and Mrs. Patterson laughed together.

"Elisha," Cousin Pat declared, "is a most inconsistent and absurd young man, behaving more absurdly than usual because he's in love."

Now, days later, Dr. Kane could hear her pleasant voice pronouncing him absurd. Never more so than at this instant. But young he was not, and it would be his death to wait any longer for that chit, Maggie, to beckon. Ready to shake her until her cloud of hair tumbled around her shoulders, he stumped off on numbed feet.

Once in New York, however, absence made his heart forgive and grow fonder, if possible. His first errand took him to Stewart's to order the latest in traveling bonnets sent to her. That done, he could settle down to his tasks for the expedition. He had written her he was at Delmonico's, but no letter came. He did not expect one.

8. IS THIS THE FACE?

AT THE Brooklyn Navy Yard, in the shadow of a big line-of-battle ship, rode his little hermaphrodite brig, the *Advance,* half-hidden by a projecting wharf. Not his really, but Grinnell's, an inconsequential item in that magnate's fleet of ships. She was so very small. Kane felt, as on first sight of her long ago, that he could straddle from her main hatch to her bulwarks. But Frobisher and Baffin had achieved fame in ships not half her size; nor boasting half her virtues.

On the First Grinnell Expedition she had responded gallantly to the most reckless tactics, and, sturdy as she was responsive, had withstood the worst concussions of hummocking ice.

"An ice storm," he told Mr. Grinnell where they stood beside the little vessel, "combines the horrors of tempest, explosion, and earthquake. With the impact of floe on floe, tables of white marble are thrust into the air by invisible machinery. They pile up under a ship's bows; crash against her hull with frightful force; heave her right out of the water."

"She weathered it well."

"A few scars."

"On her iron stripping." Mr. Grinnell only tolerated iron. "But the oak in her double hull is sound as ever."

A brig within a brig, his stout *Advance,* her outer sheathing of two-and-a-half-inch oak covered with a second of the same wood.

"Built to haul machinery so they put the best British oak into her," Mr. Grinnell said, not for the first time.

Nevertheless, the Navy had improved materially on her original structure in fitting her out for her first Arctic effort. Forward, from keelson to deck, she had been made a mass of solid timber, clamped and dovetailed, for seven feet from the cutwater. She could spare a foot or two of her bows without springing a leak. To keep the ice from forcing her sides, she had extra beams running athwart her length at intervals of four feet. Her very deck was doubled with a packing of tarred felt between, and her entire interior lined with cork for protection against condensing moisture, bane of Arctic existence. Her strips of heavy sheet iron extended from bows to beam as a shield against the cuts new ice could make in the hardest wood. Some of these plates the mechanics were busy replacing.

"The Fair Augusta needs touching up." Ly smiled at their figurehead, a little blue-gowned girl whose pink cheeks sun and salt spray had faded. He sometimes imagined she resembled his dear, wicked little Maggie, who had not yet written, not one hasty word. Idly Kane began to sketch the Fair Augusta while he and Grinnell watched the workmen.

After some minutes Grinnell, glancing at the drawing, said, "Mrs. Grinnell declares Augusta is your only love, but she really isn't the beauty you've made her."

To his shock, Ly saw he had drawn a living, breathing vignette of Maggie. So much for his ability to keep his secret. As calmly as he could he answered, "She is, sir, in the eye of this beholder," and by an effort let this evidence of his infatuation stay carelessly in view.

Fortunately, the Navy Yard commandant himself came up just then with a letter for Dr. Kane. To Ly's pleased surprise it was from Henry Brooks, great oak of a man and boatswain on the *Advance* during the first expedition. Brooks, now serving on board the *Macedonian,* had heard Dr. Kane planned another search for Sir John Franklin.

"Wants to join us," Ly told Grinnell. "He was Captain De Haven's second officer, you remember. If I get him, I'll make him my first." He could not resist handing the letter to Grinnell to read, particularly one passage:

> *I don't know any man I would sooner sail under. As I was with you in the first expedition, I would like to be with you on the second.*

"That's quite a tribute," Grinnell said.

"It makes me proud, coming from such a man. I'll ask Kennedy to assign him to me, if it's possible. The Secretary of the Navy has really done everything to help."

"I expect so," Grinnell agreed dryly. "Kennedy assured me he would stretch his authority wherever possible in your behalf."

With the small *Advance* and big Brooks he would have such a pair of stalwarts that Kane wanted to shout with pleasure. He had been, the first voyage, highly flattered by Brooks's friendship. When De Haven's expedition had been stuck fast for months in a great ice floe the size of Washington Square, riding like a shanty on a raft before wild gales, Dr. Kane drove all the crew to exercise, as an anti-scorbutic. On his own scrambles over the ice Brooks was his constant companion and Brooks's broad back his easel for sketching. Once they had flown kites (built with clumsy, cold-stiffened fingers) in a gale that howled like the dog chorus of outer Constantinople. Frolicsome as schoolboys, they had not looked the part, their rough beards framing faces pasty white after sunless months, their grips so feeble the kites almost pulled away.

The boatswain seemed to share Ly's scientific need to find cause for any puzzling phenomenon. Or else he had tagged along to keep curiosity from killing Kane. One afternoon in January the temperature had risen by four o'clock to twenty-four below and the moonlight was intense. Far off Kane could hear a sound like surf. He had clambered over the side to track it down, Brooks at his heels.

On they plodded, to be brought up short by a noise like a quarry blast. There followed the clatter of broken glass from the area they had traversed. Again a burst was heard, while a dark smokelike vapor rose up in the moonlight from the same quarter. Retracing their steps, they found no sign of a rift in the ice, but next day that section of the floe was quite gone. He might have led Brooks to his death, but the boatswain was still willing to follow Elisha Kane!

If only he could get Morton as well! A great contrast to Henry Brooks was Morton: shrewd, observant, with no considerable bodily strength or dignity, but wiry tough, and an excellent hospital steward. That first voyage Morton apparently decided before the *Advance* reached its first Arctic halt that his chief patient would be the ship's own surgeon. Kane had been perpetually seasick, and crippled by a flare-up of his demon rheumatism. His heart behaved so badly he slept sitting up. Thus Morton would find him mornings.

Soon the steward was seldom far from his side, perhaps on orders from their captain.

Ly thought nothing of his own condition, sure it must improve shortly. But it worried De Haven. When they encountered in Disco harbor an admiralty transport about to sail for England, De Haven suggested his surgeon go with it.

"You can certify yourself as unfit."

"Is that a command, sir?"

De Haven had studied Kane's face. "A recommendation."

"Sir, I understand my own case better than any other doctor." Ly paused to imply "or any layman." "Now we've reached calmer waters, I'll be done with *mal de mer*. As for my chronic affliction, I have a theory that it benefits from extreme northern latitudes. Will you allow me to experiment on myself?"

The brawny De Haven looked down at him, puzzled by the "invalid" Kane. He said heavily, "I can't stop you."

Within a fortnight Dr. Kane was fit for the hardest duty, and for months the busiest, and, physically, the ablest man aboard. His major crisis as a surgeon had been De Haven's nearly fatal attack of scurvy. The big man's old wounds opened and suppurated. He was delirious for days. Only his determination kept him alive. Today he understood the "ailing" doctor better.

But Kane could not have pulled him and his other cases through without Morton. He appeared faithfully every morning carrying a tin basin of water, mushlike with snow. In this mixture, with the aid of a hard towel, Ly rubbed his stiffened body into pliability or, on his worst days, Morton did. Morton could keep him going. From wherever he was in the Navy, he must be borrowed.

Riding back to Grinnell's for dinner, the magnate waited while Ly stopped in a music store on lower Broadway to buy some new songs for his mother.

"It is my father's dearest joy to have my mother sing for him as she did in their courting days." As Maggie would one day sing for her Elisha.

"The Judge told me of his very charming romance."

A sheet of popular music displayed in the shop stopped Ly in his tracks. On the cover of a cheap twopenny song entitled "Haunted Ground" was Maggie's madonna-like face. Lest there be any doubt as to her identity, underneath was printed "Margaretta."

He was a weak fool to be caught in the midst of his grave purposes by a childish Circe whose name was a byword.

Sternly he put Maggie out of mind to labor late every night on memorials to Congress, letters to influential politicians, to scientific societies, to generous friends such as George Peabody. To all he made clear his need of funds, since his was not officially a Navy expedition. Only Peabody responded.

Early every morning he got his racked body onto a horse and the horse onto a ferry for the journey to the Navy Yard. Or he rode to a brickyard to inspect a kiln for making his own pemmican, or to a factory to look at patented stoves. At the gunsmith's he could not order the guns he wanted, until he had more funds. (In the end, he might have to borrow them, and he hated to borrow a gun. A weapon should be a man's own, an extension of his right arm.)

Then a prolonged snowstorm halted work on the *Advance* and curtailed his rides. He did paper work until he was sick of it. The third night of the big snow the soft flakes fluttering at his window seemed to beckon him out into the night and onto Broadway where a winter carnival had burst out. He could hear the music of the sleigh bells calling him. Besides, he needed the exercise.

On the street where the Snow Queen held sway, by torch or lantern light, sleighs of all sorts dashed merrily along. Broadway's omnibuses were replaced by vast open sleigh stages filled with pink-cheeked passengers laughing at everything—at the conductor scrambling around on his projecting wooden shelf to collect the fares; at the luckless males whose tall beaver hats fell before the snowballs of sidewalk urchins; at the lucky males into whose laps pretty female passengers were sometimes tumbled. The very babes were on runners, ensconced in carriage sleighs.

He remembered the snow caught on Maggie's long, shadowy lashes the day of their first drive together. How she would sparkle in this scene, her warmth turning the snow on her face to dew! She would be spangled with light, snuggling beside him in a smart Albany cutter as they flew through this gay hubbub.

Full of longing for her, he turned with a sigh toward his hotel, picking up a newspaper from a boy who stopped stacking snowballs in a pyramid only long enough to attend him. In his room, when

Ly was finally settled in his robe, toddy in hand, from the close-packed ink-dark pages of the *Herald* the word "RAPPERS" leaped at him.

A poor, miserable printer had cut his throat with a knife used to correct proof. The coroner's jury ruled he had done so, "while deranged as a direct result of attending circles at Mrs. Fish's on Seventh Avenue." The dead man left a widow and one orphan. There had been another child. When it died, its father, the widow testified, "frequented circles at Mrs. Fish's. Each person was supposed to pay a dollar each night of meeting. My husband was not able to, so she let him in without paying. She sometimes does."

It gratifies that woman's sense of power over her dupes to dispense this "charity," Ly decided angrily. Maggie, too, he had caught enjoying the headiness of the séances, particularly when she had celebrated idiots under her spell. He deluded himself if he thought she would give up such delights for his sake.

"The jury recommended," he read further, "that the Grand Jury take action to suppress meetings at this and other houses named in the testimony."

There were worse shocks to come. Bennett, in a scathing editorial, questioned the great dead being "habitual confidants of an obscene female in one of our streets." He did not think Grand Jury action was needed. The police could simply arrest the knockers now as "loose, idle, and disorderly persons," and put an end once and for all to such tragedies as this suicide.

In brief, Maggie might, on her return to New York, be hauled up with prostitutes and other low creatures and he be helpless to protect her. He had got himself in this miserable situation by his love for a notorious, sly little girl who cared so little for him she had not bothered to write.

Well, he would write! He thrust to one side of his desk the accumulation that littered it and began his farewell letter to his love. In words of cold regret he told of his humiliation at seeing her face on a twopenny song cover; of his outrage at reading that her sister had been charged publicly with criminal culpability in a suicide; of his scorn of her profession which might lead to her being arrested as a disorderly person, and which had already allowed her to be labeled "obscene," in print. Harshly he wrote, to convince not Maggie but himself this must be the end:

"You are not worthy of a permanent regard from me. You could never lift yourself up to my thoughts and my objects; *I* could never bring myself *down* to yours. This is speaking plainly to my dear little friend who sometimes thinks she loves me more than a friend."

Too seldom to justify his foolish hopes. Only a love powerful as his could impel Maggie to a new life. Her passive affection was not enough. *She* would not suffer over parting.

"Maggie, darling, don't care for me any more. I am sold to a different destiny. Just as you have your wearisome round of daily money-making, I have my own sad vanities to pursue. Remember, then, as a sort of dream, that Dr. Kane of the Arctic Seas loved Maggie Fox of the Spirit Rappings."

He buried his face in his arms. He would not weaken, but he must see her just once more, hold her camellia face between his palms and kiss her baby-soft mouth good-by.

"I will leave shortly for New Brunswick and go by coach to Trenton so that I can be with you at one o'clock on Sunday."

Sunday at Webb's, a saddened Margaretta came slowly out of the inner room. Her lids were swollen from weeping and her lips trembled as she put out a pale hand.

"Maggie darling!" She had suffered at the thought of parting. His every nerve and muscle came joyously alive. Maggie loved him!

"My little bird! Forgive me, dearest pet, and love me. Oh, love me to the end!"

"Ly, I'll work hard, I swear, learning to be a good wife to you. Mama don't believe it, but I will."

Each of them, Mrs. Fox thought, talking to himself, not hearing the other. It would be funny if it were a laughing matter, as it wasn't. She was sore afraid when she thought of facing Leah. The doctor didn't know yet, but back they went to New York tomorrow. Business in Philadelphia hadn't been brisk.

When they left the somnolent red-brick town Maggie wore Ly's ring. He brought her three to choose from. She selected a diamond set in black enamel; gloomy-looking, her mother said, but Maggie had seen one like it on Mrs. Patterson, her only sure model of gentility.

9. DO AS I BID YOU

MRS. PATTERSON soon learned that the best schools accepted pupils only from the best families, and the second best were hardly more lenient. At one such, when she had confided Maggie's identity to the headmistress, the woman asked, "The Spirit Rapper?"

"Only you would know."

"For the first week—with luck. The modern young woman is not," the headmistress continued, "the timorous doe that masculine poets portray. She is a ferret who would dig out the truth and mischievously inform her parents. Unless Miss Fox rapped as the price of secrecy. That *would* demoralize discipline."

"She intends to adjure the spirits."

"Ah, but will they adjure her? No, I can't risk it."

Mrs. Patterson would continue her search, she promised Ly. "But —your Maggie's schooling has been interrupted for so long, she'll be far behind the other girls. Wouldn't a governess be better? Have you thought of Lizzie Turner? And her mother, Susannah Turner, an exemplary woman, teaches music."

"Should I know them?"

"Turner is that Scotch farmer near your Aunt Lieper's. The daughter's as homely as sin but an excellent schoolmistress. Maggie would have her own piano and pets, with Aunt Lieper to check her progress."

Her plan seemed too well thought out for sudden inspiration. "You haven't talked to Aunt Lieper?"

"Dear, no! But she's putty in your hands, as we all are."

"Except Mother, and she'd tell Mother at once." His mother's brother's wife was not always tactful with her sister-in-law.

"No, she'd enjoy keeping the secret. At least until you've sailed. And when you return, Aunt Jeannie will be so grateful to have you back, she'll allow you anything you wish."

Ly was not so sanguine. "Try a few other establishments before we consider the Turners. What shall I bring you from New York?"

In New York next morning, he dispatched a dozen pairs of French kid gloves to her. Usually he enjoyed selecting feminine fripperies, but not today. He had awakened depressed and stayed so. Why, when he was to meet his love after weeks of separation? Perhaps it was the grim January weather. Under a dun gray sky, the city's once-lovely blanket of snow looked like a dirty sheet on a slattern's bed. As he gave the address to the cabby he knew he really suffered a morbid fear of being seen "at Mrs. Fish's on Seventh Avenue." If only he could meet Maggie elsewhere!

Maggie was not there. Mrs. Fish opened the door. "Come in, Doctor. I want a word with you."

In the parlor, she pivoted to face him. The thick draperies so shut out the feeble light that he could hardly distinguish her heavy features.

"Dr. Kane, Maggie's always been nervous. So Ma spoiled her until Mag thinks she's quite the lady. She returned from Philadelphia worse than ever, wrought up, refusing to take part in our receptions—"

His dear child was obeying his injunctions!

"—until forced to. Now she says she's going off to some female academy, with you paying the cost. Why, I don't know, or maybe I do."

The cheap cynicism of the semi-literate kept this woman from believing in simple kindness. Ignoring her vile insinuation, he said, "I think Maggie worthy of a better life and will help her to achieve it at my own expense."

"Better life!" Scorn rang in her voice. "God has made us the chosen ones to bring revelation to the bereaved." She swooped down from this height to ask, "How is my sister to support herself once you've turned her into a butterfly?"

"In any good academy, Maggie will be trained to occupy, with womanly grace, any station in society." Then to placate the Gorgon, he stated his intentions. "When I return from the Arctic, I hope to make her my wife."

"If that's so, why didn't Maggie meet your parents in Philadelphia?"

His own sense of guilt made him flush, but he said with a glibness that appalled him, "My mother is in full mourning, so I introduced

Miss Fox to my cousin, Mrs. Patterson, instead. She accompanied us on all our drives."

"I'm relieved to hear it. Maybe Maggie's reputation isn't gone."

"Not yet." He should not antagonize her, but she drove him to it. "Not until her miserable profession causes her to be denounced in a police court. Before that happens, I hope to see her in a more wholesome environment."

"I wouldn't give that for your hopes." She snapped her fingers. "Because Mag ain't going to any academy. I forbid it."

"You are not, fortunately, her guardian. I have your mother's promise that Maggie will be freed from a life she detests."

"Ma made such a promise?" Her voice rang stridently. "She's just a simple farmer's wife not used to"—her voice cracked and she paused to control herself—"your sort. But you don't fool me. This is all a ruse to get Mag away from the protection of her family. Well, it won't work!"

At the words a chorus of approving raps burst out. Mrs. Fish threw back her head, her teeth menacing in the dusky room.

He waited until it was quiet and then took out his purse. "If you'll tell me your charge for a private séance, I'll leave the money in the hall, together with a card for Miss Fox."

"You—"

Her face mottled with rage, her breath short, she appeared on the verge of apoplexy. As a doctor, he should attend her, but he moved toward the hall. To his relief, Mrs. Fox and dear little Kate, her nose reddened by the wind, came in.

"Dr. Kane!" Mrs. Fox's face expressed guileless surprise. "I declare I didn't know you was in town."

"Didn't Miss Maggie get my letters?" He had written the day and the hour of his arrival in at least three notes to his love.

"She didn't say. Kate, did Maggie get the doctor's letters?"

Kate shook her head, eyes wide. Mutely she warned her mother not to say anything. There was only silence in the parlor, but Kate sensed her sister's presence.

He quickly scribbled on a card, "Little bird, I *must* see you!" and thrust the message into Kate's muff. A second card he dropped on the tray to deceive Mrs. Fish, saying aloud, "I'll return for the afternoon meeting when Miss Fox will surely be here."

Mrs. Fox followed him to the stoop. "Been trouble. Mag and Leah ain't speaking. I pray for help."

"You poor woman," he said gently, and ran down the steps, feeling he fled some loathsome place.

Arriving for the afternoon "circle," unsmiling he paid his dollar into Mrs. Fish's own hand. She could say nothing before the crowd. Several there expressed pleasure at Miss Maggie's return. Margaretta smiled with effort but her performance was easy and brilliant. When she had the faithful goggling at a hand bell that moved around the room, apparently without benefit of living hands, Ly scribbled "a question for the spirits," and passed it to her.

> To teach the Tigress not to interfere with our correspondence, follow me out. I will wait at the next cross street.

He had barely reached his waiting cab when Maggie came running to him, a thin shawl around her shoulders, her little slippered feet drenched with slush. He wrapped her in his coat and told his cabby, "Drive anywhere."

When her teeth stopped chattering, she said, "I couldn't go upstairs for a wrap or she'd have beaten me to the front door. Oh, she'll be in a state, our Leah will!" She laughed gleefully.

"Maggie, look at me!" He must impose his will on this irresponsible child or they were lost.

Eyes wickedly bright met his.

"You must refuse to rap for her, refuse absolutely. She is using your beauty to attract men to her house. If she can't use you, she'll let you go."

"It isn't my face, Ly, truly, it's Kate's and my powers. Leah's raps aren't nearly so strong, and the bells won't ring for her. Now Kate's doing automatic writing, and Leah's frantic jealous, but people think it's wonderful so she has to let Kate do it."

"Maggie, don't babble that nonsense about 'powers' to me. You *know* the spirits have nothing to do with it."

"Perhaps not." She bent her head. "Ly—"

Was she about to confess her fraud? He waited, curiously unwilling to learn the truth. Could he conceal it, even for his love's sake, when it might save the sanity of hundreds, the very lives of others?

She said, however, "Then what causes the rappings? I don't understand that German professor's talk of Odic Force, but it's something strange." She frowned in sweet perplexity.

"It may be," he conceded. Her eyes widened in surprise. "Have I told you my peculiar power," he asked, "revealed to me by a fakir in India, a wise old man?"

"No." She studied him warily.

"He told me, long ago, when I want the true answer to a question, I should think intensely about it for a few moments and then to hold my hand up to the light of day. If it appeared almost transparent, the answer was 'true'; if dark and heavy, 'false.' "

"Elisha, you're teasing me!"

"No!" He would scorn to read his future in patterns of sand or tea leaves, in the fall of stars or of cards, by any familiar method, but illogically he believed the Hindu.

"Does Maggie love me?" he whispered, and closed his eyes to will with all his power that her affection for him would grow every day enduring and ardent.

"Look!" He raised his hand to the small window of the carriage and his fingers glowed. With a joyful cry he clapped her face between his hands, thrust his fingers into her hair, kissed her eyelids, her temples, her soft mouth.

"Elisha, stop!" She was excited but frightened, too, with reason. "Do take me back."

Instantly he directed his driver to Seventh Avenue. "Dearest pet, forgive me."

She patted his hand in an absurdly motherly gesture. "You do confuse me, Ly. Are all men so changeable, first scientific and then superstitious, one time stern and preachy, the next—" She couldn't give a name to his recent display, but smiled shyly up at him. At her most artless, she was most captivating.

"I warned you I was an inconsistent creature. I'll demonstrate it again. I am forever lecturing my child on proper deportment. Now I want you to do what no lady should: meet a gentleman clandestinely. Maggie darling, I must see you away from that house! Where can we meet secretly? Before I leave for Washington."

"I don't know—"

"Bring Kate for a chaperone," he urged. They were nearly there.

"I'll work out some arrangement and write you, signing a name that woman won't recognize. What shall I call myself?"

"Cousin," Maggie said, thinking of Mrs. Patterson whom Ly admired so. "Sign your note 'Cousin Peter.' "

"Dearest Coz!" In a sterner voice he commanded, "Meanwhile, don't rap. Not ever again."

"I can't stop yet, Ly." She looked nervously out the window. "Leah said Kate and her didn't intend to keep me in idleness. Besides, you're not the only one that's going to Washington. Kate and I have been invited to rap for practically the whole Congress. I could see you there," she concluded softly, "far from Leah."

"When?"

"In February."

"But I'll have left by then and be lecturing in Boston!"

"We may not go until the middle of the month."

He expected to return to the capital in March. He would arrange to go toward the end of February. Then he and Maggie could have an idyllic time away from his family and the worst member of hers. In Washington with its spate of notables who would notice them? He sighed happily at the prospect of a little love and peace at once.

Down the street he could see the Foxes' clients straggling out of that notorious house. He kissed her cheek, but did not help her out of the cab. Instead, he sat well back, hidden from prying eyes.

For two weeks his official duties kept him from New York and Maggie, but "Cousin Peter" wrote several times urging her to begin walking out regularly with Kate, so that one day she could, while on a "routine" airing, meet him without arousing the Tigress. Late in January, he detailed another plan in a last-minute letter.

"Maggie, do you know Satler's Cosmoramas on Broadway near Twelfth Street on the right-hand side going down? If you and Kate will walk past it at exactly four o'clock on Saturday afternoon, I will be there. The cosmoramas are a sort of picture gallery, visited by the best ladies. If you and Kate do not like to walk past—"

For all their youth, some brute might take them for "cruisers."

"—go into the picture room and amuse yourselves looking at the paintings until you see me. You have to pay twenty-five cents' admission, so don't forget your purse. I will bring a supply of *pocket handkerchiefs.*"

Maggie was so responsive to artificial emotion, the paintings depicting sad incidents might move her to tears, as the true tragedies of her victims never did.

A note from her awaited him at Delmonico's. Politely she declined to meet him. If he called at her home, however, she would be happy to go out with him "as I have no other engagements during the day." Alone or with Mrs. Fish as chaperone? Had Leah dictated the message? He tried another tack. Again Maggie declined. She had learned only too well her lessons in deportment. But this time she gave as an excuse an appointment at her dressmaker's. She was acquiring, he smiled to see, the art of the ladylike hint. So he promised to send a carriage to take her there where he would meet her. For the afternoon he wrote out a most formal invitation.

"Give my compliments to your mother and tell her that with her permission I should like you and Kate to devote the rest of the day to a fine ride with your friend."

After a rush of appointments, speeches, dinners, he deserved a holiday. He had not averaged four hours' sleep a night for weeks.

At the dressmaker's, when that furbelowed female left the room and Kate was bent over a tray of trimmings, Maggie kissed him with such fervor that it made up for the rectitude of her behavior. The strange mixture in her of child and woman, of simplicity and cunning, of passionate impulse and extreme self-control would forever entrance him.

10. THE LIGHT OF LOVE

HUDDLED under a throw, Kane lay on the sofa in his Boston hotel room, listening to his heart rattle. It racketed worse than usual, his fever having flared up. At tonight's lecture, would that organ be audible to the first three rows? Making him sound the automaton he felt, a marvelous talking machine whose engine wheezed and pounded. He wondered if he were becoming lightheaded.

That would never do for Boston. He had been afraid no sound Bostonian would pay to hear him over such rival attractions as Emerson, Blitz, and Alboni, but he was every night astonished by the size of his audience and its aggregate age.

Only a few youthful faces punctuated the rows of solemn-visaged matrons and wistful old men. The old men made him feel they longed to go with him to a climate even colder than New England's. To the city's famous bluestockings, a live Arctic explorer who was also a scientist allowed them to crane at a curiosity the while they improved their minds. Besides, they associated him with the noblest of living women, Lady Jane Franklin, and asked, their eyes moist, what he had heard lately from that heroic wife.

How horrified they would be to learn the woman he wanted most to hear from was the notorious little Spirit Rapper, Miss Margaretta Fox! Well, he had heard today. The longed-for letter lay where he had dropped it beside his couch. Angrily he crumpled it into a tight ball. Small comfort his fickle girl gave him.

At least he now knew, after sending three telegrams, a set of Honiton lace, another of French work, and five letters, that Miss Fox had arrived at Mrs. Sullivan's boardinghouse in Washington. She, in turn, knew he was alone and ill in Boston. What had she written him? Not one of her stilted schoolgirlish notes, all milk-and-water affection, but an account of her life in Washington, calculated to torment him.

Her reception the evening before had been attended, she reported, by several officers from the diplomatic corps. Those glittering ornaments of capital society came not to hear orphic utterances but to ogle the little sibyl.

"I believe they took me for the 'spirit,' for they stared at me so incessantly I nearly fainted!"

He could picture her distress: eyes modestly cast down while she blushed most becomingly; a rosy flush that set off her flower-petal skin and cloud-dark hair. The gentlemen saw through this affectation of shyness. One of them loudly asked if Miss Fox had not attended last night's ball.

"I swear," he said to his friend in a *voce* not at all *sotto,* "I saw her there looking almost as lovely as she does today."

"When I replied I was not at the ball, he said if the enchanting creature he saw there was not myself, it must certainly have been my apparition. He was a Frenchman," Maggie concluded.

Austrian, Pole, or Hungarian, it made no difference. Washington boasted an infinity of braided and shakoed dandies, ready to flirt with Maggie during the fortnight before he would arrive. And Maggie— He must write Kate, urge her to keep a little fire in the ashes of his memory. But it was no use. If he doubted Maggie's fidelity for two weeks, how could he trust her to wait faithfully for a year—or longer—if the *Advance* were trapped in Arctic ice?

Stiff as the robot he imagined himself, he hobbled to the lamp and turned up the wick. Slowly he raised his hand, and holding it palm outward before the sputtering flame, closed his gritty, burning eyelids while he asked if his true love would be true. He waited, his breath rasping. Then, reluctantly, he opened his eyes and saw his spreading fingers silhouetted as blackly against the light as if he wore a mourning glove.

Dressing for his lecture, he derided the idiocy of his hopes. Once and for all he would give Maggie up, but the very instant he swore it, he yearned to feel the tendrils of her hair on his cheek, her warm mouth under his. He could not abandon her, not now, not ever.

As he climbed down from the Baltimore cars and took a cab to Mrs. Sullivan's, Ly felt, as always, that he had arrived not at his country's capital but at a pretentious village straggling across the landscape, the forever-unrealized dream of Brother Jonathan, rural megalomaniac. The Capitol Building, as it had been since his boyhood, was still unfinished, and the Washington Monument stood a stump far from its apex. Houses were always abuilding along the avenues, big and bigger hotels going up, with nothing, official or private, ever completed.

He nodded to two acquaintances, hoping neither noticed he was passing the National Hotel where he usually stayed. But he must, with whatever impropriety, be as near Maggie as possible. As his coach turned off Thirteenth Street onto F, he saw a line of carriages drawn up before Mrs. Sullivan's. The Fox Sisters were conducting a well-attended "circle" and he was greeted at the door by the detestable raps.

A bevy of boarders leaned over the stair rail, listening for any sound from the tightly closed parlor. A heavy-set woman with a hairy mole on her chin greeted him.

"I'm Mrs. Sullivan and you'll be Dr. Kane." She yelled for a black boy to carry his bags, and as they started up, a reedy young man by the newel post called the rappings "Humbug! Pure humbug!"

Mrs. Sullivan stopped and turned. "And who're you, pray, Mr. Swisher? The gentlemen in there"—with a broad sweep of arm she gestured toward her barricaded parlor—"are important government officials two little innocents could fool that easily, though they can't take in Mr. Swisher, a copyist at the War Department, hired not for his brain but for writing a brave hand."

A young woman tittered and Mr. Swisher flushed to his wispy side whiskers. Kane wanted to defend the fellow's skepticism but dared not antagonize his landlady. He must insinuate himself into her good graces, win the freedom of her house. While she made sure his fire was laid and his bed and towels in order, Mrs. Sullivan talked darkly on.

"The things those children tell you no mortal man could know. Me departed husband named for me his village in the ould country when not a soul as wasn't born there ever heard of the pitiful place."

But a letter from one of the deceased's Irish relatives could have been left on the hall table for sharp young eyes to see.

Mrs. Sullivan was saying, "It was himself sure, that told me the name he cut on the tombstone which he finished one day and was gone the next."

"He was a monument maker?" If so, this was an only too hideously suitable abode for the Fox Sisters.

"My late husband kindly obliged with beautiful gravestones, though his work for the government's buildings paid more. He had that soft a heart!" She started out, but halted to add, "Miss Maggie's been waiting like a cat on hot coals for you and it's sorry she is there's a most important séance this night with John C. Calhoun. Himself set the time at seven sharp."

Ly almost said, "But Calhoun is dead!" when he remembered that in her book the quick and the dead could set appointments.

"The wonderful old fire-eater looked like one of the great apes his last days in the Senate, speaking not a word, with his black eyes staring out of sockets like pits and white hair all over his face. To think he's been rapping like thunder in me own parlor these four days, ringing bells and playing the guitar like the angel he is now."

Extraordinary behavior for Calhoun, but no odder, Ly supposed, than Caesar stopping a hole to keep the wind away.

"Tonight he swore to write a message in his own hand for Governor Tallmadge. Heaven help Miss Maggie if she's not there to receive him. Pull the house down, he would. So don't be delaying her!"

Kane agree not to trifle with so majestic a shade, and in a rustle of voluminous skirts Mrs. Sullivan left him. He pulled off his outer garments, loosened his cravat, and shed his shoes. Then, exhausted from the jolts and jars, the foul air of the railroad, he threw himself across the bed to rest before he saw Maggie. Tomorrow he would take up his official duties. Tonight was for his dear.

He awoke to find her kneeling beside him moistening his shirt front with her tears. "That cruel letter you wrote, Ly, after you looked at your hand. How can you be so mean? Your letter made me take on so, Mama and Katie didn't know what to do. I thought I had lost you forever!" Her wail was music to his ears.

The sadder her plaint the happier he grew. Sleepily he nuzzled her fragrant hair, encircled with a possessive hand her slender throat, and in a smiling voice said, "I'm not lost, darling pet, but right at hand, for days and days of happiness together! No more tears for you or black moods for me, but a lovely secret time."

At Webb's, he once lectured her for taking him into the back room of the Foxes' suite because it contained a bed. "A lady," he had told her sternly, "never conducts any gentleman, not her husband, son, or doctor, into her bedroom. Never!"

"You're my doctor, Ly!" she had said, laughing.

Now, how badly he practiced what he preached! His love had come into his bedroom, and he did not order her away, but, staying in bed, drew her closer and closer until she lay beside him, his passionate child.

The former senator from New York, former governor of Wisconsin who might have been president in Tyler's place had he not declined to run with Harrison on the Whig ticket, waited nervously in Mrs. Sullivan's parlor. He regretted again, as he often had before, that the rappings had not developed the year he made his fatal decision. The spirits could have told him General Harrison would die. But that was past, and tonight an incalculable future lay before him.

He jerked down the waistcoat that persisted in climbing his broad frontal expanse, and realized he had faced the hazards of national politics and frontier office more calmly than tonight's séance. He must control himself. Drawing up to his full height, he breathed deeply and exhaled sonorously ten times. Then N. P. Tallmadge seated himself, and firmly grasping the chair arms, surveyed the scene of this week's unforgettable events.

Only a boardinghouse parlor, if better furnished than most. Just as the Fox Sisters were only country girls, though more innocent and sensitive than the average. Their rural simplicity the snobs took for ignorance, certain clergymen among them. How quick the clergy were to forget that Christianity, too, began among the lowly! In fairness to them, he must admit few ministers had met the young ladies, and the newspaper accounts, indeed the recommendations of his own good friend, Judge Edmonds, had not really prepared him for the Fox Sisters. Such dewy purity possessed of such divers powers!

How did they endure the strain of their mission? This week of shocks had worn him out. In their innocence was their greatest strength. They did not comprehend their own Odic Force.

But, then, learned scientists were unable to grasp the theory. Or refused to recognize the *od,* that subtle fluid, existing with magnetism and electricity, and found in fire, heat, and the human body.

Produced by the chemical action of respiration, digestion, and decomposition, it issued in the shape of a pale flame, shot with sparks and veiled with smoke, visible only to persons of a peculiar vision.

Open-minded seekers after truth comprehended the idea easily. The *od* was material in nature, he reminded himself, but invisible just as certain sounds any hound dog can hear are inaudible to men. Easy to understand—for anyone who wasn't a scientist. Those fellows! They had cried "folly" at Fulton's steamboat, "humbug" at Morse's telegraph, and "insanity" at Gray's iron road. Now they scorned the greatest of modern discoveries: spirit communication.

Once it was firmly established—the first firm step taken perhaps tonight—its value to mankind would be incalculable. For sentimentalists such communication meant only that the bereaved had their dear ones restored to them in spirit. For philosophers, however, it had profounder implications. In the happy future the leaders of government, industry, and the arts would enjoy at all times the counsels of the great dead. John C. Calhoun could continue his influence in Congress, an influence purified of its earthly dross, refined by the Eternal Light—

The entrance of Miss Kate and her mother interrupted his flow of thought. As the girl curtsied awkwardly, Mrs. Fox said Miss Maggie would be right down. "Been lagging over her dressing. Primping at such a time." Kate threw her mother a surprised glance.

The governor told the good woman he was pleased at Miss Margaretta's taking pains in robing herself for "this signal occasion. We have yet a few minutes until the hour the great man named," he said, consulting his watch. The hand that held it trembled. To cover this weakness, he threw an easy smile at Miss Kate.

She hung her head in embarrassment, which wasn't like her. The Fox Sisters were usually neither forward nor timid, but quietly assured, a nice balance for girls so young and conspicuously placed to maintain. Their mother was no help. She alternated between talking over-freely and shrinking in fear when the demonstrations became violent. Just as now she was in a fluster over Miss Maggie's delay, turning every second toward the door.

"Don't fret, madam. She'll be punctual."

He hoped this petty incident would not disturb the aural atmosphere. Beyond the closed doors the hall clock began to chime. On its fifth stroke, Maggie opened the door and slipped in, looking prettier than he had yet seen her.

She wore a deep blue grown, with fine lace at her throat and wrists, but the dress did not account for her aura, which heightened every childish charm. Her cheeks were pinker, and her eyes bluer, her small teeth whiter than ever. She fairly shone with happiness. There was clear triumph in the carriage of her head, held high as a flower in first bloom. He did believe, if he concentrated completely, he might actually see the Odic light outlining her trim figure. Certainly she radiated something the blindest scientist must see.

He took her hand and said, made confident by her bright face, "Tonight will be your greatest demonstration, my dear!" No medium had yet brought in a spirit strongly enough for him to write.

"Not mine, sir, nor Katie's, but Senator Calhoun's," she corrected sweetly.

A proper answer. As she took her place at the table, he saw her study from under lowered lids her mother's angry face. Then Maggie, too, hung her head, but not in embarrassment. The naughty girl was hiding a smile. He could not see her mouth, but he glimpsed one dimple. Slowly it faded. The candles flickered, and the flame stretched tall as the silence in which the four of them sat was shattered by a series of impatient raps. John C. Calhoun was there.

11. THE WASTED BRAND

AS LETTER by letter the great man rapped out his forever-honored name, Tallmadge came alert for signs of trickery. So far, in nearly a week of séances, he had detected no untoward movement or hint of strain in the two girls. At times they hardly paid attention, Miss Maggie lost in a daydream or Miss Kate's shining eyes fixed on a far-off shore.

During the months that he and Judge Edmonds had investigated the manifestations, no medium showed such powers as these children —the first chosen instruments of the spirits and still the most sensitive. He learned that his first visit. Was it only last Monday? He had lived a lifetime since!

That private séance Monday was barely begun when an unidentified spirit ordered them away from the center table, large enough to seat ten to a dozen. While he and the Foxes watched, the table glided back and forth across the room. A marble rolling on the floor would hardly have aroused less excitement in the sisters.

Their mother, though, exclaimed, "You ever see the like?"

He admitted he never had. Then the table rolled back into place and slowly one side rose from the floor until the top was sharply canted. Gently it was lowered again.

How much strength would it take to play with that massive-looking piece? He tried to lift it. It refused to budge. Over his shoulder he called to the Foxes, "Help me!"

Obediently they joined in his vain pulling and hauling until Kate mildly suggested, "Best ask the spirits' permission."

Of course. He said aloud, "May I please raise the table?"

"Yes" being rapped, he took a firm hold and lifted it with such unexpected ease he almost fell over backward.

Kate giggled and apologized. "I wasn't laughing at you, sir, but them. They do such funny things!" To her the shades of the dead seemed a crew of practical jokers.

Perhaps she really was laughing at a joke played not by the dead but the living. Well, he'd test them. With no outsider present to see him make an almighty fool of himself, he'd use N. P. Tallmadge for the weight in his experiment, all two hundred pounds of him.

"Can you raise the table entirely from the floor?" he asked the Unseen.

"Yes."

"Will you raise me with it?"

"Yes. Get me the square table."

"Me" he noted; only one joker. "Who are you?"

He as well as Mrs. Fox checked the answering raps. "John C. Calhoun."

That had been a shocker. He had introduced himself to the ladies as a former governor of Wisconsin and a friend of Judge Edmonds of New York. How then had these people, new to Washington, learned his admiration for the dead southerner?

Remembering Calhoun in his last days, his great voice a croaking whisper, his eyes hot coals in his head, the flesh burned off his bones with fever, Tallmadge faltered.

"Get it!" was thumped out angrily.

"Don't vex him!" Mrs. Fox warned. "Fetch that one." She indicated a cherry tea table by the far wall.

It appeared to be sturdy enough to bear him. So he had climbed aboard, sitting cross-legged like an idol on a pedestal. The three Foxes pulled up chairs on the three sides facing him and placed their hands on the table.

It quivered as with an electric shock. Then one side abruptly rose six inches from the floor, as best he could judge. He had to grab the edge to keep from sliding off. More slowly the other side rose until the top leveled off. There he sat, riding the air like a Persian prince on a magic carpet.

The table's elevation forced the little girls to raise their arms to keep their hands in place. As he looked down at them, they reminded him of puppies begging for scraps. He wanted to laugh and cry at once. The spirit, sensing he was closer to hysteria than any sane adult male should be, set the table down.

Before he could clamber to his own two feet, a steady rapping began. "What's he saying?"

Maggie enjoined silence. When the sounds had ceased, she said,

"He commands you to return tomorrow night at this hour, bringing three bells and a guitar."

"What sort of bells?"

"Any sort, so long as we don't see them beforehand. The spirits worked out this system to protect us from false accusations."

"You wouldn't believe the low-down things some people say," Mrs. Fox added.

For Tuesday's séance he picked bells of different sizes, the largest a dinner bell with a brass handle. The guitar he borrowed from the daughter of a Virginia congressman. She had wanted to tune it, but that he hadn't allowed. In its discordant state no human could play sweet music on it.

Maybe the music he heard Tuesday had been in his own addled brain. At Calhoun's bidding he turned a bureau drawer upside down under the cherry table and on it set the bells. The ladies had not touched anything.

That done, they had drawn to the heavy draperies at the windows, and waited interminably. In the quiet he could hear the girls' soft breathing and the candle's sputter. Besides the lighted gas fixture they needed the candlestick, Katie explained, for him to use under the table if he wanted.

With no warning the bells at his feet commenced a slow chime. Soon raps on the walls, the floor, the bureau drawer beat an accompaniment in march time. Gradually the tempo was speeded up until the march was martial and stirring. Just as gradually it slowed down, the raps muffled and solemn, the bells ringing from afar, like church bells tolling a magnificent funeral dirge, fit for a hero. Then all sound died away. He had opened his mouth to ask in a whisper if the ladies, too, heard that ethereal concert, when the bells burst into violent jangling.

A bell pressed his foot, his ankle, his knee, before it was whacked against the underside of the table. The candlestick jumped at the blow. Calhoun rapped, "Take the light and look!"

Terrified, Tallmadge crawled down to obey and found the wood badly dented from a blow, given, he thought, with the heavy brass handle of the dinner bell. The force of it really frightened him. He was ready to rush like a craven from that dreadful room when Calhoun commanded him to lay the guitar on the drawer.

Tallmadge wiped his hands with his handkerchief before he

picked up the instrument. Would he ever be able to return it? Or would it be smashed to splinters?

To reassure him, the gentlest symphony was played on it, now swelling into an angelic chorus, now receding into the distance until it was a song heard across a dark river while stars twinkled overhead. His fear was also receding when he felt a hand press his knee.

The ladies sat with bent heads, their hands clasped as if in prayer. (Not that he could suspect them of so outrageous a liberty.)

In emphatic raps the message came: "It is my hand that touches you and the guitar." The pressure on his knee ceased, a hand brushed the guitar strings, and the dead statesman was gone. Tallmadge also departed, a badly shaken man. To make sure he wasn't hallucinated, he'd bring witnesses tomorrow.

On Wednesday he brought with him two long-time acquaintances of Calhoun, both generals and South Carolinians. One had been Calhoun's friend; the other, General Waddy Thompson, his foe. Or, rather, Calhoun his, simply because Thompson was a Whig, though an ardent nullifier. To Calhoun, eternal Democrat, a Whig was a Whig. He had thrown his enormous influence against Thompson and defeated him. Tallmadge hoped Calhoun's life in the circles of light had softened him, or he might insult Waddy.

Tallmadge had other causes for uneasiness. "You understand, gentlemen, Calhoun may not appear. We can't simply summon him."

Both his guests chuckled. Thompson said, "Take a foolhardy man to *summon* Calhoun. From a conference with the Almighty, providing He is, as the Senator always assumed, a Democrat."

This blasphemy made Tallmadge perspire again, in February. Mopping his forehead, he warned, "Do be serious or the spirits may get out of hand. They once tied six knots in Edmonds' pocket handkerchief."

"Most terrifying thing I ever heard!"

Doggedly Tallmadge warned, "They hung a violin around his neck and beat him in the face with the bow."

"For fiddling while they burned!" The generals laughed uproariously. Thompson continued, "It's my belief the little rappers, if they aren't humbugs, are witches like those wenches in Cuba, calling up the damned with their spells, dancing half-naked, and shrieking like crazy."

"I'll thank you not to insult innocent children by such a comparison," Tallmadge said, stiff with disapproval.

"Look, feller, I meant no disrespect for your new religion nor the young ladies."

More circumspect misses the generals had never met, Tallmadge noted with pride, as the little girls received his guests and seated them at the big table. The pretty ceremony concluded, the air was abruptly rent with raps. Tallmadge had the satisfaction of seeing Thompson jump, then stare transfixed at the table, where the Unseen whacked away, making glass pendants on the lamp jangle.

"I'll get the candlestick again before he topples that fancy lamp. We have to pay all breakage," Mrs. Fox said matter-of-factly, as she lifted the lamp to safety. Katie, her head cocked like a bird's, was listening to the raps.

"We need a Bible, too, not one of ours," she finally reported.

"I have a pocket version." Waddy Thompson fished a worn small copy from the skirts of his coat.

Kate refused to touch it. "Please give it to Governor Tallmadge. He heard what the spirit commanded."

Thompson suddenly asked the empty air, "Who are you?"

He was answered immediately. "John C. Calhoun."

"He commands us," Tallmadge explained, "to turn a drawer upside down under this table and lay the Bible on it."

Both generals, at his insistence, examined the drawer's firmly dovetailed corners and tightly fitted bottom. When Thompson gave it a resounding thump, immediately the Unseen thumped the drawer, and Waddy nearly dropped it.

"You put it in place," Tallmadge ordered, holding the candle while Waddy upturned the drawer under the table and laid the little Bible in the exact center. He was breathing hard when he resumed his seat.

"Have your minds on the spirit of John C. Calhoun."

They bent their heads to concentrate, but were distracted by the spirits beating out "Hail, Columbia," on the backs of their chairs. When the rhythmic tattoo ceased, Calhoun spelled out, "Look!"

Waddy Thompson reached the candle first, and the three men nearly bumped heads scrambling under the table. The little Bible lay open. Keeping the place, they lifted it up.

"The Gospel According to Saint John, Chapters II and III," Thompson told the ladies.

"Ask the spirit what he wishes you to read," Miss Maggie said, eyes wide.

"Do you want us to read Chapter II?"

"No."

"Chapter III?"

"Yes."

In a fairly steady voice, Thompson read the first seven verses, and was halfway through the eighth before a loud "yes," was rapped.

"*'The wind bloweth where it listeth, and thou hearest the sound thereof, but canst not tell whence it cometh, and whither it goeth: so is everyone that is born of the spirit.'*"

A window drapery billowed as his voice fell away. He asked uneasily, "Is that window open?"

Mrs. Fox shook her head.

"Draft somewhere," Waddy said, whistling down the wind.

In the middle of the eleventh verse the raps stopped him. "*'Verily, verily, I say unto thee, We speak that we do know, and testify that we have seen; and ye receive not our witness.'*"

Tallmadge took this for a direct reproof to him who had not accepted Calhoun as witness but had brought in fallible men instead. Because he lacked faith.

That was the dead statesman's final word. When he was gone, Tallmadge almost felt the room clear, as the air does after a thunderstorm. Katie gave a relieved sigh.

On the stoop outside, Waddy Thompson began arguing with himself. "Don't know what to think. Very open and respectable. Girls could be trained magicians, though where they learned in upstate New York I couldn't say. Edmonds saw them there?"

"Three years ago. Just farm children then."

"Barnum couldn't have foisted them on the community?"

"No. Their history was known."

"Prodigies of learning?"

"What are you getting at?"

"Devilish smart to turn to just the right page of the Bible. My Bible at that. Trained magicians and Bible students it ain't human to expect two little girls to be. Thought you were taken in, Tallmadge. Now I've fallen into the same boat!"

So Waddy, too, would go back to that boardinghouse parlor. But not with him. Tomorrow night, Tallmadge vowed, he would go alone to show his trust in the greatest of the lately dead.

In reward for his trust, Calhoun on Thursday tried to write a message. The pencil had broken under his effort.

Angrily Calhoun had rapped, "Power not enough. Meet on Friday precisely at seven. I will write then."

On the paper there were a few jagged marks.

Now the appointed hour had come. Kneeling as solemnly as before an altar, he laid fresh paper and a silver-cased pencil on the drawer. Then in a calm voice he told the revered spirit, "I want your friends to recognize your hand."

"They'll know the writing," the Unseen rapped impatiently. "Have your minds on the spirit of John C. Calhoun."

Afterwards, Tallmadge swore he *heard* the rapid movement of pencil on paper. Then the papers were rustled. Raps like a peal of triumph commanded him to look. He found the sheets of paper under the drawer and somewhat disarranged, the pencil near his feet. For some seconds, he could not read the top sheet:

"I'm with you still.

John C. Calhoun."

There was no mistaking Calhoun's script. Tallmadge yelled for joy and rushed off to Waddy who went with him to the dead senator's own son. The young man stared at the message in his father's well-remembered hand.

"It is his writing, Governor. This is frightening."

Several others agreed the hand was Calhoun's or an excellent forgery. "And, since Tallmadge watched their hands, forged by children holding a pen with their toes!" Waddy snorted down the possibility. "Easier to believe in spirits than in such nonsense."

The news traveled fast over the capital's grapevines. By Monday more than one huddle on the floor of the House was discussing not legislation but the little Fox Sisters. Their séances were more crowded than ever, to Elisha Kane's annoyance. He spent his days pursuing congressmen he must avoid evenings at Mrs. Sullivan's.

12. TO FEED MY FANCY

THE Washington winter, Ly discovered, was worse for him than Boston's. The penetrating damp of the fogmire along the Potomac plagued his bones. He needed Morton but could not get him detached for duty outside of New York. So Ly sent for Francis, the family's second coachman and general handyman, who proved a comfort. He tended Ly gently as a woman, located a presentable carriage and pair for Kane's drives with Maggie, and stirred up chafing-dish suppers for the lovers when the tiresome evening séance was over.

Then Ly's little bird flew to him to nestle her head on his breast, while he held her delicately boned body on his lap in drowsy content. The day's end found him exhausted but happy, as he was now. Lifting Maggie's thin little wrist between thumb and forefinger, he said, "We must plump up my partridge, Francis."

Francis, never looking at the pair ensconced in one chair, said, "That we will, sir. This dish now, maybe she'll eat."

"Sniff that, little one. Doesn't it make you ravenous?"

With closed eyes and smiling mouth, Maggie sniffed and murmured "ravenous."

"For an Irishman, Francis, you cook like a Frenchman."

"There's more Frenchmen in Ireland than census takers find."

But the rarest delicacy left Maggie indifferent, as the champagne did not. When Francis twirled the bottle in its bed of ice, the rustle made Maggie's eyes fly open and her nose wrinkle as though bubbles already tickled her nostrils. When the wine was at last cold and the food hot and Francis stood ready to pop the cork, Maggie's laughter trilled.

"Oh, Ly, I dote on champagne!"

"But you must never, never drink it except in the company of preachers and doctors."

For he was her "preacher," still sermonizing his dear convert; her doctor unable to cure himself of love sickness. Perhaps he should not, in either capacity, encourage her or Kate's taste for champagne, but it seemed to him a harmless beverage, and Maggie's face, a little flushed with wine, was the rose in each thorny day. He wished, he told her, he could live like one Bostonian, who kept a medium in his house.

She lifted her nose from her champagne glass to say severely, "But a great scandal, I should think."

"Not in Boston, where a certain few people can do anything without incurring criticism. It's well known he only visits her twice a day with a long list of questions for the spirits."

"She can't be very pretty."

"Oh, but she is. I was taken to see her—"

"You said you were ill the whole time in Boston!"

"—on one of my better days. In fact, I was strong enough to keep a straight face while she made the chairs dance and the tablecloth twitch"—Katie came in to fetch her sister and he held out one hand to her, while with the other he grasped Maggie's slim fingers, and concluded—"twitch like that." He nodded toward the cloth on their little supper table. Its skirts swayed and jumped erratically.

Maggie stared in horrified astonishment, but Katie, laughing, said, "Do it again, Lish," and again he made "unseen" fingers pluck at the cloth.

"Like all the mysteries of your trade, it has a natural cause. This!" He drew from under the table a crude "tiara" of radiating wires which he had slyly fastened to one knee. "The Boston medium wore such a device around her ankle."

"As you enjoyed discovering," Maggie said coldly.

To feed her jealousy, he drew Kate onto his lap and gave her a sip from his glass. "Now, Katie, you tell *me* Maggie's secret."

"The only one that I know you know, too. She slips up here far oftener than Ma knows. Poor Ma thinks we're both asleep this living minute."

"Tell me how Maggie's cabinet operates."

A relative of Mrs. Sullivan's had that morning been installing the awkward piece. Whatever wires and levers, false walls, or trap doors were built into it would be capital gossip tomorrow, unless his silence was included in his bill.

Ly's speculations about it had distracted him all day from more delicate and exact apparatus, which the Coast Survey Bureau was loaning the expedition. Together with the theodolite and the Barrows dip circle from the Smithsonian and the self-registering barometer from the American Philosophical Society, they would provide him with the best new scientific equipment, whatever else the expedition lacked. But he had not, because of Maggie's cabinet, been in a mood to appreciate his good fortune.

"There's no secret about that, Ly. It's just a cabinet, mine as much as Maggie's. Shut up in there, we can't possibly see the questions written at a circle."

"Or hear them either?"

Katie had confided in him their ability to hear "mental" questions, since most sitters in their concentration unconsciously half-whispered them. Such smothered sounds the sharp-eared little Foxes picked up in the silence of the séance room. General Waddy Thompson, Kate said, actually whispered his queries aloud.

"Surely even there you'll hear Whispering Waddy?"

Maggie, her face pink with annoyance as well as wine, said in a shrew's voice, "He's a famous man, but you think he's a fool to be taken in by such artful frauds as Kate and me!"

"Worse than artful. Unheeding children," he said soberly. Kate on his knee did not stir, but her head drooped on her long, slender neck. "Too young to comprehend the pain you inflict. If I thought you did, I would detest you both."

Kate said gently, "We're always very careful not to let people get too upset."

"You are?" They nodded together. "How can you be careful?" His tone had an edge. "You can't control the spirits' answers. Or can you?" He had caught them out!

There was a momentary silence. Kate's face was turned away from his, but behind Maggie's dark eyes he saw the shutters stealthily drawn. She said lightly, her shrewishness banished, "Oh, we never ask really bad questions."

"Say they're mental, none of Whispering Waddy's, but really inaudible?"

"It's not difficult. When a sitter is wrought up, we don't let the spirits reach them. We're the mediums through which they speak, and if we choose, we can shut them out."

"It makes them angry," Katie declared, "the spirits, I mean.

Sometimes they pinch me hard!" Her countenance as open as the day.

Maggie slid her dress off one delicate shoulder, exposing a lurid bruise. "See where I was hurt last evening. By a willful spirit."

Her smile challenged him. He himself had put that mark on her, but he could not, before Kate, hurl the lie in her teeth. He must punish her for her impudence if ever he hoped to master her. Abruptly he dismissed her, like the schoolgirl she should be.

"Run along now. It's past your bedtime." He set Kate on her feet as Francis ceremoniously opened the door. Maggie left with no farewell word or glance, but Kate kissed him awkwardly.

He and Maggie had agreed, earlier that evening, to drive out next day for dinner. At the appointed hour, a cocky old gentleman answered the parlor door. "Miss Fox is engaged in a private séance."

"Miss Fox had a prior engagement with me."

The old nonentity resembled several congressmen. "The young woman's time is not her own, y'know. The spirits can't be denied."

"Neither," Ly said angrily, "can I. Take this note to her!"

On a scrap of notepaper he wrote with such emphatic dashes he fairly slashed it. "Maggie, you are a d–d humbug! I refused a dinner at the French minister's—the Count de Sartiges—for the pleasure which you now deny me. Send your mother at least."

When Mrs. Fox did not come, he knocked again, so truculently the door shook.

This time the old gentleman said, "Young man, go away! Miss Fox is in a trance. It would injure her to be roused too sudden." Then the door was firmly shut.

Rage so agitated Ly's heart that he reached his room gasping from the effort. Francis kept him in bed next day. He missed several vital appointments, but Maggie was in loving attendance.

"Truly, Ly, I was in a trance."

At the word he turned his face to the wall.

"You don't believe me?"

"No. I've never seen you in a trance. Show me. But first bring me pins to prick you with."

"No!"

"Then trance me no trances."

"But I vow they didn't give me your note, Ly."

"On your honor?" Honor in his little cheat?

"Cross my heart, Lish!"

Next morning he found his note, rolled into a tiny ball, hidden in her hair receiver. She did not see him find it as she languidly brushed the enticing cloud of her hair, twisting the mass of it into a thick rope she began to pin in a low knot. He leaned over her.

"You're in my light, dear Ly. How can I see to fix my hair?"

By that silken rope he yanked her head back until her mouth gaped with pain. "You're an artful liar, aren't you?" He held up the crumpled note.

"Yes, Ly, yes! You make me lie to you! To keep you from being angry with me."

"Just as you make me love you, though I know you are a liar and a fraud and a cheat!" Holding her head cruelly back, with each epithet he kissed her mouth and arched throat.

When he let her go, she sat unmoving, her hands in her lap. Looking down at them, she said, "I lied because I didn't want you to learn what happened at that séance. Now I don't care. Because I'm not so afraid for you any more."

"*For* me?"

"I had a nightmare that frightened me. You were lying all covered with snow and I thought you were dead. I tried to find your breath with a mirror but it broke. I had to know, Ly, if you were going to die in the snow."

A dream had driven him to Webb's Union Hotel that autumn day. How could he condemn her? "Go on."

"You forbade me ever to ask about the expedition at a séance. So I told Governor Tallmadge to ask Calhoun if I fell into a trance."

"Maggie!"

"I was in a trance," she insisted, looking not at him but into the mirror. "I didn't know what Calhoun said until afterward. He said you would get farther north than any of your predecessors—I can't even spell the word—but you would come back safely. *To me,*" she whispered. "He didn't say that. I said it to myself."

He studied her reflection as carefully as she herself was doing. "You really believe this?"

She nodded at herself. "It was Calhoun. His writing proved it. He wouldn't lie as wicked spirits do. So you will come back, Elisha! You will!" She whirled around to cling to him, spilling happy tears on his waistcoat. He could not be angry that she had found some comfort in her own mummery. It almost made him believe in her.

But more often his plans for Maggie reminded him of his struggles with batch after batch of dough which he was trying to "rise" in cold temperatures.

Morning after morning, he went to the Navy Medical Bureau to mix dough with laboratory exactness. Ly knew he was a figure of fun as in elegant waistcoat and with sleeves rolled up he measured and stirred, using this formula and that, hopefully setting each batch outdoors to rise.

"It's almost as cold outside now as it is next a stove inside Arctic winter quarters."

"Maybe that's your trouble," Dr. Harris, the Bureau chief, would drawl. "Weather's too mild. Better wait for a cold snap."

No matter what the ingredients, his dough stayed a flaccid mass, stringy and sour.

"Let 'em eat cake," Harris advised. But Ly kept stubbornly at it. Fresh bread might prove an anti-scorbutic.

The hours he waited for his dough to rise weren't wasted. Rummaging around the Bureau, he had begged from Harris drugs and medical apparatus worth at least two thousand dollars. He had also learned how to make out requisitions for rations and commutations for the ten Navy volunteers detached to him. He must get these forms to Kennedy while that helpful gentleman was still Secretary of the Navy.

Within a month there would be a change of administrations. General Pierce was committed to economy. Not only would he discourage the unofficial help Ly had been receiving from the Navy, but he might also veto any bill to provide Dr. Kane's expedition that dreamed-of fifteen thousand dollars. But Ly would persist to work on Congress to the very end, just as he clung to his dreams for Maggie. He always had been stubborn.

Next day not Maggie but three of his congressional supporters dined with him at Gautier's. Mellowed by an excellent dinner, they agreed to a final effort on his behalf, though, "It ain't smart politics, Doctor, to use the people's money to help Lady Jane find any Sir John. We're a democratic country."

Leaving aside the humanitarian aspect, the expedition's only practical value, they pointed out, "will be the nautical observations you bring back to New England whalers—if you come back. Are southern planters likely to favor money for that?"

On such petty considerations were government decisions made! Ly's boot heels struck sparks on the paving bricks as he stomped back to Mrs. Sullivan's. Maggie's talents were better attuned to the times than his. Perhaps he should leave her to her peculiar success, rather than force her into an unnatural course.

13. IN ALL DECEIT

THERE WAS A fat packet of mail from the Judge next morning. His father wrote to say Ly might as well come home. "The great days of Jackson are gone, the men of vision dead. Polk was a modest, hard-working little man, but Taylor and Fillmore! Now my own party has put an idler and a drunkard into the presidency. Mrs. Pierce, I hear, begged him to refuse the nomination, believing the capital would present constant temptations to tipple. She regards the recent tragic death of their son as a punishment from God for inebriety. That should pitch the fellow deeper into drink! I enclose letters from the British."

In January Ly had asked the Admiralty for details on the gutta-percha boats the English used on Arctic portages. So many pages in response made him open the envelope eagerly. Inside was a lengthy missive from Sir Francis Beaufort himself, famed deviser of the Beaufort Scale for measuring wind velocity. As if that signature were not enough, the first sentence referred to one of Kane's idols. The Lords Commissioners had given Beaufort, he wrote, "immediate commands to call upon Sir John Ross," etc., etc., "to furnish Dr. Kane with every helpful suggestion."

Kane felt a rush of warmth at the mention of rough, eccentric old Sir John Ross. Except for Franklin, there was no one he would rather meet in the Arctic. Never would he forget their brief encounter on the First Grinnell Expedition.

The breeze that August day in '51 had freshened into a gale as the *Advance* plowed ahead in Lancaster Sound, lookouts on every side, for fog had closed in. The short and excessive sea had fetched away everything on deck, even anchors, and the little cabin was afloat. A sudden glimpse of a high mountain shore, white with breakers, forced them to lie to suddenly. Not until next afternoon could they resume their track. Then, at three in the morning, a topsail schooner towing a launch was sighted. When Kane reached the deck, the *Advance* was nearly on her, for they had shaken out their reefs and again drove before the wind. The little schooner under a single topsail fluttered over the waves like a crippled bird. Presently an old fellow, a cloak tossed over his night gear, appeared in the lee gangway.

He bellowed above the winds. "Ahoy there! We are Her Majesty's ship *Felix,* Sir John Ross commanding."

When Ly had replied for the *Advance,* the Englishman sang out in triumph: "You and I are ahead of them all."

It was true. Of the many vessels on the search that summer, only the Yankees' *Advance* and the *Felix* had reached that point. As for the rest of Her Majesty's ships, Penny's squadron was somewhere in the gale behind them; Austin's at Pond's Bay. As the English officer spoke, a short, square-built figure came to his side. "Sir John Ross," was announced. Ly could hardly voice a reply, he was so moved at seeing the fabulous hero, his red face clear in the bright Arctic night. He appeared little stricken by his years or wounds (he was said to be scarred from head to foot) but greeted the Americans with a boyish wave.

As the *Advance* pulled away, Ly stood watching the fading figure of the gallant old man who had already led two polar expeditions, performing on one of them the unparalleled feat of wintering four years in the Arctic. And here he was again, embarked in the search for his lost comrade. Kane's captain, De Haven, came on deck.

"That was Ross in the *Felix,"* Ly told him, "and we're just off Admiralty Inlet where they picked him up seventeen years ago."

"Damned small place, the Arctic," De Haven pointed out.

That was proved true within the week when five of the searching vessels all rode within the same quarter mile. Kane had visited his hero aboard the *Felix*. As long ago as 1847, Ross had volunteered for the search, anticipating even then Franklin's "detention"—*his* word.

"I told Sir John," Ross shifted impatiently, restless to "get on with it" in spite of the ice barrier that had temporarily halted the several ships, "that any sound or inlet may, by caprice or even *routine* of the seasons, close up, and that a shutoff party must have means of falling back. I saved myself from the abandoned *Victory* by a previously constructed house for wintering. You mark my word, Melville Island is now the seat of such an asylum. We'll find them there, for depend on it," he concluded, "Franklin will expect us to follow on his traces."

The lost commander was so vividly alive in Ross's speech that Kane dared not, even now, think him dead.

Once again the *Felix* was seen on that first expedition. What mystical nonsense Maggie's followers would make of the episode!

The *Advance,* passing a sweep of coast between two capes, was making the chord of the curve when De Haven called Ly's attention to a point about six miles off. Without a glass, Kane distinctly saw the naked spars of two ships. "Brigs!"

"Penny's," they agreed. Two other officers distinctly saw with a glass masts, yards, gaffs, everything but the bowsprits of the two vessels. Then De Haven spotted a topsail schooner. "There's the *Felix.*"

They changed course, running in to speak the Englishmen when fog closed around the *Advance.* Still they stood on. When they were but three miles off, a flaw of wind drove the fog away. Not a ship was to be seen! They had vanished utterly, having been, he and De Haven were forced to admit, one of the Arctic's tricks of refraction.

Maggie's friends would have assumed instantly that the English ships were lost. Had they by coincidence actually gone down, her world would have called that mirage a ghostly portent. Instead, here was dear, hearty old Sir John Ross ordered to give Kane advice on *his* expedition.

Sir Francis himself sent charts of Baffin's Bay and several little books of tables, "showing the sun's bearings as he skims along the horizon, a ready method of ascertaining your position, provided your watch is correct."

Even Inglefield, Ly's most dangerous rival, "looks forward with pleasure," Sir Francis stated, "to meeting you in Davis Strait. He sends an ingenious shirt which when partly inflated acts as a perfect buoy in the event of immersion."

Ly chuckled at the vision of a British naval captain solemnly treading water when the ice parted under him, sustained by dignity of rank and an inflated shirt.

Admiralty men might well laugh at some of his gear, at the wolf-skin corona with which he kept his ears and forehead warm, while leaving his entire poll bare. Until he invented it, his cap was always full of frozen water, stiff and uncomfortable, the condensation turning liquid the moment he uncovered. Of course, in cold weather he hooded up, and in really bitter weather, pulled a silk nightcap over his face, covering that with a mask of wolfskin slit at eyes and mouth. In this grotesque false face he could play the Beast to Maggie's Beauty.

She ran into his room, Beauty to the life. "Ly, I have the most wonderful news!"

"You have a new frock."

"No."

"Then I'll order you one in Philadelphia next week."

"You're not leaving!"

"I must get back. Besides, you and Katie will be there shortly."

"Not next week! We may not leave Washington City until April! Because of the news you won't let me tell."

"Tell me now, sweet pet." He settled her on his lap.

"Well, you know that congressman I can never remember—"

"One man who rouses no jealousy in me."

"Silly! Well, he says Mrs. Pierce is deeply interested in the rappings, and if we're here when she arrives in March, he'll take us to rap at the White House. He says most mediums are vulgar women or *men,* and only Katie and I are ladylike enough to rap for the President's wife. Now, what do you think of that?"

"I am appalled." He pushed her off his lap.

"Why, Ly!" She pressed the back of her hand to her mouth.

"You are acquiring the airs of a gentlewoman but none of the instincts." She never could be Beauty whose virtue was compassion. "Mrs. Pierce has endured the most dreadful experience that could befall a mother." Worse, infinitely, than his own dear mother's losing Willie. "In a train wreck, the wretched woman was not allowed to die, but forced to live, unhurt, after seeing her only son killed instantly, falling at her feet so mutilated that his brains spilled out into his schoolboy's cap."

Maggie screamed and tried to run from the room, but he pulled her roughly to him. "If you are without pity for her, have respect for her husband's high office. Swear you will not rap for Mrs. Pierce!"

Transfixed by his fury, Maggie whispered, "I swear!"

"That's my good girl." His anger suddenly spent, he kissed her submissive mouth. "Put on a wrap and we'll drive out for dinner."

"Yes, Ly." Like a flower swaying in a summer breeze, she crossed to the door, and with a timid smile, left him. Graceful carriage her future governess would not need to teach her, but could spend extra time on her music, teaching her to trill the day through, his delicately boned, bright-eyed, heartless little bird.

At home, Ly roamed his father's house, drawn from room to room by his sense that only a little time remained for enjoying its fusion of comfort and unaffected elegance. The pictures could be better, since his father's liking for more than one hard-up artist had confused his judgment. Of course, Sully's portraits of the Judge and his Jeannie in youth were beyond admiration. Before he sailed, he must have Maggie painted by someone as skillful.

He stood, unseeing, before his mother's portrait, visualizing a painting of Maggie that caught the contradiction between her childish mouth and subtle eyes, when he felt a hand on his shoulder.

"I hardly recall that face in my mirror!"

"Nonsense, Mother! You were never lovelier." But mourning did not become her coloring.

"No, no! Grief has taken its toll. Soon we will have to endure again the strain of not knowing if you are alive."

"I'm your bad penny, Mother. I always turn up. How many times were you sure I was lost?" He put an arm around her slim waist.

"I can be right only once," she said somberly. Then with forced brightness, "Your father says I must not attempt to sway you from your search for those Englishmen. He says you have subordinated every other emotion to your sense of duty: your zeal for science, your ambition for fame, your love of home— It's quite a speech."

"I can hear him now." Like most orations, it contained little truth.

"I only hope," her large eyes darkened, "he does not one day find himself delivering it at a memorial banquet for Elisha Kent Kane! Where he accepts on behalf of the family the medal bestowed on you posthumously by Queen Victoria."

"Mother, what a morbid thought!"

"They're morbid, Lady Franklin and that old-maid niece of hers, that Miss Cracroft! Sending my son to his death for the sake of a dead man. I think you, too, suspect Sir John Franklin is dead. Otherwise, why are you always at the receptions of those little spirit rappers, the Fox Sisters? John said you attended in Philadelphia and Mrs. Sibley wrote about you from Washington."

So she knew. He was so inexpert in intrigue. He answered carefully, "I've always investigated supposed supernatural phenomena. Remember the Hindu fakir who gave me that robe?"

"The Fox Sisters haven't influenced you against going?"

She had not for a moment suspected one little Spirit Rapper indeed tempted him to abandon his expedition.

"I attended the circles only for amusement."

"Oh, dear." She gave a despairing gesture. "I hoped your interest was more significant."

He wanted to laugh wildly. If she but knew how significant, his poor, deluded mama! His secrecy had not only been fumbling, but also unnecessary. Nevertheless, he must be even more cautious, and not disabuse her at this late date.

"You always did have peculiar notions of fun. Lish, your father thinks you are motivated by duty," she said thoughtfully, "but I believe it is love of danger, of danger for its own sake."

He was startled at her penetration. This aspect of his nature he usually hid even from himself, considering it like a sot's craving for drink or a satyr's for women. It was in moments of greatest danger he felt most keenly alive. To teeter on the brink of disaster exhilarated him abnormally. Did not the threat to his career, to his reputation, to his family ties lend excitement to his courtship of Maggie?

His mother went on. "Remember the time you climbed the smokestack at school, when you were ten? You set the pattern of your whole life right then."

He remembered the wild joy of that episode. Surely the intensity of his feeling gave it a certain grandeur? "I didn't fall off that chimney, Mother."

"Every time I recall that adventure, I see you a little heap of broken bones at the foot of that ghastly height. Oh, Ly, Ly!" She swept out of the room, moving with the rush of a summer storm.

He did not follow her. His strongest argument he could not use: She had not feared for Willie at home, but it was Willie who died.

14. THE COMPACT

BUSY as he was in Philadelphia, he had time to be lonely, even in the midst of his family. They had never been dearer or more helpful. But where once their affections had walled him round, all the Kanes together could not close his defenses now that Maggie had breached them. He missed her most at the hour when she used to fly to his arms in Washington.

John invaded his room late one evening full of angry accusations, having cross-questioned poor Francis to good effect. His brother should become a lawyer instead of a doctor.

"You can't be serious about this little knocker, a scientist of your standing!"

"It's not yet so impressive."

"If they hear of this at Pennsylvania Hospital, I'll never live it down."

"I thought it was my reputation that concerned you."

"I'm thinking of Mother's happiness! Imagine a woman of her refinement having to receive so notorious a creature!"

"If you had ever met her, you would know Miss Fox is an innocent child whom you hope I only plan to betray."

John flushed. "You've never done that sort of thing."

"Thank you."

"That's why I was alarmed by the tales I pried out of Francis. You still haven't stated your intentions."

"I'm not accountable to my younger brother."

"Then you'll have to account to Father! I came to you first to avoid an everlasting row—if there was nothing to it." John sounded aggrieved that his consideration was not appreciated.

"Father knows I don't take kindly to dictation. I'm less even malleable than Tom, who has twice defied his Honor."

"Elisha, what about Mother?"

"Tom's Mormons didn't upset her, though many think them worse than spiritualists."

"That's not the point. Mother's in mourning, easy prey for a medium. Your Miss Fox might call the 'shade' of Willie back to haunt her, aggravating Mother's morbid state. Can't you let her recover before you inflict a worse blow? Her darling Elisha, who was always closest to her, courting a girl for months without telling her." There was deep resentment in John's voice. "She'll feel she's lost you and Willie both, her eldest and her youngest, who were always her favorites."

To quiet him, Elisha did not hesitate to equivocate. "Since she could lose me in hard fact on the expedition, do you want to make her suffer in advance? Over a misunderstanding? I have only a brotherly interest in Miss Fox, who is half my age, only a child. So I am quite willing to swear I have no intention of marrying a notorious, ignorant girl."

She would be a perfectly schooled miss, her infamous past forgotten, when he returned to her embrace!

"Thank God!" John laughed weakly.

He had really wanted a row, Elisha thought, being fed to the teeth, poor fellow, with his parents' eulogies for their eldest. This natural jealousy, however, made John potentially dangerous.

He was grateful, then, that Francis extracted from the next post Maggie's first letter since he left Washington City. She had been ill with influenza, and recuperating, was bored enough to write. He answered lovingly, telling her to call on him for anything, but cautioned, "Sign your telegram 'F. Webster.' "

He next heard not from Maggie but Kate. They expected to be in Philadelphia Thursday or Friday. Both days he took time from pressing tasks to meet the cars from the capital, but Maggie did not come. It was from the newspapers that he finally learned that the Fox Sisters would be in Philadelphia Monday, when he had appointments in New York. He could have shaken his little minx.

He pointed out the notice to John. "I'll be away while they are here. It doesn't say where they will hold their receptions, but you might find out, and go to see her for yourself." The fact that he did not know where she would be staying, the little wretch, should convince John that Ly was not her intimate.

"I have no desire to."

"Investigate my interest openly, not behind my back!"

John, very red, said, "I trust I don't need to, since I have your sworn word." For a while, at least, Ly thought he might have a respite from John's prying.

Mrs. Fox was grateful for a few days in Philadelphia before facing up to Leah with the news they never rapped for Mrs. Pierce. Maggie refused to, and Kate was too timid to rap alone at the White House. All Maggie would say was "I promised Elisha," an excuse to make Leah throw a fit. Between them two, she needed Solomon's own judgment, only it was her that was likely to be sawed in half.

Maggie was terribly restless when Dr. Kane didn't come until Thursday, having been in New York. Maggie and Kate made mightily over him. Both girls was supposed to rap that day for a lady, but Kate agreed she'd do it.

"I want to take Maggie to the piano warehouse to pick out an instrument for her very own," Dr. Kane said.

"A piano!"

There was worse to come. "There is also a handsome Newfoundland I'd like Maggie to have for a pet."

"And a Newfoundland dog!" Mrs. Fox sat down heavily. She knew them only by pictures, but if pictures was to be believed, a Newfoundland was big as a piano. Leah would have a stroke. "Big, ain't they?" Her voice quavered.

"A noble protector for my little girl when I am far away."

"But, Ly," Maggie pouted, "I had my heart set on a bird."

"You shall have one this very day."

Seemed like he was ready to give Mag the world.

"Mother Fox, aren't you coming?" Ly asked, smiling.

"You go long. I have to think." But she just sat, hoping ladies' academies didn't allow such outlandish pets *and* a piano.

"Elisha, you deliberately confused Ma so she wouldn't come," Maggie accused him when they reached the carriage.

He laughed boyishly, Maggie's dimple deepening in response. He wanted to kiss it, but there might be Paul Prys on Arch Street. "Drive out of this maze of brick, Francis, into spring's own glades. Take us to Fern Rock."

Poetry he'd be writing next, Francis thought, if he was ready to name the black woods on the old York road "glades." But, sure, love could put leaves on every tree and swear to them.

"I was serious about the dog, a big brave friend who will remind you of me."

"Preacher dear, I don't need a dog for that!"

"Dearest pet, your life will be very dull while I am gone. I won't be there to dispel your boredom with kisses. Like this—and this—and this." They were out in the country now.

"Oh, Ly, I do love you!" She fairly basked in his affection today, warm and womanly in her response.

So Francis heard nothing for a while but the smooth beat of the bays' hoofs.

"No such delicious merriment for a whole year," Ly said, holding her camellia face between his palms. "At the end of a tiresome day, no loving embrace to run to." He settled her head against his shoulder while he described her future state. "In your cold little room, your faithful dog will be waiting. You warm your toes in his shaggy pelt and dream of Preacher out on the Arctic ice, looking in his furs and beard as shaggy as your dog and just as faithful."

She giggled at the comparison.

"But"—he waved aloft a triumphant hand—"at the year's end I'll come home to my reward, my dearest Maggie, and off we'll go to Italy to thaw out."

"Elisha, not Italy!"

"Greece if you'd like."

"No, no! Italy! I've always dreamed of going there since I learned in school that Italy's always sunny."

"And its lakes are the blue of your eyes. So that's settled." He had said Italy as any lover promises to carry off his beloved to a golden land. But his chance remark might provide the incentive Maggie needed. "But for us, pet, Italy is a long way off."

"Months and months," she agreed sadly.

"Months when you will give up a life of peculiar excitement for school with its irksome regulations. You will be governed by a lady abbess, a *schoolmistress.* No more Waddys," he continued sternly, "and Tallmadges, no more wiseacre scientific asses and pop-eyed committees of investigation!"

"Oh, them!" She brushed away her devotees.

"Or Gotham dandies or Washington diplomats."

"Truly, Lish, I never cared for their admiration."

For a moment he chose to believe her. They were near Willie's glade now, so Francis had pulled up and Elisha helped his love alight. Thin sunlight dappled the woods, but the winter-dried shrubs rattled in the March wind and the trees were skeletons of their summer selves. To Elisha, the place was still beautiful, with the silver and gold of the sycamore trunks, and the deep gray-green of Willie's big rock, mossy and ancient. He spread the carriage robe on the rock, and lifting Maggie high, enthroned her there.

"Look at me, pet!" She smiled down at him. "Listen to me!"

"I always do, Preacher," she mocked.

"I have given my word," he said harshly, "not to marry an ignorant little spirit rapper."

She frowned in puzzlement.

"I now solemnly vow to marry the girl you can become. In a single year you can mold yourself into the image of my dream—if you are stronger than I."

"Stronger than you?" Her voice and eyes were alike uncertain.

"Dearest, I am a coward, afraid to face the censure of my world and marry you with your present reputation. But I ask you to defy your world, to abandon what Leah calls your 'mission.' "

"It's Leah's 'mission,' not mine, and if I want to give it up, who's to stop me? The spirits"—she flipped her hand to the gray sky—"can find somebody else to do their bidding."

"Maggie!"

She was instantly serious.

"You must also be stronger where our families are concerned. I lie to my family, deceive them like a naughty schoolboy. Break with them, I cannot. But your family I am asking you to leave forever."

She clenched her hands together, and shook her head. "Not Kate." Watching him, she said, "Kate wants to give up rapping, too, and live with us when we're married."

"So she shall!" he fairly shouted, he was so pleased. "Darling Kate—" Kate could help Maggie hold to her resolution. "Don't see her at that house, though, my pet. Once you are under my protection, never go there, but meet her elsewhere."

"Ma doesn't like that house either, and when us young ones give up rapping, she can go back home like she's always wanted.

Without Kate and me, Leah's circles would grow mighty small." She smiled in joyous malice, her eyes narrowed.

His kitten could be a tigress, too. "Not to spite Leah, but for love of me you are giving this up, Maggie. Only for love of your future husband and master! Say it."

Her face was transformed again. As she widened her eyes, they were shining. "My master! Ly, I want to tell you something."

"Tell me, dearest." He put an arm around the curve of her thigh where she sat on the shoulder-high rock.

"That first day, you looked so distinguished, I thought how wonderful to be your wife, if only I wasn't so young. Then I day-dreamed you adopted Kate and me. But Kate said you were too young for that. Now you're going to be my husband, father, teacher, preacher, everything!"

"Your master!" he exalted, and pulled her down from the rock. "Kneel," he commanded. Startled but obedient, she knelt. "Say after me, 'I will give up fame, the excitement of the séances, all my family but Kate, to endure boredom and loneliness, working hard for love of my dear master.' "

Word for word she repeated it, submission in the very line of her lovely neck.

Gently he raised her to her feet. "Never forget our compact," he abjured. "It is a charm to bring me safely back."

On the return to town, he laughed and teased her the whole way, so she would not think life with Ly all solemn oaths and compacts. Francis, listening, trusted their long talk at the rock had more sense to it than the jokes they shrieked over like children.

15. THE BETROTHAL

MRS. GRINNELL'S guest dozed on the library sofa. The firelight banished his pallor but she thought again how wrong it was of Mr. Grinnell to encourage the Doctor's Arctic adventuring when it was sun and warm milk and fresh eggs he needed. He was thirty-two and a genius some said, but to her he looked a frail boy, sleeping with his hand against his cheek. "Here's your milk punch, Doctor."

Awake, he was almost too alive and knowing, like Mr. Dickens when he lectured here. She went to the window to look again for the carriage. "Will Miss Fox come today, do you think?"

She was so curious about the little rapper. Every time she sent the carriage for her it returned empty, with a note saying Miss Fox could not possibly come. She couldn't be so friendly with the Doctor as gossip reported or surely she would have called when he was ill.

"Miss Fox has many demands on her time and knows I'm not an earnest explorer of the spirit world. Only this one." He smiled wrily at his hostess.

Mrs. Grinnell wondered how his mother would have received Miss Fox. Mrs. Kane had come from Philadelphia the instant her son was stricken. For a while they had almost despaired of his life, and at the crisis his mother hardly laid down her head. Only when the Doctor was clearly recuperating would she leave for home. A more devoted mother no man ever had. So devoted, perhaps, that no young woman would satisfy her as a wife for Elisha. Certainly no one as—as—*conspicuous* as Miss Fox. "Now, Doctor, do drink your punch!"

It was tasteless as life without Maggie and Maggie he had not seen for weeks.

Washington without her had appeared a forlorn village, its people a crowd of pickpockets. For memory's sake he visited Mrs. Sullivan's and his third-floor room stood desolate. In Maggie's room, the mirror before which his little pet used to brush her tumbledown hair reflected emptiness. The cabinet was gone from the parlor where he stood longing to hear just one rap!

In Philadelphia, he could talk about his love only to his cousin. Mrs. Patterson continued to urge him to put Maggie with a governess in the country, rather than in a boarding school. He had come to her view and gone to see Aunt Lieper. She agreed, perhaps a little too readily, to arrange everything with the Turners, "admirable people."

"My aunt's interest," he wrote his little bird, "will prevent any misconstruction. This plan will cost money, my dearest dear, but that means nothing if you show yourself worthy of my love. You will have every incentive, living in a cheerful home where you are the only boarder.

"Miss Turner is a good plain girl, with whom you can go as you please; her father, a rough, broad Scotsman; her mother, very well bred and a trained musician. Living with them, you won't feel lonely, pet, nor shy either. They're not too grand for comfort."

He had insisted that she see the place and the people for herself. "I will meet you Thursday to take you to the Turners. If you and your mother are satisfied, you can be settled in your new home by the first of May."

He had been worn, sick, and thin as a lath from his efforts for the expedition that April Wednesday when he came home to find Cornelius Grinnell waiting. There was also a note from Mrs. Fox which Francis handed him surreptitiously. He ripped open the note. The ladies declined to come.

Cornelius, seeing his face, asked, "Is it bad news, Lish?"

Leah was behind this. Leah in her strident voice had dictated this refusal to poor Mrs. Fox, caught between the Devil and the deep blue sea, appropriately embodied. He could not leave Philadelphia right now, but he must get a letter into Maggie's hand. By Nealy?

"Nealy, I need help desperately. In a matter I can't entrust to any of my brothers."

Now and in the future Nealy could be helpful if he would, forwarding to Maggie Ly's letters from Greenland, handling the funds Ly would leave for her schooling, advising her when she was troubled.

There was such anxiety in the Doctor's face, Nealy would do

anything to ease it. Whatever he did would be little enough. He had wanted to go on the expedition, but his father, willing to risk a ship, had refused to venture a son. "Do anything I can. Is it about Miss Fox?" There, it was out. He shouldn't have said it.

At her name a dam burst in Ly. All his hopes poured forth, his torments and lesser ills, together with such a spate about Maggie, her present charms and future virtues, that Cornelius was carried along on the flood. He treaded water as best he could, catching at such flotsam as floated past.

"There'll be a devil of a row with your family. . . . Your father's a hard man to cross. . . . My father's as bad in a cooler style, and he'll side with the Judge. . . . It helps, Mrs. Lieper and your Cousin Patterson knowing."

Nealy reached solid ground finally. "Lish, listen, I'll help all I can secretly. But when the ruckus comes I'll stay out of it. Because of your mother. Always admired your mother."

The Doctor made an impatient gesture. "My mother always grieves for the wrong reasons. Maggie is right for me. My parents, your father, the world thinks it noble"—his lip curled—"of me to save a grizzled explorer. Is it ignoble, then, to rescue a girl in dreadful straits?"

"Put that way— But, Lish, don't hold me responsible for her progress. Leave that to your aunt. She might not take reprimands from me, Miss Fox, I mean." Nealy looked too young and uncertain to reprimand his dog, and Ly had to smile.

He wrote a long, long letter for Cornelius to give Maggie. But words on paper, Ly knew as he scribbled them, could never reach her heart. Only his voice in her ear, his demanding physical presence influenced that earthy miss.

As soon as he could, though he had a high fever, he had journeyed to New York. In ghastly state he had appeared at the Grinnells'. Work on the *Advance* was in the last stages and he had said he would stay with them at Bond Street while he checked final details. First, first he must see Maggie.

She had been in a séance which the maid refused to disturb. Disgusted at the *hogs,* the *swine* who kept his pearl from him, he had returned to the Grinnell house in a passion and collapsed on the stoop. Morton fortunately had come over from Brooklyn to meet him, and carried him in. A night's rest—

But it had been two weeks and more. He was so ill his family had been summoned. When they were most worried, he was happiest, wandering in his delirium over Italian fields with Maggie, standing with her on mountain peaks while the sun set in swirling gold and turquoise.

Mrs. Grinnell interrupted his brooding. "Dr. Kane, the carriage is here with a young lady, too young to be Miss Fox—"

"Miss Fox is very young." As he always forgot. She had not come before because Leah would not allow it. But today she had flown to him, his dearest child.

When Mrs. Grinnell hurried out, all he could think was that she must show Maggie the wonderful mechanical bird from Switzerland. In its golden cage, it preened its feathers and trilled for minutes at a single winding.

He went mornings to the Navy Yard during his convalescence, but afternoons he took Maggie and Kate driving without interference from Leah. The two sisters were even allowed to attend the theater with him and Cornelius. Perhaps Mrs. Fish felt an invalid did not make a convincing villain.

Kate finally explained it. "Our dear cousin, Caleb Brown, is so ill, she doesn't have time to bother about us."

Brown, a good simple farmer, had accompanied the ladies to New York in lieu of the stubborn Fox. Ly liked him and was sorry to hear he, too, had been ailing.

One unblemished May afternoon he drove his dear girls to a greensward overlooking the Hudson, where they picnicked out of a lavish hamper. Maggie wore the rosebuds he had brought, tucking one into his buttonhole. Only dear plain Kate was unbedecked.

The three of them stretched lazily on the carriage robe. His head in Maggie's lap, he announced, "I have written a poem. Since two ladies cannot escape on foot and unescorted from this isolated spot, you have to listen." With a flourish he drew out a sheet of paper. "It is entitled 'Dialogue between the Sentimental Preacher and Practical Maggie,' and is, I trust, a speaking likeness of them both.

"Preacher: Maggie, I've watched the tender feelings welling in thy breast.

"Maggie: This wretched frock! It always slips and leaves me half undressed.

"Preacher: I've longed to make life's stream a fountain clear and bright.

"Maggie: How can I fix my hair, dear Ly, if you stand in the light?

"Preacher: And now I've found a rural home, away from toil and strife.

"Maggie: Yes, and an ugly governess to lead me 'such a life'!

"Preacher: A home, my Maggie, where your heart and mind will grow apace.

"Maggie: And nobody but country bumpkins come around the place!

"Preacher: A home of peace, where every thought can center, love, on me.

"Maggie: And sour old maids and rainy days and you upon the sea!"

"Exit Preacher in a huff and Maggie laughing as she sings out, 'Italy! Italy! Italy!' "

Maggie reached eagerly for the manuscript. "Give it to me, Ly! I want to keep it forever."

"Not until you prove you are entitled to it." He rolled out of reach and, sitting up, took the rose from his lapel. "Catch this in your mouth!"

Obedient as a puppy, she leaned forward, mouth open, and caught it.

On his knees before her, he took the flower and kissed her. "In Italy they say it's a sign of a happy marriage if a maid catches with her mouth a rose her lover throws her."

Maggie pushed him away. "You see, Kate? Anything from Italy or India or any far-off place he'll believe, but nothing from upstate New York."

Kate nodded wise as a little owl. "Too humdrum. Elisha only believes in magic when distance makes it magical. That's why he doesn't want you schooled around here, but off in the country, like a beautiful orphan in a novel."

Maggie liked to read romances, so he did not protest, but let her see herself in the heroine's place.

Returning with them to Seventh Street at dusk, he saw a paring of moon over Maggie's shoulder. "Wish on it, pet."

The pale golden crescent was reflected in her dark pupils. Then she sighed. "I've wished. Shall I tell you what for?"

For his safe return and their happiness ever after, he hoped, but wanted to hear her say it. "Tell me!"

"I wished for a little dog," she said seriously. "I'm afraid of big ones, and Miss Cushman has a dear little poodle she can't take back to England and offered to give me."

He should be used to such jolts. They were again acting out their roles in his poem. He could only consent, and she must have gone late that evening to get the little beast.

At any rate, he was there when Ly called next day: a poodle named Tommy whom no one else would have taken for the gift he was. His hair hung down over mean little eyes and he hated Ly on sight. He lay limp as a rag over Maggie's arm until he noticed her caller. Then he snapped at Ly.

"Oh, Tommy, be good!" Maggie wailed. "Today of all days." Her eyes were red from weeping. "Caleb's taken a turn for the worse. He may not live through the night."

"I had no idea—"

"Nobody did or Kate and I would never have gone on a picnic! What if he had died when we were away? He was always so good."

"He is not dead yet, dearest."

She shook her head despairingly. "Coming to New York when Pa refused and wanting to marry Leah to make up for Fish's meanness—"

Ly wondered how the gentle Brown could love his termagant cousin.

"She would listen to him! I don't know what we'll do without Caleb." She leaned over the newel post like a maiden in an old mourning picture over a tombstone. "He's asking now to marry her."

"On his deathbed? But then he doesn't know he's dying." Wasn't Fish still the woman's legal if errant husband?

"Oh, yes, he does!" She burst into such a torrent of tears that Tommy wriggled free and ran upstairs. When Ly had stemmed the flow with his handkerchief, Maggie said, "You can tell by the look in his eyes," and would have started crying again.

"Maggie, go to him now!" Kane spoke sternly. "Tell him to beat death off. He can win if he has the will to live! I've done it more than once, this last time because of you."

At that she clung to him. "When I thought you might die, I promised God I'd never rap again for anyone in mourning, if he let you live!" Her little chin set. "Leah couldn't make me either."

"You never told me!" All these days they had been together, she had said nothing, the strange, secretive child. Oddly, he could not imagine her praying.

"Only Kate." She pulled away and dabbed her eyes. "Maybe it will give Caleb courage if Leah marries him. She's brave, too. Can I say you said so?"

"Don't involve me. But if there is anything I can do for Caleb, send me word. Perhaps my own physician could look at him." He was suddenly aware that Mrs. Fish stood on the landing. He bowed to her and quickly left.

Sometime that night Mrs. Fish married her cousin. Before he died, Maggie wrote in a tear-blotted note, he told Leah to trust Dr. Kane. "Leah, you take the Doctor's word. He's a real gentleman," Caleb had said.

For that, Kane felt he must pay his respects to the dead. In a black cravat and borrowed black waistcoat he entered the Fox parlor, its air heavy with the scent of tuberoses. The mourners all turned as if he were awaited. Maggie leaned toward him, but kept her place beside Leah, monumental in a thronelike chair.

When Kate led him to the coffin, Maggie again leaned forward as though urging some course upon him. What did she want him to do? What did the circle of mourners expect? With bowed head, he tried to sense the situation.

For them, Caleb had become a powerful presence, such as he never was in life. Did Maggie wish her master to acknowledge before the dead man the pact between them? To Leah, particularly, Death was the godhead of her cult, if cult it was.

He went to Maggie, and, taking her hand, said, "Caleb trusted me. Before him I swear to marry you when I return from the polar seas, and to be true to you until I, too, am dead." Not, he thought, the enduring time it sounded.

In profound silence the mourners waited when he had finished. For Caleb to rap approval or denunciation? No sound came except, at last, a long, floating sigh.

Mrs. Fox later asked *his* permission for Maggie to accompany Leah to Rochester with Caleb's body. With his impromptu ceremony, he seemed to have accomplished what he had been attempting for months. Maggie was under his protection at last. Freely he consented to let her go. Then, not to lose the advantage he had gained, said, "But tell me now on what day, after she returns, I can take you both to inspect the Turner household?"

"Don't see as we need to make two trips, Doctor. Like Caleb said, we can trust you, and if you say the Turners is a good place for Maggie, I'll just go the once to see her settled."

Jubilant at getting his own way with a clear saving in time, too, he almost kissed the placid lady. The *Advance* was nearly ready, her crew almost complete, and everything not yet done must be done in haste. Mrs. Fox should begin at once to prepare Maggie's wardrobe. "Does she have a suitable trunk?"

"Valises. She ain't had clothes enough before to fill a trunk until you began giving her so many."

He would purchase the finest trunk in New York for her. He would also arrange for her to sit to Fagnani when she returned from Rochester. He might sail without many things he needed, but not without a portrait of his dear child, his very hope of happiness.

16. SWEET SORROW

THE brawny young fellow from Chester waiting to see Captain Kane shifted from foot to foot. He tried leaning against a capstan but the offshore breeze was too brisk for him to hold that pose. Standing in the shadow of the big *North Carolina* was probably the coldest place on deck but there he was out of the way of the men toting stuff aboard the little brig.

She was so miserably small. That's why he was in a cold funk. Dr. Kane had spoken of her so glowingly, Hayes hadn't expected such an almighty small boat.

"Our expedition boasts the ablest men, finest equipment, and stoutest ship, my tested and true *Advance*."

Well, here she was, and she wasn't much.

His first sight of the expedition's commander had fazed him almost as much when Dr. Kane stopped at Chester last week to ask Isaac Hayes if he still wanted to join the search. Kane's Navy surgeon had failed him and he needed someone. Anyone. Even a medical student. A wonderful chance for him, Kane had said.

Hayes, listening, couldn't get over Kane's being so small and delicate. Just recovered from a near-fatal attack of his old rheumatic fever, he planned to set right off for the Arctic, which was clearly insane. But Kane, his eyes piercing as a hawk's, made you forget the invalid and see a born explorer.

"I won't be your chief patient, but our whaling man, McGary, may. The strongest are hardest hit by scurvy, you know."

Hayes didn't. But he did know Kane had survived worse diseases in China, Africa, Egypt, for all his curled chestnut hair and dandified waistcoat. His nose was strong and his forehead high and broad, and Hayes could easily picture him in a parka.

"If you join us," Kane promised, "I'll leave all doctoring to you."

He might go back on that when he found out how little his substitute surgeon knew. But Ike could bone up nights. They'd be long enough.

That steward Morton stuck his long, bony face out of the cabin door to hail in another man. Isaac heard the steward mutter something about a "country sawbones." Well, Chester wasn't that inconsiderable, even if that fellow thought Hayes was.

Kane had said that Morton, "my invaluable hospital steward," would be able to give him "every assistance." Sounded as though he could run the whole Pennsylvania Hospital by himself. When he liked a man, the Doctor was really warm about it.

Once he had agreed to go, the Doctor got down to brass tacks, telling him what gear to bring, right down to his underwear!

He also said, "Bring books worth several readings, drawing materials if you sketch, a musical instrument if you play, anything to occupy your mind and your mates'. The most baleful effect of Arctic night is mental. Of course, the meteorological and other readings will keep you and me and Dr. Sontag busy."

"Another doctor?"

"A superbly trained astronomer. We three will keep the most complete records ever to come out of the Arctic! They would justify our voyage. If we reach the Open Sea, however, and you prove to be the Balboa who first views it, you will be forever famous!"

Only after the Doctor had been gone several hours did Isaac realize he had hardly mentioned the lost Sir John Franklin.

There was Morton's horsy face again and this time he beckoned to Hayes. Awkwardly, the medical student ducked through the cabin door. Kane, in high good humor, sat smiling at a table, a tall, scrawny fellow beside him. Kane wasn't in uniform but wore pale gray broadcloth with a chestnut-colored waistcoat.

"Dr. Sontag, may I present our ship's surgeon, Dr. Hayes?"

With a jerk of his Adam's apple the astronomer bowed. Young, too, Hayes noted with relief, shy, and a foreigner besides.

"We trust you brought none of Scott's works along," Kane said. He and Sontag laughed.

Hayes didn't get the joke. "You don't like Scott?"

"Not as passionately as Bonsall, another of our stewards, who just staggered aboard with Scott's complete works. So the rest of you can jettison yours. I'm a Thackeray man myself, but Morton here reads Dickens."

"Today I ain't reading nobody. If you don't need me, Cap'n Ken," Morton said, "I best go along. There's a deal to do."

"Don't forget the pet bird I took over last evening."

"Not likely the little miss will allow me to." Morton vanished.

Did Dr. Kane have a ward, Hayes wondered, picturing her a child with golden curls feeding a canary.

"Dr. Hayes"—Kane's tone was abruptly formal—"I have written the Secretary of the Navy, requesting for you the commission promised the surgeon whom you replace. We won't receive a reply before Tuesday, but no matter. On such an expedition Navy men customarily leave their pay behind. There will be no place to spend it. If, therefore, your pay is waiting when we return, well and good."

There's another "if" to it, Hayes thought, "if" we return.

"If not, you'll be paid from the expedition's funds." On their triumphant return, he could raise the money needed to pay off his non-Navy men, Kane decided, more easily than now. And there was always his father to draw on.

Hayes cleared his throat. "Are those funds ample?"

"Not precisely." The Doctor gave a thin smile.

"Well, then, I'll go along without pay, if the Navy turns me down." He was surprised to hear himself.

Kane's eyes became so bright it embarrassed Hayes a little. "I couldn't allow such a sacrifice. You'll need money to set yourself up in practice later."

He's convinced we're coming back, Hayes realized with a rush of relief.

"But I will never forget your offer."

"I, too," Sontag said with a bow. "It was noble."

Hayes felt his neck and ears turn fiery red. The funk he had felt on deck was entirely gone.

"Examine our scientific library for yourself," Kane was saying, "most of it loaned by the Smithsonian. Medical books you need in addition, you can draw on Mr. Grinnell to purchase."

He knows his surgeon is still a calf not yet weaned from his textbooks, Hayes realized from this, and he doesn't mind!

His hand on Ike's shoulder, Kane conducted him to the minute space allotted the ship's surgeon. "My own quarters on the first expedition," his tone was nostalgic, "you will share with Sontag. The two of you can make it very snug."

Isaac dragged his gear in, whistling cheerfully. Not many young sawbones had such an opportunity.

By ferry and bus Morton hurried to Fagnani's. He had told Cap'n Ken he didn't like that Eye-talian painting him. Mebbe the Judge did want a portrait. Mebbe he'd regret it later. That Fagnani painted Clay and Clay died. He painted Webster and Black Dan was gone. Zachary Taylor, and where was old Zach now? Seemed like Fagnani had the "evil eye."

As for his painting Miss Maggie, whatever would he make of her after painting nothing but statesmen on their deathbeds? He wished the Doctor had settled on a daguerreotype of her instead: quicker done, more like, handier in size, and no evil eye. Not that you suspect Fagnani to see him in his fine house with a proper wife sitting there; an Everett connection she was, the Doctor said.

"Oh, Morton, I'm so glad you've come! Mr. Fagnani hasn't let me move for hours."

"Do not move now, I say! Just here," the artist daubed a shadow under her lower lip, "a little angel kissed the young madonna I paint."

Popery, that sounded like. Morton craned to see an angel's kiss.

"Is it like me, Morton? Mr. Fagnani won't let *me* see."

"You would pose me a simp. I do not paint the simp."

"A simpering girl, you mean, Mr. Fagnani," his wife said.

"All the same." He shrugged. "She is young-ger, but beautiful as the Countess Guiccoli, who I paint when she is marry to that stupid Boissy, after Byron was dead."

"We do not refer to Byron before ladies."

"Such a country! But"—he shrugged—"in Italy, young girls do not read nothing neither."

"I'm going to Italy someday," Maggie announced.

Right now, Morton warned, they were going to Crooksville and they better hurry up about it.

"Tell the Doctor, the Captain, what he is, the portrait is ready Monday as I swore by God. Where all is snow and ice, she blooms like an Italian rose."

Working over Maggie's mouth when they had gone, Fagnani thought the Doctor's taking this little chick, Margharita, under his wing, was like kind, loving Marie Isabella's care for him in his youth. Queen of the Two Sicilies, she had many little chicks, but a special warmth for Fagnani, who had such a precocious talent for love like this miss. But the business was not to be discussed with Mrs. Fagnani.

What with Mrs. Fox bawling orders at him, Miss Maggie and young Kate wailing together, the trunk heavier and the dog meaner than he expected, Morton clean forgot the bird. Miss Maggie's tears kept the Doctor from noticing it was missing from her cargo; but Morton knew he'd hear about it later.

"Don't cry, petty. You must be my brave girl."

"But, Ly, whatever will I do without Kate?"

She would not weep so copiously at parting with him. To one so young a sister was naturally dearer than a lover. He was, besides, her stern master, exiling her for her little sins of ignorance. "Only a year, petty, and then we'll all be happy together."

"A whole year!"

At Philadelphia, to his relief, Francis waited with a closed carriage. This evening Dr. Kane must be invisible, since he had *not,* officially, left New York. Maggie and her mother went to Crooksville tomorrow without him, but tonight was Maggie's. Not until Sunday would he arrive to take formal leave of his family.

The carriage threw him and Tommy into too close quarters. When the little beast snarled, Maggie slapped at him with no intent to hurt. "Such a bad dog! Ly, whatever will I do if he bites the Turners?"

"Send him back to New York with your mother."

"No, no, I won't give him up! Darling Tommy, I won't let them separate us." Now she wept at parting with her lap dog.

Ly's nerves, rubbed raw by weeks of illness, overwork, and frustration, jumped irritably. Once they reached the hotel and the iced wine Francis had surely not failed to provide, his annoyance would vanish in champagne bubbles. They had rooms at the Girard House, where Dr. Kane was too well known. But he was determined their last evening should not be spent at Webb's Union Hotel!

"Put your veil down," he warned her as they entered the Girard. Nowhere in the lobby did he see a face he knew, fortunately.

In their suite, Maggie's tears stopped the instant she discovered the supper table laid in the parlor with champagne bottles nesting in a bucket of ice. "Ly, how lovely! Ma, see, we're having a party!"

Mrs. Fox eyed the bottles. "I don't hold with drinking."

"Dear Mrs. Fox, it's only champagne."

"Wicked French stuff. But the flowers is pretty."

She was persuaded to test the wine's innocent character, and "kind of liked it." After a glass with her supper and a glass or two later, she was soon drowsing, red-faced, in the parlor's biggest chair.

Her charges hardly heard her snores. They sat cheek to cheek at the little table, the scent of roses and wine in Ly's nostrils, the taste of Maggie's tears on his lips. He had kissed away the gentle few she at last shed over parting with him.

"Dearest, what is it!"

Abruptly, she turned her face away to say in a cold little voice, "It's lonely and hateful in the country. I got away from Hydesville, but now you're making me go back to the same kind of place. I won't have Katie, I won't have anyone!"

"That's not true, petty," he told her gently. "If you grow too lonely, write to Cornelius Grinnell. He will escort you to New York to see Kate and your mother. But never sleep in that house now that you are under my protection. You have other friends you can stay with, friends I approve. If you have any doubt, ask Nealy. You can rely on him."

"Yes, Ly." But her little body was still tense in the circle of his arm.

He reached for the champagne. "Drink this toast, pet. 'To Ly, who will return to such fame no one will deny him anything!' "

Her voice warmed as raising her glass high she repeated his words. When she had downed her wine she was smiling again.

"Break the glass," he commanded. She smashed it against the latrobe burner and laughed excitedly.

Mrs. Fox stirred and opened one eye. "Tipsy, the both of you—" She drowsed off again.

"Now for my toast: 'To Maggie, who will make herself a prize for any hero!' "

"They vow you're a hero already."

He had never felt less heroic. Almost angrily, he smashed his glass.

Mrs. Fox heaved herself up then. "Now, that's enough. Such canoodling and racketing I never saw and time it stopped. Time we was in bed with that coachman coming early. And, Maggie, you cover up that bird of yourn. Singing like it's noonday."

"My bird! Where is it? That wicked Morton forgot it!"

Ly promised to send the bird and other forgotten treasures. "To Chester by Tuesday when Mr. Turner can fetch them. The same day my little barque will be plowing through trackless seas."

Maggie flung herself at him. "Don't go, Ly, don't go! "

He rubbed her cheek with his. "Calhoun said I would return safely."

"You don't believe it, so how can I? Don't go!"

In one of her always-unexpected displays of passion, she seemed to melt into his very bones. Stroking her neck, her fine-boned spine, he murmured: "I believe this: Cling to me, lean on me, hope in me, *trust me,* and I'll come back to you."

Unseeing, he walked along the empty corridor, down the empty stairs, and out of the Girard House, the evening as unreal as a dream. He and Maggie had parted, perhaps for the last time. He wanted to turn back, but there was no turning back for Elisha Kane.

17. THE AWAITED DAY

THE great day dawned at last, cool and bright, and Ly woke with, surprisingly, no stiffness in him. Morton found him on his feet, leaning far out the window to con a lovely sky.

"A good breeze to take us far from life's complications."

"Yes, Cap'n Ken." Morton smiled broadly.

Ly whistled as he scrubbed himself, but his mood was neither so cheerful as he sounded nor so clear. He was at once eager to escape and sickeningly unready. If only he were not leaving Maggie unsettled in mind, uncertain in behavior! His trills reminding him of Maggie's bird, he broke off. That bright-eyed creature had caused almost his worst moment in a wretched week.

"There's some of them complications waiting downstairs, sir," Morton warned him. "Reporters."

"Are they asking odd questions?"

Had any of them been on his trail when he escorted the Foxes to Philadelphia on Thursday? Or during his sudden trip Saturday? Perhaps he had been seen chasing that damn bird. He could say he was taking it as a gift for his mother or Bessie. But how explain his visit to Crooksville? He was such a poor deceiver, they might catch him out, and set off a scandal of major proportions.

"What *are* they asking, Morton?"

"I reckon they want something to quote in schoolbooks in case you don't come back, Cap'n Ken," Morton said.

Kane in relief grinned like the schoolboy for whom he was to set an example. "Go down and tell them Dr. Kane will see them aboard the *Advance* this morning, together with his intrepid crew. Don't forget to say 'intrepid.' It's their favorite word for us."

"I'm jes intrepid enough to say it, Cap'n."

Fortunately not Kane but his brig had been the reporters' chief interest since she was moved from the Navy Yard to a more public mooring opposite Grinnell and Minturn's. So they had been clambering over her, writing authoritatively about her and nowhere near Delmonico's when Mrs. Fox had come panting from the cars straight to him.

"Doctor, Mag's in a state. Setting by the window of her room, holding Tommy, and saying if she can't go home, they'll jump out together soon as you've sailed. I'll have to fetch her home. I give my word, so I'm telling you first." Her broad face was lumpy with misery.

He jerked to his feet so quickly that he tilted his worktable. Letters, documents, and requisitions with which he had been frantically trying to cope slithered all ways. He grabbed at an inkwell and missed. Clutching the empty air, he said, "No, Mother Fox. Maggie *must* be resolute!" The word rang hollowly.

"She veers with the wind, Mag does, though she stuck it out against Leah about the rapping. Maybe you could of made her stick to the Turners if you had got her mind set."

"If I go at once—" Reaching Philadelphia late he could ride out to Crooksville early Sunday, returning at the hour when his family was expecting him. He grabbed a valise and thrust his papers into it. His father could take care of these and Brooks of the work aboard the *Advance*. Once again he was scamping duty for Maggie's sake. "Since her bird hasn't gone yet, I'll take it."

At the door Mrs. Fox had halted. "You shouldn't be running off to Maggie right now. Papers is full of Dr. Kane this and Dr. Kane that. Maggie ain't the girl you need, that's the truth. You give her up, I'll say you was in the right. She'll get over it."

He rose heavily, his love like a weight on his wrists and knees. "Maggie, yes, but I might not."

"I allus felt sorry for you," the old woman said.

As he got off the cars in Philadelphia that night, clutching an unconcealable bird cage, the cage door slipped its catch. Instantly Maggie's pet made a swoop for freedom. It had not flown far, but from perch to perch, just out of reach. Maliciously, it led him on. Again and again he had failed to net it with his top hat, by an exasperating fraction of a second while station loungers guffawed. Having reduced him to panting dishevelment, the bird finally soared off.

Early Sunday the Turner household was hardly astir when he

arrived. Dew on the roses and honeysuckle smothering the porch had made the air almost unbearably sweet. By the village clock rising above a line of willows it was not yet seven.

Mrs. Turner had recognized him at once: Mrs. Lieper's nephew and a famous explorer. She quickly buttoned her neat dress at the neck. "Why, Dr. Kane! We heard you were going to the Arctic again."

"I sail Tuesday. Since I was in the neighborhood to bid my aunt farewell, she suggested I use my influence with your homesick charge."

Its nature was all too clearly shown when Miss Fox, barefoot, a thin wrapper over her nightdress, flew down the stairs. "Ly, Ly, you've come to take me home!"

Fearful lest her unmarried daughter come to this—unusual—scene, Mrs. Turner said, "We can talk in the parlor."

He led Maggie into a room fresh and pretty in the country style. "Dear child, why mope for a gloomy New York house when you can live here?" Taking her little chin in his hand, he said firmly, "That's no fit home for you! Besides, all your hopes depend on your staying here and studying hard. So does the very existence of one dear to you—or is he forgotten already?"

"No, Ly! I'll love you—him—until I die."

Mrs. Turner nearly smiled, but Dr. Kane's face gave her pause.

"Dress yourself and we'll walk in the garden."

"Yes, Ly." She had not obeyed her mother so readily.

While she was gone, Mrs. Turner, at the Doctor's request, summoned her daughter Lizzie and with them he discussed Miss Fox's education. He had given so much thought to every detail it was obvious that not Mrs. Lieper but he was the young woman's sponsor.

"Her moral and musical development will be in your charge, Mrs. Turner, while you, Miss Lizzie, will cultivate Miss Fox's understanding, dormant now through deliberate neglect."

His searching glance shook Lizzie a little, but she said firmly, "I'll do my best, sir."

Studying her face, he nodded. "Your best should be very good."

On her fair, freckled skin, her blush showed brick red, most unbecoming with her sandy-auburn hair. He looked away to give her time to recover herself, and Maggie stood meekly in the doorway.

In the garden he saw she was still near to tears and banished them by his account of her bird's escape.

"He led you a merry chase!" She laughed quite happily.

"So have you, my wicked child. But here's an end to it."

At his tone, her face sobered. "Yes, Ly." She began at once to talk in a very grown-up manner about her studies.

Yes, he approved her studying German. "A noble language." He added, smiling, "I speak not a word of it and I want you to outdo me in something besides good looks and spirit trances. Dear pet, it won't all be work. You can read poetry and dream of me, study your globes to find where faithful Ly is, sing your heart out and"—he caught her hands and the blue veins showing against her white wrists made him say—"exercise!"

"Piano exercises?"

"No, no, physical exercise. Romp at least three hours a day in the open air, rain or shine. Don't spare me shoemakers' bills but wear out dozens of pairs while you laugh and play and grow fat."

"Not fat!"

"I want a rosy-cheeked little maid waiting for me, not a pale, strait-laced automaton. I made that clear to Mrs. Turner. Stay here four months. If then you still dislike it here, you are free to go where you choose. You are free, Maggie, of every bond but love."

"I am?" she asked doubtfully.

"Every oath you swore was for love of me, and for my sake you will be my good brave child."

"I'm not brave!" Her mouth twisted with terror.

"Petty, what is it?"

Looking down at her clenched hands, she told him. "My last night home, Katie and I wanted to find out—if you were coming back. A dead sailor talked to us. He said you saw his grave in the ice by a high cliff. Is it true? Did you see John Torrington's grave?" At the name, her glance struck his, demanding the truth.

It made him feel colder than he ever had in Greenland. As plainly as if the rudely chiseled stone stood at his feet in that sunny garden, he saw one grave at Franklin's last-known winter quarters: "Sacred to the memory of John Torrington, who departed this life January 1st, A.D. 1846, on board the H. M. ship *Terror,* aged twenty years." Had the sailor in his dream finally spoken, not to him but to Maggie?

Shaking Ly's arm she said wildly, "He said they were all dead, all Franklin's men, and you would die in the snow, too. Don't go, Ly!"

His chill did not abate but his mind cleared. The graves on Beechy Island were described in his book. There was also an engraving of them based on his sketch of the three headstones. His book was not yet out, but a printer or a proofreader or the engraver, any of them might be infected with the spiritualist mania and attend Kate's circles. That suicide had been a printer! There was nothing supernatural here. Katie had unconsciously used something she heard.

This explanation would not satisfy Maggie. Only a flat denial would serve. "I never saw his grave nor heard his name."

She wet her lips. "Torrington sounds English."

"The Devil is always plausible. By disobeying my wishes, you gave him a chance to frighten you, silly child."

She nodded slowly. "Maybe I am a witch and it was the Devil."

"No! you are my own sweet witch whom I have wrested from him!"

She had looked around her as if seeing the garden for the first time. "Here I can believe that, when you are here, too, Ly. So come back soon. I'll wait, I truly will."

When he was in the saddle, and leaned down at the gate for a last kiss, she responded with a fervor that almost matched his own.

At nine o'clock on Tuesday the *Advance* was towed into the stream and anchored astern of a Sardinian frigate. At ten Dr. Kane stepped aboard, cheered by the throng that crowded the water front and by everyone on the steamer, *Union,* which the New York Lodge of Masons had chartered to accompany him down the bay. On deck, his crew could hardly move for the horde of visitors. These he gave a confused greeting and very shortly bade a hurried farewell as a spanking new tugboat, the *Titan,* chugged up. Then the *Advance* weighed anchor, the *Titan* took up the slack in the hauser, and his brig, with a slight shudder, started slowly out the North River.

Twenty miles down the bay the Masonic craft left them, after giving three ear-splitting cheers for heroes who had not yet proved their mettle. Kane hoped there would be as tumultuous yells on their return.

The Voyages

18. NORTHWARD

THEIR STEAM TUG, THE *Titan,* FELL OUT OF SIGHT JUST BEFORE night closed in and with it went their last tie to land. Kane on the bridge turned to stare up at their press of sail, white against blackness. As they at last plowed northward he should be experiencing the happiness he had promised himself once the *Advance* was under way: To leap the deck for joy and with a glad if faulty heart welcome the hazards before him.

But the morning's elation was gone and he was left with gnawing uneasiness for Maggie and the expedition both. He had not had time to be sure his wayward pet was surely settled, and yet the little he had spent with her he should have used hand-picking the rest of his crew. Instead, he had let McGary, his Second, sign up five from New York's water-front flotsam: Godfrey, Blake, Riley, Whipple, and Hickey, the cabin boy. Only names to him, and yet the lives of all might at some juncture depend on one of them.

By what malign fate had he experienced first love at the very instant of his greatest chance for fame?

At his elbow Brooks in his deep tones reported, "Weathering to starboard, sir."

The *Advance* quivered under the first flick of the approaching storm. A splatter of rain brushed Kane's cheek, its warmth a reproof. By now, they should be north enough for sleet or the last of the Arctic's spring snows. As the ship began to take the swells with her old easy roll, he felt the first queasy turns of his most faithful malady.

"Keep all possible sail. Trim only as you must, Mr. Brooks," he said sharply, and hurried to his cabin.

Brooks, understanding the captain's impatience and haste, too, smiled affectionately after his retreating figure.

Kane barely made his cabin. Morton wisely had a basin out, and in proper privacy the brig's captain was thoroughly seasick.

His attack over, he lighted the lamp above his minute desk. In the light, Fagnani's little madonna smiled down at him. Sternly, he looked away, and dipping pen into ink he did not yet have to thaw began his journal by listing his men.

Out of seventeen, only three, Brooks, McGary, and Morton, had ever seen the Arctic. Brooks and Morton he knew of old. McGary was a New London whaler and should be stanch. But how would the rest stand up to the perils ahead? Jeff Baker, the youngster he had enjoyed on hunting trips at home, might bear no resemblance to Baker the man, confronted with the Arctic's frozen echo of earth.

In the galley he heard Schubert, their French cook, singing "*Aux gens atrabilaires.*" What would that child of the boulevards make of black craters in a white land, ringed by ghostly pinnacles bathed in an eerie light? Sontag, their astronomer, should find that landscape familiar.

Its pull was so strong if inexplicable, the British had a name for it, "Arctic fever." Brooks, Kane suspected, suffered a touch of it. That great burly fellow was not on this voyage only because of Elisha Kane. And McGary, pig iron where Brooks was oak, what drew him again to the North he had seen many times on a Baffin's Bay whaler? What lured him from the hearty meals and comfortable beds of home? Was their captain's own anxiety for speed due entirely to the lateness of the season, or in part to his desire to see if the reality resembled his fantastic recollection?

He banished speculation and set down a plain account of their stores and equipment: five boats including the metallic lifeboat donated by its maker, Mr. Francis; lumber to house over the *Advance* in winter; simple tents of India rubber and canvas; several sledges, some built after the British Admiralty model; a large library and as fine a set of scientific instruments as the British could boast.

For provisions: two thousand pounds of well-made pemmican, a parcel of Borden's meat biscuit; a quantity of exsiccated potato and of pickled cabbage; of dried fruits and vegetables, though none of the more valuable and costly preserved sort; ample Navy rations of salt beef and pork, hard biscuit and flour; several barrels of malt with an apparatus for brewing; and a moderate supply of liquors.

That reminded him he must tell the men in the morning the three simple rules governing this expedition.

Late that night Henry Goodfellow, uncertain at the wheel and grateful that Mr. Wilson, officer of the watch, stayed at hand, heard, during a lull in the wind, a man retch violently. A slight figure staggered against the rail and then pressed on to the bridge. When the seasick man came into the circle of light, Henry was startled to recognize Dr. Kane, wrapped in a cashmere robe. Pale but composed, he inquired their course and examined the log.

"Can't we carry more sail, Mr. Wilson?" he asked impatiently.

"Aye, sir." She might pitch as well as roll if pushed too hard, but the Captain was the one who was seasick, Wilson thought, as he went to bellow orders.

Kane patted Goodfellow's shoulder. "Doing all right, Henry?" Another young friend like Baker, how was he faring in the fo'c'sle?

"Fine, sir." Henry felt wearier than ever in his life, but he had found he was neither afraid nor clumsy as a sailor, and there was triumph in that. He also got along well with the men, though he went warily with Blake and Godfrey, obviously bully boys.

"Your first voyage and you're not seasick. I always am, and will be until we reach Greenland." Kane laughed at himself and with something like his usual quick, bold step retired to his cabin.

Later, as he went off watch, Henry again saw the Doctor on his way to check the log again. Didn't he ever sleep?

By morning they had run through the blow into a fine, brisk day. Kane, wrapped in his old buffalo robe, reclined on a tarpaulin-covered box on the quarter-deck, watching the men work the ship. The big fellow with the insolent air was, McGary said, an East River boatman named Godfrey.

"Says he made three times in tips what we pay, but was running from a woman. Could be the law after him, but he's brawny."

"Blake?"

"An experienced sailmaker out of Baltimore. Cooks, too. Whipple's a Limey. From Hull, sir. If he survived the fo'c'sle of a Liverpool packet, I reckoned the Arctic couldn't skeer him."

McGary had done well enough in filling out the crew. Hickey, their cabin boy, was clumsy but good-natured, and Riley was showing himself an average seaman, a better man aboard than Stephenson, the Irish patriot, whom Kane had enlisted. No longer young, the gentlemanly Irishman was having his difficulties, though he persisted manfully. Goodfellow and Jeff were different cases altogether; used to more comfortable surroundings, but young enough to be adaptable.

The Captain retched again and was hardly over the throes when Morton appeared with a clean bowl. "My poor Morton!"

"You may be tending me 'fore we're done, Cap'n. Wantta go below for a rub?"

Morton's ministrations made him feel almost human. He must speak to the men before his malady overtook him again, he told Brooks, who called all hands on deck.

"For a jawing from the Captain," Godfrey whispered to Blake. At McGary's glare, his expression became mock respectful.

"As you were told before signing on, this is not a Navy expedition—though many are Navy men—nor do we follow Navy regulations. In the Arctic, I found such procedures unsuited to the life. In winter quarters, for example, men and officers live and mess together. You can eat what I do, but probably won't, sailors being addicted to that abominable mush of salt pork and biscuit called 'scouse.' "

Not until he smiled did they laugh, he had pronounced "abominable" so explosively.

"So the strongest sailors may be stricken with scurvy, while the frailest escape, if they eat with me messes of lichen and moss, gull livers and other tidbits."

They laughed readily now.

"On this expedition we have only three rules. They will be rigidly enforced. The first is law aboard any ship: absolute obedience to the man in command. For us, it also applies on land, where, on some forays, the leader may not be an officer, but a dependable and resourceful sailor. Nevertheless, as my deputy, he must be obeyed as though your lives depended on it—which—they—will!"

The final words cracked as sharply as a dog whip around the ears of the pack. The very sound of them sobered the men.

"Our two other rules you may, out of ignorance, think priggish. We drink spirits only when dispensed to us. The effect of alcohol on the body during intense polar cold can be disastrous. Only a doctor can decide when a dose of brandy will help or harm, so our store of liquors is in Mr. Hayes' charge." The young surgeon pinked up as the crew all eyed him. "Those of you who smuggled spirits aboard are advised to turn them in now to Mr. Hayes."

Here a hangdog expression, there a defiant one, told who had hidden a bottle or two. That liquor would be gone before the *Advance* settled into winter quarters, so he did not press the point.

"Finally, the officers will punish habitual profanity. Fright or injury may shock any man into an oath. Such offenses will be overlooked, but not continual, careless blasphemy.

"Our survival will depend largely on God's grace. No skill of your officers, no muscular prowess of yours can protect you from the Arctic's treachery. But God's hand may stay your foot at the brink of a hidden crevasse, may loose the crunching maw of the ice pack, or halt an onrushing berg in its tracks. We will have many miraculous escapes if we begin now to propitiate the Maker of them."

Kane stood silent for a minute, his eyes moving from face to face. Watching him, Stephenson thought it odd how the Captain, though the smallest man on board, seemed to loom over them. He had, for all the drag of his seasickness, that twill in the muscular texture which gives tight little fellows more size than they measure and more weight than they weigh. Abruptly, Kane went below.

With more than one uneasy glance northward, the crew dispersed, Tom Hickey surreptitiously crossing himself.

Mr. Wilson, their sailing master, put the brig into St. John's in eighteen days. The little Newfoundland settlement was gay with bunting, its inhabitants dressed in their best and waving British flags in welcome. The Governor, brother to the head of the Admiralty, was especially cordial, and Kane perforce gave the first day over to official hospitality. The second found him haggling for meat like a thrifty housewife, now that it was too late and his purse too lean.

He was grateful when Governor Hamilton presented him with a handsome team of Newfoundlands he could not have afforded to buy. Kane sank his hand into the lead dog's silky coat as he listened to the Governor's speech, and wished he could have provided Maggie with just such a magnificent guardian in place of the detestable Tommy.

They were at sea again in fine June weather, swinging north along the Labrador coast, its low hills somber under a bright sky, when Whipple from the crow's-nest yelled, "Iceberg off the starboard bow!"

All available hands had been busy marling the recently purchased beef and mutton; boning the fresh chunks, rolling and tying them with twine, and hanging the rolls in the rigging to dry. From every spar hung cones and balls and cylinders, like Christmas ornaments on an unseasonable great tree.

At Whipple's cry the men were instantly on their feet, clutching twine, knives, and hunks of meat as they squinted ahead. Kane, wondering if Whipple would know a berg if he saw one, moved to starboard. A berg could look like a low-lying cloud and conversely, a cloud like a berg, but Long Tom was right. The North's first sentinel rode well within view.

At sight of the mammoth Kane felt the excitement of the novices, but differently. He experienced the exhilaration that comes not at first encounter with an awesome spectacle, but on second view.

They were advancing upon a huge oblong cube of pure but not dazzling white, a monolith waiting only the chisel to become a floating Parthenon. It disdained to glitter and rode tranquilly amid waves that tossed the little *Advance* as though she were a gull. Men and officers watched magnetized until the berg was far astern.

The younger officers wore a thoughtful look at mess that night, but McGary, chuckling, said, "More chatter in the fo'c'sle over one berg. Afore they're home again, they'll see 'em thick as chickens in a dooryard."

Kane smiled. "An amusing but inadequate image, Mr. McGary. To me, any berg is impressive. Bonsall, to celebrate meeting our northern friend, break out a bottle of my claret. Schubert's ragout deserves accompaniment." Delmonico's never served better, Kane thought, his malady having subsided almost with Whipple's cry.

"Friend, sir?" Mr. Hayes asked, incredulous.

From the bemused faces Kane knew he must explain. "Friend, indeed. As whalers do, we will fill our casks from the fresh-water pools found on many bergs. We will anchor in the lee of fixed bergs, and make tow horses of moving ones time and again."

"Tow horses?"

"You all know that a mature berg extends much farther below water than above. Hence it responds more readily to deep-sea currents than to surface action created by the winds. A berg will drive defiantly into a contrary gale, cutting a path through wind-driven floes. By making fast to such a steed, we will traverse otherwise impassable ice."

McGary nodded. "Set your lines right, keep a tight rein, and away we go. Better'n steam and cheaper, ain't it, sir?"

His practical Second put it more effectively than he.

Two nights later fog from the Greenland side swaddled the brig. A man couldn't see across her beam. Whipple in the bow felt at home. Like old England, seeing stuff this bloody thick but without no danger of bashing another ship. They hadn't seen a sail since Newfoundland.

Suddenly the gray-white curtain ahead was rent by a towering black prow. With a deafening crash, the bow pitched up violently. Shrieking his choicest oath, Whipple was tossed over backward, cracking his head against the capstan as jib boom and martingale came down around him. The brig keeled to starboard, but catching herself, slid into open water as the berg veered off.

Ohlsen, the carpenter, reached Long Tom, where he lay bawling obscenities, only a second or two before the Captain came up.

"You ain't dead yet if you can cuss so. You stop. Here comes the Captain. Just the jib boom, sir, I can fix right up. This fella ain't hurt."

"My head!" And Whipple gave his fluent opinion of the berg.

Kane probed with skillful fingers. "You've a good tough skull. Take more than that to dent it, Whipple, isn't it? And your powers of imprecation haven't suffered."

No more bergs were met as they plowed northward, the days steadily lengthening. Imperceptibly twilight yielded not to night but to dawn. The sun drifted below the horizon, like a Fourth-of-July balloon aflame, illuminating the *Advance* with a fierce light that crimsoned the sheets and the faces of the men. Quenched by the sea, it went out, only to rise within the watch, cool, shimmering, and pale.

For several days Kane noticed men off watch lounging on deck when they should be sleeping. On duty, they worked groggily. So he spoke to them again.

"I hear green hands complaining there isn't night enough for sleep. There will be less shortly. So you must learn to sleep in full sunlight, in order to perform your duties as smartly as the officers theirs, and *on exact schedule.* If we do not keep careful account of time, the expedition itself would be lost. Some of you know enough of navigation to realize that.

"Perpetual sunlight is small discomfort; unending night a harder test of your mettle. By your ability to adjust to the first, I can decide if you are man enough to face the second."

As they dispersed, he noticed that fellow Godfrey wore one earring in the piratical style. "No ladies around to admire, so get rid of that. It could cost you your ear farther north," he warned drily.

Lounging in his bunk, not sleeping, and still wearing his earring, Godfrey announced to the fo'c'sle it didn't take him a day or a night either to size up the Captain—"A pint-sized dandy."

Bonsall opened one eye. "Mr. Brooks who sailed with him before speaks most respectful of Captain Kane."

"Navy stuff, bowing to the brass. You're Navy, too, and a trained bootlicker. Not me. I'm my own man."

Bonsall looked at him speculatively. "You never been in the Navy?"

"Not me." Godfrey spat.

"A sailor named Godfrey figured in that mutiny on the *Somers.* He got off, I think. Leastways, I never read he was hanged."

Godfrey dropped from his bunk and swaggered toward the ladder. "You read too much, Bonsall," he said carelessly.

Brooks saw the riverman disobediently on deck and gave orders that Godfrey on watch be kept humping. "Let him do two-three men's work, he'll sleep." Brooks, like the Captain, favored useful punishment.

Steadily the little brig pushed north. Her log read:

June 23—latitude, 56–7; longitude, 52–12; wind, at four hours, calm—at 12 hours, E. 6—at 20 hours, E. 7; atmosphere, b. c.; current (true direction, N. 69 E.; velocity, 0.49).

June 24—latitude, 57–11; longitude, 51–58; wind, at four hours, E. 5, at 12 hours, calm. . . .

19. STRANGE PORTS

ON JUNE 26 the brig rolled through a cold and dripping fog, the men shivering at their tasks and muttering into soggy beards. Kane, from the ache in his bones, sensed the Greenland coast.

"Nearing Fiskernaes."

"Aye, sir, but not in a hurry in this weather."

The later the better, to Brooks's mind. The Captain was putting in for supplies and dogs. Newfoundlands were all right, but those damned voracious huskies– On the first expedition they had littered his deck, gorged two pounds of flesh a day and then tried to eat the shoes off your feet. Why, in '51, when a crewman aired his mattress on deck, the brutes tore it to rags and et it!

At daybreak they stood outside Fisher's Fjord, and Godfrey, who had just dropped off, was hauled out of his warm bunk to row Mr. McGary in for a pilot. Beside dripping, moss-fringed cliffs the river-man pulled steadily.

"Not much draught and you got to thread your way through these here islands." McGary waved at them. "Takes an Eskimo."

With McGary in it, hardly draught for their boat, Godfrey thought. His bulk almost set the skiff in the water. Eight miles he said it was, but it sure seemed longer. Then McGary pointed. "Fiskernaes."

Godfrey, turning, saw across a shore of wet pebble a handful of huts clustered around a red-and-white frame house with green blinds and a flagstaff. Not a soul was in sight. "Call that a port?"

"Bigger'n some you'll see."

By the time the skiff scraped bottom, the shore was crowded with Eskimos like furry ducks—dumpy and short-legged—quacking excitedly. When Godfrey stooped over to beach the boat, they laughed. When he looked round to see what was so funny, they laughed louder. The dried-fish-and-dried-filth stink of the place hitting him, he screwed up his nose. The crowd giggled hysterically. So he was a freak fit for Barnum's Museum, but they were funnier.

McGary set right off to find Lassen, the Danish Superintendent. With nothing to do, Bill looked the crowd over carefully to see if everything wearing trousers was male. The Captain said the women wore britches, too. The riverman's roving eye picked out a few plump figures with near-pretty faces. He winked at one, and the betrousered piece, turning to nudge her companion, revealed a sleeping papoose on her back. Leave it to Bill to smell them out.

When McGary, Lassen, and an elderly Eskimo finally came up, a little Husky without a papoose was riding Bill piggyback while he jiggled her in gallop rhythm and bellowed "Camptown Races."

"You—" McGary's cold gray eye expressed blasphemies.

Bill dropped his rider so she thumped on the shingle, and the crowd howled.

For a broken jackknife and other considerations the elderly Eskimo agreed to pilot the brig, and in the pale of evening she stood before Fiskernaes, her rigging silhouetted fragilely against the sun-cleared chilly sky. When Kane came ashore, he was astonished to see the Eskimo women in their fanciest garb, brilliant with beading and handwork, assembled there. "God-free!" they yelled out to the ship. "God-free!"

"Your sailor makes very funny with them," Lassen said stiffly.

The Danes' relations with the Eskimos were amiable but moral, Kane knew. Officials intermarried with the natives, but never debauched them. Together with Lutheran and Moravian missionaries, they had improved the moral tone on that whole coast.

As Godfrey's little rider galloped up and down to catch the sailor's distant attention, Lassen added, "Husband out hunting."

Bill, Kane assured him, would be kept on a tight rein.

All the brig's boats were soon put to loading the Captain's purchases of fresh and salted cod, stock fish and crepe fish, of shark oil in barrels, and cod livers for the dogs. So the Eskimos' amusing friend got ashore only long enough to load and light out.

He had to satisfy his admirers with quick stunts behind McGary's back. He would pull down the corners of his mouth and leer at them cross-eyed or, giving his ears a stiff jerk, seem to cause his jaw to drop and his tongue to hang out. When they shrieked with laughter and McGary turned, lowering, Bill was loading another barrel into the skiff.

"Can I help it they think it's funny when I stoop over?"

Seemed to Bill he made more and harder trips than any other crewman. The worst was hauling out the dogs Kane bought. The brutes stank worse than the fish, and their teeth terrified him.

It was dawn when Captain Kane finally shook hands with Lassen and brought to the skiff a roly-poly clutching a handsome gun. "McGary, this is Hans Christian, a skilled hunter who is joining us. Besides his wages, I have agreed to give his mother a couple of barrels of bread and fifty-two pounds of pork. Will you see to it?"

"Aye, sir, send the skiff right back."

Another blasted row! If Bill weren't so tired he'd have sworn in the Captain's face. Around McGary's bulk the Husky boy spied the funny man. "God-free!" he beamed, and held out his new gun.

"That," Kane indicated the gun to his Second, "and the gift of a new kayak have made me munificent in his eyes. He and the kayak will be very useful to us, skimming fast after prey our clumsy rowers could never catch."

McGary nodded and gestured toward their weary oarsman. "Slow as Bill here. He's only fast with the ladies."

Baffled by calms or light adverse winds, they were nine days reaching Sukkertoppen. It made Fiskernaes look like a port. At the foot of a wild isolated peak, a low, dingy compound with tarred roof and heavy gables was set in a rocky gorge. This was the "Governor's Mansion," connected by a stairway with clusters of mud-brown Husky huts.

The *Advance* arrived at midnight, when the strange light of Arctic summer night, very like that of an eclipse, bathed all in gray except the crimson northern sky. Packs of dogs howled at them from the beach and Brooks loathed the place on sight.

But the Captain was highly pleased with it. There he was able to buy dog harness and a good stock of reindeer skins cheap.

"For fifty cents apiece, Brooks! Several are *bennesoaks,* skins of the largest males, which make invaluable sleeping bags."

He had also bought several pairs of the crimped and seamless sealskin boots the natives wore. These he distributed to the crew as if they were wonderful gifts. "More proof against wet than any made by sewing," he explained to the dubious men.

Saturday they beat to the northwest against a heavy gale which subsided too soon. It took the next six days to reach Proven, where it lay sheltered by hills that were really monstrous rocks with no earth to mask their wrinkled, grinning ugliness. Summer came on so slowly here that the water line was still fanged with ice. Jeff Baker at the wheel never viewed a gloomier spot.

But the Captain, coming up, said in a warm voice, "I have real affection for Proven, Jeff, and for all who inhabit old Christiansen's Husky House. A real Eskimo home where in winter that patriarchal old Dane lives not just with his wife and all *his* descendants, but with his wife's mother and her children, grandchildren, and great-grandchildren."

"How many is that, sir?"

"Every time I tried to count, a canary bird and a sick bitch with a family of whining puppies kept getting in my tally. That was three years ago. There must be several more children now. They all live in a room fifteen feet square, just high enough for a grenadier without his shako." Kane laughed delightedly.

"Where do they sleep?" Jeff asked, bewildered. The Doctor didn't sound at all like his fastidious Philadelphia self.

"On a shelf of plank pine which runs around three sides of the room and serves as sofa and communal bed. There *is* a loft overhead for guests. I'll take you to visit my shrewd old friend."

An iceberg had found its way into port and for Kane its spire rose pleasantly as that of a village church. Jeff admitted the resemblance. Kane, studying the shore, said, "They have the summer lodge up. Take a look."

He handed the glass to Jeff, taking over the wheel himself. The Doctor never followed the seagoing etiquette in which McGary was instructing the landlubbers. Jeff hoped McGary wouldn't see him as he tried to spy the structure Kane indicated.

"That big tent to the left. Made of reindeer skins."

"Oh, that." It might have been a shelter for animals. Jeff reached for the wheel with an uneasy glance over his shoulder. McGary stood right behind them. He gave Jeff a conspiratorial wink.

In port, the little Doctor and the big Dane clapped each other heartily on the back. "Mama said you coom. A captain you are. So ve celebrate like last time American Yuly Foort."

Late for the Fourth, but it would give the men their last chance for amusement, so Kane agreed, and together they planned a Husky ball to be held in the loft of the storehouse. "Ve have eggnog vroom eider eggs. I make."

But first the Captain must finish his fur buying, turning the skins he already had over to Madam Christiansen who rounded up a circle of Eskimo seamstresses. When Kane came in later to watch their bone needles flying, making reindeer hides into parkas and sealskins into pantaloons for his men, the Dane's Eskimo wife gave him the great news of her small world.

"Una marry good Husky. Frederick also." Her daughter, Una, beaming, displayed her chubby little daughter. Kane had already been shown Fred's summer tent and new rifle, and only after those, his new wife and newer son. "Is good," Madam said.

Kane wished his own family would accept with such biblical simplicity a man's taking in marriage the girl he wanted. His own dear girl he must write at the first opportunity. Since Newfoundland, he had not written her a word, he had so many official letters and reports to prepare. Some way, he must find time for a long, loving letter.

The grand ball shook the loft rafters. The women in their sealskin pantalettes and brilliant cotton monkey jackets from the settlement store reminded Schubert of the Amazons of Paris. He saluted his partner as "George Sand" to Kane's amusement. Fred Christiansen and Mr. Wilson, the brig's sailing master, both brought guitars which the latter played with facility and spirit. The Husky girls were more adept at the polka and quickstep than the Americans, who made up in enthusiasm what they lacked in grace. Godfrey swung his giggling partner until she spun like a ball of fur, and Blake, stomping amazingly, trod on the tail of a rat whose squeals were lost in the din. The rats had been so long in possession they hardly bothered to move until then.

Such fraternizing was all very well, Kane thought, with these civilized southern Eskimos. Those farther north were another breed, ready to lie, cheat, steal, or, on sudden impulse, kill you—as they did each other. Such children of nature could, he was sure, be held in line by white man's magic, but only if their awe of white men was not dispelled by familiarity. He must make his crew understand they should be friendly but never intimate; another rule that might seem priggish, when in fact their lives depended on it.

In dealing with the northern savages, he needed a skilled interpreter. Christiansen, standing with him watching the dancers, said Carl Petersen, vice-governor at Upernavik, was the best man. "But he von't go. For Captain Inglefield, he von't leave his son. Only one he got now. His other boy die vhile he go vit Penny."

Kane felt all at once impatient for this rowdy dance to end, so he could start for Upernavik to try his powers of persuasion on Petersen. He itched to succeed where Inglefield had failed. It would be a good omen. Between here and that last outpost, however, he must buy more dogs.

The brig in Brooks's charge half-sailed, half-drifted up the coast while Kane in the whaleboat picked up dogs at a dozen small settlements. He handled them as easily as any Eskimo. With a firm grip, he shut a dog's snarling mouth, muzzled it with twine, tied the brute's fore and hind legs together, and pitched him into the boat. Not a man in the crew, not McGary would try it. When the whaleboat headed back for the ship, the oarsmen rowed with a nervous eye on the writhing heap of dogs at their feet.

You had to say that for the little toff, Godfrey admitted to himself, he could handle huskies.

At Upernavik, Kane spent too much time signing up Petersen, working harder on him than on a Boston audience or a southern congressman. But he triumphed where Inglefield had not. Petersen would be good for little besides interpreting. In Disco several years before, while firing a cannon on King Christian's Day, the piece's premature discharge had left him with a permanently stiffened hand and wrist. But Penny had, nevertheless, found him useful in '50.

Though he followed British example many times, in one major respect he was departing from it. Kane would not sail off into icy space, as Franklin had, leaving no chart of his course. If the *Advance* and her crew needed rescuing, those who came after would know exactly where to look. This information he would intrust to the Judge, the one man his son could rely on to lock it away from dear ones as well as officialdom—until time to produce it.

So for days Kane had been working, when none of his men was around to see, on a lengthy report for his father. In it, he not only spelled out his intentions, but included marked maps and sketches of landmarks to guide where maps came to an end. Late his last night at Upernavik he wrote an affectionate covering letter.

He could almost see his father's gay smile and curling forelock. A tough fighter, one of old Hickory's own and, like his hero, at once ruthless and deeply sentimental. If only he had had time to enlist the Judge in Maggie's cause, he would have defended her as ardently as General Jackson had Mrs. Eaton. Not that there was any parallel between his delicate flower and that overblown rose, Peggy Eaton!

Now, at last, though it was very late—or rather early—he could write his little pet. His note to her was pitifully brief, but even so, Morton interrupted before he was done.

"You up early, Cap'n Ken, or ain't you been down?"

"Our last chance to post letters, Morton."

"You best come to breakfast."

Routine must be maintained. He would finish later. He found the mess agog at the number of bergs in sight in July! Sontag, the scientist, had counted them: 216.

"Such shapes!" Dr. Sontag said. "Like mushrooms, like ferns, like fantastic birds. Worn so by the waves, by the currents?"

Kane nodded. "And with some thawing by the summer sun. Were none of them pitted where rocks gradually melted into them?"

Sontag nodded eagerly. "One with a long, spotted neck, Whipple called a 'bloody giraffe.' "

Wilson said, "I had no idea we'd see so much ice all at once, sir."

"Not really heavy ice," Kane said. "Exceptionally open water here, wouldn't you say, Mr. Brooks?"

Brooks agreed that the sea ahead looked very promising and Mr. Wilson went up to stare bemused at water the experts called "open."

The Captain hurriedly addressed his packet of mail. On what he thought was his note to Maggie he scrawled a postscript, preceded by a sketch of a pointing hand. The significance of the hand his dear pet would grasp. He was interrupted again before he could put each piece into its lined envelope. But finally he had everything ready. Maggie's he addressed in care of Cornelius, the rest to Mr. Grinnell himself. Then off his mail went on the long journey half around the world to home.

20. IN THE ICY MOUNTAINS

ON JULY 27 they neared Wilcox Point but could not yet see beyond it into Melville Bay when a heavy fog closed down. There was big ice near and no mistake. With all sails reefed, the *Advance* still moved steadily, carried by the currents God knows where, Brooks thought helplessly.

When the sun finally dispelled the fog, Wilcox Point was far to the south, and the little brig, well into the bay, stood surrounded by bergs beyond counting. All around, their spikes and domes were lined in endless tiers. The men gaped until McGary's bellows roused them from paralyzed amazement.

"So now you seen Bergy Hole as the whalers name it. Lower the boats!"

By a whole day's towing with both boats, they crawled out of there and were rewarded for their labors by a good wind. Kane decided instantly to take radical advantage of it.

From here, whalers and explorers alike always hugged the shore to reach Cape York and the North Water by a landward route. But August was almost on them. He had noticed the land ice decayed and broken. It would clog the inshore track.

"Why not stand to westward until arrested by the pack ice and then *double* the Bay by an outside passage?"

McGary and Petersen looked dubious, but Brooks nodded. He remembered the *Advance* that first trip had been caught by floes on the inshore track. Just about now, too.

They beat rapidly through tolerably free water for two days. Then an offshore breeze drove an ice field in their path and Kane gave the first order to tie to a north-moving berg. It took eight hours of heaving and hauling at hawsers and oars to plant the anchors and pull the brig within lee of the monster. It had not towed them a ship's length when, with violent crackling, ice lumps the size of walnuts peppered the deck and the crew.

"Cut us loose, McGary!"

At his own command, the Captain himself wielded an ax on the nearest line. The brig was no sooner free than in a mighty convulsion the face of the berg fell in ruins with the noise of artillery fire, barely missing the *Advance*. More than three hundred fathoms of whale line and all their effort wasted! The weary men had to take to the boats again to haul the brig along. They were learning ice navigation the hard way.

Next day, caught in another fog, they moored to another berg to keep from drifting. When the fog lifted, there were two polar bears on a floe alongside! It was two in the morning, but so light that the Captain and McGary took to the quarter boat, and to cheers from the excited men, bagged one bear while Petersen and Dr. Hayes in the Red Boat got the second. The big carcasses were hauled aboard, their dirty yellow pelts streaming blood.

"This is something like!" Blake said, but it fairly turned his iron stomach to see the dogs, nearly insane over the raw flesh, ferociously devour the lot.

For two days they shifted their lines or "fasts," as Jeff learned to call them, from berg to berg, moving erratically ahead until finally they tied to such a monster that it was a moving breakwater that kept a steady course northward. The floes fell away on either side of it, leaving a wake of black water a mile wide. They began, however, to swing closer to land than Kane liked, land that was a wall of glacier. Any fluke might thrust them under it. He climbed to the crow's-nest to look for a promising lead. Spying one around ten that night, they parted with their "fast" friend.

They were no sooner away than the night sun, rising over the berg's crest, kindled dazzling fires on every part of its surface. The light turned the floes through which they bored into a resplendency of blazing carbuncles and rubies and molten gold.

The brig crunched steadily through this jewelry, its noisy progress arrested now and then by tongue ice the men cut out of the channel with saw and chisel. Kane, still aloft, would spot one clear pool here and another there, while Brooks rumbled orders that sent the brig zigzagging from opening to opening.

Four days of this, the Captain hardly coming down to sleep, saw them through the Bay ice into the North Water. Ahead, they had open passage to Smith's Sound. Cramped and weary, Kane dropped to the deck. Brooks waited with a broad grin.

"Made the crossing in only eight days! A record, sir."

"We've made up lost time, at least." If he could send a letter to Maggie now, he could do it with a full heart and clearer conscience. For the first time he smiled back at her portrait before he fell into his bunk, not waking until noon next day.

As he came on the bridge, they were passing the Crimson Cliffs of Beverly with their sinister streaks of blood-red snow. Stephenson, the mannerly Irishman, asked, "Is it really red, sir? Or only an illusion."

"Lichen. I went ashore to see two years ago and the color is due to lichen." He enjoyed explaining the Arctic's vagaries to his men.

To another watch he pointed out Hakluyt Point with its incredible six-hundred-foot shaft of gneiss. "An Arctic obelisk." Capes Alexander and Isabella, the gates to Smith Straits, their precipices rising a city block, he called "The northern Pillars of Hercules."

They seemed to challenge a sailor's right to pass, and the crew stood silent while the little *Advance,* darkened by towering shadow, glided silently between these headlands. Gulls and eider flashed white over the water.

"As picturesque as white sails over the Mediterranean," he said to Riley at the wheel.

"Yes, sir, for the size of them." Riley neatly pinked his Captain's image in flight.

Smiling, Kane made for the crow's-nest again. By now the men should be used to seeing him there more often than on the bridge. But who else could do the conning? Only he or Brooks, no climber, would recognize, for instance, the smoky radiance of the atmosphere ahead as iceblink found over heavy floes. A freshening headwind was driving ice down from the north just as the *Advance* was crossing the line between the known and the unknown.

Inglefield was supposed to have rounded Cape Hatherton, but his charts had already proved shaky. They would scarcely become more dependable farther north. Before they entered the ice in an area no white man had yet reached (except possibly Franklin) he must set up a line of retreat.

As Kane hurried down to give the necessary orders, Henry

Goodfellow decided that the Captain moved in the rigging not with the swinging ease of a sailor, but with the scramblings of a small boy in a gnarled apple tree. He really had none of the awful dignity sea captains were supposed to possess. It was not the men's respect so much as their interest that he roused. What set him really apart was his tireless drive toward his goal.

"Mr. Brooks!"

Look at big Brooks, coming on the double. "Aye, sir."

"Iceblink ahead. We will leave emergency supplies on the mainland in sight of Hatherton. Ice can't bury a landmark that size. Use the metallic boat."

Under Brooks's direction the little boat was loaded with an exactly calculated store of provisions, tidily stowed and lashed down. Then over the side it went to be towed by a crew in the Red Boat. Goodfellow saw Jeff Baker at one oar, happy to take part in their first cache. There went the Captain, too. If Kane had a weakness, it was his never really delegating authority. As a scientist, Henry decided, he was used to checking every step by his own observations.

Ashore the men overturned the metallic boat so it became a housing for its own cargo. Then they buried it under rocks, stones, and sod, and crusted the pile with sand and water, the Captain laboring with the men.

"There!" Kane brushed wet sand off his mittens. "Frozen, that should withstand wind *and* bears."

"Aye, sir, if it's thick enough to fool the bears' noses. They smell it out, nothing they can't get through. Remember the limey's iron casks we found they smashed?"

Such a long speech from his first officer might persuade the Captain to more piling and plastering. But he said, "Ice and snow will cover that, Brooks. It will do." The panting men smiled in relief until Kane said casually, "Now to the west cape on Littleton to set up a cairn."

There, after a nasty row, they built a regular little monument. "High enough to catch the eye of any searchers," Kane said.

Jeff looked at it with sudden shock, as if it were his own headstone. But when they hauled up an American flag, and the banner unfurled on the midnight breeze, home seemed not so far away, and Jeff cheered as heartily as the rest.

Soon they were back on board, their stout little ship plowing north against wind and tide. Within two hours she encountered the ice pack. Despite all her twistings and turnings it pressed her closer and closer to a Greenland shore that failed, Kane saw, to conform at all to Admiralty charts. They were at last piercing the rim of the unknown. To find what? His Open Sea? Any trace of Franklin? What solutions to what mysteries?

He was thinking like a medium, his little medium. In his cabin he told Maggie's portrait, "But mine is the real other world, not your humbug world of the spirits!" Laughing in excitement, he leaned over to kiss her teasing mouth.

His "piercing" must in fact be patient prodding. Ahead was solid ice except for a blue-green streak along the shore where the tides had torn a narrow, irregular channel. Up this the *Advance* worked her slow way.

They could rarely use sail, Mr. Wilson discovered. Most of the crew weren't even aboard, but out on the ice with McGary. From the crow's-nest the Captain called orders to tow or track or warp as needs be, and Brooks relayed his commands to McGary.

To towing with the boats, Wilson was accustomed. Warping at least resembled docking a ship at home, though it was done here for a different purpose. Here, when loose ice crowded the brig, a hawser was fixed to firm land ice ahead and the vessel inched forward from the capstan, Brooks and a few men taking turns at the bars. Out on the ice, the rest with oars and spars poked the brig at beam ends or astern to nudge her around tongue ice.

Tracking, Wilson really disliked. Then the men were hitched into harness with shoulder belts called "rue-raddies" by which they dragged the brig along, as if she were an Erie Canal barge and the men patient mules.

When there was any wind and the Captain saw clear water ahead for as much as a ship's length, he ordered Wilson to crowd sail for "boring," or ramming the ice. Then their hard-nosed little ship might bound back on her rudder or crash through so handsomely a half-dozen men were marooned on a floe. Twice in a day that had happened. Each time Kane scrambled down to make sure McGary picked them up in the small boats. The crew were fast learning to ride a floe as casually as a river raft at home.

That night, when the ice crew came aboard sodden and weary,

Kane clapped the men on the shoulder. "It's tiresome and dangerous work, but you're proving up to it. See that headland?"

It didn't look as distant as Wilson suspected and Kane knew it to be. The Arctic light was deceiving.

"If we're there tomorrow, I'll be satisfied. Mr. Hayes, I recommend dry clothes and a tot of whisky around. You agree?"

"I a-g-g-ree, sir." Hayes spoke through chattering teeth, dripping where he stood, and the men thought it a great joke that the sawbones shared in the prescription. In this grinding work officers had to lend a hand and Hayes had been caught on a floe.

A full day's hard labor found them hardly nearer that headland. Suddenly the pack pushed the *Advance* into an unmarked inlet while fog like cotton wool crept over her. The watches spent the night wading through it.

Kane laughed to see Tom Hickey stepping high as if the stuff caught at his ankles. "Never seen such," the cabin boy said, amazed. "Oughter call this Fog Inlet, sir."

"Your name for it will go on my map, Hickey. Any landmark," he called to all the watch, "is ours to name. No one has been here before us!"

From his jubilant tone his men would never suspect his inward mingling of fear and fury that the *Advance* might be beset here for the winter, far south of his hoped-for goal.

God was kind. A sou'wester next day blew off the fog and shoved the pack and the brig with it out into the clear. At least the Captain called it "clear," though Goodfellow saw more ice than water.

For four more days they strained toward that chimerical headland. It must be vastly higher than even Kane had thought to be seen from such a distance. After an eternity of sweating labor, they passed it, and he and Brooks agreed, over the charts, they were beyond Inglefield's northmost point and this being mid-August, could press on some distance before winter forced them to tie in.

That day they entered a narrow reach, attended by curvetting walruses that mowed the sea ripples with their tusks and presented their sphinx faces to the visitors without humor.

"In shore in such numbers they usually portend a storm," Kane warned Wilson. A stiff southerly wind was steadily increasing. "In the lee of that ledge ahead, we can harbor safely. McGary!"

He had McGary send out one, two, and then three hawsers to

massive rocks at the water's edge. When the brig was snug, he retired, Brooks assuring him, "This wind will blow us a passage clean to the Pole, Captain!"

His big friend was unwontedly enthusiastic over a little favoring wind after days of duller travel. But Kane, before he stepped over the companionway combing, also regarded lightheartedly the sinister sky and the moaning and whistling shrouds, though he did notice their faithful dovekies were blown away and the dogs already howled. He had Brooks's word that the dogs were well secured. If they got loose in a blow, skidding and yawping all over the deck, it would be the devil's own catastrophe short of shipwreck. They were his only concern as he went below.

By morning the wind roared like a lion. Ice had crowded out the walruses and rubbed and pounded so violently against the brig, that she strained hard at her lines. Anything loose above deck was swept away, including their anchor buoys. The storm heaved a great mass of ice over the bow. It smashed on the deck not far from where Kane stood, covering him with ice chips and spray. He shook most of it off but he was still dangerously wet, must change, his footgear at least.

He stood barefoot in his cabin, when he heard their smallest line, their six-incher, part with the snap of a cord breaking. The brig shuddered and then steadied to the pull of the two remaining lines. He was hurrying into dry socks when he heard a second line go with a metallic twang that meant the whale line. He was pulling on his sealskin boots when McGary lumbered awkward as a walrus down the ladder.

"Cap'n, it's blowing the devil and I'm afeart to surge."

Kane, still more scientist than seaman, had to think what "surge" meant: feed out the single line, a magnificent manila hawser ten inches around, that still held. The strain on it must be unbearable by now, but any slackening of that mighty rope would give the storm wicked opportunity.

On deck he found the crew in a huddle watching that cable, a massive harp string on which the wind played a deep aeolian chant. "Its death song," he muttered, almost as the strands gave with the crack of cannon fire. In the smoke that followed the recoil, the brig was dragged out into the wild ice, at the mercy of the plunging pack.

His stout ship steadied, there was nothing like her, and they tried to beat back through the ice-clogged tidal channel. Two hours' vain struggle and the storm still pressed them dangerously near a point where the strait narrowed insanely. Heavy ice tables clogged the passage between shore cliffs on one side and their ledge on the other. To keep some command of the helm, they must let the brig go freely where she would otherwise be driven. So they let her scud under a reefed foretops'l.

"Wind her a little, Mr. Brooks! Drop anchor!" Hold her back from her doom, he wanted to cry out.

But there was no withstanding the torrent of ice that followed her, streaming along like an avalanche, thrusting everything before it. Their rudder would go, their stern be stove in if they stood against it. They had only time to fasten a spar as a buoy to the anchor chain before they let it slip.

"So goes our best bower."

"Yes, sir," Brooks said, and made it sound profane.

Down they went upon the gale again, scraping along a lee of ice at least thirty feet thick. One floe to which McGary tried vainly to hook a line was by measure more than forty.

"I have seen such ice only once before—"

"I never seen the like," McGary said.

"—and never in such rapid motion."

"Hope I never do again," McGary said.

Just then one upturned floe rose above their gunwale, smashed in their bulwarks, and deposited a half-ton lump of ice on their deck. The brig hardly dipped her bow before this onslaught.

Beyond the floe ice against which the *Advance* slid and thumped stood a line of bergs. Toward them the storm drove her. "She may be dashed to pieces against them, or they may prove a refuge, McGary."

"Aye. Look, Cap'n! They're a distance from the floe edge. Open water between."

The crew, too, had seen it, and yelled exultantly as the gale swept the brig toward this passage and into it. Then, with an eddy of wind against the lofty ice walls, she lost her headway. At that instant they saw the bergs were not stationary, but moved steadily toward the brig; on their own momentum, contrary to the storm, advancing toward the floe ice. The brig would be crushed between the two.

Only minutes before the ice had seemed to part as miraculously as the Red Sea for the Israelites. Now, they all waited in silence for sure destruction.

Then Kane spotted a broad sconce piece, a low, water-washed berg, driving up behind them. Its roots as time-worn as its crown, it moved not with the deep currents but north with the storm. For all its reduced state, it was still more massive than the heaviest floes and might batter a path for them.

He could only say "McGary," and point to it.

"Yes, by God, sir!"

Brooks at the helm maneuvered the brig so the sconce could come alongside. As it pulled rapidly up, McGary, agile as a cat for all his bulk, planted an anchor on its slope, and with legs braced held on by a whale line while Kane scarcely breathed.

Their noble tow horse, whiter than the pale horse that pursued them, hauled the *Advance* bravely on. Spray dashed over his windward flanks and his forehead scornfully plowed up lesser ice. But the advancing bergs narrowed their channel to forty feet.

Brooks roared, "Brace the yards!" The cross spars at his bellow were turned obliquely, just in time to clear the cliffs on their port side. Their port quarter boat was swung from its davits within seconds of being crushed to splinters.

Then they were through that devilish strait, had swung in the lee of a berg to shelter from the storm, and ahead was an open lead. Kane, as he turned shaking from the rail, saw Riley and Hickey, the cabin boy, on their knees thanking God. They were not alone in their prayers.

A flaw in the wind soon drove the brig from shelter, and the gale speedily carried her to the end of her lead and into the ice again. Sometimes they escaped its onset by warping. Other times they scudded wildly through half-open drift. When the ice closed so fast they could neither warp nor scud, the brig's strength and buoyancy alone withstood the pressure. Isaac Hayes, who had once scorned her, learned that day to love the little ship.

Her jib boom snapped off at the cap, her barricade stanchions carried away, she came at last to rest in a pool of open water beyond a lofty cape. Between her and the gale a berg had anchored itself to give further protection. Exhausted, her crew turned in, but not her chief officers.

Kane was too exultant and yet too anxious to sleep. "Ten miles nearer the Pole than we were this morning, Brooks! Near disaster turned into solid achievement!"

"Aye, sir."

But the gale was not yet broken and the floes pressed their defending berg hard. Where he stood with Brooks in the stern, the ice could be heard crashing against the base of their white mountain. Then he saw that towering peak sway toward them.

It always struck him as horrific to see a berg somersault when tides or storm altered the balance between its glittering superstructure and its keel. A berg diving easily as a seal was as shocking as a mountain dancing. But this— He watched their berg tilt until its pinnacle hung directly over his little ship and knew he looked at death.

The berg lurched, lurched again, and then, with a quick jerk, swung erect, its position altered just enough to allow the floes to circle its flank and smash the *Advance* astern. When the red-eyed crew hit the deck, they found their brig's rudder wrecked, the pintles torn from their boltings, and the wheel useless as the nips began.

The first shock came on her port side. She rose half out of the water to let that assault pass. But on came a veteran floe, a vast table twenty feet thick, and behind it other immense blocks, rank on rank, pressing under her keel and thrusting her sidewise straight at the berg that was lately her shield.

The face the berg presented to them was an inclined plane that descended deep into the water. Up this incline the brig was thrust as steadily as if a giant steam-screw-power forced her into dry dock. With shock after shock jarring her to her very center, she was lifted in her precarious cradle up—up. In another instant she would be driven too far, and tumble over on her side into the tumultuous sea. Up— The men felt her sway.

Then one of those mysterious relaxations Kane called the pulses of the ice set in. Gradually, gently, she was lowered into the water, clear except for rubbish ice, and carried toward the shore. From the moment she began to climb until she was safely settled, but for the groaning of her timbers and the sough of the floes, Goodfellow thought you could have heard a snowflake drop on her deck. For some seconds after there was intense quiet. Then the crew's yells were deafening, while tears streamed down McGary's face, a horrendous sight.

He brushed them away and bellowed for volunteers to take a line ashore. In no time the brig was made fast. Indeed she grounded when the tide fell and would have heeled badly but for a detached mass of land ice grounded beside her, which shored her up even as it stove in her bulwarks. Mr. Wilson decided he would never in this world get used to the insanities of ice navigation.

He was also perpetually surprised at the endurance shown by their semi-invalid captain. With that great oak, Brooks, and Iron Man McGary, Kane had, Wilson calculated, been thirty-six hours on deck. Yet, as he went below, the Captain hardly looked tired.

Brooks noticed him staring after Kane. "Fools you, don't he? Did me the first trip. He'll outwear McGary before we're done."

21. A THING APART

THE *Advance* rode out the rest of the storm in the lee of that great headland, which was in fact the cape they had labored days to reach. The face it showed them was a sullen black cliff a thousand feet high with an ice belt like a dead-white beach along its base. It circled a deep bay which ran well inward. Beyond this, another cape jutted.

"We won't approach it directly. I'm not ready to risk going adrift in the pack ice so soon again," Kane said. "Mr. McGary, pass our towlines to the beach."

Harder but safer, the crew agreed as they clambered into harness again and pulled in rhythm to a tune Bill Godfrey started. They sweated under their furs in spite of increasing cold, but worked well for knowing no one too good for this chore. Brooks and even the Captain took their turns, a startling and stimulating sight. They made three miles the first day.

The next, they traversed only a single mile when the tide fell so sharply that the brig grounded, heeling over until she reached her bearings. When she rose at 10 P. M., the men were ordered out on the ice again and hauled not so heartily, a steady snow dragging at them.

"In August," Bonsall said with disgust, "snow seems someways more unnatural than the perpetual ice."

Wednesday it still snowed, but they kept tracking until the brig grounded at low water; then, when the tide lifted her, pulling in harness again. Thursday the snow stopped but left a pasty sludge that hid cracks in the ice through which the men sank knee deep, barking shins on sharp edges despite thick fur boots, the oozing blood stiffening their socks. The temperature continued to fall and the air was so bitter cold they breathed shallowly and sang not at all. Friday, when the brig grounded as usual and the men tumbled into bunks at such a slant half the crew had to brace themselves in their sleep, Hayes spoke hesitantly to the Captain.

"Some grumbling among the men, sir. The want of rest, the cold, our slow progress–"

"Most discouraging," Kane agreed briskly.

"Perhaps if we turned southward to winter–"

"You are probably not the only one looking southward."

"I haven't discussed it, sir," Hayes said quickly.

"I'm sure you haven't." Kane smiled. "But *I* must. Mr. Brooks, assemble the officers in my cabin."

It was ridiculous to hold a conference at a 45-degree angle. Kane listed against his small desk and considered what he must say. He could not blurt out the simple truth: So far they had only sampled peril and would not be real explorers until they learned to risk their lives as a day-to-day thing.

All but Brooks took their places self-consciously, but the Captain showed himself so ready to listen that they soon talked freely. All but Brooks favored wintering to the south.

"Take another gale to get us farther north, Cap'n, and don't seem like we'll get it so late," McGary said. "Winter practickly. Two inches a new ice on her hull now. Temperature dropping all week."

Kane nodded. "I am loath to recognize the signs, but it does look like an early winter. Dr. Sontag, our northmost position?

Speaking carefully, the astronomer reported, "Determined by the sun's lower culmination if we can so term his midnight depression, in this bay, we are latitude 78° and 41′."

His listeners looking only blank, Kane explained, "In brief, we are already farther north than anyone has reached, except Parry on his Spitzbergen tramp. We could retreat in triumph."

Someone sighed in mistaken relief.

"We need tell no one that this expedition's officers, except for Brooks and myself, were ready to turn back at the first difficulty," Kane said sharply. At their shocked faces he modulated his tone. "The dangers are equal either way, gentlemen. It will be as hard to withdraw now as to advance. Nowhere to the south did I see a suitable winter harbor, nowhere a point from which to launch our spring searches, nowhere a sign of Franklin. That way lies failure! While just ahead–" He let them finish the thought.

"Could have a southerly gale tomorrow," Brooks declared, and then in his large, kindly way both excused and encouraged the rest.

"They're new to this life, sir, and don't know how chancy Arctic weather is. Most of the men are raw, too."

"You know, Brooks, I think the men, being used to hard labor, have taken our troubles rather better than the officers."

McGary sputtered that he could work hard as any hand.

"Maybe so," the Captain said, "but stick with me and you'll be a slimmer man, Mister, when next New London sees you."

They all laughed at that.

"You were forewarned," he continued, "that we did not follow regulations, that you would be more navvy than naval officer. But one Navy law holds. Your captain is held responsible for success or failure. In this instance, we lose more than we gain if I accept your advice." Patiently he repeated, "Life would not be easier to the south. Worse, the distance we have so laboriously crawled would be lost. So we will warp to the next headland."

He searched each face, detecting on none any real disaffection. More easily, he continued, "From there I can see for myself the best starting place for the spring searches. At the nearest shelter to that point we will go into winter harbor. Is this acceptable?"

"Might as well be killed for a sheep as a lamb," McGary conceded.

"You would be poorly cast as either, Mister, nor am I the man to lead his flock to slaughter."

They were laughing again. Kane felt he had weathered well a small tempest.

On the heels of this minor triumph he faced major disaster. At high water itself the brig went aground on the rocks and stuck there even at night tide, always the greater. They might never get her off!

"She must be lightened instantly. Put ashore everything portable, Brooks. Fast, man, fast!"

All hands laid to, and that job speedily done, the boats were brought alongside and heavier objects, "ponderables," lowered into them, their remaining heavy anchor into the quarter boat. The rudder they sank astern. Heavy hawsers were run to a fixed berg and they were ready for heaving on the morning tide. Until then Kane could only wait, while the men snatched at rest.

Around three the lightened ship heeled so abruptly that the men were thrown from their bunks, the cabin stove was pitched over, and hot coals spewed onto the deck. It began to blaze smartly. The men ran for the fire buckets but there wasn't time.

Sontag, on the watch, was wearing a heavy pilot-cloth coat. Kane held out his hand. "Your coat, Doctor."

Without a word the astronomer peeled it off and Kane used it to choke down the blaze until water arrived. When he finally returned the badly charred garment to its owner, Kane said softly, "Sacrificed for a good cause. The powder is stowed not far off."

The next afternoon heavy ice at her stern shoved the *Advance* free of her shackles, while splintering her rudder. At five she floated easily, the men tracking until low tide at ten when she was aground again. After a hot supper the crew turned in, quite inured to this mad progress.

But Wilson brooded over the abuse the brig had taken: she had a hard time on those rocks, had been high and dry the last two tides, and had grounded no less than five times in three days! It was light enough to see the sailing master's face, and Kane, coming up, said without preamble, "Except for a portion of her false keel, there is no real injury. Her broken rudder and one shattered spar are easily replaced. She'll get us there and back again."

"And so will I," the gleam in his eye seemed to say to Wilson, "though I, too, have suffered some damage."

"I believe you absolutely, Captain," Wilson said earnestly.

The morning of August 29 they reached the northern headland. An ice belt surrounded both it and a small bay beyond. Kane and Brooks studied the long reach of ice through their glasses.

"Broken in spots and difficult to traverse, but practical for miles, Brooks."

"Looks so, sir."

"Shall we take McGary for a little walk? Ice that holds him—"

"I know your little walks, sir, but McGary don't."

McGary set out cheerfully, sure he could tire the Captain, if not Brooks. The ice proved solid but complicated with drift. Kane wore a long waist scarf, like a Hindoo's cummerbund, to keep the cold from intruding at the waist of his pantaloons. Its ends floated martially on the breeze ahead of McGary, who returned winded after fourteen miles, while the Captain showed no strain.

"I'm a sailing man," McGary said, panting, "not *used* to footing it. This time, Cap'n says we take a boat till she's stopped. *Then* we walk. Brooks and me are going—" He'd show the Captain yet.

"And I," Sontag added himself to the list.

"Morton, of course. Gives us four. Cap'n wants seven. I'll take the first three from the crew."

Blake, Riley, and Bonsall spoke at once. When they went below for extra socks, the tin cup and sheath knife apiece that were to be their only gear, Godfrey said, "Bonsall's a born toady, but I never took you for one, Blake."

"Maybe I'm tired of sleeping at a slant or tired of your gab. Maybe I want to show I can keep up with him."

"Me, I know I can, see?" Godfrey boasted.

"You ain't likely to prove it the hard way," Bonsall said.

Their best and lightest whaleboat, sheathed with tin to keep the ice from cutting through her, Ohlsen, the carpenter, was fitting with a canvas cover. A sledge was already stowed under her thwarts. In addition, they took buffalo robes for sleeping, a sail for a spare cover, a single extra suit for the whole party, pemmican and a soup pot, and lamp for the mess. In three hours they were off. Some smart aleck had christened her, Brooks heard, "The Forlorn Hope."

She proved so to McGary her first day out. Pack ice in front and along one side, an ice wall on the other forced them to haul her at high tide up on the ice belt. They pushed on by sledge.

Their highway was a broad shelf of ice overhung with lofty cliffs. Huge blocks of ice dotted its surface and long tongues of rock thrust across their road. They worked around these easily but were harassed by streams that cut gorges down which the sledge had to be carefully lowered, carried through icy water, and dragged up the opposite side.

When they camped that night, their tent, once buffalo robes were spread and the cooking lamp lit, was surprisingly cozy. Dry socks replaced wet. Hot tea and pemmican were downed with relish. Soon only the smokers were awake, musing over their pipes while the sleepers snored around them. The next night they were settled as comfortably when their wakeful captain saw water seeping in under the tent lap. The damned excessive tides of the region had caught them.

"All out! All out!" Everything that couldn't stand a wetting the sleepy men piled on their buffalo robes and held high.

For hours they held up those sagging robes, waiting for the tide to ebb. Suddenly the Captain, in rolling tones, proclaimed them, "Eight Yankee caryatids, up to their knees in water, an entablature supporting their household gods! A handsome monument if we freeze in this position."

It sounded almighty funny, whatever it meant, and they whooped with laughter. McGary's belly shook with it, and they whooped again. At least it stimulated circulation, Kane thought.

The water dragged itself away finally and they went back to sleep, none the worse for their ordeal. But the glacier that blocked their path the day after proved a harder trial. Its icy sides were steep and a slip would send a man into watery depths far below.

"Our shoes are too smooth. Wrap cords around like this." Kane deftly wound his own. "Gives traction for crawling, but take it slowly." Belly on the ice, he inched forward.

"Like a God-damned ——ing caterpillar!" McGary exploded, and immediately followed. Kane vowed later that the Second rocked his way across. His spectacular blasphemy went unreproved.

On the far side they had to portage. Brooks, as their strongest man, carried the theodolite, sixty pounds of mechanism in an angular mahogany box. "A dubious honor, Brooks," the Captain said. "We lesser men can only take turns with the dip circle." Blake, Riley, and Morton in conspiracy saw he never took his turn.

When they were forty miles and five days out the Captain decided they progressed too slowly. "We'll do better on foot, leaving the sledge and tent here. Each man carries his buffalo robe and pemmican. Except Brooks, who has the theodolite."

To their deep satisfaction they made twenty-four miles that day, and, since it was not much below freezing, slept in the open without discomfort. Next afternoon they came to a perfectly open bay.

"Not a scrap of ice in her! But there's ice out in the strait."

"Listen!" Far off they heard a steady roar. Without a word the Captain at a dogtrot swung around the inner sweep of shore, Sontag like a gazelle leaping at his heels.

"Almighty hurry, the Cap'n is in. Danger, maybe?"

"A discovery, I think. He does like to discover things for his map," Brooks said indulgently.

When they reached the headlong pair, Kane was jubilant. He flung out an arm toward his find. "Probably the largest in North Greenland. Half mile wide here," he yelled above the roar of a tumultuous river that plunged over a bed of rocks. "We'll camp here, and ford it in the morning."

McGary was glad to hear it, not being built, like Sontag, for leaping gracefully from rock to rock.

Bonsall came up, excited. "Flowers, sir, over there!"

The whole party ran to stare down, oddly stirred, at small clumps of Arctic flowers nestling in dirt pockets in the rocks. Kane and Sontag squatted to study them.

"So late their growing!"

"Solar heat thrown off by the stones helps. Festuca and other tufted grasses, mostly, but those purple flowers are lychnis and the white stars—"

"Chickweed!" Bonsall beamed at the homely sight.

"Here's a solitary hesperis." Kane touched it with gentle forefinger.

Sontag carefully collected specimens, but the Captain's handful were, he said, for salad. "Cress, related to the mustard family. You eat mustard greens at home."

Blake, who was from Baltimore, admitted the charge. But he ate no such piddling things and he ate them boiled.

"In the Arctic, they're medicine, raw. Never cook them." The Captain ate his with enjoyment, the men stoically.

Over his salad Kane named the river "the Mary Minturn, after Mrs. Grinnell's sister." The men were pleased. The name "Minturn" took them back to New York's water front, to the *Flying Cloud* tall at her moorings and other ship, "Grinnell and Minturn" ships.

"You're with a Grinnell ship now," Kane reminded them.

They slept well that night, lulled by the sound of running water, but liked the river not so well next day when they plunged through the icy torrent. Midway to the next cape they came on a lesser stream with trampled lichen along its bank.

"Deer! They've fed here recently," Kane declared, but, though they watched to a man, they saw no deer and ate no venison.

Beyond that cape lay another bay with another headland on its far side. "Seems like we been here before," Blake said.

"Not only we ain't but nobody else ain't," Riley answered.

The Captain's comment rang familiar. "If I could get to that headland, I could see—"

Like he was so farsighted he couldn't see nothing close up, Riley thought. Such as Brooks tiring, him being forty anyways, and that theodolite heavy for an old man to lug.

"New ice," the Captain said, "and far from safe. But with tact I could cut straight across the bay, tact and a wiry man or two for company. The rest can recruit here."

Meaning chiefly Brooks and McGary, who wasn't wiry. Riley, nodding, volunteered even before Morton. When Kane clapped him heartily on the shoulder, Riley was that proud to be going, his grin was so wide his mouth hurt!

Equipped only with the Captain's pocket sextant, his Fraunhofer telescope, a walking pole, and three days' food, the trio set off. For all they had to walk on eggs, they came in a surprisingly short time to their goal. That cape, Kane said, was the highest visible from the brig. "With my glass I could see it from the crow's-nest. There's no mistaking its configuration."

Once there, he wasn't ready to stop. After a good night's rest he set them a stiff pace northward, clambering around the cape and on to a headland a thousand feet high. Atop it, he spent an hour with his telescope and his chart. He had them use the glass, too.

"You're looking across the eightieth parallel. Don't ever forget it. I never shall!" He propped his paper on Morton's back, told them, while he mapped it, what they saw. "That's the other shore of Smith's Sound over to the left. That great dusky wall may be a glacier. If so, it's the world's greatest!"

Reaching far to the north-northeast was a vast sweep of land he named for George Washington. Its most projecting point bore 14° by sextant from the farthest hill on the opposite shore. Between stretched solid ice. From the crest where they stood, Kane studied the long lines of hummocks dividing the floes like the trenches before a beleaguered city. Beyond a stream of bergs formed an almost impassable barrier. Beyond them, the ice seemed unobstructed. But the Arctic's deceits could make a thousand bergs appear a smooth, attractive plain. With a sigh he dropped his glass.

Nowhere had he found a better place to winter than the bay where the brig now rode. Walled by headlands which stood a barrier against moving ice, which secured the harbor from wind, eddies, and drift, it was nevertheless open to meridian sunlight. On one rocky islet the dogs could be housed, on another the observatory set up. The streams in the depths of the bay which had harried them on this trip would be a boon next summer, melting the ice around them, freeing the brig for her homeward voyage.

This decision made, he became anxious to return to the *Advance*. His party being of a like mind, they traveled with a speed that proved fortunate. Snow and wind at gale force met them as they came in sight of their ship. Through flurries of stinging snow they hurried aboard where Kane briefly announced his decision.

Down in his cabin, when his eyes met Maggie's, he was shocked to realize he had for days scarcely thought of her. At home she had reminded him of an Arctic flower, but here no Arctic bloom brought her to mind.

22. ONSET OF NIGHT

THEIR mooring he named Rensselaer Harbor to please his family. As for Maggie, whatever else happened, her portrait was hung at his "Rensselaer."

Mr. Wilson, a Griswold connection, said "that's a York state name."

"My father's mother was Alida van Rensselaer," Kane explained, "so our home place was named for her. Since I was the one," he told his mess with a smile, "set on reaching this bay, I have appropriated the right to name it."

The conversation made him remember uneasily his father saying once, "Be democratic in choosing your friends, but a thorough snob when you choose a wife, Elisha. Your mother is the only woman I ever saw as beautiful, well bred, and brainy as my mother." The Judge would not consider Maggie a suitable successor to those two.

"But I do, my darling," he assured her portrait, "and I am the one who must make the choice. You are mine!"

In a few weeks his Arctic Rensselaer was transformed from a bleak solitude to a place of comfort and cheer. Ohlsen and Petersen had housed in the deck of the *Advance* and built, on the Captain's design, a roomy cabin below to serve as a common, commodious dormitory. Later it would be Schubert's galley as well. To increase their living space, their supplies were moved to a storehouse of ice and canvas on a nearby islet.

The freezes of early September cemented the floes around the ship, affording men and dogs easy come and go to the shore. There a hut was built for the brutes, clearing the decks of them.

The most dedicated work went into the observatory on "Fern Rock," a granite obtrusion a hundred paces to seaward from the brig. The rock rose the height of the ship's crow's-nest where she stood fast, and the men had to haul straight up a good thirty feet all the rock, gravel, and water Kane and Sontag required.

At the top, though the temperature was usually fifteen above, the Captain and Dr. Sontag sweated profusely as they labored on the four walls of rock, cemented with moss and freezing water. Later, Ohlsen laid over these a wooden roof with holes and slits where the scientists calculated they were needed. Inside, pemmican casks, filled with gravel and water and left to freeze, formed rock-rigid pedestals for the sensitive instruments. Sontag supervised their installation, when McGary, huffing and puffing, managed to get himself as well as the instruments up the height.

"Finicking," McGary called the tall, anxious young astronomer. "One jolt and he's afraid the Milky Way will turn sour."

When it was all done, Kane was jubilant. "The noblest little observatory in the world, and the highest, geographically!"

Out in the open ice field a weather station went up next, built of wood, latticed and pierced with augur holes to allow free passage of air. Inside, behind screens to stop the drift of fine snow, their collection of thermometers was hung.

"Enough of them to start an Arctic branch of the Smithsonian," the Captain boasted as they suspended the biggest, his three-foot Taliabue. Its size was such that a man could stand well back and read tenths of a degree down to seventy below.

His enthusiasm made most of the men feel they were part of a remarkable establishment.

September brought, too, the return of nightfall every day. The first stars in many months relieved the long, staring days of endless sun and iceblink. There was a bedtime and a time for rising "without offending nature," Brooks said, and Kane made the home feeling complete by changing the log from sea time to the good old progression of hours beginning at midnight.

On the first of October, however, their wonderful thermometers dropped below zero for the second day; and the sun, when it found a hole in the swirling clouds, showed itself at noon hanging low over the southern hills. It cast a white light and the ice never blinked. Darkness would close down upon them before they knew it.

While there was yet time, Kane sent out two parties. McGary and Bonsall with five crewmen went north to cache supplies for the spring journeys. Hayes, Wilson, and Hans were dispatched inland to look for game and Eskimos. Where one was, the other was usually not far off.

Kane himself began to work the dogs. The Newfoundlands were no trouble, but the huskies– From the beginning he had tried to instill into these wild brutes a degree of obedience and fair play. He usually fed them himself, and the greedy puppy who snapped at his mate's food was sent flying through the air, propelled by one of the Captain's heavy Arctic boots. Fights between full-grown males he broke up fast, yanking them apart with hands armored in heavy fur mitts, cuffing one dog and kicking the other until the fight was out of them. By never relaxing his rules he was schooling them.

The crew, afraid of the dogs in a pack, though they made pets of individuals, couldn't get over the dogs' affection for their stern teacher. He, in turn, was careful never to display favoritism. The Captain couldn't afford a pet, not here. Only at home!

Now, with Petersen as mentor, Kane spent his daylight hours drilling separate teams to pull a sled around the brig. He drilled until his wrists ached from his efforts to make a dog whip as precise a tool as a fencing foil. Would he ever master the trick of swinging eighteen feet of whipcord by a stubby handle so exactly it snapped alongside the ear of a particular dog in a team of twelve?

"The snap make him obey. He don't like that noise. Next time, maybe you draw blood. My little Paul," Petersen smiled in fond remembrance, "makes such a loud snap like I myself can't."

To hear his father, Paul the *wunderkind* did everything on earth better than any other living creature. Captain Kane was competing with a child of ten.

One afternoon a misplaced snap threw the entire team—dogs, harness, whip, sledge, and driver—into chaos. Petersen laughed uproariously and Kane was trying to disentangle himself when Morton came running up.

"Cap'n Ken, three men coming. That'll be the Sawbones' party. Seven in the other lot."

"Did you ever call me the 'Sawbones,' Morton?" Petersen's laughter had a bad effect on the Captain's temper.

"No, sir! Mean to say 'Mr. Hayes.' "

"Right. I'll go meet them."

Even Morton was still so unaware of the Arctic's infinite treachery it had not occurred to him that this might be McGary's party returning *without* four members. But, no, that was Hans running ahead. "Reindeer!" the boy shouted.

They had not killed any, only spied them afar. They had encountered no Eskimos, only come on sledge tracks. Ninety miles inland they were stopped by a great glacier.

"I assure you, sir, it rises four hundred feet." Dr. Hayes, all too conscious that his party had accomplished neither of its objectives, offered this news in lieu of success.

On October 10 the sun made its last appearance over the southern hills, its final bow cut short by a curtain of clouds. Next day at noon there was a reddish dawn which never broke, followed by a few hours of pale, unnatural light. Through it Kane peered anxiously for signs of McGary's party.

A handful of men came plodding into view. Kane counted them. Thank God, all seven were there! They, too, were stopped by the glacier where it hit the sea. Nearby, on an island, they had stowed eight hundred pounds of pemmican and other precious stores.

"On the seaward side, Cap'n, away from the water them new bergs lash up. Allus thought they dropped like rock fall off a cliff. But that ain't the way of it."

"How is a berg born?"

"Well, it ain't there and then it is, sir. Just rises up before you. Breaks off under water, she does, and then up she comes, a hell of a thing to see!" The Second became slack-jawed in remembered awe.

"Venus rising from the foam," Kane murmured.

"More like a great cow calving, with the newborn berg heaving and bawling, trying to get its footing and falling over and coming up again mighty unsteady. When a thing that size carries on so, it's a sight bigger fuss than a ship launching." Embarrassed by his own loquacity, he concluded, "Well, anyways, the stuff is cached in a cave on the island, sealed tight agin bears."

"Very good, Mister. I've never seen a berg born myself. Perhaps I'll be so fortunate before we leave."

With his rolling gate, McGary strutted off. Kane smiled, and thought the man who recommended that chunky little whaler had done Elisha Kane no small favor.

Dr. Hayes, sent out again by his commander, this time to deposit a self-registering thermometer to the northward of Marshall Bay, returned with news of a second failure. He had Morton and Blake with him. Their second day out, the surgeon reported, "To my great mortification, I found the thermometer broken."

Kane put up his hand as if to ward off a blow. "It was an invaluable new instrument and its readings would have been of great scientific interest, Doctor."

"I know, sir. It—it must have happened when we lashed the sledge. I wrapped it in woolen and placed it in the center of the sleeping bags and buffalo robes— It looked safe."

"In handling delicate scientific instruments there is always danger." Kane could not entirely suppress his exasperation. "Put the whole story in your report, since we must account for our failure to use it." Hayes should have let Morton load that sledge.

Now morning came with a false dawn that shot up streaks of browns and grays the men found strange beyond their traveled experience. The insidious advance of darkness seemed to have a fascination for them. Kane noticed Blake, Hickey, even the insensitive Godfrey stop to stare silently at the black masses of the hills, starkly clear for five, then four, then three hours a day, their patches of white snow glaring over the bay of shelter. By the first of November the only light was a grayness at noon.

As steadily as the dark advanced, the cold intensified. Below decks the lard lamp, designed to stretch their fuel supply, provided a moderate temperature. But its warmth was not pure blessing. Their quarters were humid as a laundry tub. Moisture clung to every beam, and though Bonsall had built troughs that kept the drops from falling into their berths, the air stayed clammy.

It drew Kane's rheumatism to his knees like iron dust to a magnet. Half-crippled, for two days he tossed in his bunk, before deciding his only cure, as always, was exercise. With Morton's help, he struggled into his furs, while Hans hitched the Newfoundlands.

Announcing that he wished to measure the height of the cape on the bay's far side, he said, "Jeff, you and Hans come with me. We'll take sights during the noon twilight."

Both lads needed the exercise as much as he. They were taking the loss of the sun hard: Hans, homesick as he faced the winter night far from his people; Jeff, not only among strangers but also in an alien world.

With an expertness that gratified him, Kane gave the whip to the dogs. They darted off, their driver riding the runners, the boys trotting alongside. At the shore the team balked. The rising tide crunched the floe against the shore ice, spewing up pebbles of ice as methodically as a factory machine does bolts. Through this barrage the dogs would not charge, until Hans carefully guided the lead dog through. Then the rest followed, while Kane and Jeff lifted the sledge onto the ice shelf.

It was level as a wharf. They made the five miles to the cape in less than an hour. Hans held the dogs, while Jeff and the captain tried to scale the cliff face. They climbed only fifty feet when it became too steep and smooth to traverse. "Goes up a good four hundred feet higher," Kane estimated.

Jeff nodded mutely.

Backs to the cliff, they rested. Before them a vast leaden dome arched over a floor of ice, empty as a church at midnight. But against the granite wall behind them the roar of distant artillery reverberated. Only, it couldn't be artillery.

"Ice hummocking, forced upward by pressure of currents and tides," the Captain explained, "at times acting in union, again as opposing forces."

"Yes, sir." Jeff searched the vast field of shadowy white for some sign of this violence. There was none, though the thunder rolled, one clap sounding so near he shrank as if there had been a burst of lightning.

Far to the right a pinpoint of light suddenly pierced the leaden gray. Not a star; more like the lighted window of a cabin seen by a man lost deep in the forest.

"The brig?" Jeff pointed.

"Someone's hoisted a lantern up the mast," the Captain said in a pleased voice, "to light us home."

As they turned to make the descent, one of Kane's rheumatic knees caught, throwing him off balance. He grabbed Jeff's arm. The younger man quickly used his whole weight to steady his chief, and Kane could feel the boy's body quivering.

Not a week later Dr. Sontag on his noonday check at the observatory had to carry a lantern. At the weather station the thermometers read only twenty-three below, but at Fern Rock the magnetometer burned his fingers fast when he touched it, and the warmth of his face clouded the sextant arch and glasses with hoarfrost.

In the quarters Jeff and Bonsall discussed the first issue of the ship's newspaper, *The Iceblink,* a wax-and-ink publication for which the Captain had drawn the masthead showing the *Advance* in her winter harbor.

" 'The winter night has set in.' I'm a great hand for reading," Bonsall said, "but I favor reading something I don't know."

"I didn't know it would last three months." Ninety days! The sun itself would not appear for a fortnight after that. The thought clamped hard on Jeff's heart, making it hard to breathe.

"What I'd like to read is a way of reconciling this dark with the Good Book. You remember how it was. First the world was dark as here. Then God said, 'Let there be light.' He divided the light from the darkness, not onct a year neither—"

Jeff murmured, " 'And the evening and the morning were the first day.' "

There was a burst of laughter from Godfrey, lounging in his bunk. "This place ain't in the Bible! God wasn't proud of the job He did around here. He wants it forgotten, not snooped out by—"

"That's blasphemous." Bonsall knew he shouldn't let Bill Godfrey rile him, but rile him Bill always did.

"Just philosophy," Godfrey said loftily.

"Of a paltry sort," the Captain said from the doorway. "You do better with your muscles than your mind, Godfrey. Let's see how you fare in the Fox Chase I'm organizing. Up on deck, the three of you! The course runs from galley to capstan and the 'Fox' with the biggest lead after ten laps wins a fine Guernsey shirt."

"It's on my back now." Godfrey added after a pause, "sir."

Jeff rose up determined to beat the insolent bully. He felt himself somehow Kane's "champion," as kings had theirs. But Bill won handily, sporting his prize at mess. The men eyed it glumly. It was strange, Kane noted, how Godfrey, while doing nothing positively objectionable, managed to be a disturbing factor.

He worked well, but had developed no special skills. The rest had, and during this time of enforced confinement the men made all manner of gear for the spring journeys. Brooks was preparing canvas. McGary played tailor, his stitches small and neat for his hams of hands. Whipple proved an excellent cobbler, while Bonsall tinkered, making oil lamps after the Icelandic pattern.

For most of the officers there was an endless amount of paper work, all of it coming at last to the Captain. Nightly he examined and approved Dr. Hayes's log, Dr. Sontag's weather chart, Mr. Wilson's ice measurements, and Bonsall's tables of tides and temperatures prepared under Sontag's guidance. He himself developed his sketches into paintings, at which the men craned. Then, late into the night within the vaster night, he wrote in his journal.

His little pet was surely busy over her paper work, too, though not into the small hours. Then, he hoped, she dreamed of him who passed oddly dreamless nights himself when he did sleep.

23. END OF WINTER

ON HER WAY downstairs that late December morning, Lizzie Turner halted at the empty little room. The table with its closed books, the bed with its smooth counterpane, the old courting mirror with its blank face bothered her. She hitched her shawl around chilly shoulders and told herself again that Maggie was seventeen and a woman. If a grown woman forgot her promises, neglected books and teacher, too, for her fashionable friends, was the teacher to blame?

In Dr. Kane's eyes, yes. Those eyes had weighed her fidelity and been satisfied. When his glance had met hers, without words they had come to an understanding. Now she was failing him!

There was dust on the bureau. Polishing its smooth surface harder than need be, she glimpsed her own homely, wind-burned face in the mirror and rejected it, choosing to see instead Maggie's impassive face as it had been those last weeks. What could any teacher do against such apathy? But was it apathy that made Maggie sit, hands folded, ears unheeding, through an entire lesson? Sitting, book open, head bent, never turning a page; hardly moving for hours? Or was it iron control over nerves drawn too taut? The question plagued Lizzie.

Maggie had not been so at first, but, after a few tears, perfectly attentive, eager to work. For French, she had a flair, but it was German she was determined to master.

"Dr. Kane knows *everything* but German. Make me learn it, Miss Lizzie."

They had worked hard, their progress as slow as a mare's on a gumbo road. Her music was as facile as her French, though she slurred the trills and hardly attempted big chords. "My hands are too small, Mrs. Turner!"

Ma was patient but persistent. "Reach for those chords, Miss Fox, and you can play them."

Those days, when Pa came with the mail Maggie's dark head had turned with happy expectancy. Twice in Mr. Grinnell's letters there were enclosures from the Doctor. Then Maggie flew to her room, and after a dozen readings, returned, radiant, to say, "I can't study today, Miss Lizzie! I'm too happy! Let me work at my singing."

Ma had stayed at the piano while her pupil sang like a bird for hours. After dinner the second time, Ma said quietly to Lizzie, "She'll hear once more—from Greenland—then for months no word will come. Hard for her to endure, she's so young and impatient. She'll need help, Lizzie, through that trying time."

Parts of that second letter Maggie read to her. The Doctor's staccato style was so like him, Lizzie could almost hear him speak. His cheerful commands inspired Maggie to work harder on her German, but she wasn't really a good student. As Lizzie came to know the girl's mind, she grew puzzled over her success as a knocker. Maggie was not clever. If she was a fraud, as sensible people supposed, how had she fooled the credulous? They doubtless fooled themselves. Since the telegraph, people believed anything.

Exercise, about which the doctor had been most insistent, Maggie had always shirked. Lizzie, to whom the weather was all one, found Maggie forever excusing herself from a walk, usually because of that dreadful little dog. It was "too hot for Tommy. See how my poor dear is panting"; or it looked like rain, "and Tommykins can't abide rain."

When they did walk, Tommy was an everlasting nuisance, yipping at every living thing: colts, cows, chickens, and finally a skunk. When they returned from that ramble, Ma told Maggie to scrub him.

"But, Mrs. Turner, I'll get that horrid smell in my hair!" You'd never think her a farmer's daughter who had smelled skunk before.

Ma smiled. "Who's to do it, Miss? Lizzie or I? He's not ours or he'd be better trained. A lady's pet has manners to equal hers."

Reluctantly, Maggie had bathed him, but not thoroughly, so he was banished to the woodshed. She had mourned over him yowling in his jail, and baby-talked to him through the cracks, but it was Pa who finally scrubbed him, before Ma knew it. Maggie's sly smile over that made Lizzie cross with her for days. Miss Fox was altogether too sure of wheedling her way from any male.

During this to-do Maggie seemed not to notice that the Doctor's

Greenland letter had not come. Of course they had been told not to expect word before October, when Inglefield was due to return from the Arctic. But young Mr. Grinnell had added, "though a whaler may bring word before then." Lizzie immediately began counting on a whaler. Whalers were thick enough around Baffin's Bay in summer for the Doctor to hail one. She was encouraged by Mr. Grinnell's writing in August: "We shall probably hear from the Doctor by the end of next month." By whaler, Lizzie nodded.

Maggie said dreamily, "If they have a piano aboard—"

"Aboard a whaler?"

"No, dear silly governess! Aboard the Grinnell's yacht. Didn't you notice his letter was dated 'The Yacht *Albion,* Newport'? If I'm a guest on it next summer and there *is* a piano in the grand salon, I'll sing for his mother, Mrs. Henry Grinnell."

"Better begin now to practice for it," Ma said drily. Maggie had been negligent about practicing on hot days, and, besides, Ma didn't encourage her to put on airs. They were contrary to the sensible program the Doctor had laid down.

Maggie's sidelong glance at Ma contained so much malice that Lizzie was startled. That evening Maggie wrote Mr. Grinnell, but not until Pa had taken her letter to the post did she announce, "I asked permission to enter Miss Willard's School at Troy next month. Dr. Kane said I was free to go where I wanted and Miss Willard's is most elegant. I have lots of friends in Troy. I met the Boutons when Leah and I held receptions there and later I—visited—I—"

Suddenly every trace of color had ebbed from Maggie's face. Knocking over her chair, she ran headlong to her room. They heard wild weeping and Lizzie had wanted to go to her.

"No, Lizzie," Ma said firmly. "Let her be. I think she regrets that foolish letter."

Lizzie thought Maggie wept because she was lonely, never seeing a familiar face. But Lizzie obeyed her mother until, in the night, she heard Maggie crying as if her heart would break.

"Maggie, dear, we're your friends, too, fond of you as the Boutons. Ma only reproves you when you do something the Doctor might not like. Believe me, Margaret." Lizzie lighted the lamp.

Maggie lifted a tear-ravaged face. "I'm not lonely! I'm frightened, Lizzie! There are terrible people in Troy! I forgot them when I wrote Mr. Grinnell, and I can't tell him about them, ever. Such things don't happen to girls he knows. But don't let him take me to Troy!" She clutched Lizzie in plain terror.

What in the world *was* all this? Lizzie wrapped the coverlet around Maggie's shoulders and said in a sensible voice, "You just tell me, if you can't tell him, and I'll help you, dear."

Maggie twisted around to stare at the black window of her room as if something malignant lurked outside. "That time I visited the Boutons horrible men hung around their house, hiding behind bushes and trees, waiting a chance to burn me for a witch. The Boutons and their friends stood guard with guns night and day, because the sheriff wouldn't go against a mob, he was too afraid. Finally Leah came. She's mean but she's brave, and she helped me crawl away one night. I forgot that until I mentioned the Boutons."

"Forgot it? How could you forget such a horrible experience?"

"I only forgot it was *Troy*. Mobs have come after Kate and me other times. At David's farm—I can't remember where else, I've been so many places. It wasn't the mobs frightened me most. Once Captain Rynders and two men came to a séance—"

Lizzie had read of that arrogant bully, ringleader of the bloody Astor Place riots. "Rynders!"

Her tone made Maggie smile scornfully, her little face hard. "Oh, the spirits chased him off!" Then she flung her arms around Lizzie's neck. "Don't leave me, Lizzie! I'm not used to being alone. I always had Kate to keep me company in the dark. Ly shouldn't have taken me away from Kate!"

"I'll stay by you, child. And I'm always in the next room." Lizzie turned the tear-soggy pillow and smoothed the sheets.

Lying awake while Maggie slept, secure at last, Lizzie understood the Doctor's determination to help this poor child. The man who was so nobly risking his life in Lady Franklin's cause would respond chivalrously to Maggie's plight. Taking her under his protection was one of his finest deeds, and Lizzie resolved to make his hopes for the girl come true.

In the morning, however, when she reminded Maggie to tell Mr. Grinnell she had changed her mind, Maggie said she didn't guess she would! She seemed to have forgotten her tearful confidences as she had the Troy episode. Did she deliberately dismiss incidents from her memory to shield herself from reality? Or did she genuinely forget?

When Mr. Grinnell wrote advising against the change, Maggie, her face aglow, handed the note to Lizzie. "Now I can stay with my dearest Lizzie." She gave a happy sigh.

Lizzie's bafflement increased with every week in October as Maggie's indifference to her lessons also grew. The weather was generally perfect, the woods a patchwork of color, the sky a bright clear blue, but Maggie was also indifferent to walking. She went no farther than the garden bench, sitting, hands folded, never looking when Pa returned with the mail.

The Greenland letter still had not come. Lizzie's own anxiety made her pray silently as she went about her tasks. "Protect thy servant, Lord, on the great deep! Conduct him to safe haven, and send him back to his dear ones, we beseech Thee, Lord." Was Maggie praying, too? She gave no sign.

About Maggie's apathy, Ma said gently, "Suffering takes people differently. This may be her way—to wait in a solitude of her own making. It's surprising in one so young, but she isn't an ordinary girl, Lizzie."

She wasn't one single girl in Lizzie's mind but by turns a frightened child, a frivolous minx, and a secretive woman.

The last week in October Inglefield was back in England. But no letter came. Mrs. Lieper did.

The Doctor's aunt settled herself firmly in the most comfortable chair. "First sing to me, Miss Fox. Elisha loves to hear a woman sing."

Ma was nervous, Lizzie could tell. But Maggie performed well technically, though she sang without any expression, like a little music box letting Mendelssohn's sweet, sad melody ripple forth.

"Don't be so stiff and unfeeling, child!" Mrs. Lieper commanded. "And smile occasionally."

Maggie's smile was forced.

"Are you well, Miss Fox?" Mrs. Lieper leaned forward.

Her hand to her temple in a gesture of confusion, Maggie said, "I don't know." Panic showed in her eyes and was gone quickly.

"She's pining for Elisha, Mrs. Turner. Elisha wouldn't like it at all, dear child. He wants a happy, lively young woman waiting when he returns."

"If he ever does," Maggie said evenly.

"Don't say such a thing! Heavens, they can't kill Lish, though it's been tried often enough. No Eskimo could best him, believe me! And a berg is just a large chunk of ice."

"Yes, ma'am."

"You can take his old aunt's word he'll be back. Ask your spirits if you don't believe me."

Maggie smiled in her secretive way. "I vowed to the Doctor never to rap again." She seated herself, hands folded, but this time Lizzie saw they were clenched together.

Mrs. Lieper eyed her. "She needs a change, Mrs. Turner. Is there a sensible friend you could visit, Maggie? Not your family."

Maggie appeared not to resent the slur. Mrs. Lieper was overfrank at times. "There's Mrs. Walter."

Ma nodded. "Dr. Kane spoke favorably of her."

So it was agreed that Maggie would invite herself for a little visit. Her letter brought Mrs. Walter to Crooksville in haste.

"*There* you are, and so pale, dearest! Your letter frightened me half to death. We must get her away, Mrs. Turner. You and Miss Turner have been making her work too hard. At least I hope that's all that's wrong. Of course, dear Dr. Bayard will make certain. An excellent man, but then, you'd expect that, wouldn't you, with his brother American minister to Brussels? Surely there's nothing really wrong, is there, dearest?"

"No, Ellen, I'm just tired."

"You see! I said it was overwork. You've been taxing her brain too severely, Miss Turner."

Surprisingly, Maggie laid a loving hand on Lizzie's. "No, she hasn't, Ellen. I haven't worked hard enough. I'm tired from waiting. Waiting weeks and weeks for a letter from the Doctor."

"A naughty man," Mrs. Walter said, "but then men are all so thoughtless. I never approved his sending Maggie to such a *quiet* place. She really isn't accustomed to so much *quiet*. Unnatural for her."

"He had her best interests in mind," Ma said stiffly.

"Oh, men! They never understand women. My husband was as kind a creature as ever breathed, but he never understood me. It made him quite cross when I changed the furniture or my coiffeur or the cook, just for a change, which a woman simply must have now and then. We'll give Maggie a change, and back to her books your dear little pupil will come, much refreshed."

"I trust so, and so does a more important friend."

"Yes," Maggie said, turning to Lizzie. "Open any mail from Mr. Grinnell to see if there's an enclosure. I don't expect there will be." Head down, she left the room.

They followed to help her pack, Mrs. Walter rattling away. For all her chatter, the woman took over the packing and did it efficiently though now and again she paused to frown at some of Maggie's things. "Is Maggie allowed money for new clothes? This bonnet"—she held it out scornfully—"will only do for the cars."

"Maggie's money is in her keeping. If she needs more, she can draw on Mr. Grinnell."

"The Doctor's generous, I'll allow," Mrs. Walter said. Lizzie held her tongue, but it took grace.

When Maggie had been gone two weeks, Ma wrote to inquire when they could expect her. Not for another week did they hear—from Mrs. Walter. Maggie had suffered a severe illness, brought on by mental disquiet, but was recovering nicely and should return before long. There was no mention of a letter from the Doctor, surely the best medicine for Maggie.

November had dragged unendurably. Their uneventful mail was a daily torment. There was no word from the Doctor, and not a line from Maggie. Lizzie began to regret refusing that post at Mayhew Academy. That they were paid for lessons never given only aggravated her state.

Mrs. Lieper stopping by for news of Maggie—or Elisha—couldn't see Lizzie had cause to fret. "Don't blame yourself, for goodness' sake! The child's as difficult as Elisha at her age. Mental illness, you say? Brain fever from worry over Ly! A quiet puss, but a deep one."

"Secretive" would be a more exact word than "deep," Lizzie thought; never showing she was frantic for news of the Doctor. If she was improving as Mrs. Walter said, perhaps a letter had come. Mr. Grinnell, knowing Maggie was in New York, would take it to her. No one would bother, least of all Miss Fox, to tell Lizzie Turner, who had met Dr. Kane only once, that he had at last been heard from.

By the middle of December Ma was disturbed enough to write Maggie a gentle reproof. She reminded her of the solemn promises they all made the Doctor. These the Turners had tried to fulfill, and

Maggie, too, at first. "But how shall I account to that noble-minded friend for this lapse from duty? Ask your heart if it be right."

Lizzie had spent Christmas praying feverishly but had not prayed since. Now, two days before the New Year, she leaned her head against the cold glass of Maggie's window. The white and lonely landscape outside could have been the Arctic except for the Crooksville road cutting a black line far to the right. Over its frozen ruts Pa was coming at a sharper clip than was safe. He must have news. Of Maggie's returning, or perhaps— Lizzie started to run down.

"Letter from Grinnell," he bellowed at the kitchen door.

Lizzie, sure that it was the October letter, opened it before she saw it was addressed not to Maggie but to "Mrs. Susannah Turner." There was no enclosure.

Ma read and let it fall to the table, her mouth pursed.

"What is it, Ma?"

"It's young Mr. Grinnell asking if Miss Fox has returned. He knows she's been in New York—she probably asked for money—but not that she's still there. Mr. Turner, my patience has limits!"

Pa smiled. "I never tried to reach them."

"If my letters won't recall her to her duty," Ma said firmly, "perhaps Mr. Grinnell's influence may. I will advise that young man to spend no more of Dr. Kane's money until he learns precisely what Miss Fox intends." Her firmness threatened to dissolve in tears.

Pa patted her shoulder. "You just do that, Susannah."

Find out, Lizzie wanted to cry, if word has ever come from the Doctor. Find out, find out! Looking down, she saw her big, awkward hands were clenched as tight as Maggie's that day she sang so mechanically.

To the crew of the *Advance,* assembled for a Christmas celebration, Dr. Hayes preached an acceptable sermon. Morton mixed an even more acceptable punch. Schubert had worked such magic with plain marled beef that the Captain ruled it must be followed by a bumper of champagne for every man.

But studying their haggard, pasty faces, he found absolutely saddening the effort each made to be boon and jolly. His poor gallant crew! Only Schubert and Morton were now free of scurvy. The rest, himself included, suffered that blight to a greater or less degree. All had aged, too, an Arctic night taking harsher toll of a man than a full year elsewhere in the whole weary world. Not one of his crew was, however, in sore straits.

He wished he could say the same for his dogs. Over the laughter of the men he heard the brutes baying at the light from the cabin as if it were the moon. Whatever possessed them had appeared first among the huskies. Although native to the Arctic, they had been quickest to weaken.

It began with the adults in the Eskimo pack fighting viciously among themselves. Soon the males were devouring the sluts' puppies before the best could be culled. Petersen, nursing along a fine pair of white pups, was finally bitten by the mother.

"She froths at me," he reported in alarm.

"Hydrophobia can't develop at this latitude," Kane assured him as Hayes dressed the bite. "Germs die in this cold. But I'll order her shot before she attacks the Newfoundlands." His ten mighty Newfoundlands were the very foundation of his search plans. "We'd better move them aboard ship."

Then some of his cherished ten had grown queer, too. Cerberus, patriarch of the den, died mysteriously of a sudden. His successor, Old Grim, took to wandering off, at first for a few hours, and then over night. Three days before Christmas, while Kane was exercising the dogs, Grim had broken loose.

The Captain yelled for Hans. "Grim's loose. Is he there?"

"Can't see, Docto Kay-en."

"Get a lantern quickly." Kane maneuvered the rest of the team safely back to the *Advance*. With Hans and Morton, he had tried to track down the vagrant. The dog's trail swerved shoreward about six hundred paces from the brig.

"Here he go!" Hans scrambled over a jumble of ice and snow. "And here." When they came up with the light, the Eskimo's moon face fell. "No track!" The snow had been drifting. There the trail ended. "He come," Hans insisted, sure Old Grim, an outrageous sponger to whom the men sneaked tidbits, would return to such a happy feeding ground. But Grim had not been seen since.

January brought the most intense cold on record. In fact, the chloric ether in one thermometer froze solid.

"It cannot be!" Dr. Sontag said. But it undeniably was.

His astonishment prompted Kane to record the temperatures at which various chemicals aboard froze: spirit of naphtha at −54°; oil of sassafras at −49°; oil of wintergreen flacculent at −56°, solid at −63°.

The men were awed by homelier aspects of the cold's force. To cut sugar with a saw; butter and lard with cold chisel and mallet; pork and beef with a crowbar and handspike amazed them.

Morton with a grin reported, "Don't know the temperature, Cap'n Ken, but put it down London stout and Old Brown sherry both froze solid in certain lockers. Their owners takes it hard!"

Kane laughed dutifully at the joke and went up to the dogs. Several were worse. Old Flora, his favorite Newfoundland bitch, was peculiarly affected. In the dim light he saw her pacing, head down, and when he went to her, she walked right into him, who was solid, though she had swerved carefully to avoid invisible objects.

He had not noticed Tom Hickey in a corner until the boy quavered, "You can almost tell, sir, the size and shapes of the divils she dodging."

"Nonsense, boy. It's all in her sick mind. Don't hang about, watching. For the sake of your own mind, keep to your work!"

Watching Flora himself, he understood the cabin boy's fears. There she swung wide of a stocky individual just McGary's size, edged around a slight ghostly Elisha Kane, to stop and stare up at a tall specter. Brooks? He broke the spell the sad dog cast and went angrily below. Where was his vaunted superiority to Maggie's dupes? They had lost loved ones, he only a few beasts. Yet he was seeing spirits, stirred not by a sly, sweet girl, but poor mad Flora.

He was also more morbid than Hickey, Kane thought late that night when, sleepless, he crawled from his bunk to go again to Flora. Over his sleeping clothes he pulled his fur-lined cashmere, over that his buffalo robe, and moved quietly through the quarters. On deck it was cold as death and black as pitch. He felt for a lantern.

When the noses of two silent dogs nudged his hand, he almost yelled. The instant he struck a light, they began to leap and whirl in exuberant delight, eerily making no sound. Not pleasure, but their sickness made them fawn and slaver. In a moment they might fall into sullen lethargy, followed by hours of howling and dashing about as if pursued. After her initial endemic spasm, Flora had become generally lethargic, rousing only to eat voraciously.

She lay lethargic now in a corner, not hearing his soothing words. "Good dog, good old girl—"

Perched on a barrel, he brooded over her and all his failing brutes. Abruptly she staggered to her feet to plod a zigzag course, moving deep into shadow, then out into the light, in and out, in and out, and around—what? Unseen obstacles in an irregular line like ninepins that have survived the first bowl.

His worry was aggravated by his helplessness. The dogs' disease wasn't hydrophobia, but true lunacy which no doctor could cure. The endless night had dimmed the minds of his poor beasts.

From the darkness on his left came three faint raps. Again they came: rap-rap-rap. Shocked alert, he identified the sound. A dog dreaming of fleas that were not there—it was too cold for fleas—had scratched them. Rap-rap-rap. He saw a hind leg jerking in the shadows. That he should for an instant imagine anything else showed again that the night was eroding his own mind.

Without delay he retreated to the warmth of his bunk and the feeble light of his heating lamp. Maggie smiled at him, more live and real than his own pallid face in a mirror.

"Believe me, I will return to you!" he whispered to her. Her lips seemed to move in the faintest caress. "No!" He closed his eyes to the lunatic beguilement, and opened them to pick out with care every stroke of Fagnani's brush. That exercise of will done, he slept.

By the middle of February Flora was dead. Her long agony had affected the men. Even the most insensate, like Bill Godfrey, tightened his muscles when Flora gave one of her infrequent but infinitely mournful howls. Kane should have had her killed long before but did not. So many dogs had died he could not kill another. That was his rational excuse. In fact, he used her madness to test every night his own powers of resistance to the dark.

When on the last day of February the first rays of the sun struck the *Advance,* nine of his Newfoundlands and thirty-five huskies were dead. Of the entire pack, only six survived, one unfit for draught. So much depended on this handful, Kane began at once training them to run together, while Ohlsen built a smaller sledge.

24. SPRING SOWING

IT WAS STILL bitterly cold, though the sun, equinoctial now, glared beneath the horizon like a smelting furnace. Around the northern head of Rensselaer Bay a party of men pulled a loaded sled over chaotic ice. Now Kane could see them, now he couldn't.

Through the black months unseen tides and intruding bergs had pushed and heaved massive blocks of floating ice in a mighty torment. This eruption the all-powerful cold had arrested in the very moment of turmoil, leaving in the frozen sea jagged ridges that crossed and recrossed to make a labyrinth. Through these hummocks the sunken sun cast long, blood-red shadows that further confused the maze. For minutes the intent watcher could detect no sign of life on the vast scape.

Then the little party emerged in silhouette on the side of a mound. Lifting and pulling and guiding, the men had nursed the burdensome sledge up the hummock. Now they were working it precariously down the other side. They resembled foraging ants that, having come upon a huge crumb under the harvest table, are engaged in the terrible exertion of hauling it home over the fearsome terrain of the dooryard.

But his men were outward not homeward bound. Sent to stock a base up forward, they represented not the harvest, but spring sowing, though Spring, late as it was, had scarcely shown her face. Kane in the crow's-nest knew the snow was still so dry and grainy the sled screeched over it as if it were fine beach sand. The men in harness moved by fits and starts, less facile than the dogs he had counted on to haul this load. Kane could feel the strain of their effort in his own legs as they dragged inch by inch northward.

There, they were finally rounding the head of the bay, just eight hours since they left the brig. Most of that time he had followed them with his glass. Exhausted, he climbed down, smiling to think that Brooks, like a moving locomotive, was hard to stop.

He had been equally hard to start, putting off, on one excuse or another, the loading of the sledge for several days. To Kane's sharp query Brooks had answered: "For this late, it's cold even for the Arctic, and I just thought if we wait till it warms up a bit, we'd get farther north and quicker if we didn't start yet."

Kane had almost smiled at his First Officer's earnest paradox, but the matter was too serious. "We can't afford further delay."

The sledge with its stores of pemmican and other supplies, topped by a boat—in the happy event of finding open water—had refused to budge at first. The harder the men pulled, the deeper its runners cut into the snow crust. Brooks muttered, "Too cold."

His captain knew, too, that excessive cold increased friction on the runners. "Try again, boys. Once she's started—" He threw his own weight at the rear and the sledge creaked forward slightly.

Bill Godfrey, among the bystanders seeing the party off, had swaggered up to put his shoulder to the load. The sledge started with a lurch, pitching the straining men up front into the snow.

As they scrambled to their feet, Bill roared laughing. "Takes a man to get that thing started."

Kane said coldly, "You'll have a chance to show how you are on the long pull." His irritation slipped over into his command to Brooks. "Transfer the load to the Faith, Mr. Brooks. The sledge with the broadest runners should have been used."

The Faith started easily enough, and the party was off to a chorus of cheers from the men and yapping from the dogs. His beasts would have their turn next, carrying him and one crewman to the outpost Brooks was to set up ten days out from the brig.

Traveling light and fast, sleeping very little, Kane could reach Brooks's base in a third Brooks's time. If he took along that braggart, Godfrey, the fellow's stamina would get a real test. From the top of the housing Kane saw McGary returning from the routine observatory check.

"Staying low," the New London man called. "She's minus forty-two, Cap'n. Barometer's high."

"Better than the other way around," Kane shouted. He went below whistling.

The following days he spent giving the dogs warm-up runs. They worked well together. A steady rise in the temperature also cheered him. With the supply party out a week, the thermometer stood at a neat minus seven. The next day Kane, driving his team to inspect a fox trap, discarded his face mask as a gesture toward the coming spring. Returning, he found to his shock that his cheeks were freezing, and needed Hayes's help when he reached the brig.

A sober McGary came up to them. "Minus forty-two again."

"Damn it, McGary, this is the end of March. The weather should be above zero."

McGary looked startled at the Captain's near-profanity. "It ain't," he said laconically. "Your face bad?"

"It's nothing. And I intend to allow nothing to delay me once we get word Brooks is on his way back. It *must* warm up."

He had ordered Brooks to send two men on ahead, men able to out-travel the rest, say Petersen and young Jeff. With no load they should reach the *Advance* from that ten-day station in half Brooks's time. They should be here, Kane estimated, in a week.

So he went grimly ahead with his preparations, though the thermometer stayed stubbornly low. Late the night of Brooks's twelfth day out he was catching up on entries in his journal while the men sewed away at moccasins or busied themselves at other tasks.

Morton came up with a handsome pair of fur stockings. "Figgered you might need these, Cap'n Ken, seeing the weather."

"They're handsome indeed." They appeared to be made of dog's hide.

"Sort of a memento," Morton said, "of Old Flora."

Kane almost dropped them. Over their heads they heard footsteps, then stumblings down the hatchway. Three figures reeled through the door. One said in a stiff voice, "Fear—ful trouble."

"Sontag!" The man was barely recognizable. Kane rushed to him. "Who's in trouble?"

"All—but—us." Each word seemed frozen.

His companions had already toppled. Then Sontag, too, collapsed into the sleep of freezing and utter exhaustion. It was almost minutes before Kane could identify the other two, their features were so swollen: Ohlsen and Petersen. Kane shook Sontag back to some consciousness. "Where are they? Brooks, Jeff, Schubert, Wilson? Dead or alive? Tell me, man!" He had to slap poor Sontag's suffering face to get an answer.

"By the ice . . . frozen . . ."

"Are they dead?" Almighty God, almighty God, no!

"Sick . . . Hickey stays by them."

Kane had forgotten the cabin boy went, too, the brave boy. Sontag could tell them nothing more, so with hot tea Kane and Hayes worked to rouse Ohlsen. The rigid, half-conscious carpenter yielded an agonizing word at a time.

"Hummocks . . ."

"Where, Ohlsen?" Where weren't there hummocks in that labyrinth?

"North . . . east."

"How far?"

"Forty . . . fifty . . . mile."

"Ohlsen! Ohlsen! Give us a landmark to guide us. A landmark!"

"Berg."

"How high? What shape? What color?" How many hundreds of bergs forty, fifty miles to the northeast and in the shadow of only one, a tiny tent hidden by drifts?

"I show."

"You are in no condition to be moved. Tell us! Hayes, get more hot tea. No, brandy might be dangerous. Ohlsen, tell us!"

He muttered something in Swedish, then in a loud voice, "I show."

"We'll have to take him. He's our only hope. Hayes, keep working on him. Morton, you work on the others. McGary, we'll use the light sledge. Who'll volunteer for the rescue party?"

Astonishingly, Ohlsen was the first to speak up. "I go."

Godfrey and four others volunteered almost together. In a matter of minutes Little Willie, the men's name for the light sledge, a name it hurt their captain to hear, was ready. Amid a package of pemmican, one buffalo robe, and a small tent, they propped Ohlsen, wrapped in dogskins and eiderdown. The men put their shoulders to the *rue raddies* and the rescue party pushed off. It was forty-six below.

With the strength of desperation they passed the head of the bay before light. Thereafter Kane occasionally slipped out of harness to run to a point of vantage. Ahead was desolation. Icebergs stretched in long, beaded lines across the next bay. The hummocks were piled higher than a standing man. Only rarely could the party thread through them. Most must be painfully climbed.

After sixteen hours Ohlsen awoke. Kane bent over him. "Do you see the landmark berg anywhere?"

Ohlsen, his head moving slowly from side to side, squinted long at the glittering array. "All the same." It was as if, Kane realized, the carpenter were looking at a vast crystal rock in a hall of mirrors.

Ohlsen could give them no sure help. Instead, Kane must try to think like Brooks. They came at last to a long, level floe, sure to attract his First Officer, weary of the endless hummocks. Kane ordered a tent raised, and Ohlsen, freed from his bag, to keep moving.

"To halt is to freeze." The carpenter, barely able to stand, plodded in a circle. The temperature was minus forty-nine, and snow drifted before a sharp northwest wind.

"Here," Kane told the rest, "we fan out, man by man. They crossed here, I'm certain. At any sign of them, yell!"

The men groped their way irresolutely, each one fearful lest he himself, losing sight of the others, be lost like Brooks and his party. Drifting snow would cover their tracks. For hours they searched. Had they really fanned out, they would have been miles apart. But their fear and their natural tendency to travel in circles kept them together. So all heard Hans's shriek and came puffing up. He pointed excitedly at a broad track in the snow. "Sledge!"

Was it really a sledge track? McGary shook his head. "Trick of the drift." But it was their only clue, and Kane ordered it followed. They lumbered on—how long?—until Blake yelled, "Footprint!" On this they all agreed. Their pace quickened. They came to a hummock swept clean by the wind, the trail lost. Godfrey swung up onto it. Instantly he bellowed, "Flag on ahead!"

In his terrible hurry the Captain fell twice and hardly knew it. He hardly felt his heart's wild pounding or heard the roaring in his ears. He only saw a fluttering little American flag hanging from a tent pole almost covered with drift.

His men beat him to the goal and then silently lined up on each side of the tent, waiting for him to discover what lay inside. With his remaining strength he pushed away the snow and crawled through the flap. In the semi-darkness lay four men. Alive? There wasn't room to stand and he was too weak to rise anyway. He croaked, "Brooks?"

The dear, familiar voice rumbled, "We were expecting you."

"Brooks!" Kane could not stop his tears.

Then Jeff declared staunchly, "We knew you'd come."

"Jeff boy! Wilson and Pierre, are you all right?" He reached for their hands, but before he touched them fainted on the robe that covered the four.

He awoke to the penetrating warmth of brandy.

"Mr. Brooks said it would bring you round, sir."

But Brooks was the sufferer here, not the prescriber of remedies! In the babel of voices Kane could not think clearly. It was McGary who sat him up, got spirits down him, that he knew. Then, rubbing his eyes, he saw no one moved. Boxing his ears, he reduced the babel to dull ringing, and peered around the dimness in the tent. All about him men rolled in skins or sleeping bags were strewn like logs. Others slept squatting in the corners, exhausted.

"Henry." He leaned over Brooks. So strong was his First Officer's feeling for Navy discipline, it was the first time Kane had dared address him by his first name. Brooks, thinking the Captain spoke to Henry Goodfellow, did not answer. "Henry Brooks!"

"Sir? Aye, sir. I know we failed. Didn't get far enough. It was the hummocks. Never could get through to clear ice. Kept crossing hummocks. I'm very sorry, sir."

"Don't think of it, my poor fellow! What's important now is getting you back to the brig. Are you up to the ride?"

"Yes, sir."

"It may be hard on all of you. Jeff, how do you feel?"

"Not too bad, Ly, I mean, Captain. Just numb and sleepy. Is that all right? It's worried me a little." His voice faltered.

It was desperately not right, but Kane did not say so. "McGary, get everyone but the sick on his feet at once. We must run for the ship."

Outside, he beat his own aching limbs into life and made each man McGary shoved through the flap stomp his feet, swing his arms, and beat his breast to knock out the menace of sleep. When the four stricken men were strapped to the sledge with everything piled over them for covering—robes, tents, tarpaulin—the trek to the brig began.

Now the hummocks that had halted Brooks must be crossed by rescuers carrying four sick men. On the way those hummocks had looked taller than a man. Now they appeared a full story high. In many places the ridges rose up in parallel ranks too close for the sledge to run between them. Then the rescuers had to use their ropes as suspension lines for swinging the burden from top to top. At such points Kane was in terror lest a man at the ropes weaken and their precious freight hurtle down.

Here and there a man began to falter. Drifting snow hid gaps in the ice through which more than one dropped to his waist or deeper. To lessen this danger, Kane had the strongest take turns at the lead belt, probing a passage. Then John Blake on the lead plunged into a drift and lay there.

"Get up, Blake. Get up, I say! It's death to sleep!" Kane boxed the side of the fellow's head, and grasping him under the armpits, hauled him out of the snow. He was mildly surprised to find he could do it. "Go to the rear a while. Bonsall, you take the lead."

When he turned to hand the line to Bonsall, he saw a half-dozen others slump onto the snow or throw themselves on it as if its soft white were a featherbed.

Bonsall pleaded, "Wind's down and we aren't cold, just sleepy. Three minutes' rest will fix us, sir. Just three minutes."

Hans sat stupefied, a ball of blubber. Tom Hickey, the brave boy who had stayed with the sick, sat on a block of ice, bolt upright, eyes closed, mumbling to his mother or perhaps it was the Virgin. They were all so far gone, they must have a breather, and before long warm food in them. Thank God for McGary!

"McGary, pitch a shelter and allow these men four hours' sleep. Not an instant more. Then get them moving. I can trust only you to keep that watch."

Deep satisfaction showed in the whaler's face. "Aye, sir."

"With one volunteer, I'll push on to the tent on the floe, and get drinking water and hot soup ready. Who'll go on ahead with me?" he called to those still on their feet.

Without surprise he saw Godfrey come right up. "I'm your man. Anything to get moving—sir."

25. WHITE AS A SHROUD

A HALF-HOUR out the going became easier or else Kane had begun to tap those inner resources that he had drawn on in more than one past extremity. The stinging pain behind his forehead was gone, and he and Godfrey crossed hummock after hummock without a stumble.

Suddenly an open floe stretched before him as far as he could see. Ly's pace quickened. He moved better than he had in months, steadily, with an even, quick step that was a pleasure. Godfrey, who had been following in silence, Indian style, came abreast and they began to talk. For the first time Ly found himself conversing easily with this strange man.

"It is getting warmer."

"It is warmer and the wind is down."

"So it is."

"Our tent can be no more than nine miles off now."

"The sun is rising fast."

"It is dazzling to the eyes."

For some reason they found it best to speak in simple, declarative sentences. Even while Ly spoke, he seemed to hear what he said coming from afar. Yet the sentences looked familiar, every word, as they marched across the snow in front of him, the letters tall and evenly spaced and leaning slightly forward.

"They lean into the wind as you and I are," he said to Godfrey, and they both laughed.

Certainly he recognized those sentences for he had brought them right out of the copybook in best free hand.

Now, before his eyes, they changed to italic characters. Right above each one was the French translation in black bold face:

"Le soleil est—"

Maggie, in her sweet childish voice, read very carefully. He held out his hand to encourage her, and squeezing her small palm in his warm grasp, encouraged her to jump from word to word.

"The sun is dazzling."

"Le soleil . . ."

But now Godfrey was grasping his arm and pointing. "That a bear ahead?"

The sun was so bright Ly could not see until he squinted his eyes nearly shut. "I see a white bear—a great Arctic bear."

If it were white, how could he see it against the diamond-studded snow? Then the bear moved.

"Let us track it."

That was Godfrey's voice. It was not a sentence from Maggie's French book.

"He is taking his time."

"Then we can overtake him."

"We can have him for supper."

"I believe he is waiting for us."

"No, he is moving toward our tent."

"Now I see our tent. It strikes a shadow against the sun."

"The sun—"

"Le soleil!" Maggie's voice rose in triumph as she pronounced the word in a perfect accent. She turned to him, laughing.

"The bear is already there. He has beaten us."

"He is overturning the tent."

"Hurry! He will tear up the blankets and eat the food."

"Hurry! We must save the blankets and the food."

At half-past five in the afternoon the two men reached the halfway tent. They crawled under reindeer skins and slept.

His beard being pulled awoke Kane. Godfrey stood over him with a large knife.

"Did you get the bear, Godfrey?"

"There wasn't no bear."

"It got away?"

"Never was there."

"The big white one near the tent? You saw it!"

"Bill Godfrey never did." The fellow sneered scornfully. His eyes were glazed. "Bill Godfrey only heard Kane say he saw one."

"What are you saying, man? Put down that knife!" Kane tried to leap up. His beard was frozen to the reindeer hide.

Godfrey shook his head to clear it. "You're stuck, sir. I'll cut you loose." He began hacking away, as though he were cutting burlap from a case of pemmican.

Kane submitted in silence. He said finally, "We cached a bottle of spirits here."

"I got it, sir. It was froze."

"Then strike a fire and thaw it."

"Bottle broke. But the fire is struck, sir, and water's thawed." He crawled through the flap and returned with a measure of drink. When Kane gulped it greedily, the riverman gave a sly smile.

The water was tepid but the brandy in it warmed Ly's gullet. He smiled in turn. "Arctic snows are flavorsome melted."

"Freezin' didn't hurt nothing but the bottle, sir."

"A brew to do the men good."

"I know, sir. Tried it first myself." As always Godfrey must have the last word.

But not about the bear, Kane decided, though that could wait. "Get more snow on for soup." He busied himself breaking up pemmican for the pot.

A shout was heard before the soup was hot. Hans half-ran, half-stumbled toward them. "Docto! We here. All here."

As they came in sight, Ly began to count them. One . . . two . . . three. . . . With the three by the tent that was six. Seven . . . eight . . . nine. The prostrate forms on the sled were but lumps of blanket and hard to count. He grabbed Godfrey's brew and ran to them.

They lay in tandem, the foremost man sitting between the legs of the man behind him, resting against his chest and that man between the legs of the third and so on, giving each other warmth and a little comfort. Brooks at the rear was braced against the handles of the sled. He nodded toward the lump leaning against him. "Needs help."

The man's hood pulled open disclosed Jeff's dead-white face. The half-closed eyelids only wavered toward wakefulness. Kane forced a little of Godfrey's mixture between the boy's lips. Then a little more. Warmth seemed to reach him.

"Home." The word came from far down in Jeff's throat. "Glad." Then he said distinctly, "Never saw the river meadow so green."

Let the boy dream happily not of the brig, now within striking distance, but of his true home on another face of earth. They must get him to the brig soon. "Wilson, Schubert." Ly touched Brooks's shoulder in a spasm of fear. "Mr. Brooks, there are twelve!" There should be thirteen. Who was that other one? But he should not have asked Brooks. The poor fellow was ill. Confused, he called, "Ohlsen!"

But Brooks answered first. "With you, sir, we make thirteen."

That was it. To cover his embarrassment Kane ordered rations around and three minutes' sleep for every man. Then the party, together again, pushed across the last hummocks to enter an avenue of icebergs ranged like opposing chessmen on a fantastically compressed board.

An angry god having crushed the board between his hands, the knights could not make their stately turns, nor the bishops slide obliquely. Kane strained to see the Pinnacly Berg—a great Gothic king. From its vaultings and arches they could sight home. Draw up to checkmate him and the game was won.

Now Kane saw the unmistakable landmark clearly. Far off in the sky, but not set in blue. It was framed in black as though he viewed it through a telescope. Now the telescope turned in his hands, throwing off at the far end whirling black circles that spiraled around the mighty berg and then contracted to engulf it. It was gone.

Beside him Hans gobbled up a mitten full of snow. Kane cuffed the wretch for his stupidity and when the fat boy looked up imploring, his lips were bloody.

One of the whirling black circles caught Kane up and sent him aloft. It turned white as it rose and through its core he saw his men far below, floundering and falling. He saw himself making the rounds, goading, prodding, rousing. "Keep moving, Hickey. Godfrey, give the boy a hand. Steady on." He saw himself move forward with giant steps, when all the time he floated high in a glittering ball from which the whole icescape lay spread before him. There was the Pinnacly Berg and beyond nestled the brig. . . . He watched steadily, but it did not vanish.

"Bonsall, move ahead to the brig. Tell Dr. Hayes to come meet us. But first to prepare for surgery."

Why had he picked Bonsall who was falling often now at the lines and stood near exhaustion? But Bonsall, to his surprise, scampered off as if he were Mercury, winging his way into the whirling blackness. Then the dark spread and spread until it reached Kane where he stood trying to beat it back, to keep it from closing down on the poor men.

This time no one needed to rouse him. He knew his three minutes' rest was about up. "Thank you, McGary."

He opened his eyes to find not McGary but Hayes leaning over him. "Dr. Hayes—" Kane swung his eyes from the surgeon's anxious face to the foot of his bunk where Maggie smiled down. "How long since we reached the brig? I seem to have slept hours."

He tried to struggle up, but Hayes held him firmly. "I'm the doctor here. Those were your first sensible words in four days. You've been delirious with a high fever and we feared—"

"I never die," Kane said sharply. "The men?"

Bonsall had reached the ship speedily and Petersen and Whipple had gone with the dogs to pick up the failing party. Dr. Hayes had received them on board prepared for all eventualities. All were in such suffering that it had been difficult to prescribe at first, Hayes confessed. The load had been too much for one green surgeon, Kane thought. If only he himself had been on his feet. "I know, I know."

Who could not see because of snow blindness and who had to be led to his bunk from sheer exhaustion? Who could not walk for frostbite and who had not the energy to do so? Whose mind wandered from the dangerous shock of pain and whose from seventy-two hours' exposure to weather nearly fifty below? But Hayes seemed to have handled everything with judicious energy, administering morphine freely, and brandy and food in moderation. There had been four amputations, two minor and two major. Hayes had sweat over them, the first in his experience.

"Brooks lost a foot, Wilson toes, Schubert most of a leg, but if you listen I think you can hear him singing."

Far off Kane heard a lilting tune. His smile faded as he sensed Hayes held something back. "Jeff?"

"A leg, too, but I think he's all right. It's tough on such a young fellow."

Hayes himself was all of two years older. But it was a bitter thing for Jeff. "Take me to him." With Morton's help, Hayes carried the Captain to Jeff's bunk.

The boy's face brightened. "Ly! Sir! I'm glad to see *you*. We were worried." Jeff's face was flushed and when Ly took his big-knuckled boy's hand in his it was hot and dry.

"And you, Jeff? Feeling better?"

"I guess so. But I won't be much use to you after this."

"You can do important scientific work for the expedition."

"Yes, there's that," Jeff agreed, after a swallow.

On Hayes's arm Kane made the rounds, all the patients touchingly pleased to see him and at the sight too obviously cheered about their own recovery. It was unfair to Hayes who had managed very well. Shockingly weak, Kane crawled back to sleep. Near midnight Hayes roused him.

"Baker's fever is way up. He's delirious again. I've tried everything."

The boy's babblings were incoherent most of the time, but once he seemed on a hunting trip with Ly. Against all arguments, Kane refused to leave his side that night. On into the morning he stayed, bathing Jeff's forehead with snow mush, fighting his fever with drugs.

By noon Jeff was quieter. Just as Ly rose to go at last to his bunk, the boy was seized with a dreadful spasm, arching his back and clenching his teeth in agony.

"Jeff!"

The boy opened eyes that showed utter awareness of the truth. Deep in his throat a cry tried to tear its way out, but his jaws were locked. Ly lifted him, held him tight to his breast as if at once to keep him from going and to give him love where he went. Jeff slid back into a coma from which mercifully he never roused.

That strangled cry still rang in Ly's ears the day a rough procession of men, many sick, none entirely well, bore Baker's body to its rest. They carried the improvised coffin of deck slabs as evenly as they could over the broken ice and up the steep side of Fern Rock to the Observatory. There, on the pedestals that had served the transit and the theodolite, they laid it while Kane read the service and sprinkled snow on the dead in place of black dirt from green fields.

When the coffin had been pushed into a vault in the wall, and the men, at Kane's command, filed out ahead of him, the sight of Henry Goodfellow, whose parents also were Kane's friends, reminded him of Jeff's father and mother. They had let their boy go along with the hero of his childhood because they relied on Ly to bring him safely back. Dr. Kane had failed them. Weakling that he was, he had been down when Jeff most needed him, and Jeff had died.

Kneeling by that cold mausoleum, Ly prayed the Lord to make him stronger.

But he discovered very soon he needed more than strength; he needed greater skill and wisdom. Though he searched the medical books, he found no remedy for the erysipelas that Schubert developed in his stump.

The disease put an end, finally, to that gay soul's singing. Once more Captain Kane led a stumbling procession over the ice and Jeff Baker was no longer alone.

26. THE LETTERS

IT WAS March before Maggie returned, so subdued and pale that Lizzie became instantly protective. Ma was more impressed with her new seriousness.

"I do think Mrs. Walter has been a good influence."

"Not on her health," Lizzie said. "I'll just take her some milk and a piece of that pie."

Maggie began at once to confide in her governess. "Dr. Bayard said I got sick from keeping shut up in myself. At home I could talk only to Kate and without Kate I couldn't talk to anyone, even you, Lizzie, though I knew you were kindhearted. After that night."

It needed no further identification.

"Every day a letter didn't come I grew more frightened. The Doctor was forever writing me and I thought if he didn't, it was because he was dead."

"An arbitrary and morbid notion."

"I'm not very good at thinking," Maggie said, as if it were a subject like arithmetic, "and when I'm frightened, I freeze up as if I were fast in the center of an iceberg."

"Thank goodness his letter came to thaw you out." Lizzie tried to smile. Perhaps Maggie would read parts of it aloud. Her hopes mounted when her pupil took a scrimshaw box out of her valise. Spouting whales and arching waves encircled the iceberg that ornamented its lid.

"Oh, I didn't get a letter. That's why I took a turn for the worse in New York. Then Mr. Cornelius Grinnell called and explained everything. I don't think I'll get sick again."

"What did he say?"

"That I couldn't expect mail from Greenland as if it were Albany. The Doctor might have dispatched a whole packet of letters by an Eskimo who just threw it away and went bear hunting. Eskimos are *very* unreliable. Or maybe his letters missed the last ship out in the fall. They don't go back to Greenland again until late spring, so I'm not to expect a letter before July, Mr. Cornelius said. He didn't laugh at my not understanding geography, but you must teach me, Lizzie. Dear Kate brought my old letters to comfort me. She was hiding them for me from my sister Leah. Kate put them in this pretty box."

"It's most appropriate." What did the two little girls think their older sister would do with the letters?

"Every day I read one, pretending it just came. Then I seal it up again and put it on the bottom, so when it comes to the top, I have to open it. I'll answer every one, and save them for the Doctor, after you've corrected them. I hardly ever wrote him before."

"A lady acknowledges mail promptly," Lizzie said automatically. This letter game might help distract Maggie until late summer; and her teacher.

They worked with the globes the first morning, so Maggie could see how far word from the Doctor had to travel—from Greenland to Denmark to England to America, most likely. They found the point where the Doctor was last reported. Latitude and longitude took on new interest for Maggie when Lizzie said, "If the Doctor reaches a higher latitude than anyone else has, it may make him more famous than finding Franklin."

"Just for crossing an imaginary line?" Maggie could hardly believe it. "How will he know when he does?"

The science needed to determine a ship's position near the Pole Lizzie was not prepared to expound.

They soon settled into a satisfactory routine. Mornings were for English grammar, foreign languages, and a little practical arithmetic. Maggie, no longer encased in ice, showed a voluble calm as hard to penetrate. As if she's wrapped in rippling water, Lizzie thought.

After their noonday dinner Maggie napped, Lizzie reading aloud to her until she slept. Then came her music lesson, followed by a walk—without Tommy, who, praises be, had been left with Kate.

Evenings Maggie answered the Doctor's "latest" letter. Her New York friends wrote frequently to keep her from dying of loneliness "on that dismal farm." Once she was unkindly sent an editorial expounding the fruitlessness of Dr. Kane's search.

Maggie nodded. "Sir John said they were all lost, and my last night home that sailor told Kate and me it was true."

What sailor Lizzie did not ask. "The Doctor wants the rappings forgotten."

"I seldom think of those days." Maggie made them sound long, long ago.

Friends also mailed her reviews of Dr. Kane's book when it was published. The critics' eulogies interested Maggie more than the book itself. Cornelius Grinnell sent her one of the first copies, enclosing the Doctor's card. This Maggie carefully put in the scrimshaw box, but the book she only leafed through. "The pictures are pretty."

A pallid word for the Doctor's dramatic sketches of polar fantasy, to Lizzie's mind. "Maggie, you really must begin to read it, so that you can discuss it intelligently with the Doctor."

"So many hard words! Lizzie, read it to me!"

So at naptime, one late March afternoon, their improving reading was Chapter I of Dr. Kane's personal narrative of the First Grinnell Expedition. Maggie dropped off all too soon for Lizzie, who proposed continuing evenings. "Ma and Pa want to hear."

Pa was particularly taken with the book, making Lizzie reread exciting passages, but even so by mid-April they had reached Chapter XXI. A few pages earlier Maggie, a little drowsy, had frowned at the beloved author's mention of Beechy Island, as if the name were half-familiar. To Lizzie's exasperation, she went off to bed just as the British and American explorers together had come on traces of Franklin's winter quarters.

Naptime next day Lizzie was eager to begin. By the second page Maggie's lids drooped. Lizzie read firmly on, " '... a messenger was reported. The news he brought was thrilling. "Graves, Captain Penny! Graves!" We were instantly in motion.' "

Maggie's eyes half-opened.

" '... the headboards of three graves ... occupied a line facing toward Cape Riley, distinctly visible across a little cove.' "

"By a high cliff with ice all around," her pupil said in a shrill voice. "Go on, Lizzie."

Made uneasy by Maggie's manner, Lizzie hurried through the inscriptions on the graves of W. Braine, Royal Marine, and John Hartnell, A. B., both of the crew of the *Erebus*. Maggie stared up at the ceiling, waiting. Was there something she *expected* to hear?

The last memorial " 'was more grave-like, more like the sleeping places of Christians in happier lands than the others. It was inscribed: "Sacred to the memory of John Torrington—' "

"Torrington!" Maggie sat bolt upright, her eyes wild and accusing. "That was the sailor's name. He told Kate and me Dr. Kane had seen his grave, but Lish denied it. He lied to me, Lizzie! He lied!" She grabbed the book from Lizzie's hands and glared at the drawing of the desolate scene. "It's just like the sailor said. It was Elisha who lied." Her face a mask, she thrust the book back at Lizzie.

"Don't say that!" Lizzie's voice was sharp with indignation. "If Dr. Kane said he never saw the grave of anyone you talked to at a silly séance, do you know what he meant?"

"What he said."

"He meant you didn't talk to the real Torrington, but to some demon. Your spirits are all devils, if they're anything!"

Surprisingly, Maggie conceded, "Some of them could be. But Ly's own book proves Torrington told the truth. That's why I believe him and know the Doctor lied." She moved rigidly to a chair by the window, and crouching there, said, "Right under that tree he stood and lied to me, when I trusted him over anyone, even my own mother. That was the last time I'll ever see him. Torrington said Ly would die up there, and I believe *him,* now."

Neither from that conviction nor her chair could Lizzie budge her. She sat stiff as a cataleptic, staring out, and would not come down to supper. First Ma and then Pa went up to reason with her. To Pa's every argument she answered, "I'll never see him again."

"Probably not," Pa said, making her jerk around to look at him. "If you starve yourself to death before the brave lad returns, of course you won't see him. If you want to be alive on the great day, better come to supper."

She obeyed, but hardly ate, and went upstairs right after.

"Gone up to look out at that damned tree," Lizzie fumed.

"Elizabeth Turner!"

"To keep Lizzie from swearing at it, I'd best cut it down." Pa smiled. "Though it makes a nice piece of shade for the cows."

"No, Mr. Turner." Ma looked thoughtful. "Let it stand as a reminder that Dr. Kane is human. Any man will lie if pushed too far, and Maggie's spirit nonsense must have been a great trial to him."

When Maggie came down next day, dark shadows under her eyes, Ma drew her into the parlor and shut the door. She explained later, "I suggested that Maggie visit Mrs. Walter for a week. Perhaps she and other worldly friends can make Maggie understand a public hero may have some private weakness and be the dearer for it." To further her gentle plot, she wrote Mrs. Walter.

A week to the day Maggie returned from that visit. Her anxious governess went with Pa to meet her. Maggie wore a new bonnet. "A miracle it isn't all over soot."

"Most becoming. The violets set off your eyes."

"Not as well as gentians. Dr. Kane says my eyes are like gentians, but the milliner hadn't any." Apparently Dr. Kane's word was again to be relied on, even in flattery.

On the long ride home she told in detail how Mrs. Walter was doing her house over "in the new mode." With rosewood and red satin, tapestry carpets, and gilt gas fixtures. "She has a buhl cabinet for a whatnot, and I'm to beg a souvenir of Dr. Kane's explorations for her to put in it. She wants us to be married from her house with Dr. Bayard giving me away, and a reception after. The idea may upset my mother but I can bring her round. Lizzie, don't you think smilax and white rosebuds in festoons would be lovely draping the hall banister? Perhaps Elisha will insist on camellias. He says I'm just like a camellia."

"A neat little bouquet he makes you sound." Pa turned round to grin at her. "How many other kinds of flowers in it?"

"You're not supposed to be listening, sir!" Her tone was arch.

Well! Late that night Lizzie and her mother talked over this development. "Dr. Kane doesn't want a fashionable wife, but this phase of hers may pass before he returns." Ma didn't sound at all sure.

But Mrs. Walter seemed to have made Maggie's coming marriage so real to the girl that she worked in earnest for the smilax and rosebuds in festoons. In two months she made more progress than in the preceding ten. Her grammar became instinctive. She read for herself and "quite liked Scott," and she began to collect recipes.

Mrs. Turner was so pleased she declared Maggie had earned a rest when Mrs. Walter invited her in June to spend July in the mountains. Maggie herself left almost reluctantly. During her absence, a letter from Mr. Grinnell arrived. It contained an enclosure addressed in the Doctor's staccato hand.

"Whatever shall we do? Precious as this is, I cannot risk it's being lost."

If he were lost, too, and this proved his last word! Lizzie, holding it tenderly, said, "Maggie must come for it."

A telegram summoned her. In two days she was there, running in half-laughing, half-crying, her bonnet fallen back, her hair tousled, by no means the modish damsel. "He did write, he did! Dearest Ly! Where is it, Mrs. Turner?"

"Here, silly child. Dry your eyes so you can see to read."

"I haven't a handkerchief. I always forget and Elisha used to carry extra ones on my account." Recollection made her cry again.

Ma wiped her tears and stood, handkerchief dangling, while Maggie read. It took so little time that Maggie turned the letter over to see if there wasn't more on the other side.

She wet her lips. "It's very short." Childishly she counted the lines. "Not as many as the months I've waited."

In Philadelphia Judge Kane puzzled over the postscript to Elisha's otherwise highly serious epistle. He had drawn a hand pointing to the words: "Love. My last word is 'Love.'"

More suitable as a lover's postscript to a childish sweetheart than as a conclusion for Dr. Kane's confidential report to his father. He must have meant it for Bessie, thinking, as brothers will, his sister still a little girl.

27. MEA CULPA

BEFORE they had buried Jeff, before Kane had even turned away from the boy's deathbed, his sorrow had been rent by such a surge of hope that his heart could hardly bear it.

Whipple had burst into the quarters, shouting, "People halloaing ashore. Too big for Eskimos. Tall as white men!"

Morton grabbed the Captain, rushing heedless into the cold. "You outta your head, Cap'n?" He bundled Kane into a heavy parka, while such crewmen as could walk struggled into theirs.

They crowded behind Kane up the companionway. On deck he squinted into the light. Grouped on the land ice at different levels, some singly, some by twos and threes, like figures in an opera tableau, stood thirty to forty strapping fellows. Their lances, thrust at rest in the snow, heightened their theatrical look. A party of Franklin's men, surviving as he had been sure they could by adopting Eskimo ways, had come on their enfeebled "rescuers."

His vision blurred by tears of excitement, Kane moved out onto the ice, arms wide in welcome.

At this gesture an echoing chant filled the air, "Hoah-ha-ha" and "Kaa-ka, Kaa-ka," repeated over and over. This wild babble was not the hail of Englishmen!

Disappointment like gall in his mouth, he said, without turning his head, "Petersen, does this frightful noise mean anything?"

"Eskimo greeting. It says 'We are here.' "

They were, indeed, and whether for good or evil had yet to be determined. But he must show the white men's peaceable intent. He walked farther onto the floe, waving his arms to prove he carried no weapons.

The tallest man in the group leaped down to meet him. Oddly, as the fellow approached, he lost his Patagonian proportions and assumed more normal size. Standing beside Kane, however, he proved a full head taller. Under a hood of mixed white-and-blue fox pelts his swarthy face had stern dignity and his black eyes were piercing. He was obviously their leader.

Petersen interpreted for Kane. "We search for white men. Have you seen white men, many white men?"

The chief's stern dignity vanished like a bubble as the Eskimo broke into uncontrollable laughter. Kane, startled, waited for an explanation, when the fellow could finally manage to speak. "He say never saw man white as you."

A pasty, sickly white after an Arctic winter! The chief and his band must not find out the weakness of his poor crew.

"His name Metek."

"Metek," Kane acknowledged. Pointing to himself, he said, "Dr. Kane," and held out his hand.

Metek took it, solemnly saying, "Docto Kayen," before he broke again into laughter. Then he and Petersen jabbered together. "He and his men out on ice for first walrus hunt of spring. Go home now, bellies full, sleds full."

The chief gestured with his lance, a formidable weapon made of narwhal horn spliced to give added length and heft, its tip unmistakable steel. The dog-team leaders had stabbed theirs into the ice and tied their yelping lunging dogs to these "posts." At Metek's gesture, up came these spears and all the others, as the band scrambled across the ice toward the brig. A forest of lances speedily waved around Kane. Was Metek's gesture a signal?

"He say he and men go on ship now."

Where they would outnumber his crew two to one if every man were well and on his feet! Discovering this, they might take over the brig, carting off its contents at will, and the brig itself piece by piece. Timber was worth more than gold in the Arctic. Better to present them with small gifts, making them friends, than to allow them, as enemies, to take the lot. Better still, bargain with Metek as chief, swapping what Metek coveted for walrus meat and dogs. Thus he could turn danger into advantage.

"Tell Metek only the chief will be honored with a visit to my cabin. My men will feast his here on the ice."

Metek grandly waved his men back and with a broad grin followed Kane. As they passed the ship's surgeon, McGary being too far off, Kane said, "Dr. Hayes, our other guests are not to set foot on board. But don't use gunfire except at my command."

In the quarters, Metek, childlike, fingered everything: the Captain's chair, his desk, his pens, his swinging ink bottle. He squinted with the utmost disbelief at Maggie's portrait, peering behind the canvas to discover the creature lurking there.

"He say, 'Magic,'" Petersen reported.

"Witchcraft," Kane agreed, laughing. "Here, Petersen, tell him this fine steel needle is for him."

Metek, rolling it between his fingers, pleased at the feel of the metal, pricked his thumb, and marveled that it drew blood with so little pain. He pricked himself again and laughed uproariously.

"Before he bleeds himself to death, say I will give each of his men a needle in exchange for two sledge loads of walrus."

Petersen interpreting, Metek beamed approval, clasping Kane's hand in a somewhat bloody grip to seal the bargain. Next, the Captain produced a steel stave from an alcohol cask. In sign language he showed how several lance heads could be cut from a single stave. "One of these in exchange for a dog."

Four dogs for four staves, Metek agreed, and wanted to take staves and needles to his men at once.

"No. Tell him feast first and when his band is ready to leave, then we will have a solemn exchange of gifts."

Out on the ice the crew had set up an improvised table, loaded with such delicacies as the brig's galley could provide, among them white bread and sugar lumps. Over a coal fire corned pork was parboiling. The Eskimos fingered a few things, but soon withdrew to gorge to their own taste, squatting in circles around their sleds, each man with a chunk of raw walrus before him.

From this he sliced a long thin piece, and, inserting one end of the greasy strip in his mouth, began chewing. Tirelessly, impassively, he sucked in the fatty lengths, resembling in the process a piper who inhaled rather than blew on his instrument. So engaged, Metek's band looked far from menacing, and Kane's uneasiness began to wane.

This inhaling continued through the night, though now and then an Eskimo stopped chewing to sleep, head on chest; or to move to the coal fire, marveling at the black lumps, too hard for blubber, which nevertheless glowed red.

By morning they were bloated and sluggish from their gorging, but at first light up and ready to leave. Kane and Metek made ceremonious exchange, after the chief had shown his hunters how easily the magic needles drew blood. Kane was allowed to choose four dogs, and given not only a generous supply of walrus meat, but also the sled on which it was piled.

When Metek had indicated the fine points of that conveyance with its sides and runners of walrus bone and tusk, Kane, to whom it was beautiful as purest ivory, said, "Tell him he is great chief."

Metek grandly agreed, and promised to return soon with more walrus. Then they were gone as suddenly as they came.

Surely their splendid physical condition was proof that some of the lost Britons, given as much sense as Eskimos, could have survived in this area; that he and his men could recover full health with their aid. They could supply meat and more dogs, even help in the search.

"Pardon, sir, but that blasted crew made off with an ax, a saw, some knives, and has broke in the storehouse."

While apparently interested only in eating and sleeping, they had managed those sly thefts and might return to perpetrate more. "Set a watch, McGary. But don't raise a gun until you mean it. Keep that deadly magic in reserve."

Not all the band had, in fact, gone. Three sledges were found hidden behind hummocks, and next day five of the hunters appeared without Metek.

Kane and Petersen went to greet them with seeming cordiality. "Tell them they may come aboard and will receive gifts when they return the missing articles."

Loudly they protested they had stolen nothing, and left, cannily scattering. Two of them traveled by way of the storehouse where they tried to hoist a coal barrel on the shoulders of one. McGary confessed he fired small shot "to help them on their way." The men who left by another route cut the India-rubber boat to pieces —for its wood. Their next Eskimo caller must be sternly dealt with.

Kane was disconcerted when he had his hostage, an agile, elfin youth who drove up in open day. He was far handsomer and more sprightly than any other native they had seen, and his sled and team very smart.

"My-ouk I am," he declared with obvious pleasure in the fact, and said he lived at Etah. Metek and the rest had come from there, but My-ouk, with beguiling frankness, professed to know nothing of the missing tools and ruined boat.

"Tell him," Kane said sternly, "he will be shut in a dark place until he speaks truth."

My-ouk displayed only surprise at this, and was thereupon imprisoned in the hold where he refused to eat and wept and talked sadly to himself. By night his spirits lightened and he sang: a brief *solfeggio* repeated over and over. Each time it promised to grow into a melody, but never did. It haunted Kane in his bunk. He would question the lad again in the morning, and let him go.

But he was already gone, having lifted the hatch under the very noses of the watch. He also abstracted his dogs and sled. The Captain officially reprimanded the watch, but in his journal wrote: "My-ouk. Etah. My bird is flown." As he closed the book, he was humming that snatch of notes in a minor key. Surely, such a lilting start could be brought to song. Maggie's face caught his eye, and he tried all day to work out a melody.

The sight of other humans besides their pallid selves stirred his men into life almost as much as the coming of spring and the sun. If Metek's men could hunt now, so could he and Hans, Petersen said. They rigged a mobile ambush—a white screen atop a rude sled—and pushed it ahead of them until they slid within range of basking game. Thus concealed, Hans got four seal in one day, and on the next two days brought in ptarmigan, rabbit, and a reindeer.

So they did not need the walrus which Metek, of course, failed to deliver. Fed on fresh meat, the well among the crew grew heartier, and the ailing improved steadily. It was time, Kane decided, for the big push; first to McGary's cache by the great glacier, then across smooth ice to the American side and on around a big bay whose existence Kane inferred. The outlet to that bay might lead straight to his Open Sea. It would take all of May to reach, and all of June to return, but such a discovery would be the expedition's crowning achievement.

The threat of an Eskimo raid must not deter him, though he could spare only four able-bodied and six disabled men to guard the *Advance,* and ready her for sailing. Some of his invalids could help Ohlsen a little in dismantling their winter snuggery. But not Brooks, whose stump had not yet healed, nor Wilson, still down. He never visited with those two, never thought of Jeff or Schubert, without berating himself. His incurable optimism had made him trust Arctic weather to hold fair in March! If he failed this time, four brave men would have suffered in vain.

The last Wednesday in April McGary's party led off with the big sledge, the Faith, lightly loaded until they reached the first cache. Thursday, Kane and Godfrey followed with the dog team—three of his own survivors hitched with Metek's four. Whatever Godfrey's character, on the trail he kept to Kane's speed. They made excellent time—though Kane often stopped to sketch. Red sandstone piled a thousand feet to make turreted castles, ruined towers, whole antique cities casting black shadows on the whiteness below, his pencil could not resist. Their second day out they caught up with McGary's quintet.

Huge drifts began to plague them. At the brig there had been only four inches of snow, but here they floundered to their middles, had to portage the sledge, and beat a path for the dogs. But they were almost to the great glacier and their main cache by early May.

At 79° north Kane stopped to record a towering column of greenstone on the brink of a deep ravine. As smooth as if cast in bronze for the Place Vendôme, it rose nearly five hundred feet from a pedestal three hundred feet high. As he drew it, he felt cold under his furs, though it was only five below zero. He had also noticed dropsical swelling in his legs, a scurvy symptom. But the drawing was one of his best. Labeling it "The Tennyson Monument," he stowed it carefully.

It was for the men in his own crew that he named the ice-surrounded islands they came on next. Beyond, their view was obstructed by a lowering cape. When they finally encircled it, there was the great glacier.

Nothing had prepared Kane for the sight. Far into the distance—at least sixty miles—stretched a mighty wall of dazzling crystal. It made the Great Wall of China puny, the Pyramids ant heaps, Niagara a pretty waterfall. Somewhat pyramidal itself in structure, it rose by giant steps to its crest, cliff on cliff of glittering ice, sunlight pulsing on every facet.

He despaired of drawing it. Black and white could never record its flashing color. There were no trees to provide scale for its mass. His men looked like ants where they circled the cache at its foot, disturbed ants staggering in a line toward him.

They yelled "Bears! Bears!" and a little feverish, he thought bears pursued them. But no, McGary was saying that bears of foulest lineage, procreated incredibly, had pawed aside stones it took three men to set in place.

"Stop swearing and tell me the worst."

"See for yourself, Cap'n."

On swollen legs, Kane lumbered to inspect the damage. Their biggest autumn cache was entirely stripped, iron casks smashed and rifled. The great store of pemmican they had planned to stow at each stage on their outward passage for use on the return journey was gone. So was every drop of alcohol for cooking. It was simple disaster.

No captain had better men. They volunteered to ration their remaining food and push on to his Open Sea. "Leastwise," Godfrey said, "until we catch those blasted bears and eat them."

Not stopping, they traveled eight more miles before pitching their tent. Kane, taking an observation for latitude, suddenly stiffened in agonizing pain, and reeling, fainted. He came to almost before the men reached him, and realized he had suffered a convulsion like the dogs' last winter. In the warmth of the tent, after he downed hot broth, the spasm seemed to wear off, but in the morning his legs were still rigid.

"That will wear off, too," he told his men. "There's smooth ice to the American shore. Can you haul me, strapped to the sledge, until I recover?" Strapped, he wouldn't hinder them by falling off.

If he could go on, they could, they stoutly declared.

The weather stayed moderate, but his weakened body could not resist cold at all. When they camped that night by the bay he had known would be there, he found his left foot frozen. Some hours later dream and waking became confused. He was sure of struggling up once, Whipple and Stephenson helping him toward the tent flap. He could not remember reaching it, and came to next in McGary's brawny embrace.

"Get you on the sledge, Cap'n. Then back to the brig."

Toward the brig there were high drifts his weakened men could never get the sledge through. Stay on smooth ice by the American shore, he thought he said, smooth as the skating pond near Rensselaer. Skate to his Open Sea, that was the way. Here was Maggie gliding beside him, though he had mistaken her at first for My-ouk, because she was singing My-ouk's *solfeggio.* The crew—

He could hear them talking and tried to count the voices. All his crew were not here! The most helpless he had left to the mercy of Metek's band. Brooks lay strapped to his bunk, legs rigid, with a lance point aimed at his throat. "Back to the brig!" Brooks expected him to come. "To the brig!"

"Aye, Cap'n, almost there."

McGary always answered the Captain's ravings. Seemed to steady him like, while they kept going, day after day. Another day they'd be there, if the men held up. The Second gauged the rest by Morton, the toughest. For the Captain, Morton would go till he dropped, and that boy Hickey had showed guts before. It was Riley, Stephenson, and that lazy Hans as surprised the Second, struggling and hauling and lifting the Captain in terror of his dying before they reached the brig, and them as near dead as him.

Nine days out of the unnamed bay the little party stumbled aboard the *Advance,* Dr. Kane's face so black and swollen that Isaac Hayes did not know him.

After a week of night sweats, dropsy, and fever, Captain Kane, propped up by pillows, entered in his journal the failure of another mission. Around him, invalided, lay four of the men who had saved his very life.

Hayes diagnosed the Captain's attack as a malevolent combination of typhoid fever and scurvy. Kane blamed it on the Captain's incurable haste. Had he waited a week longer they would all have been stronger, the weather milder, their chance of reaching his Thalassa enormously greater. But no, moving at his usual headlong speed, he had nearly doomed the expedition to total failure.

Only a month remained for future forays. He himself would be fit for none. Whoever discovered his Open Sea, it would not be Elisha Kent Kane, a punishment justly deserved.

28. TRIAL OF STRENGTH

ISAAC HAYES, at last assigned to a search journey, felt like a dog loosed from his leash. He had labored long months in the sick bay, with small thanks. The men seemed to resent his ministrations, even the kindly Brooks whose foot *had* to be amputated.

"The air will do you good," Kane said drily.

The Captain's nose twitched at the stink of the unwashed and ailing around them, the high smell of slop buckets and burning tallow. Outside the brig, bands of soft mist hid the tops of the hills. The unbroken transparency of last month's atmosphere had given way to the pearly sheen of Arctic summer.

"Since I am confined to the sick bay," Kane continued, "I may as well tend it. You're the only man in good physical condition, aside from Godfrey. Here's what I want." Kane pointed to a wide gap in his map: the "American shore" across from Rensselaer Bay. Their last foray, his men had scarcely touched it before they had to cut back to the brig with their unconscious captain. "We can't leave without searching there."

Hayes, who didn't believe any of Franklin's men lived, nodded perfunctorily.

"If you find no trace, you can still bring back readings and soundings to correct Inglefield's charts."

He'd be the first man to push through there, Ike saw, and his youthful face glowed. He'd worked hard for just such a chance, almost from the day Kane talked in Chester about the Balboa who would first view the Open Sea. If only Kane had said, "Dr. Hayes, you're just the man for this important task!" At any rate, he was going, and this time he'd show the Captain—

"You will take Godfrey with you."

That braggart; maybe he'd show Bill Godfrey, too.

On a promising day in late May he and Bill set a fast pace out from the brig. Their lead dogs, a pair of powerful, wolfish iron grays

Kane got from the Eskimos, plunged forward with bounds more like a lion's than a dog's, carrying along the rest of the team. Bill handled the brutes well, having picked up the knack on his trips with the Captain.

Pleased at their progress, the surgeon, when they camped that night, offered the sailor his blue glasses. The opalescent sunlight was hard on the eyes.

"Those things any good?" Bill asked skeptically.

"They really help when you're facing into the sun. You should have them, since our success depends upon the driver's skill."

"Put it that way," Bill said, and quickly took them.

By flattery he could be kept in hand, be driven as hard as he drove the dogs.

Before noon next day Ike began to pay for his gesture. His eyes felt gritty, full of sand where no sand blew, and his eyelids heavy. But they continued to press northwest in flashing style.

The third day his blurred vision made it painful to use the sextant. As if that weren't trouble enough, fog closed down. When it finally rose, the American shore lay only twenty miles away, but between reared an ugly ice barrier.

"Bill," he called, standing legs apart, jaw set, "ice like that stopped other search parties, but we're going through."

Godfrey, looking at him, said, "Sure, Doc. Sure thing."

At the first opening in the ice wall, they turned in, leaving behind their last "straight" mile for days. Hours on end they twisted and turned, or crawled up and through a wilderness of ice piled twenty to forty feet high and covered with drifted snow.

Bill's whip no longer crackled. He coaxed and hauled the dogs along with a patience that astounded the surgeon. He cursed, Hayes cursing with him, when harness or lines broke or the sledge capsized on top of a ridge, tumbling dogs, sled, and cargo over and over into the drifts below. But, mumbling continual blasphemies, Bill time and again reloaded their cargo, mended the lines, and started on. Ike almost liked the fellow.

That night they found a cramped hollow where they built a cozy snow house. As Hayes was falling away into sleep, Bill said low, "You keep squinting, Doc. Your eyes going bad?"

"A little troublesome. All right in the morning."

"Take the glasses. You need 'em worse."

Hayes smiled at Bill's playing Sir Philip Sydney. "You'll need them if you don't keep them," he warned.

"Not me." Godfrey shoved them roughly toward him.

When Ike roused a while later, Bill was patiently picking knots out of the sledge lines. They got hellishly tangled on this kind of going. "Georgian knots," Bill said.

In the morning, Hayes's eyes would not open. He heard Bill stirring. "Is the water warm yet?"

"Pasted shut, ain't they? Kind of swole, too."

The surgeon fingered them lightly. "So it appears." Caked matter washed away, his lids stayed shut. The pain was agonizing. "We'll have to lie over until I can see." He kept his voice steady.

To maintain strength, he ate, though the pain was so sickening that he barely held food down. Then he wrapped a clean sock over his eyes to shut out every splinter of light, and, teeth clenched, lay waiting a letup to this nerve-rending misery.

Bill crouched in the doorway. "Do some work on the lines. Never seen such a —— mess. Shorten any more, the dogs can't pull. Using me a strip from the top of my pantaloons for leather." He talked steadily, with time out only to feed dogs and men again; talked to down his own fear that "Doc" might give way and scream.

"All us in this frozen hellhole," Bill soliloquized, "because that cocky little bastard wants to play hero at home and abroad with Queen Victoria saying he done a far, far better thing than any living American, if he ain't dead by then and all with him."

"None of that talk."

The sailor went on without a pause. "Old Franklin never got caught this far north, dead or alive. Died south of here in a commodious cabin, of heartburn, maybe, or gout. His crews, using common sense, got for home like we should. Or joined the Eskimos, every man picking himself a nice roly-poly piece to keep him warm."

"This far north" were the only words Hayes really heard. He repeated them softly, and his agony seemed to subside for an instant. "When we reach shore, I'll take bearings."

At that Godfrey's voice trailed off. "He knows now," Ike thought with grim pleasure, "the Doc ain't gonna holler."

At nine-thirty that night "the Doc" got one eye open, and they started on. Within the hour it was shut again, forcing them to pitch camp. For a day and a half they holed up, Hayes at times setting his teeth into the skin of his sleeping bag to stifle any moan. Panting, he said to Bill, "I'll be a better doctor for knowing real pain at firsthand."

"Oughta be damn good, sir."

Not "Doc," but "sir." Isaac Hayes smiled. The angry red sea that had lashed his brain for hours, was it subsiding a little? Sometime that night he really slept and woke with both eyes open. "Bill! I can see! Let's get moving, to make up lost time."

"Aye, sir, on the double."

Perhaps it had not been a total loss.

A foggy day and misty, for which Hayes gave thanks. He had no other reason to be thankful. The ice maze forced them to travel twenty miles to get two miles nearer the American side. When they stopped in their erratic course to rest the dogs, Bill reported uneasily, "Can't see so good. Blurs out at twenty paces."

"Fog and mist, Bill. Don't let my attack get you nervy."

"Me nervy? Not me."

But he crawled sullen and silent into his sleeping bag, forgetting to feed the dogs, and he slept doubled up as if from scurvy cramps. Hayes took care of their beasts and went off on foot to explore a track for tomorrow.

On and on he tramped, kicking wide tracks in the snow crust to mark the way. He was curiously rested. Although his eyes still watered and burned, his body had greater spring than ever in his life. He would make a landing on that shore if he had to drag Bill on the sledge. Just as he swore this, he came out of the maze onto a smooth old floe that ran for miles straight to land.

Eight days out from the brig, the frozen, tumbled sea that had swallowed them disgorged Ike and Bill on the edge of the Big Unknown. The sledge had capsized so often that it needed a complete overhaul. Their supplies were low, and Bill was in poor shape. But tomorrow Isaac Hayes would scale the high crag that overhung their camp and with what eyesight he had see farther north than any living man.

He roused Bill early and, leaving him to work on harness and sledge, began his climb. The rising sun he could see only through an agony of squinting. Had Balboa's eyes troubled him? On a ledge Ike paused. Below, where he heard the dogs yelping, all was bleak and in shadow. A heavy mist swirled in from the frozen sea. But over a shoulder of rock up ahead what he saw made him catch his breath. The sun had caught the cap of a lofty peak.

Finding handholds almost by instinct, he scrambled up the side of the bluff for a better view, and then a better one, reaching, finally, a table hundreds of feet up. The mist hid everything below, but to the west–

It was as though he stood on the brink of a midsummer thunderhead. Behind and beneath blackness boiled in turmoil. Out of this angry dark rose lofty masses of white to red that rolled back and up to a serene blue. Isaac Hayes, discoverer, stood alone, looking upon peak after peak of a great mountain chain that forged northward as far as his tormented eyes could see. And beyond.

If only he had fifty pounds more pemmican! Below, the land ice to the north ran smooth and solid as it followed the coast paralleling his range of pearly mountains. Tomorrow or the day after might bring them to the northern outlet Kane had predicted; the next day to the Open Sea itself. If they sacrificed one of the dogs—

Reluctantly he abandoned this panorama of sweeping light for their dark little camp. Bill had made the sledge fairly sturdy and with a whiplash had repaired the lines.

"The land ice to the north will be a treat to the dogs after this past week," Hayes said, not looking at the sailor, but slapping one of the lead grays.

"North?" Bill's jaw dropped. "Jeez, Doc, we got only three days' grub and the brig more'n a week away."

"I'd hardly take the same route," Hayes said with a scornful laugh. "Once is enough!"

"My scurvy cramps," Bill cast wildly about, "and my eyes is worse. Won't help none to starve our way back, if we get back."

"We can kill one of the dogs if needs be."

"The Captain is counting on this team for other searches most likely. Rather have you lose a man," Bill said gloomily.

That gave Ike pause. He stood looking from the dogs to Bill and back to the dogs. If he spent either recklessly, it would be worse than the broken thermometer. And if he did not exhaust his own strength, he might have another chance to push north. Who else was in as good condition? None of the other officers.

"We'll take his pets safely back to the Captain," he said with a smile. "Harness them up and put about for the brig."

Midday on that first lap the sun poured so directly down that there was no relieving shadow on the shimmering landscape. Hayes's eyes worsened. Bill was rubbing his own suspiciously. Fortunately the snow was blown smooth and hard enough to let the dogs carry both men and make speed. They sped across a deep bay bounded to the south by the most enormous snout of rock Hayes had seen the entire voyage, except for Sanderson's Hope, near Upernavik. This was Hayes's Hope, part of *his* mountain chain, his own landmark when he went north again.

They camped under this towering cliff. Suddenly Bill, who had stumbled around settling the dogs, cried out, "Doc! Doc! Where are you? I can't see you! Can't see nothing! You hear?" He screamed the last words, loud as a woman in labor.

"I hear," Ike said coldly, close to Bill. "They probably hear you at the brig."

Godfrey sucked in his breath, and clutched at the surgeon's parka. "Doc, listen, the pain ain't much, but I can't see! Can't see to drive, but don't leave me behind, Doc, don't leave me!"

"Have you gone crazy? Of course I won't leave you. By morning you'll be all right."

Hayes got the fellow into his sleeping bag, and while he warmed pemmican and coffee for them both, Bill kept calling out to him in childish terror of being alone. He insisted Ike pull his own bag alongside. "So I can hear you breathe," Bill said cannily.

As he lay nursing his own eyes, Hayes thought Bill's fright at a little snow blindness out of all proportion.

Sensing this, the sailor said, "I didn't take it good as you, but Christ, the idea of being blind scares hell out of me! Me, an old bum shuffling along, whining for pennies! Cut my throat first. Never see the girls again, smiling up at me, hitching up their garters, switching their sassy little asses at Bill Godfrey. I been their boy, Doc. They're crazy for me!"

Hayes laughed. "I'll see you recover for their sakes!"

"You just do that, Doc." Bill spoke in ludicrous earnest. "Funny thing, with this bandage on I keep seeing one girl and she's none of mine. She's the Captain's."

"Who on earth are you talking about?" But Ike knew.

"That girl over his bunk. Tending his lordship before we left, emptying his slops, rubbing his feet, I seen her there, smiling like she's up to no good. That minx ain't his style."

This description outraged Isaac Hayes. The face over Kane's bunk was a tender young madonna's, mysteriously wise. "Because you're starved for a woman, you read your own low desires into the face of a pure, innocent girl," he told Bill hotly. "Keep your filthy tongue to your own sort and leave her alone, if you want me in earshot."

"Don't move away, sir!" Godfrey clutched at the surgeon's sleeping bag. "No offense meant."

They lay silent, but neither breathed in the deep rhythms of sleep. After a while Bill said almost timidly, "I don't think you know who she is, sir. That's a fact."

"But you do!"

"Sure. Cap Rynders–"

"Who?"

"Rynders, boss of the Five Points Gang–"

"Were you one of his thugs?"

"Didn't say so. Everybody around New York knows Rynders. Well, he's got her picture, too."

"That's preposterous!"

"Swear to God it's so. You can buy her picture plenty places. She's one of the Rochester Knockers, the pretty one. Rynders was hired once to break up a séance as he'd have enjoyed doing. Get his mitts on the girl, too, see? By God, if the rappers didn't scare him off, Rynders himself! Devil takes care of his own, he says, and hankers for her worse than ever."

"Kane's picture isn't a cheap print. It's an oil painting–of his ward, I think." Hayes remembered something about a bird the day he came aboard the *Advance*. "She couldn't be one of the rappers! Such an association," he chose the word carefully, "would ruin a scientist of Kane's standing."

"So he ain't human. Never thought he was, the way he draws Eskimo girls like they was specimens. I'd settle for a little Husky right now."

"You settle down to sleep or you'll never see another."

But Isaac himself was too excited to sleep. Godfrey might be right. If the girl was a rapper and a scandal developed– Mr. Grinnell would want a scientist of unblemished reputation to make the official report of the Second Grinnell Expedition. Kane himself had been only a ship's surgeon when he wrote the report of the first one that had persuaded Grinnell to back this voyage. For a man without any weaknesses there was a real future in Arctic exploration.

Their next stage was a nightmare, with the snow so deep and wet the dogs could haul neither man, and Bill worse. Laboriously Ike led the team, Bill holding onto the sledge while he stumbled after, falling frequently, and wet through. When they halted at four, Ike fed the dogs their last scrap of pemmican, leaving only coffee for the men. Bill had fallen flat when they stopped, and Ike, dragging him to his sleeping bag, was determined that this sodden lump should not keep him from reaching the brig.

Oh, Ike wouldn't leave him, though a rescue party could easily be sent. He'd drag Bill the whole way, making him forever Dr. Hayes's henchman. To do it, everything inessential must be jettisoned: sleeping bags, cook lamps, extra garments, everything but their rifle, instruments, and one pair of sealskin boots to feed the dogs.

That way, in the morning light, he lightened his load a good fifty pounds and piled the whimpering Godfrey onto the sledge. "Shut up, shut up," the surgeon muttered impatiently. "Try to head the dogs out from the shore."

At midchannel the snow was firm enough for Hayes to ride the runners, but a fog settled down and his eyes, so swollen that the lids would not close as once they would not open, strained in vain to see Cape Sabine, their southern landmark. That night he fed the team the shakings of their bread bag and the scrapings of their lard cloth, mixed with scraps of sealskin boots. He and Bill had only coffee again. Hunger was weakening Ike more than he dared admit.

Without explanation he rode the sledge, too, on their next run. "Can't see, for the fog. The dogs can take us. They must know their way to the brig from here. Smell it, likely." It was foul enough to reek for miles on the pure polar air.

On and on they went. So long as the dogs held out, there was no cause to stop: no food for men or animals, no bags for a warm rest. Thank God, the dogs ran like brutes possessed.

At one in the morning welcoming hands lifted them aboard the *Advance*. Ike was carried in to Kane where he lay on his bunk.

There was no hint in the Captain's voice at his shock. Poor Hayes's eyeballs were a mass of blood and purulence. Kane took the young surgeon's hands hard in his.

"You have weathered your initiation magnificently!" Kane's voice rang through the quarters. "I can't tell you how glad we are to have you back. You have been greatly missed, Doctor."

Such warm words made Isaac regret a little the ideas he had entertained about the Captain and that girl. Was she smiling compassionately down on him?

29. CELEBRATION

THE CAPTAIN insisted Hayes rest two full days before making his report. Even then, it had to be oral, Hayes's eyes recovering more slowly than Kane expected. Sitting with his cherished map beside the strong and youthful surgeon, Kane wondered if he'd have to watch those eyes. They might prove a serious weakness.

Hayes poured forth the details of his journey in impressive detail, Kane checking everything against Hayes's log.

"You did extraordinarily well, plagued as you were with snow blindness. The mountains are an important discovery, another indication of a northern outlet to Smith's Sound. How was the ice between here and your southmost point on the American side?"

"Entirely solid. We saw no open water."

"Then we have time for one more effort! My last throw, at the rate spring is advancing." Kane's voice rose. In hope or desperation? "We must defeat the great glacier, push beyond it into that outlet, and from there—"

"Straight to the Open Sea!" Hayes raised up on one elbow. "Let me lead that party, sir." If only he could see Kane's face!

Kane's voice was over-hearty. "If we had more time, you'd be the very man. But we can't wait for you to recover as completely as you must to make such an exhausting trip. Your eyes might be permanently injured. Neither you nor I are up to it, so we must do with the men we have."

Ike fell back on his pillow. Damn his eyes! Whose he meant he was not certain.

Kane was ticking off names too glibly. McGary, Hickey, and Riley were all sound enough. "Bonsall's scurvy knee is mending. They will be equal to the provision party which goes only to the glacier."

Who would push beyond? Hans, the Captain was saying. His pet Eskimo, fat, hale, lazy, and bootlicking. But he was only the dog driver. Who would be the real leader?

"Morton, who is recovering rapidly, thoroughly understands my theory of the Open Sea, he's heard me expound it so often, poor fellow. I'd trust his judgment as I would my own."

Morton! He wasn't an officer or even an educated man, just the ship's steward. But he was the Captain's crony, his personal nurse, privy to Kane's secrets which he hid behind a deadpan face. This was too pat. Kane must have decided on Morton before his ship's surgeon had even returned, sick or well.

So it was Morton who went. On Kane's order, he pulled no line. His strength, like the dogs', must be husbanded.

"You're paying now," Morton baited the others, "for the nursing I give you this winter."

"Small nursing you done for me," McGary said.

"A little goes a long ways with a patient your heft."

Truth was, McGary was nothing near as fat. Like Cap'n Ken said, the Arctic had leaned him down. Even so, his stocky figure stood out in the group Morton waved back to before he and Hans plunged into the wilderness of fresh-struck bergs at the glacier's foot. He sure wished McGary was going along. For company, he'd take the Second to any man aboard the brig; for holding on to the bitter end, only the Cap'n himself was McGary's beat.

Hans surprised him though. It was the Eskimo every time who found a way through the damned hummocks. Smart in his stupid-looking way, Hans was.

The morning of June 19 they shinnied up a high berg, and what they saw made Morton scrabble for his compass. "Some way we got ourselves turned about. Must be south we're headed now."

No, it was straight north, and what he saw proved Cap'n Ken had the right of it. Must be warmer the further north you got, from the way that ice plain was spider-webbed with black-water channels. The wind was mild and the dovekies so thick that Hans come near to catching one by its little red legs. The glacier was far behind and in its place was land, real land, with only a scattering of snow patches on it.

Hans driving, they picked their way past the black leads to the point where the "sea" narrowed to a thirty-mile channel with big capes each side of it. This was the Cap'n's "outlet." Right again he was, but the ice under them was getting rubbery.

"Easy to starboard," he yelled, and Hans geed the team wide to make safe landing. They hugged the shore, plain gawping at open water all round, lively with ducks. They swarmed up and flew north.

"North!" he yelled at Hans. "You seen that? Got to get where we can see past that cape to starboard."

It was so rugged the Cap'n should name it for Old Hickory as would please the Judge. They tacked the sled around it on one runner along a ledge seventy feet up. Tricky bit that was, but they come down to broad land ice so smooth they made fifty miles before it disappeared like a road petering out in the middle of nowheres.

"Take the rest of the way on shanks' mare," Morton said, but Hans didn't know what a mare was. "On foot!" So they tied up the dogs and footed it, breaching inlets and creeks by jumping from rock to rock, or by ferrying over on a handy chunk of ice. "Like Eliza." Hans laughed without really getting the joke. Then Tood-la and four other huskies caught up with them. "Told you to tie them dogs good, stupid. How we gonna feed 'em?"

But that afternoon the dogs scared up a bear and her cub. Morton nicked the pair easy and there was meat for all.

Across the bay was one of them headlands like Cap'n Ken was always pushing on to. "Another Gib for size," Morton told the heathen boy, who never heard of Gibraltar. "From the top of that I could see quite a spell. Shortest way is straight across the ice."

Hans shook his head. Too rubbery for the fat boy, so off he went by land, which took longer. Morton, stepping light, traveled the quivering ice. His Gibraltar being a sight too steep to climb on the near side, he tried crawling around to its north face but was stopped dead where the rock dropped sheer down. He could hear water lapping at the foot of the cliff. What water it was he'd have to see some way.

He backed down to try another way round. Up a couple hundred fathoms a knob stuck out. Standing there, he'd be as good as in the crow's-nest. Squirming along, he made it, and pulled to his feet.

Cap'n Ken should of been him. Here it was, enough open water to make even Brooks happy. Far as he could see north wide-open water, and even with the Cap'n's glass, no end to it. A swell from the north was raising whitecaps on its surface, and far below he could hear surf breaking against that cliff. He did wish the Cap'n was there, especially to see the rain cloud over to the northwest, the first such Morton had seen in the Arctic. Trees and rain clouds was two things he found he missed, which was peculiar in an old Navy hand. The mountains lying under that cloud were stacked like cannon balls clean to the Pole.

"Hans!" he bellowed, but only the gulls nesting in the cliff above his head clacked in answer. Ivory gulls they was, and those birds out over the water was molemokes, for sure. Silver-backed gulls by the thousands circled the waves below, diving for fish.

If this wasn't a sea, Morton never seen one. That fact determined after considerable thought, Morton gave three cheers for the Doctor and three for his Open Sea, and from inside his parka pulled the two flags Cap'n Ken had given him "for such an eventuality." His fingers all thumbs, he tied to his walking pole first the swallowtail flag of the *Advance* herself and then the Masonic flag, the Cap'n not having an American flag to spare. As they fluttered in a real sea breeze, Morton's throat choked up, and he was glad that fat Hans wasn't nowhere round to see him crying. Hans would of laughed, likely. Eskimos thought every living thing was funny.

Morton reckoned what really broke him down was Cap'n Ken not being there, when the little fellow had counted so long on finding his Open Sea.

All during their tiresome trip back Morton rehearsed his speech. "Flying Cap'n Ken's colors high as I could wave 'em, with a nice little north wind blowing full in my face, I viewed the scene." He would pause here so the crew could cheer, and then for Brooks's benefit go on like this: "Open water as far as eye could reach is what I seen, with room for our brig to stand anyways Mr. Brooks pleased, with a whole fleet of brigs maneuvering around her. There she was, gentlemen, the Polar Sea, plumb where Cap'n Ken predicted we'd find her."

He could hardly wait to see the Cap'n's face. As for himself, the Navy'd likely give him a rise in grade.

Morton's speech had the crew stamping their feet and whooping, the Cap'n yelling like a schoolboy and pounding Morton's back, McGary shaking his hand till he like to wore it out.

Then Cap'n Ken made a speech, too. "I need not tell you all the longest day of the year is lately past. An equinoctial storm may any day free the brig from the icy isthmus in which she is now caught. While Morton went north, I sent Mr. McGary south. He reports the ice is breaking up at a very satisfactory pace. There is open water to the south as close as Fog Inlet. Between there and this great Open Sea the ice now stretches, as I said, in a narrow isthmus. Soon it will vanish and the *Advance* will be homeward bound with great news, great news!" His face shone. It almost had some color in it again.

The crew yelled at the mention of home, yelled again when the Cap'n ordered a dram of spirits around, yelled a third time in honor of the day it was. Outside, a moist and flaky snow fell, but the weather couldn't change the date. This was the Fourth of July, which was why the Cap'n couldn't let Morton take their American flag.

30. DECISION

THE ICE which for ten months had held the *Advance* in a vise was so rotted that the brig swayed with the tides, and McGary felt a sailor again. Melting snows off the higher icebergs cascaded in a water spectacle that reminded Stephenson of the fountains at Versailles and Goodfellow of the one in City Hall Park. Bonsall, sent to pick up the pemmican cases Brooks's disastrous depot party had abandoned, found water pooled on the surface of the ice.

"Tricky as a marsh meadow," he warned the two men with him, and pushed on whistling, "Who wouldn't sell a farm and go to sea?" First thing he'd do back home was buy a snug little farm. They did not find the pemmican.

Blake and Whipple, ordered ashore to gather the stunted Arctic greens—lichen, young sorrel, andromeda, draba, and stonecrop—that the Captain ordered everyone to eat, pranced back chanting, "We've been a-maying," and made even Ohlsen laugh.

The carpenter was mysteriously busy installing a false keel on their big flat-bottomed whaleboat, *The Forlorn Hope*.

"That thing going to sea, Swede?"

"All I know is Captain's orders."

The Captain was gone with Hans for a look at the ice to southward. From the brig, not a lead could be seen, but open water must be creeping close now.

"It's ass backwards not knowing what's to the south. Everything charted from here to the Pole practically, but not our way home," Godfrey grumbled from his bunk, his eyes still bandaged. Hayes's eyes were bandaged, too, although Kane said the wrapping might come off any day. He hardly heard Godfrey for listening to the cheerful tattoo set up by the snowbirds swarming on the storehouse.

From far off came the crackle of the dog whip. The Captain was returning. After supper Hickey led the surgeon in to a meeting of officers that Kane had called: to give orders, undoubtedly, for the homeward voyage.

Kane, looking at their expectant faces, realized what a shock his news would be. Better to get it over with. He said without preamble, "The ice is solid for thirty-five miles below Rensselaer Bay. There are a few driving leads for another twenty-five miles. Only then did we come on broken ice with clear water beyond. In sum, the brig is at present sixty miles from freedom."

They sat motionless. Then McGary stirred on his haunches. "But, Cap'n—"

"Oh, you were right about Fog Inlet. However, the breakup has advanced only four miles since you were there."

"In two months," Wilson said.

"Time is no indication," Kane pointed out sharply. "The real breakup hasn't commenced. For Penny, it came early in June, for Austin, not until the middle of August. For us—who knows? But when it comes, it will come fast."

Brooks said hesitantly, "We're eighty miles north of them." He shifted his crutch, his eyes on his captain.

"We are indeed!" Kane smiled. "May I remind you, we were able, a year ago, to force the brig through the pack to this point as late as August 28? So our release may come as late as September 1. Sometime in the next six weeks."

His listeners sighed in relief. Where they had expected the worst, they were given the half-bad. But Henry Brooks decided that the Captain knew well the really big danger: If the ice between here and the North Water broke up too late, winter would catch the brig in the pack, far from shore, fuel and provisions low—

"So I have time to collate my records," Dr. Sontag said.

"What's another month?" Wilson agreed. His stump would be healed when the *Advance* at last spread canvas and her sailing master took over his rightful task.

"Meanwhile," the Captain announced, "I will try to reach Sir Edward Belcher's squadron at Beechy Island to beg supplies for our homeward voyage."

Brooks nodded. The Captain was really going to scout out a line of retreat if the worst came.

They all knew of Beechy, the British depot point six hundred miles away on Lancaster Sound. Worth the distance, since Belcher had four ships with him and two other English vessels were somewhere near. They visualized a cluster of masts, every ship packed with the comforts that attended British explorations. But of the officers, only Morton and McGary would go with Kane.

"Ohlsen had been readying the *Hope's* keel. Her rigging I leave to you, Mr. McGary." He dismissed them all, but Brooks, leaning on his crutch, lingered. "Well, Henry?"

"If you get to Beechy safe, don't come back, Doctor. You can send a rescue force from there. Another winter might see you in as bad shape as me. This one's gone hard on you."

"Henry, when that stump can bear your wearing an artificial foot, you'll be the best man on board, as always. Trust me, mine ancient, to take care of us both." He reached up to put his hands on Brooks's broad shoulders. "When the time comes, every man will have his chance to try for home, if he wants. But I myself can't abandon the brig while there's a chance to save her, next year if not this."

"She's a stout ship."

"Come up on deck and make your apologies to the Fair Augusta for trying to tempt her captain into deserting her."

His mind half on their mutilated little heroine of a figurehead, who had lost the tip of her nose and one breast to the mauling ice, he listened to McGary's plan for the *Hope*.

"Only a New London whaler would risk such a spread of canvas, McGary. But you'll be handling her."

Brooks and Wilson agreed that the Second was mad when she was finally rigged. "Figure it out. On a whaleboat twenty-three feet long with a six-and-a-half foot beam, he puts first a light cotton foresail—" Wilson was ticking the canvas off.

"With a twelve-foot lift!" Brooks shook his head.

"Then a heavier mainsail of fourteen-foot lift braced by a sprit." McGary pronounced it "spreet," and it was eighteen feet long.

"Plus a snug little jib." McGary's madness gave the two crippled officers more to talk about than they had had all winter.

"Like you stay-at-homes to see how she takes the wind!" McGary retorted.

"One good breeze will take her—right up in the air," Brooks rumbled. "Ever thought of using a balloon instead?"

Ohlsen devised a cradle to lift her onto their sledge, the Faith and all hands who could walk helped drag the monster load the full sixty miles to open water. It took five days. Then their miniature fore-and-after was afloat, performing in a style that made McGary bounce. "Ain't she a sight?"

Clogged as the water was with drift ice, she managed to clip along. Kane felt he had never experienced lovelier motion.

"Wish them two could see her!"

They were all in high spirits. For crew, Kane took his sturdiest: Riley, Hans, and the strong, awkward cabin boy, Hickey. They laughed wildly at everything, like boys on holiday. Kane himself felt a little heady at the thought of Beechy. A bath, a decent dinner, a bottle, and the conversation of his betters, the veteran English captains, were ingredients to make a heaven. From there he could dispatch news of Morton's discovery, and send letters to his family, and to Maggie, his lovely child.

In the midst of death and desolation he thought of her only spasmodically, but with reborn life and hope he could write of his persisting love.

Their first landfall was the point where they had stowed the metallic lifeboat. That cache was still intact, a good omen, and nearby they came on a group of rocky islets whose sky was dark with ducks. This was their breeding season. With guns, stones, even their bare hands, the *Hope's* crew instantly became, like the Van Nests in Knickerbocker's *History of New York,* "desperate robbers of birds' nests." They gorged themselves on duck eggs and, loading their boat with game, made for Flagstaff Point.

Their flag was still there, flying bravely if in tatters, and the men cheered. Kane was silent, remembering Jeff had helped run up that banner. He could see the boy's happy face.

As they stood to the southwest under full canvas, plowing obliquely out of Smith's Straits into Baffin's Bay, McGary's exuberance subsided. The Second had every sailor's distrust of open-boat navigation, and for all her show of sail, the *Hope* was a whaleboat. Her knifelike bow buried itself in the troughs of the short, choppy sea that took all McGary's expertness with the steering oar that served for a rudder. "Heavy gale makin', Cap'n."

"Already made," Kane yelled above the wind.

For twenty-four hours a ferocious norther buffeted the *Hope,* saved time and again by McGary's instant skill. Their oilskin deck cloth was torn and leaking. They nearly foundered, and bailed desperately. Had the oar been handled wrong for one instant, they would have been lost. When the wind finally hauled eastward, they scudded before it toward the inshore ice, the pack now their refuge.

The storm was gone, but it left the ice tight around them. For three long days they resorted to tiresome ice navigation. Then the sun shone again, the pack relaxed, and keeping inside it they sailed steadily for Lancaster Sound and Beechy until the ice again closed.

Tirelessly his little crew fought their way through the floes against capricious weather. Now it was sunny and warm, now raining and bitter cold. Leads opened and closed like traps. Once the *Hope* was in an alley between towering ice masses when some freak of the currents sent opposing floes surging toward each other, head on. They met like phalanxes of white elephants, their tremendous collision showering the crew with spray and spinning ice fragments while the *Hope* was borne upward on the accumulating rubbish until she rode high above the water, and for twenty minutes hung there.

When she was at last lowered to safety, McGary complained, "Can't keep ships of yourn in the sea, Cap'n."

Kane heard himself laughing like a madman. "In a ship that really flew, I could reach the Pole!"

Thereafter McGary developed a trick that would have amazed even New London men. When he saw two floes coming on slow but deadly sure, with a small pull of his oar he turned the whaleboat across the lead, pressing down her bow as the floe advanced astern. As that floe slid under her and lifted her bow above the level of the ice field, she would spring right out of the water to ride out the nip astride both floes!

The first time he did this, Kane and all gaped. When he had hauled her onto the ice as often as a dozen times a day, they took it as easily as an English huntsman a leap over a hedge.

But it was hard on the *Hope*. She had developed a leak that kept one man constantly bailing when they came finally to a dead halt about ten miles from Cape Parry. Not a lead showed. Westward several tall bergs were frozen fast. Kane reached for his spyglass. "Let's have a look."

He and McGary clambered a hundred feet up the nearest berg. For thirty miles to south and west the ice lay solid and motionless, lifeless as desert sands at high noon. Kane handed the glass to McGary whose face, as he looked, grew impassive as the ice.

"Unnatural kind of ocean, ain't it?" was his only comment.

"An unnatural season!" Kane burst out. He strained to see in the distance the smoky wreaths and spirals that rise when ice is breaking up, turning the horizon as brown as if a prairie-grass fire raged afar. The horizon stayed a clear, infuriating blue. "Inglefield found open water here two years ago. A year ago we stood to the north at this point clear of all ice. Now look at it!"

"Almighty solid."

"If the breakup shakes the *Advance* loose from her present moorings, we might get this far and no farther. Or if by then this barrier showed any leads, warp into it and be caught by winter!"

"Better off where she rides than stuck here."

As they tramped the four miles back to the *Hope* where she lay on her beam ends, her belly scarred, bruised, and limp as a beached whale's, they agreed that the brig could not get home this year.

"In such cases, isn't it the rule aboard a whaling ship that the captain's authority ends and it's every man for himself?"

"Heard it," McGary acknowledged.

"If the breakup comes too late, I shall so inform the crew. Any who choose to will be free to strike for Greenland."

"You going, sir?"

"No, Mister, I stay."

"Reckoned so. Reckon I will myself. Cozier aboard ship."

"Don't decide until the time comes."

"Decided when I seen that ice. Solid, water ain't my element."

So he would have McGary, Morton—unless he ordered that faithful soul on his way—Brooks, and his other amputee, Wilson. How the rest would decide he could not predict. It was not a choice between life and death, as some might think. He would warn those who went that conditions were against their reaching the Greenland outposts.

Grown fat on auks, eider, and scurvy grass, the crew of the *Hope* worked her almost to the brig, going the rest of the way on foot, using their poles to cross on the rocks. Their sudden appearance startled Whipple.

"Too big for Eskimos! White men," Kane called, smiling.

He reported only their failure to reach Beechy. None of the *Hope's* crew mentioned the terrible ice. Perhaps the seamen missed its significance.

Kane set everyone to work moving the *Advance* into a better position for the high tides due in two weeks. The ice blasted from her sides, she was warped a mile to the northwest and made fast. Her wintering spot was marked with her name and dates painted large on a cliff face. On its crest they buried Jeff and Schubert under a pyramid of rocks that was at once gravestone and cairn. Nearby they sealed into a hole in the rock Kane's report to the world, enclosed in glass. They also marked the site of their dismantled observatory. During this "packing up" Kane watched the weather.

The signs were ominous. The snowbirds had flown south, the poppies were wilted, young ice was forming fast. By mid-August it could support a man and the gales had not come. Twice Kane had stumbled on Petersen in whispered conclave with Hayes. The time had come for the men to choose.

When they were assembled, he explained their situation exactly. He himself would not abandon the brig. "She is not my only consideration. There is no way to withdraw our entire party safely. Between here and Beechy a tremendous ice barrier lies athwart Baffin's Bay at Lancaster Sound. The boats, then, are useless. By sledge, the journey would be perilous if all were in perfect health. At our present half-strength it would be disastrous."

Petersen shook his head in disagreement.

"Without having seen that ice barrier, you think otherwise, Mr. Petersen?"

"For years I know Baffin's Bay," the Dane said with faint scorn, "summer, winter. You let me, I lead you back safe."

Kane smiled. "I won't let you lead me into those ferocious wastes, but any man foolhardy enough to attempt it is free to go. You have given me all you bargained for and more."

Certain of his men, set to argue that very point, appeared taken aback, but Dr. Hayes, arms akimbo, asked, "Won't the withdrawal of some give all a better chance to survive?"

Kane's smile was broader. "You must decide on entirely selfish grounds, Doctor. Going or staying, we will none of us play the hero. To those who go I will give the best outfit I can spare, their share of the supplies, and my blessing. In return, I will ask them to renounce in writing all claim on those who stay."

That requirement made several shuffle their feet uneasily.

"If the ice halts them, they will be welcomed back like brothers," he assured everyone.

Suddenly he wanted the fainthearted on their way. With a half-dozen resolute men he could hold the brig more surely than with three times that number to any degree disaffected.

Young Hickey blurted out, "I'm staying, sir. I seen that ice. An' staying with you—"

Kane cut in quickly. "No, Tom, don't decide now. All of you think it over for twenty-four hours. Then each man will announce his free choice."

His own course was ordained, though he had been too stupid to realize it and had allowed himself foolish dreams of Maggie. "A whole year!" he could hear her wail, his child to whom a year was an unconscionable time. He could not expect her to be true for two years. But all this had no bearing on his course. His responsibility was to Brooks and the rest and to the *Advance* herself. There was a bittersweet savor in it, akin to his taste for the smell of danger.

The men when they assembled next day were painfully self-conscious, but their captain only curious, almost eager, to know their respective choices. Mr. Brooks, he announced quickly, before Brooks could refer to that unhealed stump, would stay with the ship.

"Mr. McGary?"

"Likewise."

"Our Second Officer, a magnificent sailor, was never a great walker. Mr. Wilson?" Young, reserved, suffering his disability keenly, Wilson had touched his captain these last weeks.

"I'll be here," Wilson said with a crooked smile.

"Dr. Hayes?"

"In view of the perils you said would confront the withdrawing party, I feel it my duty to make sure they have medical care, knowing those aboard the brig will have your expert services. Against my inclination I go with them."

That young man, Kane decided, hungered for leadership, and hoped to achieve it on a long, dangerous sortie. He might also gain a little personal fame by being the first to announce Morton's discovery. "A noble sacrifice," Kane said, straight-faced.

Hayes blushed.

Petersen, sure he understood the ice better than any American captain, would go, believing he led the party. Hayes might change that. Of course the Dane was homesick for his boy. But Hans, likewise homesick, chose to "keep with Docto Kayen." Sontag, perhaps due to Hayes's influence, would go, and to Kane's distress, Bonsall, too, the only Navy regular to withdraw. Kane assured him it was not against regulations.

"I'll give you a letter, Steward. Ohlsen?"

He desperately needed the carpenter to build their burrow within the hold, to find fuel for them, to repair the sledges and small boats that might prove their last resort, and to keep the brig seaworthy, if she finally escaped. He wanted to urge the good, grave Swede, "Stand by me!" But Ohlsen also had a wife and children at home.

"To make sure I go home to my family, I abide now with Captain. In long pull, safer so."

"That's what I say," Hickey declared loudly.

"I'll remember your vote of confidence." To his death he would remember it.

Godfrey and Blake would go, as Kane happily had expected. Riley, a better man than either, went along with them, he said with a hangdog look, and Whipple, likewise. McGary snorted in disgust. Of the water-front men he had signed on only the cabin boy, Hickey, stayed. Stephenson, who had never belonged aboard ship, was leaving, but Kane's own young friend, Goodfellow, a natural sailor, stayed. Except for Bonsall and Riley, the best men stood by the *Advance*.

In his satisfaction, Kane gave the withdrawal party an over-generous share of the stores and medical supplies. "Shall we share the medical books, too?" he asked Hayes mischievously.

Isaac sensed the Captain was almost elated to have them go, and it made his sleep uneasy the night before departure. Bonsall in his bunk knew himself a wretch whom Sir Walter Scott would scorn, but he couldn't face the long night again. With the observatory dismantled, August Sontag felt he was of little further use and his going would mean one less man to nurse, one less mouth to feed. "If I were stronger, if I could shoot good, I would stay," he told Hayes.

Whatever the inward doubts of some, on the last Monday in August the withdrawal party marched off with the confident step of men sure of their purpose. In a few hours they were out of sight.

Late Tuesday someone scrambled onto the deck of the *Advance*. Kane went up quickly and there was Riley, panting as if he had run hard.

"Didn't like the look of things at their first camp at all, sir. So I lit out for home. Let me sign up again, please, sir?"

"Glad to have you home, Riley," Kane said.

31. BY BREAD ALONE

WHEN IT came Henry Brooks's turn to read at Sunday service, they had arrived at the Book of Ecclesiastes. The First Officer rose on his good leg, propped the knee of his stumped one against a bunk board, and began the words of the Preacher.

" 'What profit hath a man of all his labour which he taketh under the sun?' "

His voice stuck a bit at the phrase which had special meaning for every man there. "—under the sun," he repeated.

The light was fast leaving Rensselaer Bay now in mid-October. The sun no longer reached the *Advance*. Only the northeastern headlands and the pinnacles of the bergs far out on the floe showed a yellow glow at noonday. All else was dark shadow outside; and inside their communal igloo, down in the bowels of the brig, only the wavering lard lamp staved off a midnight within a midnight.

Kane, standing in his furs before the stove, hands clasped behind him to catch its warmth, filled the silence created by Brooks's hesitation. " 'One generation passeth away, and another generation cometh; but the earth abideth forever.' " Stopping himself, he said, "I'm sorry, Mr. Brooks. But the sayings of the son of David are as full of quotations as a scene from *Hamlet*. Please continue. I believe there's more about the sun in the next verses."

"Yes, Captain." Brooks adjusted his position to throw more of the flickering lamplight on his Bible's fine print. "Yes, sir," he nodded after he had found his place again, "you're quite right. 'The sun also ariseth, and the sun goeth down, and hasteth to his place where he rose . . .' "

How many there prayed to see that sunrise? It was the sun's going down, Kane had felt from the first, that sent half his crew on the desperate journey south. Those who had stayed— Their prospects for food, warmth, and health were infinitely poorer than in the first winter, but what his faithful fellows dreaded most was the opaque world settling about them. They dreaded it like approaching blindness. They dreaded it worse than its attendant scurvy.

" 'The wind goeth toward the south, and turneth about unto the north . . .' "

Wilson lay on his back, hardly listening. Something had gone out of him when recurring scurvy opened the lesions on his healing stump. He was Kane's worst case, though far from his only invalid. Even Morton and Hans, as able-bodied a pair as Kane knew, suffered touches of scurvy already, before the winter was fairly begun. But they combated it with cheerfulness and hope, the best remedies save sunshine and green victuals.

" 'All things are full of labour; man cannot utter it . . .' "

Labor was the very essence of Kane's plan for their survival, launched almost as the withdrawal party vanished from view. For the ten who stayed, nothing would have been so demoralizing as abandoning familiar routine. So he had insisted all watches be kept, absurd as the order was in their situation, because it forced the men to be busier, now they were so few, than before. He had also ordered tidal and temperature readings and stellar observations taken regularly.

"Dr. Sontag and our observatory may both be gone, but we need not give up this important work. We'll set up a simple weather station on the ice near the brig, and our records will be a major scientific contribution," he had told Brooks in a carrying voice.

In full view of his men he made his journal entries every night. If he doubted other eyes than his would ever see those pages, he did not let it show in his face.

" 'Is there anything whereof it may be said, See, this is new? It hath been already of old time which was before us . . .' "

Together with old ship's routine he was using the old tried ways of Eskimos for surviving the cold and the dark. The burrow in which they now convened, smaller than the Judge's study at home, was an igloo of moss. By the sledgeload in bitter weather the men had cut and scraped moss from rocks and cliffs first to pad the quarter-deck and then to line this hut below. They entered it by an Eskimo *tossut,* a tunnel that required a man, when he had descended the hatch to the hold, to crawl on all fours into the brig's living quarters.

Goodfellow had given it the pseudo-poetic name of "Ben Djer-back," which amused them all.

To heat their igloo, they burned wood from the body of the brig herself. With Ohlsen he had gone over her as carefully as a property appraiser looking to her purchase to determine what could be sacrificed.

"We'll need every stick she can spare."

Ohlsen had drawn a long face. "A trim ship like her ain't got no spare wood."

"Nonsense. She's dressed for heavy weather. We'll strip her to bare necessities and take our chances next summer."

Ohlsen continued balky as they stood in the shadows of the ice off her beam to study her profile.

"Figure it for yourself, Ohlsen. We face five months of winter, and need, on an average, seventy pounds of fuel a day to keep the quarters just above freezing. With our coal almost gone, that means a ton of wood a month. Where had we best begin?" He might as well have asked the carpenter whether he'd prefer an arm or a leg amputated.

"Big shame, but if you order, we take outer deck planking."

"Good. That will make an imposing woodpile right off." They carefully weighed each day's allotment.

Of game, they had hardly enough to weigh, so with Hans the Captain had gone seal hunting. If the Eskimos could find seal, so could they. But Kane, green at it, had driven too close to a family of rough gray seals. The shaky ice gave way under the sledge. Cutting his lead dog, Tood-la, from the traces, Kane had fallen into the water with him. Tood-la scrambled out safely, but the ice crumbled when Kane tried it.

While he had paddled around the circumference of the hole in search of ice that would hold him, Hans on firm ice prayed like a good Moravian, in Eskimo and broken English. Each time the ice crumbled under his captain, Hans ejaculated, "God!" and then resumed his prayers as Kane paddled to another spot. Looking across now at Hans's round face where the boy struggled to follow Brooks's words, Kane smiled at the memory of that day.

But he might not be here to remember had he not hit upon a scheme for escaping. Bracing one foot against the submerged sledge which held steady, he had put the nape of his neck against the ice and carefully inched up. His wet jumper slid up the surface until, with a desperate push, he had launched himself onto the ice, his process reversing a ship's launching. They got no seal, but Eskimos appearing at the brig not long after had provided some fresh meat.

Brooks's voice rumbled into his reverie. "'There is no remembrance of former things . . . neither shall there be any remembrance of things that are to come with those that shall come after.'"

Oh, but there was, Preacher! He had been just now remembering and around him— Goodfellow, propped on one elbow, listened earnestly. McGary, settled solidly on his haunches, was attentive beside Ohlsen, absently fingering the teeth of a saw. Every man worn and wan, but alive, almost only because of remembrance and of remembrances to come.

"'And I gave my heart to seek and search out by wisdom . . . all things that are done under heaven; this sore travail hath God given the sons of man to be exercised therewith.'"

His present travail was over those sons of men called Eskimos. Where in the vast darkness had they vanished? He tried to attend Brooks, but his thoughts pursued the errant natives.

When they appeared at the brig so soon after half his men had left, the circumstance seemed menacing. But they had, in the pattern of the world's most artful diplomacy, made friendly overtures, accepted hospitality, and stolen a little for which they promised to make amends when threatened by a judicious display of force.

It had all happened before, but this time it came to a different conclusion. This time, both sides had agreed to a treaty of mutual aid through the winter night. The Eskimos promised to sell or lend him dogs, to take him or his men along on the hunt, and to trade fresh meat for knickknacks. The white man, in turn, swore not to use sorcery against Eskimos (convinced he was a wizard, whose love was a witch!), to shoot for them on the hunt, to welcome them aboard the brig, and to trade with them. Both sides vowed to be brothers forever, and the village of Etah, assembled, ratified the treaty.

On its ratification, the Eskimos had presented the white men a walrus flipper weighing forty pounds. More walrus had been procured when Hans, Morton, and he had hunted with them, enough to feed his men and dogs for a month. Now every ounce was gone, and so were the Eskimos, without a trace. They had walked away as casually as a child leaves off playing a game. Where, where were they?

" 'For in much wisdom is much grief.' " Brooks gravely read the closing sentence of the lesson. " 'And he that increaseth knowledge, increaseth sorrow.' "

Sorrow lies in the full understanding of knowledge. That was what the Preacher meant. But what of the suffering of innocents who only helped another to such understanding? Kane searched the faces around him. These men had set out with him and stood fast by him not to seek wisdom themselves, but to aid his search. Would not he, in the long reckoning, be held accountable for their suffering?

His prayer, "God help restore us to our homes," was said almost too feverently.

To shake off the solemnity that wrapped them, Kane called with a smile to Hickey, sitting bolt upright on the edge of his bunk behind the stove, "Up and doing, Tom! Prepare us meat worthy of the Sabbath!" He put more spirit into the order than he intended.

The boy instantly came alive, and darting across the quarters, dived into the *tossut.* He disappeared before the Captain could say what scrap, of the little they had, he thought "worthy."

Throughout the service Tom had worried over the task that would shortly confront him. Long ago Sunday dinner had been a joyous occasion for which Schubert would produce a specialty so tasty it made the unleavened Sunday service endurable. As cabin boy, Tom had been first Pierre's slave, then his pupil, and finally his successor.

The tradition of a Sunday dinner persisted in the face of barreled meat so strong that, boiling, its smell made sick men retch. As for the fruit and vegetables outside on the ice, a pitiful lot they had left. And so far past their prime that, though he cooked dried apples and called it applesauce, or cooked dried peaches and called it preserves, both came out tasteless pulp. The men thought Tom a terrible cook and were forever remembering Schubert's triumphs. But what could Tom do with navy beans, one jar of pickled cabbage, four bottles of dried-up horse-radish, and plain flour? Only the flour was good. Their meat biscuit was saved for journeying.

For fresh meat they had a single hare a month old. Not a hare since had entered Hans's traps, save one a fox found first. The foxes themselves were too smart to be caught. Three ducks were left from summer. With one of these, a cup of flour, a handful of apples, he could maybe make a stew suitable for Sunday. But until Hans shot a bear or the Eskimos brought walrus, the Captain wanted the ducks kept to make broth for the sick, served a teaspoon at a time, like medicine.

Tom was concluding his survey when Brooks said, "Remembrance," and Tom remembered that in the storehouse– He shuddered.

Yesterday, when he was following Captain Kane and Ohlsen around the brig, looking for more fuel, as they descended the hatch, they heard in the hold a sharp swish, and right after a frantic squeal. "That make even nine," Hans said, pleased as Punch.

In the feeble light of an oil lamp Tom saw him run across to kick something viciously. Then he hauled up a rat as limp and as long as a hare. Extracting his arrow, he proudly swung the creature atop a pile of dead rats, lined up head to head and tail to tail.

"An impressive catch, Hans." The Captain patted his arm.

Tom had been cheered, too. With the pantry stuff moved out on the ice where it was too cold for them, the rats made bold to run the whole ship. They particularly liked the moss packed around the quarters, and their rustling kept Tom awake in loathing of them. Worse, yesterday a rat bit the Captain himself when he tried to pull on a mitten in which, overnight, she had made a nest.

"Dress them, Hans," the Captain told him, "and hang them in the storehouse safe from the dogs."

Safe from the dogs! When the dogs were plagued with the rats gnawing the very pads on their feet! Safe for what? "Captain," Tom almost choked saying it, "we ain't gonna eat–"

"Now, my young chef," Kane smiled, "I have eaten locusts at Senaer and bats in Dahomey, both very good when prepared well and you're hungry. So would rats be. What are these rodents but noxious small deer, fatter than deer we're likely to see?"

Hans, with a wide grin, strung the long tails through his fat fingers and carried his catch out of there, while a white-faced Tom, watching him, had resolved he would never cook a rat.

On the Captain's order of a meal "worthy of the Sabbath" Tom tore for the storehouse. Inside, he needed no lantern to find the hook from which the three ducks dangled. With eager fingers he felt for the least scrawny, and clutching its legs, sped back over crunching snow. The cold, pale undarkness of noon embraced the wreath of timid smoke from the cabin's stack. The dogs set up a howl for food and a friend. But Tom in his hurry heeded neither.

The duck was delicious. Though hardly big enough to satisfy one well man, Pierre's pupil stretched it artfully into a stew for ten. The men relished each spoonful and sucked the last lick of flavor from each bone. Kane could not reprove Tom for this extravagance, it did such wonders for the men, giving them a brief illusion of plenty. Before it wore off, he must, some way, reach the Eskimos.

After dinner, in temporary well-being, his invalids napped soundly. Wilson's book fell from his relaxed hand, and the Captain, picking it up to mark the place, saw it was *Uncle Tom's Cabin,* that Abolitionist novel, open at the very point where Eliza is pursued across the ice by dogs.

Not then but later the idea came to him. Why not use the dogs he had bought from the Eskimos to track down their vanished masters? Or they might know the way to the Eskimo hunting grounds. Next day he sent Hans and Morton with a team not to Etah, but to Anoatok where Eskimos had last been seen. In that older village, its igloos built of stone and half in ruins, Morton had come on My-ouk, the singing rogue, comfortably ensconced with the wives of two other men, since he had none of his own! At Anoatok, Morton and Hans were to let one dog run free, following him with another on a long leash. The rest could be left tied up at the village.

Late that night Tom Hickey, on watch, ran in crying, "Wolf! Sniffing around the storehouse."

Kane reached for his favorite Marston rifle. "He can't eat salt pork, but we can eat wolf." He had run out without his mittens and the cold metal of his gun burned his hands. Also he had but a single cartridge. His shot struck home, however. The beast yelped, and Kane found he had wounded one of their own dogs.

"A truant from Morton's team. Only a flesh wound, luckily. He's too good a dog to lose."

"Captain, sir, he looked a wolf, he did that."

"I would have sworn he was a wolf myself."

In a few days their black dog, Erebus, also returned. Perhaps the dogs were more attached now to the brig than to the Eskimos.

Kane's plan might not be working. But within the week Brooks was calling cheerfully, "Hans and Morton coming, Captain!"

They were both half-frozen but had brought nearly three hundred pounds of walrus meat and two foxes, sufficient for his little company until the sun returned.

32. THE PRODIGALS

THE CAPTAIN, on the walrus-meat diet enjoying enormously improved health, assigned himself to the late watch. It was better for men at all ailing to keep regular hours, and, besides, he had an infinity of tasks he did best in solitude, while the others worked better for the companionship of daytime, if not daylight.

So he was asleep the forenoon of December 7 when a cry from the watch woke him. "Eskimo sledges!" Kane bounded to his feet, but reached deck none too soon. The visitors had come up fast.

In the moonlight of that noon he saw the dogs first. Then a strange Eskimo ran toward the deck ramp, gesturing anxiously. Behind him his companions lifted two bodies from the sledges. Kane had taken only a step forward when a voice hoarsely shouted his name.

"Cappen Kane! It's Petersen!" repeating more feebly as they carried him up, "Carl Christian Petersen, with Bonsall."

The returned wanderers, as cold and numb as men can be and live, he dared not take directly into the moderate warmth of the quarters. They might faint in an agony of shock. So he had them propped on buffalo robes down in the bulkhead, beside the *tossut,* and fed bread sops and hot broth to warm them. When Bonsall dozed, Kane got the story out of Petersen.

"Where are the others?"

"They all living... when we go... in camp two hunnert miles off... out on ice... Like I never seen it," he admitted, his big face sheepish.

Kane ignored the admission. "What happened?"

"Place I think we go sure, we can't get through... try another place and can't cross... days we walking around that ice... I say to try third one... food gone, men hungry, bitter cold out there... so black... they get mad, fight, argue, argue with Petersen. They call me stupid old bum and I am Vice Governor!"

"They must have been half-crazy with hunger and fear," Kane soothed the Dane's pride. "What did you do then?"

"I do nothing. That young fellow, the doctor... he says he take charge... so I go, Bonsall with, but Bonsall in bad shape... we gonna die... then Eskimos come and haul us."

Squatting beside Petersen, Kane anticipated the story in every detail, except for the Eskimos' arrival. Who could anticipate their comings and goings! "Do the others want to return?"

Petersen shook his head. "No. They want not to come... But they got to or they die. Not even old Danisher like Carl Christian Petersen can live out on such ice in cold and dark."

Kane slapped the "old Danisher"—all of forty-five—across his great mat of whiskers. "Next summer you'll get home, Petersen, I promise. And all the other poor wanderers will reach home, too, if we get them safely back here first."

The Eskimos and their leader, Kalutunah, seemed over-ready to rescue the rest of Petersen's party. Their eagerness made Kane suspect them of intending to make off with the food he had to send. But he must risk it. So he dispatched them with a convoy of boiled pork, meat biscuit, bread dust, and tea. The tea, at any rate, would not tempt them. He himself could not leave the brig's load of sick, nor spare Hans, his only able-bodied hand.

Four days he waited, at once anxious for sight of his lost sheep and dreading their return. On the fifth the grimmest processional imaginable crawled, wearily and painfully, through the *tossut*. Dr. Hayes came first. He took Kane's outstretched hand self-consciously, but could not speak; he tried to rise, but his numbed legs could not lift him and he stayed on his knees, an involuntary suppliant.

"It's all right, Doctor," Kane said, as though Hayes had apologized, "quite all right."

There followed slowly Blake, Sontag, Stephenson, Whipple, and bringing up the rear, Godfrey. When they were all in, there was hardly room to count heads. But the crowded quarters, the rank odors of boiling pork, lard lamps, and drying furs were the comforts of home to men exposed for days on open ice at fifty below. They gobbled down Hickey's meat-and-biscuit soup, his wheat bread spread with molasses, and ate the well-ripened salt pork as if it were a delicacy.

When they were fed, Kane, standing in their midst, said with commanding seriousness, "When you left, you were promised a brother's welcome if the ice drove you back. This we all extend you.

We are glad you are safely here. It will be a tight fit, but we will keep warm and we will not starve, providing every man resumes his place aboard ship fully resolved to help his mates."

As he talked, his eyes moved from man to man, waiting until each one looked his captain straight in the eye.

"Our chief concern will be to nurse the sick back to health. When the sun returns, we need a full complement of healthy men to speed us home. Our hospital facilities are poor indeed. We do not have bunks enough for everyone. So I am resigning mine to one who needs it more. I hope others here feel well enough to do the same."

But the men who had been snatched from the clutch of real terror did not wait for soft beds. Spreading their furs by the stove, they fell limp across them, sleeping like babes returned to their trundles.

Kane had Hayes, however, installed in the Captain's bunk. Then, looking at the prone figures around him, Kane tried to think what, exactly, they were to do. The igloo they had built was designed to accommodate only his half-crew, with no way, really, to expand it. Yet how could a score of hard-bitten men even breathe in so cramped a space without getting at each other's throats sooner or later? Right now it would be difficult to fuel the stove or do any other chore without stumbling over a body. They could all live here only by exercising ingenuity and patience, virtues in shorter supply than their rations.

Next morning he became aware that Kalutunah and his men were purposefully lingering. By custom, they should have left after the first meal or early in the day following. But there they sat on deck, waiting. For what? He had Petersen brought up to interpret. But Petersen did more than translate Kalutunah's few words. He apparently knew in advance what the Eskimo would say.

It all came out. The withdrawal party on their way south had helped themselves to a sledge and several foxskins and articles of clothing. The Eskimos were waiting to be repaid.

Kane drew Petersen aside. "Is this true?"

"Kalutunah made us gift of furs and sled we think. Eskimos not object. Say nothing till now."

"Petersen"—Kane kept his temper by an effort—"you know Eskimos never 'make a gift.' They always make a bargain which they see is carried out whenever it happens to suit them."

"Gift," Petersen tried to insist, but could not meet Kane's blazing eyes.

The truth was, the defectors, in a hurry to get south and confident they would never return, had appropriated the goods without ceremony, thereby not only risking their own standing, but doing callous harm to the friendly relations Kane had carefully nurtured. They did this to comrades who might, before the winter was out, be in sore need of the Eskimos' friendship.

"Tell Kalutunah we will hold a council at once!" He spoke so sharply that Petersen snapped to almost military attention.

To make the ceremony more impressive, Kane invited his guests into the cabin they had never seen and seated them formally on a red blanket, while he addressed them in ordered phrases Petersen intoned solemnly.

"My men did not steal. . . . White men do not steal. . . . In our country, men going on long journey receive gifts. . . . This ship was a gift." Kane waved an arm at Grinnell's munificence all around them. "My men thought Kalutunah a great chief who gives gifts . . . But Kalutunah strange to ways of white men . . . so white men return everything. . . . White chief give Kalutunah and his hunters gifts now they go on long journey to their own village."

The sooner the better, Kane would have liked to add. He ordered the sledge brought up and the articles stolen from the Eskimos laid on it piece by piece. Then he had Hickey bring the box of needles. The Captain dealt five to each Eskimo, giving each a ceremonial tug of the hair, native equivalent of a handshake. To Kalutunah he presented two steel knives, which the chief immediately tried out on the slab of walrus that was laid before him. All his men gorged again before departing.

They devoured a week's ration of fresh meat, just when his supply was halved by the defectors' return. Perhaps it would put them in a mood to bargain when he arrived at their huts to trade for walrus. He must go shortly, while they were still there and amiably inclined.

That mission was delayed by his experiment with pork-fat lamps. To conserve fuel wood, Kane, with Bonsall, their tinkerer, back to advise him, rigged up four burners in which he would use the rendering of salt pork gone too bad to eat. Such Icelandic-style lamps gave off some heat. Cooking for the enlarged mess could be done over them and ice melted for drinking water.

But their odor was sickening, and they consumed too much of the oxygen in air already stuffy. To relieve matters, he moved one into the bulkhead compartment forward. The open flame, sputtering in a shallow bowl, needed constant watching.

The first night the lamp was there, with one of the watch to keep an eye on it, the fellow dozed. A darting spark lodged in the tinder-dry moss. In a moment a sailcloth wall was ablaze with eight sick men nailed to their beds next door, too weak to crawl through the *tossut*.

Crawling out, Kane could see little for the smoke. While the men ran to form a bucket chain from the tide hole, the Captain beat at the blazing moss with a rifle butt.

"Damn them! Damn them! Damn them!" he said with each blow, but just whom he was damning he did not admit to himself.

Then he stumbled on a pile of furs, and grabbing them up, threw them spread out over the burning area. The first water bucket to come down he pitched at a fresh outburst of flame, and such a cloud of smoke surged up that he was completely blinded and half overcome. He groped hatchward. Ohlsen's foot struck him as the carpenter came down the ladder, knocking Kane unconscious.

The fire took the entire end of the sailcloth-and-moss wall and ate into the skin of the hulk before it was beaten down. Every man who fought it showed injuries; either from burns suffered below decks or frostbite on the bucket gang. At Christmas dinner, two days later, Kane appeared with bandaged hands, a dressed forehead—"where Ohlsen kicked me"—and without beard, eyebrows, or familiar fore-lock, all of which had been singed off.

He held a wine bottle between his injured palms. "It's the last of our Sillery and, like us, has lost its sparkle. But the spirit's there. I'll make the first toast." He raised the bottle, his bandages making it appear swaddled with a towel as Francis long ago wrapped the champagne he poured at the little suppers with Maggie. "To next Christmas at home with our loved ones!"

Taking only a sip, he passed the bottle to Brooks. The big fellow took a leisurely draught. "Tastes like turkey and cranberries to me," he said as he passed it to Hayes. "Hickey, make mine roast turkey, if you please."

Hayes, when he handed the bottle to McGary, allowed he'd have the same, "with plenty of white meat." McGary ordered "More stuffing, Steward," and around the room the game went. The stiffness Kane had noticed between the "goers" and the "stayers" seemed to be relaxing as this one ordered mutton, that one plain roast beef with his wine, one liver and onions, another boiled potato with a slice of cucumber alongside.

That was Riley. "A boiled potato would be the likes of heaven to me now." With the cucumber, Kane was inclined to agree.

There were dessert orders also, the last of them for "Watermelon—iced."

"Iced?" They roared laughing. It was a magnificent joke.

Tom Hickey, lifting the lid from the pot boiling over the stove, shouted gleefully as steam mushroomed toward the ceiling. "Anyways, gentlemen, we got plenty of what we got. Who wants more beans?"

Kane did not wait the New Year to resolve to go to the Eskimos for fresh walrus, now desperately needed. For all their Christmas merrymaking, McGary was sinking with scurvy and Brooks and Wilson weakened day by day. Only walrus beef could sustain them and some of his new patients.

With Petersen, he set out for the Lower Bay, a hundred miles off. In forty-below weather and in the teeth of a sharpening wind they made Anoatok's deserted huts, and holed up with the dogs for warmth. The gale drove the snow so hard by morning, the dogs refused to run. Men and animals once more took refuge in the hut. Their fat lamp gave little warmth, but its light held back the night.

In such a storm they must keep watch. Petersen took the first trick, while Kane slept on the rude stone that was the Eskimos' bed, his fur wrappings frozen stiff around him.

Out of nothingness he heard Petersen cry, "Cappen Kane, the lamp's out!" and opened his eyes to utter darkness. Outside, the gale whistled, but inside all was still and piercing black.

"Petersen!" he called in irrational terror.

"Here, Cappen." The Dane touched his arm. "I maybe dozed. I wake up, the light gone, and guns all outside."

They could strike a light only by firing a gun, and as usual they had stacked their rifles at the hut's entrance to protect them from the condensation in any Arctic habitation.

"But I have pocket pistol and piece of moss."

"Try igniting it."

Petersen tried vainly: click . . . click . . . click . . . Impatiently, Kane reached for the gun. As he touched Petersen's hand, the pistol became illumined. In a bluish light it trembled, every detail visible—barrel, lock, and trigger. Petersen's thumb and fingers shone out as clearly—the creases in their skin, the fine hairs just above the knuckles, the shape of the nails.

"Cappen!" Petersen's voice wavered. "Take it!"

Kane's fingers closed on the cold metal and it glowed even brighter. In his pocket he had found a scrap of paper they might be able to ignite. This time the pistol fired but the paper did not catch. In the glow, Kane could see to recharge the weapon readily.

He fired again, and the concussions bounded back from the stone roof over their heads with such concentrated force that he could feel the rappings in his very teeth. Rappings? Echoes, he should have called them. The paper still lay limp.

While he tried to think what to do, the gale outside shrieked wildly at him: "Ly, Ly, come back! Co-o-ome back, Ly!" Like Brooks, he was hearing voices. A voice.

Without conscious thought he had rolled the paper into a cone, filled it with Petersen's moss over which he sprinkled some powder. He fired, and the cone flamed up like a torch. The pistol, warmed now by many firings, slowly lost its unearthly light. He handed it back to its owner.

"Phosphorescence," he said calmly. "A phenomenal display." What his lighted hand meant to him, however, the power of science could not dispel. More, he had heard Maggie call. In the light flickering on the stone roof he saw her face as he drifted into sleep.

Next day the wind was down, but the dogs were too weak from lack of food to leap the hummocks to the south. Reluctantly, Kane turned back toward the brig.

33. ALL THE NEWS

YOUNG CORNELIUS GRINNELL was altogether too definite about the date of Dr. Kane's return. In August he wrote they expected the Doctor on October 10. Maggie began to mark off the days.

"He can't know so exactly," Lizzie grumbled. "Ships from Europe are often a week late, and from Greenland the delay might be much longer."

Her words feel on deaf ears, and October 10 found Maggie roaming the garden, waiting for a messenger with a telegram. From her window, Lizzie watched the wind-blown little figure, so pathetically sure of news.

"Oh, Lizzie, if only I were on the Battery, hearing the salute guns! They will salute the Doctor, won't they? Even if he hasn't found Franklin's men. It's so dull stuck here!" she had complained, her little camellia-white face pink with excitement.

"Dr. Kane will be better pleased to see you in Crooksville."

"It may be ages before he can come down. In New York, he could slip away—"

"Where to, pray? He knows nothing of your visits to Mrs. Walter, and would hardly call at your sister's."

"You are so tiresomely right sometimes!" With that, she ran out to watch the road.

A carriage was coming! Mrs. Lieper's. Perhaps she had word. Lizzie ran down. At the front door she heard Mrs. Lieper ask in her clear, over-loud voice, "Child, have you news?"

"No, ma'am. I hoped you did."

"Ly's old aunt will be the last to hear unless you tell me. My sister-in-law never will. Miss Turner, good morning. Is your pupil ready to be graduated from Dr. Kane's select academy?"

"Almost. We could use more time, but—"

"She wants him home, as we all do. Any reason to expect word today? The child is positively agog. It's very becoming."

"This is the tenth, and Nealy Grinnell said Ly would be back the tenth," Maggie said happily.

"He knows not a whit more than I. Nor does his father," Mrs. Lieper declared scornfully. "Grinnell's ship has been to the Arctic but he hasn't."

"Elisha said I could rely on Nealy as I would on him."

But the Doctor had not come on the tenth or eleventh or twelfth. On the thirteenth they were shocked by the loss of the Collins liner, *Arctic,* with four hundred drowned. The disaster filled the newspapers over which Maggie pored. The ship's name was really unfortunate. More cheerful news was Captain McClure's safe return to England. In the Arctic since 1850, he had been feared lost.

Grinnell's next note Lizzie found more sensible. "We have no tidings as yet of the Doctor but do not in fact expect him before the end of the month. My father says if he is not home by the end of November, he will conclude that the Doctor intends to remain another winter in the Arctic."

Mr. Grinnell's conclusion Maggie ignored. "Not until the end of November!" It sounded as if it were *forever.*

For distraction, she fairly flung herself into her lessons, conducted by the parlor window so she could watch the road. From the piano she also had a clear view. Pa said that was lucky or he'd likely have had to move it.

Theirs was a cheerful household the third week in October, when Pa, coming in with the mail, insisted the *Pennsylvanian* had gone astray again. As soon as Maggie was in bed, he brought the paper in from the barn. It told of Sir Edward Belcher's abandoning his entire Arctic squadron.

"Won't help her hearing the English left five sound ships in the ice sooner than face the winter ahead. Worst in forty-seven years, they predict. Belcher didn't even wait for Collinson."

Ma was reading the article. "Captain McClure is confident Collinson and the *Enterprise* will be heard from soon."

"Leaving the Doctor holding the fort alone. Better mislay that paper, Susannah," he warned Ma.

"But the Doctor has sailed by now!" Lizzie protested.

"If he sailed," Pa said. That paper disappeared.

So did the one for October 23 containing the first news of Eskimos finding traces of a large party of Franklin's men, dead of starvation. "Very discouraging for Margaret to learn before the Doctor arrives that he has failed in his mission," Ma said.

"Why do you both assume the worst? Those Eskimos found the remains of only one party. The Doctor may have saved the rest!"

Both her parents nodded insincere agreement.

That week Maggie began to receive a newspaper by mail. "Probably some spiritualist journal," Ma said. She did not like this reminder from the past coming just when Margaret was doing so splendidly. "I'll have to speak to her." But she put it off, conscious that they were already censoring Maggie's reading.

Next day Pa waited very late before producing the "missing" paper.

"News is worse than we thought. About what those Eskimos found." He cleared his throat. "Dr. Rae of the Hudson's Bay Company says the traces indicate 'Franklin's men were,' " he carefully read the phrase, " 'reduced to the last dire extremity of starvation.' "

"Mr. Turner," Ma's voice trembled, "let me see that—"

"Now, Ma!" Pa tried to hold it out of her reach.

The clock ticked loud while she read. Then, dropping the newspaper, she sat down to steady herself. "Burn it, Mr. Turner! At once! Maggie must never hear a syllable of this. After her attack of brain fever, I cannot risk it."

Lizzie still knew nothing definite. "Ma, what is it?"

"Like the Donners." Her mother shuddered violently.

Ma had never forgotten the ghastly tragedy that had befallen a family named Donner going overland to California. As Lizzie ran to get spirits of ammonia for Ma, white to faintness, she knew what the Eskimos had found. Pa had burned the paper when she returned.

When her mother was somewhat recovered, Lizzie said, "Ma, Maggie must be told. We can break it to her gradually, before she hears the whole shocking story in a letter."

"No." Ma closed her eyes. "No lady would mention it."

"You are only postponing the evil day," Lizzie said firmly.

"I will never discuss this horror with Margaret."

Every day Maggie did not receive a letter was a day's grace to Lizzie. The strange journal had stopped coming, so the girl had no mail at all. Not for another month need they grow anxious about the Doctor, so it puzzled Lizzie to see Maggie sinking back into her old listlessness. Perhaps she was ailing.

"Do you feel poorly, Maggie? If you do, tell Ma. We can have the doctor in. You must be blooming when Dr. Kane comes."

"If he doesn't return soon, he never will," Maggie said flatly.

"That's nonsense. I think he'll arrive shortly, but if he doesn't, it only means he's staying another year, as Mr. Grinnell said."

Maggie fixed eyes empty of any expression on her teacher's face. "Congress wouldn't give Ly any money, so he had rations for only one year. For one year, Lizzie. Did you know that?"

"Mr. Grinnell surely knows what stores the *Advance* took, and he isn't worried."

"Maybe he is now." Maggie's blank eyes met and yet did not meet Lizzie's. "Maybe Sir George Simpson has made him worry."

"Whoever he is." Lizzie frowned in genuine puzzlement.

"Don't you know? Well, I do," she said with strange satisfaction. She bent her head over a lesson she was totally unable to follow.

Lizzie soon gave up, and, saying Maggie needed a nap, tucked her in bed. She fell at once into heavy sleep, and Lizzie, disturbed, slipped out to the barn.

"Pa, in that Eskimo story, was Sir George Simpson mentioned?"

"Remember every word. Including him. Governor of Hudson's Bay Territory. He's the one sent the news to Mr. Grinnell."

"Maggie knows his name, and asked just now if I knew it!"

"How could she find it out? She's had no letters, newspapers, nothing for days. You saw me burn that paper, Liz."

"She knows something about him!" They stared at each other in the twilight of the old barn. "Pa, I'm frightened!"

They agreed not to tell Ma. At supper the pair of them sat almost afraid to think, and were relieved when Maggie went up early. Lizzie, on her way to bed later, paused at the girl's door, but it showed no gleam of light. In her own room she stood for minutes, staring out at the dismal night, cold and sleeting. The tree branches glazed with ice shone eerily.

Some hours later she was roused by a cry from the next room. She tapped on Maggie's door but got no answer. Had she dreamed that cry? Then she heard a faint rattling. Was that the raps? Weren't they louder? Or did the spirits rap more softly when they told Maggie secrets, strange secrets? In the dark hall the cold draft around her ankles made Lizzie remember this was All Hallows' Eve. But the spirits walked any night for Maggie Fox!

Lizzie's hand was frozen to the doorknob until she thought of the Doctor. He had not been frightened by Maggie's spirits, but boldly snatched the girl from their grasp. A woman whom he trusted could do no less. Lizzie opened the door.

Maggie lay huddled up, shaken by an ague so violent that her teeth rattled. So much for your irrational fears, Lizzie reproved herself as she hurried for comforters and to wake her father. The fire must be stirred up to heat bricks and make hot potions. By morning Maggie's chill had abated. Lizzie and Ma thought her asleep as they stood wearily looking down at her in the gray light.

Then Maggie, in a clear but remote voice, said, "I was always afraid of Ly's dying in the snow. I hate snow and cold and I thought freezing the worst way to die. But that's nothing compared to— When they go in search of Ly, what will they find? How can they tell who it was? From a bone in a stewpan!"

Ma burst into tears and left, but Lizzie braced herself. "What wild talk is this? See how you've frightened Ma!"

"She knows. You all do. But you tried to keep secret from me what those Eskimos saw!"

"Silver spoons, wasn't it, that they found?"

Maggie only laughed and talked more rapidly, turning her head from side to side. "Lish hasn't any fancy silver with him. He hasn't as much food or anything as Franklin had. But in the end Franklin's men turned cannibal. Watching a man sicken and fall. Hardly giving him time to die before they— They get to like the taste, don't they, Lizzie? I read that somewhere, I know I read it."

Lizzie recalled that one horrible old man in the Donner party had hoarded up more flesh than he could eat. The rescue party had left him in his nauseous lair. She felt faint.

Faster and faster Maggie's words hurried. "If he hasn't sailed, Ly's men will turn cannibal, too. They haven't enough food. They— Ly will be the first. His heart's weak, and he's a little man, Lizzie. Ly!" She sat straight up, and called wildly, "Ly, come back!"

Lizzie slapped her hard, slapped her again. "Listen to me! Before you scare yourself into fits. Will you listen?"

Maggie nodded, drawing short, jerky breaths like hiccoughs.

When she had subsided, Lizzie, sitting on the bed, said in a steady voice, "If Dr. Kane decides to stay another year, his men will live on the game he said would abound on the shores of his Open Sea.

They will live off the land like the early settlers. I can read, too, and I read his lecture about that. He took plenty of powder and shot, didn't he?"

"I don't know." Maggie, rubbing her cheek, tried to focus on Lizzie's face. "He thought Franklin's men might have done that, too, but they, they–"

"Don't start that again!" Lizzie commanded. "Don't argue. Just listen. After five years Franklin's men had exhausted their powder. Dr. Kane's men haven't, so they will hunt. With his eyes, he himself is a crack shot, isn't he?"

"I don't know."

"You don't know much." Lizzie was deliberately rude. "If you had read his book instead of letting the spirits frighten you off, you would know he brought down bear after bear that first voyage."

"He shot a tiger once in India," Maggie said quite sensibly.

But the events of the night shook the Turner household. How had Maggie found out? None of them would ask–for fear of her answer. To allow everyone time to recover, Ma suggested Maggie visit New York again. "News of the Doctor will reach her quickest there. Pray God she hears soon."

There had been no news. It was clear now that the Doctor would not return this year. Ma, when her own composure was restored, felt Maggie should also be recovered enough to resume her education.

At supper last night Ma had said, "When Margaret left, I pitied her from my inmost soul. She required a change of scene to dissipate the heart sickness that comes from hope too long deferred."

For Lizzie, crumbling her bread into small bits with nervous fingers, there had been no change of scene.

"But," Ma said firmly, "she has been away a whole month. That's long enough."

So she had written a letter summoning Miss Fox back to Crooksville. Pa took it to the post this morning. Lizzie, for something to do, went up to put Maggie's room in order.

When Lizzie was changing the lining papers in the bureau drawers, under each she found newspapers, hidden flat and smooth, several issues of *The New York Times,* a journal new to her. Frowning, she examined them. All contained news from the Arctic boldly marked in black pencil. On some, taunting comments were scrawled.

These were the papers someone had mailed Maggie in late October and early November.

Beside word of McClure's return was written, "Where's the brave Doctor?" When Belcher's abandoned his ships "frozen fast in the area of Beechy Island," Beechy was underscored. By someone aware of Beechy Island's figuring in Maggie's earlier upset. Across the first meager report of the Eskimos' findings was scrawled: "Kane was told they were dead. But he knew better than the spirits!"

The news that Franklin's men had been reduced to cannibalism drew a worse comment: "Wasn't that a dainty dish to set before Her Ladyship?" Lady Franklin, obviously. Lizzie searched for a reference to Sir George Simpson. Yes, there it was. She must tell Pa. Pa was a Scot, and what a Scotsman darkly imagines he doesn't always admit.

Gloomy editorials were also marked. "... there is little doubt the bold adventurers must spend another nine months ice bound... their great risk is the season to come. Should it be a close one, they may themselves need the help they sought to give Sir John Franklin." When word came that Collinson was safe in Port Clarence, an editorial pointed out, "Dr. Kane is now alone in the field." Below this was crayoned in ugly big black letters, "THE END."

Who had inflicted this cruelty? Surely it was that older sister "from whose influence kind friends must shield Maggie," Dr. Kane had warned them. By not telling Maggie the news from day to day, Ma had played into that woman's hands. Maggie, sensing the Turners kept the truth from her, concealed her own sources of information. So Mrs. Fox-Fish-Brown had been able to outwit them. Did she know it, and was she laughing in her dark New York house, laughing and waiting for Maggie's despair to drive her back to her old life?

Lizzie gathered up the newspapers, and taking them downstairs, put them where they belonged—squarely in her mother's lap.

34. SIGNS AND PORTENTS

IN MID-JANUARY the sun was one hundred and twenty-five days away, counting backward or forward, but time, Kane found, he reckoned in terms of sustenance for his sick. Food it could hardly be called. He took it where he found it.

There was the day Old Yellow, who stalked the darkness, his back arched like a hyena's, ate one of Jenny's pups. Those poor things would never mature to harness, so Kane pampered Old Yellow with a pup a morning until they reached the last two. These had real flesh on their bones. Kane cut them up for his scurvy sufferers.

There was the day he uncovered up forward an old bear's head, frozen harder than the stuffed specimen it was intended to become. It had miraculously escaped the rats, and thawed, the head yielded several portions of meat which he dug out to the last scrap of sinew. The firm jaw muscles his patients found particularly worth the pain of chewing against sore gums.

They all daydreamed of more satisfying food. When Hickey scraped the bottom of the barrel for a helping of pickled cabbage, seasoned with the last of the pepper, as a special dish for the Captain, he piled it to one side of the plate. Beside it he laid close a slab of corn bread, leaving plenty of room for the phantom slices of cold roast beef Kane's hungry mind put there. Room even for an imaginary endive salad. With a bottle of ale, Preston's ale, it would be a tasty meal.

He yearned for less remote delicacies. Charles Lamb's roast pig he would willingly have passed up for walrus liver, called by the Eskimos *awuktanuk,* and eaten as a confection. With little slices of walrus fat larding it, it was delicious. But no walrus had been caught or even sighted.

And his men were every day in worse shape, the weakest once his strongest: Brooks, McGary, Morton, and Riley. Long ago he had told Hayes scurvy worked that way, and wished he had not been proved so thoroughly right. Of the withdrawal party, Hayes had lost a foot and Sontag and Stephenson, Blake and Whipple all suffered a serious combination of frostbite and scurvy. Godfrey complained of his eyes, lying with them bandaged. Was he malingering, secretly inflaming them so he could hoard his strength to his own ends?

There was the glad day Petersen's traps yielded a fox. The Captain divided it into equal portions for his bedridden, and then he, Hans, and the dogs took off hopefully for Etah and the Eskimo hunters. At Anoatok, in the Eskimo tongue, the "wind-loved place," he was again halted by a gale and spent two frustrated days in a deserted hut, returning used up and empty-handed to the brig.

In that brief time his youngest men had sickened. Hickey could not keep on swollen and blistered legs long enough to cook their poor mush meals, and Goodfellow's gums were cracked and bleeding. The sick hemorrhaged seriously. He tried dosing them with his remaining brandy mixed with citrate and chlorohydrated tincture, but the hemorrhages continued. His own nose bled and he was appalled by the brick-dust poverty of his blood.

But he, their commander, was, thank God, vastly more serviceable than last year. Like all of them he needed fresh meat badly, but he could not leave his hospital so soon again. This time he sent Hans and Petersen to the Eskimos. Halfway to Anoatok Petersen broke down, Hans sturdily hauling him back. What would he have done without that Eskimo boy?

There was the day, the very next, in fact, that Hans patiently tracked rabbits up a distant fjord and caught three. He covered them so well that they did not freeze, but yielded raw-blood cordials for Brooks, Wilson, and Riley. Every man had a scrap of rabbit to eat and afterward the Captain drove his ambulatory cases up on deck for a sniff of clean air.

Their minds timid as their bodies, they were struck by the eeriness of the moonlight cutting through the rigging. The extravagant twinkling of the stars frightened them, the sudden mists seemed portentous, and they listened, gaping, to Petersen.

"I look through the mists at the stars and foretell if it snows or a blizzard come and from which way the wind blow!"

They retreated to their bunks like animals to their burrows, but his two young ones might improve with exercise. Even more than exercise, they needed a change from the depressing atmosphere of the quarters, which had, over all the other stinks, a prison smell for Kane now. Next morning he bundled Hickey and Goodfellow into furs and took them out on the ice.

"Breathe deep, Henry," he commanded Goodfellow.

"Air feels pretty sharp, sir."

"It's fresh air which you aren't used to," Kane said in a cheerful voice. "Walk the path to the storehouse and back, breathing deep as you can, and you'll feel much better."

Kane and Hickey watched Henry pad off, shouldering his gun, and breathing deep. "Tom, you come with me to the weather post."

"Happy to, sir." But the boy stumbled every few steps. Kane let him fall behind, setting his own pace.

They met Petersen returning from his traps with nothing again. "Stars, they twinkle for a storm. Air warm, mists rising. She blow from the southeast, Cappen, and bring snow."

"Have we time to take the temperature readings first?"

"If you ain't too long gone, sir," Petersen warned.

The temperature stood at only fifteen below, high indeed.

When they faced about toward the brig, Tom stopped short in horror.

"Holy Mother of God!" He pointed at a bundle swinging from a yardarm.

"Our furs, do you mean?"

"It's a hanged man swinging there, sir. I seen one once—"

"Hickey, you know perfectly well we stowed our sledge furs in a big sealskin bag and tied them high and dry to the mainmast, away from the damp and the rats."

"A hanged man dangling is a dreadful sign!" Clutching Kane's sleeve, the boy slumped to his knees in quivering terror.

"Hickey, stand up! There's no man there."

"It don't need to be a man, sir, only to have the look of a hanged man to be an evil sign. And so it looks exactly!" He sobbed despairingly on Kane's arm.

"Hickey, stop that!" He cuffed the side of the boy's head as a rough restorative. "Stand on your feet!"

"Yes, sir." Tom rubbed his furry sleeve over his wet face. Just then the low moon caught the swinging mass, giving it a red outline. A gust of wind moved it in a slow arc until the heavy weight bumped the great mast. Timber and arms rattled emptily. Tom recoiled to his knees again, praying hard. "Mother of God, Mother of God, help me to stand up for the Captain's sake!"

But he had to be half-carried, half-dragged back and pushed through the *tossut*. "The air and his weakness have affected Tom's senses," Kane explained to Bonsall. "Where's Goodfellow?"

"Went out with you, didn't he? He ain't got back."

"I knowed it! I knowed it!" Hickey threw himself on his belly, crawling toward the *tossut* to rescue Henry.

Kane pulled him back. "No, Tom," he said gently, "everything is all right. You stay here with Mr. Brooks; I'll get Henry."

From his bunk, Brooks beckoned the boy. "Stay with me, Tom, and just leave everything to the Captain. You know you can rely on him."

"I saw a hanged man, and someone will die," Hickey said.

Over the hatch this trip Kane heard the tarpaulin flapping. Rising wind drove snow from the land into his face and whistled loud through the rigging, while overhead the swinging bag thumped and thumped and thumped, an unreasonably ominous sound.

"Goodfellow!" he bellowed. "Henry!"

Only the whistling wind answered. The snow had driven back the stars. The moon had fallen out of sight. It was wholly dark.

He went back to light a lantern and then made for the storehouse. It was empty. Toward the shore the floe, dropped by the tide, pounded the land ice. Kane lumbered in a hurried circuit of the brig. Perhaps Henry had by now returned to the cabin. Below, Hickey was brewing tea as though his life depended on it.

"Henry's coming, and I have to fix him a bit of supper," he said, agitated.

"Tom ran up on deck after you left, Captain, and came back crying he saw Goodfellow," Brooks reported.

"I saw him! I saw him! I'm getting his supper now."

"He swears he saw Goodfellow making his way on the land ice, and then jump to the floe," Brooks added, the men listening.

"It's too black and stormy to see without a light, Tom," Kane said matter-of-factly.

"I saw him! He's coming, Captain. I saw him plain."

With Hans, Kane continued the search through the driving, drifting snow. Every rounded mound of ice could be his young friend, prone, and covered over by drift. It was an impossible search, but in the face of an impossible loss he went on and on. Then, at six in the morning, Henry Goodfellow walked calmly toward him, his furs packed with driven snow, his rifle still on his shoulder.

In the cabin he dismissed the fuss over him. "I just went hunting," he announced as if everyone should have known, "to get us all fresh meat, and right away I came on a herd of deer. They ran, of course, but I took after them. They ran faster and faster, but so did I. Shot down two of the biggest." He laughed heartily at the recollection. "Hans can go pick them up."

His report finished, Henry Goodfellow, belatedly hit by exhaustion and the shock of warmth, fell to the deck and, turning on his back, slept soundly. When Kane examined his rifle, it had, of course, never been fired.

His poor fellows weakened steadily. At one time every man was down flat except himself and Hans. He and Hans flourished on the rats no one else would eat. Chopped up and mixed raw with a little tallow, rat meat made nourishing little balls Kane found almost palatable. For the others, there was always, by God's kindness, a pup, a rabbit, or a scrawny fox to keep his worst cases alive.

While Hans hunted tirelessly or sawed wood to keep them from freezing, his captain dosed the sick, bandaged their running sores, bathed the feverish, tended stoves, lamps, and slop buckets, led morning and evening prayers, cooked morning mush and evening beans, and went every day to take the weather readings. The men began to fall silent on his return, and to watch him make his careful entries as if they were part of a ritual, the cabalistic signs in a spell which would one day transport them home.

35. THE RENEGADE

BY EARLY MARCH the coming sunlight mingled with full moonlight to invest the air with an ash gray. It clothed the gnarled hills and pointed out the bleak terraces. The dark and the cold now lurked in the depths of the fjords and brooded over the measureless plains of ice. But intense moonlight glittered on every crag and spire of a world Milton or Dante might have envisioned.

The unnatural light, like the pull of shifting poles on a tentative compass, made restless the minds of his sick. Dropping down from his watch on deck, Kane heard Brooks reminisce with Ohlsen in the adjoining bunk.

"Thought we never would get through them hummocks. From the time we laid down the last pemmican case, I don't remember nothing until Petersen called me into the tent. Must have gone off in some kind of fit, I guess, Swede."

"My feet hurt going back," Ohlsen remembered. "Boots was pinching." He had almost died going for help for the depot party, but recalled only that his boots pinched.

"Baker's boots pinched him, too, I recollect, but it wasn't his boots that did for him—"

"Hush, Brooks!" Kane whispered. "Let the others sleep."

"Doctor"—Brooks pulled him down—"five nights to come one year ago you crawled in on the four of us, down flat as flounders. I didn't see your boots, but for sure they was Eskimo ones."

"So they were. Now, quiet!"

"It was a hard walk, greatest I ever heard tell of, you made to save us. But maybe it was no use, with Baker and Pierre both dead, and Wilson and me near to it. The whole four gone."

"Brooks, stop that talk. That's an order. You and Wilson will both make a longer walk than mine, if we have to foot it to the Greenland settlements this summer. So rest up for it."

But Brooks, memory strong on him, fumbled in the dim light

until he caught both of Kane's hands. "Doctor, you cried when you saw us," he whispered hoarsely, "and you didn't pull up until we jabbed the stopper down in the whisky tin and gave you a tot."

There were other whisperings in the shadows of the quarters, with a disturbing on-the-sly feeling to them. He finally caught out the slyest—Godfrey and Blake. Those two were up to something, but though he added the duties of a police detective to his other tasks, what it was, he could not find out.

That week he took the risk of sending off their only hunter, Hans, to Etah. With their last two useful dogs and Kane's Marston rifle, Hans marched bravely away. The succeeding days were fine, and Kane began to hope. When Hans returned with walrus, the whole crew could recruit strength enough to haul the boats to Refuge Inlet. From there the bird colonies on the rocky Northumberland islets were within reach. His men could make a Capua of the place, feasting and sunning themselves to health. Then they could strike for home.

Should Hans fail— Men in better shape than his crew had starved to death in the Arctic in April. The Spitzbergen victims—

In the very midst of such brooding he heard Hans's voice shouting "Bim! Bim! Bim!" to the accompanying chorus of the dogs. The boy was driving a full dog team, wonderful Hans, and had also brought young My-ouk. "He be second hunter to Docto Kay-en," Hans announced proudly.

Beaming, in words and signs, they told how Hans, finding the Eskimos themselves starving, with his magic gun led them on a hunt, bringing in a fine walrus. My-ouk's bone thinness was testimony to the Eskimos' hard winter, but they had sent the brig a generous load of meat. My-ouk slept that night on a bearskin at the foot of the Captain's bunk.

Kane began at once to feed his men as much walrus as their condition would tolerate. Wilson and Riley could keep it down only in broth, but the rest he put on a concentrated meat diet. They had thinly sliced walrus heart with lime juice or vinegar before breakfast; at breakfast, blood gravy with wheaten biscuit; at dinner, walrus steaks slightly stewed or fried; and at bedtime, more raw heart slices and vinegar. Dishing out such riches made Kane happy to the point of giddiness, and he got grease smears on his journal.

But Hans and My-ouk together could find no game near the brig, and when the Captain was down to a scant two days' meat for his sick, he sent his young hunters south to the Eskimos again.

The resurgence of animal life was undoubtedly delayed by the weather. It stayed extraordinarily cold, so cold that their last firewood was now consumed, and Kane was burning their big manila hawser. Their next resort must be to the very body of the brig herself. After two winters of suffering and labor to save her, the *Advance* would never bear them to sea.

When he put Ohlsen to work cutting into her hold forward where the sick could not see what he did, the carpenter did not protest. He was too enfeebled to realize the enormity of the act.

This decision distracted Kane's attention from Godfrey and Blake, but the morning Hans left he noticed them with their heads together. Blake was down with a bad leg, but Godfrey's sickness was so obviously feigned that the Captain ordered the fellow to work at chores well away from Blake's bunk.

In the late hours of the night watch, as Kane passed Stephenson's bed to feed the stove, the Irishman plucked his sleeve.

"Captain!" Kane, bending down, the man whispered softly, "I don't like to be after worrying you, but I overheard a little plot. Two men will this day run for it. They spoke of Hans, too."

"Godfrey and Blake?"

"The very ones, sir! Is Hans in with them, do you think?"

"No. They may plan to waylay him and the team."

Without sledge and dogs, the brig would have no transport. Without Hans, no hunter. Besides, they owed their very lives to the little Eskimo. He might be killed defending the team from those bullies. But surely Blake's leg was too bad for him to make a dash!

At six Kane roused Bill to prepare breakfast. Keeping the sailor busy might keep him out of mischief. He showed some initial uneasiness, but soon went boldly over to John Blake, his grin insolent. If the pair intended to bolt, they could be apprehended best outside these cramped quarters.

"I'll try hunting in Hans's stead," he told Brooks loud enough to be overheard, and climbed into his furs.

Morton was on the watch, able to keep on his feet part of the day, thank Heaven, though he limped badly. Him and Bonsall, Kane told what to do. Then the Captain hid in the bulkhead.

Within half an hour Blake crawled out of the *tossut,* and, glancing about furtively, satisfied himself he was in the clear. Without a trace of lameness he scampered up the hatchway, Kane letting him go as Morton on deck had also been instructed to do. Without Bill, Blake would not go far, though he had cleverly fooled his physician-captain. Kane waited. Presently Godfrey appeared, accoutered for travel.

"Where bound, Godfrey?"

The big riverman leaped for the ladder.

"Halt, or I fire!" As Godfrey wavered, Kane said sharply, "Don't tempt me! I'm itching for a shot at you. Get back to the cabin, fast!"

Sullenly Godfrey obeyed, Kane prodding him through the *tossut* with his rifle barrel. Inside, while he held a gun on the culprit, Bonsall snapped handcuffs on him. Blake, lacking his confederate, soon returned on his own, Morton following. As John saw the tableau under the lamp, his limp also came back. He, too, was handcuffed.

"These men were caught deserting ship," Kane told his raptly attentive crew, "before even the rats have left us."

He went to stand behind his small desk and had the pair brought before him. Their offenses were entered in the log: "Malingering—skulking in your bunks while sicker men waited on you, taking food out of the mouths of shipmates whose need was worse—insubordination—"

"We was just going hunting," Godfrey muttered.

"Don't interrupt an officer. You'll be told when to speak. You are also charged with conspiracy and desertion. For the last, you deserve to be hanged."

"A hanged man!" Tom Hickey squeaked.

"Quiet! Mr. Brooks, will you please maintain order?" Never in their long association had he made such a show of authority over his crew. But it was needed. Besides, he was trying to think how to punish these scoundrels. He could not lock them up, lacking a jail, and imprisonment meaning little to men imprisoned, as they all had been, for months. Reduced rations? How reduce the rations of hungry men? "Have you anything to say for yourselves?"

"Honest, Captain," Bill whined, "we was coming back with walrus. Maybe we done wrong sneaking out like that, but we didn't mean no harm!"

"I'd let you go and good riddance, under other conditions. Once before I hoped I had seen the last of you, but you came crawling back. You were welcomed with kindness which you repay by deserting just when you may be of some use, when your brute strength would help haul better men home. So here you'll stay! Not at Etah, gorging on the Eskimos' meat, debauching their women, stealing their goods when you are ready to decamp, but here! If you'll swear before all your shipmates to obey and to work hard, I'll parole you. Otherwise, you hang."

Loud were their protestations of reform.

"Any slacking will bring a touch of the cat." He had never ordered a man lashed, but they cringed as if he were a hardened tyrant. "Bring the Bible, Mr. Bonsall." Blake and Godfrey made solemn oaths. "Unlock the handcuffs, and put these men to helping Ohlsen."

Without another look at them he himself went out to hunt in earnest, but found not so much as a hare to draw bead on. Returning late, he was told Godfrey had made good his escape.

"Ohlsen was too weak to stop him. Knocked poor Swede down. The first dang thing I knowed, Cap'n Ken," Morton explained, "was when I seen him running on the ice foot. I hollered, but he didn't stop, and I hain't shooting without orders."

"When Hans returns with the dogs, I'll go after him."

If Hans returned. The boy knew nothing of Godfrey's desertion, and might allow the riverman to come close enough to wrest his gun away. In a misery of suspense Kane waited and watched through the last fortnight of March. Daylight was gaining, but game had not yet appeared. Without meat his men were lapsing back into their sad previous state, and the most he had shot in one day was three ptarmigan.

He was beginning to be afraid to trust himself out alone to hunt. The slightest exertion had become an agony of effort and his mind seemed affected. Twice he distinctly heard Hans call, "Docto Kay-en!" and the second time he heard the dogs bark as well. He had struggled a dangerous distance over the ice before realizing it was a delusion.

One early April day the dawn's light showed a dog team leaping toward the brig, but still a mile off. He yelled for Bonsall. "What do you see?"

"Hans coming back, sir! It's Hans!" They stumbled to meet him, both of them barely able to walk.

But the man behind the sledge was Godfrey.

"Where is Hans?" Kane sucked air into his suffering lungs.

"Sick—*he* says." Godfrey stood unabashed as a stone.

"Too sick to come home?"

"He's right at home where he is." Godfrey smirked.

"If you've harmed him, you'll pay with your own life!"

"Don't you worry about him. The Eskimos spoil the fat little slob, just like you used to."

"Your insolence—"

"They spoil Bill Godfrey, too. Specially the women. Feed me by hand, the women do, and Hans's 'jolly nurse' has plenty of 'jolly time' for Bill." The riverman guffawed.

"Get aboard the brig," Kane ordered.

"I'm returning the dogs and the sled full of walrus, because I'm fair, see? I'll see my mates taken care of, see? But I ain't going aboard that miserable brig, now or ever. I'm going back to the hut and the woman Kalutunah give me." He started to turn, but swung back when he saw Kane's pistol leveled on him.

"I gave you an order! Move!"

Surprised, Godfrey obeyed but at the gangway balked. "Go ahead, shoot! I don't think you got it in you, Doc, to shoot down an unarmed man."

Kane and Bonsall together had not the strength to force this bully aboard. He must get help. He handed the pistol to Bonsall. "Cover him and shoot to kill if he makes a break for it."

Kane's back was a signal for Godfrey to bound away. Bonsall fired but the pistol failed to cap. Instantly Kane grabbed a rifle from the stack near the mainmast. In the cold and with his excitement it discharged while he cocked it. Godfrey, alarmed but unhurt, zigzagged shoreward. Kane's aimed ball whizzed past the sailor's head and he was out of reach.

"The hell with Kane's orders!" he shouted defiantly.

If only the rifle had not gone off prematurely, he would have been an easy target. And a dead man, his captain having murdered him.

Shaken, Kane looked after the fleeing bully. It was minutes before he saw almost in front of him his precious dogs, the sledge, and a slab of walrus of godsend proportions. What was Godfrey's game? And where was Hans?

With the walrus they had a regular feed all round, which so

heartened the crew that they downed their "beer" with cheers. This was Kane's brew of flaxseed, lime juice, quinine, and willow stems which Goodfellow had named the "Arctic Linseed Mucilage Adaptation." In a day or two, the grunts and growls of the men had a good-natured twang.

To hearten them further, he put the sick who could sit up to work picking eiderdown or cotton for coverlets that would be their boat bedding on the escape; or sewing canvas bags for the same purpose. Brooks was busy balling off twine to lay up "small stuff." With such activity while the sunlight poured through the scuttle and the teakettle sang on the stove, their quarters looked brighter than in months. Only Hans's absence cast a shadow.

Petersen was physically the best fitted to go for him, but at the very suggestion took to his bed.

"Hans may be in imminent danger!"

"Yes, Cappen, somevun should go quick for him."

But it would not be Petersen. "Somevun" must be his Captain, unsteady as he was. Happily, he was out only eleven hours when far off he saw a little figure. There was no mistaking Hans's methodical seal-stalking gait. They were soon jabbering together in a patois of Eskimo and English.

Hans had shrewdly suspected Godfrey's intentions at once, resisted the sailor's blandishments, and kept the gun out of his reach. Hans had indeed been sick. "Little veek," the Eskimo said. "Got to send Bill vit valrus." That had been sensible of him, though he thought Bill meant to use the meat to make a deal with the Captain. Baffled in this, Godfrey was back in Etah playing the great man.

The rest of the walrus Hans had stowed at Littleton Island, and needing the sledge to haul it, was on his way back to the brig on foot. The faithful soul went right off on his errand. He returned shortly in company of Metek, Etah's chief, with Metek's handsome fourteen-year-old son and a noble sledgeload of meat.

The natives told a sad tale of the winter. Its severity had forced most of them to eat their dogs. Only twenty of the brutes were left on the entire coast, the seven best belonging to Kalutunah. With that provident man Kane resolved to strike a bargain. But first he must demonstrate his power as a *nalegak,* or great chief. To do this he must bring Godfrey back single-handed.

He evolved a scheme that would amuse the Eskimos and take

Godfrey by surprise. Captain Kane might be a great white chief but he was also a small man who could fit into the furs worn by Metek's son, the boy, Paulik. Armed with a pair of leg irons and his six-shooter, Kane rode one bright April day behind the Eskimo chief.

As they approached Etah, the villagers streamed out to welcome their returning lord. Prominent among them was Bill, waving his arms and shouting "Tima! Nalegak! Tima!" as loudly as the choicest savage. An instant later Kane held a pistol behind the fellow's ear while Metek, grinning, snapped foot cuffs on him.

"You have hard walk ahead, Bill, eighty miles with those things on your feet. Get going!"

Bill looked around the circle of giggling Eskimos. A dumpy little woman, quite caked with filth, shrieked "God-free!" adding something in Eskimo which made the others roar laughing, some rolling on the snow in uncontrolled mirth.

Bill turned back to his captain whose tight smile seemed to dismay him more than the Eskimos' laughter. It apparently convinced him that Kane was at last ready to shoot him down in cold blood.

"Aye, sir," he said, and started to lumber off. An Eskimo deftly thrust a spear between his legs to trip him up, while another kicked him when he fell. Kane motioned them back, and stood with leveled pistol while Godfrey struggled to his feet.

"Keep well in front of the sled or you may get in the way of my dog whip," Kane ordered, and drove the fellow running before him the whole distance back, with only a brief respite at Anoatok, where Bill was too exhausted to make trouble and Kane too keyed up to be caught napping.

The story would spread among the Eskimos, and Bill Godfrey in the end prove an unvoluntary help to his captain. On Godfrey himself that relentless run had a most salutary effect.

36. EXODUS

QUITTING A SHIP was a fearful thing to sailors, Kane realized, frightful enough in the open sea, when the need for action in an emergency—fire, storm, collision—smothered all feeling. Quitting their ice-held *Advance* was harder. Men, no less than rats, are loath to leave a ship unless she is sinking, and the brig was more than their ship, more than their home for two cruel winters. She was the single familiar object on a bleak and alien coast.

Sailors also having a deep distrust of small boats, the men dragged their heels almost from the moment he announced they must leave by May 20. Every day after, the ice would weaken without thawing completely, creating endless difficulty for their sledges on the long pull to open water. Had they faced swimming the whole thirteen hundred miles to civilized port, his men could hardly have been more reluctant to start.

Nevertheless, by hard driving, he saw nearly everything prepared by that date. To the end he heard pleas for "one last meal aboard" or "one last night in the cabin." The most unexpected came from Long Tom Whipple, their chief blasphemer, who asked for "one last prayer."

To this epidemic of dispirits only Christian Ohlsen proved immune. He had several reasons for wanting to get home.

"From my wife and babies," he told Kane as they secured the trussings under their escape boats, "I been gone too long. They think I'm dead, maybe."

"Your wife will have a happy surprise."

"She's a fine girl, big, strong, but even so, she have hard time taking care of so much children. Four we got, all girls. Maybe I got boy now, too. My wife ain't sure when I go."

"He'll be walking and talking when first you see him."

"That's right, Captain!" Ohlsen, smiling, patted their smallest boat, the little *Red Eric,* as if it were a growing boy.

"Call him 'Eric,'" Kane said on impulse.

"Eric Ohlsen." The carpenter considered. "A good name."

They stood by their three boats, poised on the land ice to start the journey. The two big whaleboats, roofed with tarpaulin and wider than the big oak sledges that cradled them, looked ridiculously like ponderous gray ducks too fat to waddle. The little *Eric,* a mere duckling in contrast, seemed eager for swift flight.

Ohlsen made one last round testing the underpinnings. "Some of her best timber I use for them."

"So we aren't abandoning the *Advance* altogether."

"No, sir." Ohlsen looked back at the brig. "Not her."

Whipple had his wish when the entire company assembled in the dismantled winter chamber for a farewell service. Its moss walls had long since been consumed by the stove, together with many supporting timbers and some hull planking. The low sun poured laterally through a wide gap as Brooks read the tenth chapter of the Book of Numbers.

The Israelites began their march out of the wilderness " 'on the twentieth day of the second month of the second year,' " which except for the month was the expedition's starting date. Kane chose the chapter because of that coincidence and saw the men, too, were heartened to note it. While Brooks intoned the order in which the standard of each Israelite host left camp, Kane sent Hickey to haul down their own flags. The cabin boy tenderly folded them and gave them into the Captain's charge just as Brooks read, " 'I will depart to mine own land and my kindred.' "

Finally, with the cloud of the Lord upon them by day, Brooks got the Israelites out of camp, and Kane's own men appeared willing to leave.

He must say a few words but would make no sermon. "God has stood by everyone here," he said quietly, keeping his eyes from looking out toward the place where Jeff and Schubert were buried. "He will move with us during our deliverance, working through the will of each of us. That is God's way. Those who will to follow Him are saved. Those who *will* to be delivered, God will guide home.

"Make no mistake," he tried to infuse them with his own determination, "we must reach home or everything we have accomplished at such cost will go for naught. We must live to tell our discoveries."

He had been thinking of Sir John, wondering what undiscovered country he had penetrated. The world might never know.

Suddenly the brave Dutchman, Barents, came to his mind. In many ways their cases were parallel. Barents, two hundred and fifty years ago, had reached the top of the Old Continent. There he, like Elisha Kane, had been forced to abandon ship and with fifteen men—having lost two, like Kane, during a bitter winter—make his way back to civilization. But he had not so far to travel as they and he had lost another man on the way. And *Barents himself had perished.*

"Pray now that God's hand will hold us up."

Over the bent heads of his men he saw Sir John's portrait hanging on the wall. *That* Franklin should escape the Arctic. He went to remove it from its frame, rolling it into a case of India rubber where he had previously stowed Maggie's portrait.

Brooks came up solemnly with a written pledge from the men. Whatever the hardships, the undersigned would abide faithfully by the expedition and their sick comrades. The names he expected were there, but so, too, boldly scrawled, were Godfrey's and Blake's.

Up on deck Kane and his men marched ceremoniously two complete turns about the ship. At Kane's command they stopped near the Fair Augusta, their battered little girl in blue.

"Our boats will be so crowded we must ungallantly desert our fair lady, without so much as a farewell toast, since we have no spirits left." Only an emergency flask of alcohol.

"No, Cap'n! Take her. There's room." That was Morton.

"She's our good-luck piece, sir," Hickey wailed.

"Wood, ain't she? We can burn her if she gets heavy." There spoke Godfrey himself. *Burn her for a witch.*

"Very well." Kane let himself be persuaded. "Mr. Ohlsen, dislodge her carefully."

The men tramped in silent order to the boats, Brooks struggling with his stump, Hayes on his frostbitten foot. They among others he must call "able-bodied" were but a degree sounder than his four worst sufferers.

Of these four, Goodfellow was too weak to stand; Wilson could not walk on his unhealed stump; Whipple's tendons were so contracted by scurvy that he could not straighten his legs; and Stephenson was as weak as Henry. These men Kane could carry by dog sled to a hut at Anoatok. They could rest until the boat-laden sledges pulled up.

More than the boats Kane dare not load on the sledges, his dozen "able" men were so feeble. Every pound of provisions—and they were carrying fifteen hundred pounds on this exodus—he and his dogs must also move by easy stages on ahead of the men at the towlines.

They took their assigned places laughing and joking, as they adjusted the comical Eskimo goggles, making sure the slits in those wooden slats were exactly in front or a man couldn't see anything. With the sun's rays ricocheting cold and dazzling off every point of ice and snow, these were an absolute necessity.

"I'll repeat my orders," Kane called out. "While I am acting as your common carrier and courier"—they considered that a great joke—"Mr. Brooks is in charge. Under him, Mr. McGary commands the *Faith* and Mr. Morton the *Hope*.

"Crews of five have been named for each whaleboat-*cum*-sledge, with three additional men on the *Red Eric* later. You will mess and sleep with your crew, though you will all pull together on each sledge by turns. In time a single crew at the rue-raddies will be able to move either sledge"—they cheered the day skeptically—"but as yet you are too feeble. On that account, though we will keep strict routine otherwise, there will be no set hours of work. You will stop when you are tired. You'll find, though, that you're holding up longer and longer each day, I promise you. Now, 'storm along, my hearties!' "

With the best will in the world they leaned on their shoulder straps and the sledge carrying the *Faith* slid grudgingly out over the ice.

When Kane turned back to the brig to take off the first of his sick, a huge raven with a great flapping of wings settled high in the rigging. Kane recognized the marauder.

"Old Magog," that had been the men's name for him last season, "you here already?"

Ohlsen came up with the Fair Augusta on his back. "Not yet!" he shouted at the ill-omened bird, shaking his fist. "The brig is not yours yet. Men stay by her still!"

Men stayed by the brig for many a dragging day. The *démarche* from the *Advance* was not a forthright retreat. The first day his poor fellows managed to pull both sledges ahead only one mile. In four days they had advanced only seven miles. Kane himself was constantly shuttling back and forth between the brig, the crew, and the hut at Anoatok, nearly sixty miles away.

Their hospital hut there, a low stone igloo, he had prepared days before the retreat began. More cave than human habitation then, he had made it passably comfortable. On his trips equipping it he had also carried up a good half of their provisions. When all his sick were installed there with Stephenson well enough, he thought, to tend the lamps and heat their food, he whipped back to the brig to start moving on more supply bales. He had also to carry their next day's food to his sledge party.

As he approached them he almost despaired, seeing how wearily they inched their ark along. If he could not give them fresh meat, he would at least provide fresh bread and hot tea! At the ship he set himself to baking up a batch, using the recipe he had evolved at the Navy Department long ago. In three hours his dough raised impressively without salt, saleratus, or shortening, though no housewife would believe it. The fat loaves he dispensed still warm to his men. But a blizzard was blowing up and with Godfrey and another sledgeload he hurried on to his sick.

At Anoatok all was confusion, the lamps out, the snow piled so high against the door that his invalids had not strength to close it. Snow flurries had melted on their blankets and they lay sodden, too weak to improve their wretched state. Looking at them by the light of a fire of tarred rope, he saw they must have meat and his sledge crew, too. But he could not leave them! Godfrey, though unreliable, was swift.

"Take the dogs and hurry to Etah for walrus!"

Whipple heard the order. "Don't ditch us, Bill!"

"Signed the blasted pledge, didn't I?" Bill said angrily, and was gone.

Someway Kane got their bedding dry, and brewing them quarts of hot tea, guzzled with them. Then he, too, slept. He awoke some time after his watch had run down. Out of the storm came the yelping of dogs. Godfrey already? The round trip was forty miles.

"Godfrey, Cap'n. Try beating my speed some time!"

A second figure ran around the sled. "Metek, Cap'n Kayen. Walrus." He had a chunk in his arms and the sled was piled high.

All smiles, as if he paid a social call, Metek scooted into the center of the hovel where he began at once to slice and pass out strips of the dark, juicy meat to the drowsy men. For himself, Kane, and Godfrey he cut more generous slices. Kane gulped his down, anxious to take the lion's share to Brooks's party.

They were already up to Ten Mile Ravine. In spite of the blizzard and their own swollen feet, they had worked fourteen hours without stopping. Riley, snow blind, had nevertheless stayed at the drag lines. Kane pounded his back and fed him walrus by hand.

"No captain ever had such a crew! With honest meat in your bellies, what wonders you'll perform!"

More cook than captain, again he went to the *Advance* to bake bread, and make flour pudding and render pork fat. He also loaded the last hundredweight of their provisions on the sledge, and with Metek's help, took it that day to Anoatok. From there he went on later to choose the spot for their next entrepôt, and decided on the island opposite Cape Hatherton. The largest and highest of the Littleton Islands, the Eskimos, because of the amusing contour of its hills, called it Petiutlik, or "The Bobbing Seals."

Pushing on from there to Etah for more walrus—the endless miles he and his tiring dogs had traveled—he was alarmed by the rapid ice change. The snow on it was leaden gray from water seeping up and the ice fields were spotted with dark patches of thaw. A gale could transform the floe over which his men plodded, on which every pound of their provisions was piled—and their powder and ball—into a tumultuous ice pack. His freight must be moved toward Hatherton in haste and his invalids made ready to leave at a moment's notice.

He found the entire Eskimo village out on the rocks gorging auks or dozing, bloated with food, in the sun. The very infants toddled about, their faces smeared with blood or buried in the disheveled feathers of a raw bird. He let himself be stuffed with auks' livers and bedded down in the place of honor, Eskimos entangled like eels around him. With a feather coverlet over him and his hostess's two-year-old for a pillow, he slept like the dead.

Next morning, the Eskimos loaning him their only surviving dog team, he left his own tired beasts there to rest up, while he headed north again, two of the natives with him. His valiant sledge party was within three miles of the hospital hut! In better shape, they were eating more than he had calculated. He dared not dig into their store of future provisions, but there was still some flour left at the brig.

"Come along, Tom! Didn't you say you were once a baker?"

"One of the best I was, sir."

With the two Eskimos, Godfrey would haul a load of supplies to Petiutlik, while Kane and his cabin boy walked the fifty-odd miles to the brig. It took sixteen hours.

The pair spent a happy time next day in the galley, singing as they kneaded dough on the top of a big empty cask. Tom stoked their fire with volumes of the *Penny Cyclopedia of Useful Knowledge,* the only books Kane would allow him to burn though all must be left behind. Their boxes of specimens, gathered with such care, the scientific instruments which had been his pride, all left to Magog, raucous overhead.

Scraping out the flour barrel, Kane said, "That's the last of it, I'm afraid, Tom."

That improvident young soul commented cheerfully, "All the better, sir. Now we'll have no more bread to bake."

Tired, for lack of other bedding, they ripped open old mattresses and slept like vagrants in a haystack. Toward morning Godfrey came up with the team. He had not stopped at all on his long run south and back, so declared he'd turn in at the brig and walk up to the sledge party. Tom and the Captain left him snoring.

They were not two miles along when someone called.

"Bill, ain't it, sir? Sounds like his beller."

They swung quickly round and out of the curtain of snowflakes Godfrey plunged without his parka, his eyes wild. "Captain, for God's sake, wait for me!"

Bill beseeching him: "Whatever is it?"

"A hant," he was panting, "on the brig, playing a guitar."

Tom crossed himself.

"Nonsense, Bill! What ghost would haunt an empty ship?"

"It was playing one of them frog songs of Schubert's sounded like. I ain't going back for my coat."

"Then I will." As Kane snapped the dog whip, Tom tumbled hastily off the runners.

On Wilson's guitar, swinging free from a peg near a gap in the brig's hull, the wind was softly playing. Kane smiled to hear it. Bill

Godfrey didn't know what a good musician Eolus could be. The sound made Kane remember the guitar-playing at Maggie's séances. He wondered if that sly puss had used a convenient draft to her purposes. Leaving the instrument, he picked up Bill's coat and joined the fearful men. "Only the wind, Bill."

"Maybe so." Bill added with curious malice, "Heard that ghosts play tunes at the rappers' circles. Wouldn't scare you, likely."

What precisely was the scoundrel hinting? Kane dared not ask.

Within a week the sledges were well past Anoatok and into Smith's Straits, when a storm such as he had never experienced caught Kane and Petersen on the way to Etah again for meat. (The track to that native settlement, Kane had beaten until it resembled the road to church on Sunday morning.) Without warning snow wreaths so filled the air that he could not see the way. He could not even see Petersen or the dogs, it was so dark, while overhead the wind droned like a great flywheel. It almost lifted him off his feet.

"Is it a cyclone?" he yelled.

"Get holt somethin, Cappen," Petersen warned.

They ran for a great black rock to which they clung while the wind actually tore the jumpers off their backs. Inching around to the boulder's lee side, they lay spoon fashion to keep warm, the dogs flattened out beside them. When the fury had subsided somewhat, they floundered back to the sledge party. The floe! Had the floe gone? And the boats with it?

Snow had drifted so deep around the *Faith* that they could hardly find her. Brooks, emerging from cover, resembled a walrus breaking through the ice. "The floe's holding, sir! Can't believe it, but she's holding!"

"The storm's subsiding. Get started, man, get started! I must go bring down the sick."

He brought Goodfellow first, and sped back for Stephenson. The sledges were at the ice marshes now, sludge fields of snow and water over rolling, uncertain ice. It required all McGary's and Petersen's skill and instinct to find safe passage. The *Hope's* stern went through once, dragging six men into deep water. She was saved by the grim refusal of the others to let go the ropes. Kane before leaving warned them sharply to sheer well off any sign of a tide hole.

Returning with Stephenson, he passed a hole with the snow

around it trampled and the ice showing a great raw edge. A short way beyond Ohlsen, deathly pale, crouched on a hummock.

"You're hurt, Ohlsen! What happened?

"Just knocked my wind out, Cap'n. Don't stop with sled. Ice weak here. Go on, go on!" the carpenter ordered his captain.

"Stephenson, wait here quietly. I must get Ohlsen where he can lie down."

They stretched the carpenter in the stern sheets of the *Faith*, bundling him in buffalo robes. Hayes would attend him.

Brooks looked unhappy. "Said he strained himself some. Said he'd be all right."

Ohlsen's agonized breathing worried Kane deeply. "He may be ruptured internally. How did it happen?"

"We was crossing what looked just a little pool and shallow, but the *Hope's* runner went straight down. To save her, Swede rammed a capstan bar quick under the sledge like this—" The First Officer showed how Ohlsen had straddled the bar and forced it down with all his might. "When the men dragged the boat forward, he slipped and the bar snapped up, catching him full between the legs."

Kane had seen a man killed in a cavalry charge by being thrown onto the pommel of his saddle. "The worst sort of injury!"

"We seen it jolted him bad, but he didn't let go. Kept swearing and saying 'Go on! Go on! Don't stop!' Shook us to hear Ohlsen cuss. Didn't think he knew the English for a real oath, sir."

"You left him alone," Kane said angrily.

"No, sir. We left Hickey by him, but he ordered Tom on."

By good fortune, just as they reached a stretch of clear ice, a north wind blew up. "McGary," Kane yelled, "get the masts up! Use the long oar for a boom on each boat."

The men gaped, but McGary instantly understood. "Aye, sir. Get her up, you lubbers." Morton got his men started on the *Hope's* mast almost as quickly, and under full canvas, the two boats, with the sledges they were lashed to supplying the runners, ran gallantly before the wind.

Sick as he was, Whipple mounted the thwarts, to stare astonished at their mode of locomotion. "God-damnedest sight I ever seen!" he said with no reproof from Kane. All the invalids followed Tom's example, except the prostrate Ohlsen, while the well men on the gunwales broke into the familiar sailors' chorus Kane had not heard for months. It put a lump in his throat.

"Storm along, my hearty boys!" they roared in real harmony.

Ohlsen lifted a bewildered head. Kane crawled back to him. "We're ice-sledding," he explained.

Ohlsen only clutched at Kane's hand. "I done it wrong, sir! If I done it right, I save her without no trouble."

"You did save her!"

"But I done it wrong! Hurt myself that fool way. You just set me down some place." Sweat broke out on the carpenter's forehead and he wept.

Kane cradled the poor fellow's head in his arms, and said earnestly, "We won't leave you, Ohlsen!"

By the day's end Ohlsen's fever was alarming and he was at times delirious. He kept urging his son Eric, very real to him now, to "Go on! Go on! Don't stop on weak ice, Eric!"

They had sighted the Bobbing Seals earlier, and on the protected inshore channel the wind continued to sweep then along. Only when it died did they camp. Two of the men caught birds which Hayes used for a soup he fed Ohlsen. The injured man looked better. But to Kane he said, as he had to Eric, "Go on! Go on! Don't stop for this sick fool."

"We're stopping so we can all rest. Soon we'll reach open water. We need you to check the boats before they're launched."

"Boats in good shape, but not me. You go see my wife and boy, Captain. Tell her to name the boy 'Eric.' "

"You'll name that boy yourself, Christian. Now sleep."

Early next morning Kane climbed the largest dark seal-shaped hill. Far off, under the horizon, open water stretched. He ran down, stumbling and falling in his happy hurry, and met McGary returning from Lifeboat Cove. Their cache of two years ago was safe there. Perhaps they had reached a turning point in their fortunes. As if to prove this, Etah Eskimos came in a crowd to help drag the boats, saying they knew where to catch auks.

Then Hayes beckoned him. When his surgeon had given his news, Kane packed the Eskimos off to hunt birds, so he and his men would be left alone for a duty they must perform alone. Despite the Eskimos' present friendliness, Kane felt he must still hide from them any weakening of his party and Christian Ohlsen was dead.

On a sheet of metal Ohlsen had brought along to mend the boats Kane scratched his epitaph and laid it on the carpenter's breast. Then they sewed his body into his own blankets and carried it in a slow procession to the head of a little cove and consigned it, after a quiet service, into a tomb of rocks fit for a Viking. In silence they marched down the gorge to the boats, and without a word began again to drag on their lines.

Like Barents, Kane had lost a cherished man along the way.

37. ANGEKOK

WHEN THE ESKIMO hunters returned, the whole village of Etah came with them—boys of ten pushing babes on hand sledges—eager to help the "angekok," the "magic man," Docto Kayen, on his way. Gay as gypsies, the natives camped on the ice marshes.

With their nets they caught auks by the thousands, and by the thousands Kane's men and dogs consumed those tiny mouthfuls. With their sledges, they carted Kane's freight and his more precious sick steadily south. The infants squalled, the women chattered, the men spun long yarns punctuated by peals of rattling laughter, the confusion was frenzied, but they were, nevertheless, shortening the trek to open water by a good fortnight.

Kane was deeply grateful to the poor, miserable, dirty, *happy* crowd of them. Their example made his own men break into song and drag on their sledges right heartily. Gone was the moody silence of the scorbutic. How wrong he had been, as recently as Ohlsen's funeral, in suspecting these Eskimos of possible treachery! They did not know the word. They stole, yes, but as a matter of course, as gypsies do. When they could have overwhelmed his feeble crew and taken everything, they helped instead.

Men and women he once regarded as savages became neighbors he saluted by name: the faithful Metek and his wife Nualik ("Mrs. Eiderduck," in Petersen's translation) with their five children from My-ouk down to little Accomodah; Nesserk and his wife, Anak, and their brood; Tellerk ("Right Arm," and a strong right arm he proved); Sip-su, handsome as My-ouk, and Marsumak and Aningnah, Erkee, and the half-grown boys. Their very dogs helped. Since he and his crew had reached the Bobbing Seals, the Eskimos considered them their guests for whom nothing was too much. There had been no "trade," no treaty of any sort, except for a petition from Metek and his wife.

They came to him, pressing little Accomodah, their youngest, before them. He was a fat, misshapen little boy with a bleeding nose. Worriedly, they pointed to the boy's protruding abdomen. It was more than aldermanic. He was badly potbellied.

"Docto Kayen *angekok,*" Metek said.

As a magic man, Kane was expected to wave this deformity away. The boy, Kane learned, stuffed on blubber.

"No more *ossuk,*" the Captain sternly ordered. Meat the child might have, but not an ounce of *ossuk.*

For really magical effect, he then presented Mrs. Eiderduck with a lump of brown soap to be rubbed on the troubled area. "Tell them," he instructed Petersen, "I will see the boy again when we reach open water where the *angekok,* dipping his hand in salt water, then will lay it with curative effect on the boy's belly."

Metek, when he heard this, promised to hasten the progress of the sledges to the healing waters.

They reached the sea at Cape Alexander on June 18. North of that black promontory it surged with wild force. To men so long away from open water the roar of the surf was almost frightening, but the salt spray tickled the nostrils and the outlook over the indigo-blue horizon was bold and good.

Their poor boats, however, stood a painful reminder of Ohlsen's absence. Without his loving care and pat of confidence for each, even their biggest, the *Faith,* looked small and overladen. They were drawn up on the ice shelf to be swelled and calked, Brooks hobbling around shouting orders with his old vigor. He and McGary did their best on the repairs, and launched and stowed all three, while their captain took his ease. After driving the dog team an estimated eight hundred miles the past month, Kane needed a rest.

He spent the time distributing gifts. Each Eskimo received a knife or a file or a saw for a keepsake. All gear his crew were discarding he also handed out. There remained his unfinished business with little Accomodah.

The child was brought before him and immediately began to cry, wiping blood and tears on his furry sleeve. Kane took his wailing patient by the hand and led him to the semi-privacy of a table rock. Standing the boy on it, the *angekok* in his best country-doctor manner stripped the boy to the thighs and felt his belly. It was round and hard and liberally smeared with brown soap.

Kane shook his head. "Still too much *ossuk.*"

Petersen, entering into the spirit of the occasion, repeated it portentously. Accomodah let loose a new flood of tears, as Kane thumped his chest and then stood him about to thump his back.

"Come along, boy." The parents and all of Etah fell in as they moved in ceremonious procession to a sheltered stretch of beach. Passing the grinning Morton, Kane ordered, "Bring one of my silk undershirts."

At the water's edge Kane turned to Accomodah, standing naked and comic as a little idol. "Here we go!" the *angekok* gave fair warning. Then, scooping up a handful of salty water, he dashed it on the boy's belly, rubbing until the soap foamed. Accomodah squealed and tried to push away but Kane's other hand held him securely behind the rump. The watching Eskimos squealed, too, in sympathetic horror. The *angekok* obviously performed a dangerous and potent rite as he splashed more and more water on Accomodah, thoroughly embrocating his little belly.

Kane then washed the tears and blood from Accomodah's face, and held a cold wet hand to the lad's neck until his nosebleed stopped. By the time Morton came up, Accomodah was clean and dry and the only Eskimo on that shore ever to have experienced a bath of sorts.

"Now, Morton, open it out and hold it up. Petersen, tell them it is a magic shirt which will cure Accomodah so long as he eats no *ossuk* while he wears it."

When they slid the shirt over the boy's head, it reached almost to his ankles, but they tucked its bulk into his fur breeches. The feel of it against his skin made Accomodah laugh for the first time. He rubbed the silk across his middle and laughed again. Kane gave him a final curative pat on the behind.

"No *ossuk,*" he and Metek repeated together.

The weather was favorable, finally. Just before they sailed, Kane gave Metek, for his many services to them, an amputating knife, which he knew how to use, though his earlier operations he had performed with a bone instrument. To all the villagers Kane gave his dogs, except Toodla, with whom he could not part.

They were excited most by the charts he had drawn for them, showing the coast south to Cape Shackleton. Headlands and hunting grounds he indicated by sketches of landmarks and animals. In a few seasons' patient marches they could, he told them, reach a land where the daylight was longer, game and driftwood plentiful, and the natives enjoyed the use of kayaks, fish nets, and other wondrous conveniences. From their intent faces he saw they heeded his words. Metek said something earnestly.

"You come back," Petersen translated, "and lead us to better hunt."

"Tell them Hans can guide them."

"Angekok come back! Docto Kayen come back! Come back."

When they pushed off, My-ouk thrust more auks into his hands. The boy was in tears. Aningnah, too, was crying beside the tent curtain, wiping her eyes on a birdskin.

"Come back, *Angekok!* Come back . . . come back . . ." The cries, intermingled with the barking of the abandoned huskies, followed them far out into the bay.

The wind freshened as they doubled the westernmost point of Cape Alexander. From the top of the promontory now behind them a lone figure waved farewell: My-ouk, Kane was certain. Around them kittiwakes and ivory gulls and jaegers dipped their wings in the curling waves. As they dived, screaming, for fish in the beautiful water, they re-created the identical scene of two years ago.

The little fleet tried for Sutherland Island, but found it barricaded by an ice belt so steep they could not land. Kane climbed the *Faith's* mast to scoop enough snow from that high shelf to fill their kettles. They ate aboard their crowded boats and stood away toward Hakluyt.

A short, choppy sea soon swamped the *Red Eric.* Of her crew of three, Riley and Godfrey were picked up by the *Faith* and Bonsall by the *Hope.* Relieved of their weight, the little boat stayed afloat, though it responded sluggishly to a tow. Then the *Hope* gave a signal of distress. Brooks, as they came up, bellowed, "She's making water fastern'n we can bail her, Captain."

The wind was now hauling around to the westward. They could not take the sea abeam. Again Kane clambered up the mast. Ahead he saw the low gray blink of the pack. He gave orders to head for the ice and they fastened alongside an old floe on which his weary men turned in without hauling up the boats. They slept, without waking, through a cold drizzle.

Next day, when the *Hope* and the *Eric* had been bailed out, the fleet worked its way through the ice, often pulling themselves through the leads with boat hooks, or even dragging the boats bodily over the ice. At last the water opened and they bent oar for Hakluyt. It appeared almost as forbidding as Sutherland, but high tide enabled them to haul up the boats. They rigged up a tent for the sick, reinforced their bread-dust-and-tallow supper with a few birds, and through a snowstorm worked at calking their leaks.

The snow beat against their faces as they pushed toward Northumberland Island. There auks in numbers swirled around them, and a fox led them an artful chase before he escaped their guns. On and on they wound their tortuous way, across Murchison Channel on June 23, past Fitzclarence Rock on June 24. Next day they made admirable progress, Kane staying at the helm sixteen hours.

But they were by no means traveling at the speed he had hoped, and he was forced to reduce each man's food allowance to six ounces of bread dust and a tallow lump the size of a walnut. To stretch this miserable dole, they cooked the "whole boiling," as Whipple grimly joked, into a broth which was served in scanty portions through the day. At night their great restorative was tea. In the lee of a berg they would fill their kettles with snow and start the brewing. To a man they drank it by the quart, hot and strong.

So near the first of July they had every right to look for the North Water of the whalers, but around them the ice lay solid or in close pack, and when Kane and McGary took a view, they saw the land ice spread itself unbroken far to the south.

"Ain't a sight I fancy," McGary said, "but we should hit open water soon."

The next day provided their hardest pull. Their diet was beginning to tell on his men. Dragging or pushing, they worked feebly, but did not realize the trouble was due to their failing muscular powers.

"Never seen sludge that sticks like this here, Cap'n."

Then, before noon, a fog engulfed them, and they could do nothing but sit it out. From behind that curtain a gale treacherously flung itself on them, braying with the voice of a thousand trumpets. Their boats were picked up, shaken, spun around, and let down into a swelling waste of broken hummocks. The little fleet was gathered up again, and, the men in the boats utterly powerless, was borne along in a tumultuous skreed of ice and snow and water. The red, brassy face of Dalrymple Rock stared down at them through the snowy sky. They would be dashed to pieces against its foot, and Kane for the first time gave up all hope of their escape.

But it was the pack itself which the storm smashed against the rocks. With oars and boat hooks his crews were able to work their little flotilla clear and into a stretch of land water wide enough for rowing. They rowed desperately toward the land ahead.

It was walled with ice as forbiddingly as Sutherland or Hakluyt. In vain they searched for an opening and were at last forced to grapple the ice wall and wait for the rising tide. The *Hope* had stove in her bottom and lost part of her weatherboarding and all boats were badly chafed. But the gale was not yet done with them. Waiting for the tide, they kept afloat only by constant exertion, bailing out the scud that broke over them, warding off the ice with boat hooks.

At three o'clock they were able to pull the boats onto the shelf. A deep and narrow gorge opened in the cliffs at the spot where they clambered up. Too weary to unload, they pushed the boats into it. An abrupt turn in the ravine put a sheltering cliff between them and the gale. Overhead the ice-coated rocks nearly met.

"It's a blasted cave, Cap'n," Whipple yelled.

As they were bringing in the last boat, the *Red Eric,* and shoring her up with blocks of ice, an unmistakable whirr made every man stand motionless, staring up. A flock of eiders darted swiftly into the ravine. It was their breeding ground! The wet and weary men, too tired even to eat, turned in to dream of eggs and abundance.

"Weary Men's Rest," they named their crystal retreat, and stayed there three days, exerting themselves only to gather eggs and feast on them. The third day was the Fourth of July.

The storm had abated. The sun broke through. The men were restored and rested and spirits were high. Up went the flag and out came the Captain's alcohol flask.

"Hardly enough to spoil our temperance record," he said, shaking it at his ear, "but enough to flavor a patriotic eggnog."

"With less milk in it than whisky even so," McGary said.

They drank to Old Glory, to "Weary Men's Rest," and to a safe journey home, and lowering the boats almost jubilantly, pushed on south through the narrow canals between the ice belt and the floe. On one bad shore the bergs were so close packed they were fifty-two hours forcing this passage. But farther on leads began to open "specially for us," Brooks said, and July 11 found them nearing Cape Dudley Digges, a light breeze helping them nicely.

They came without warning on a glacier not laid down in any chart. Its tongue of floe extended far out to sea. Kane at first felt they must double it at all hazards. His men were too weak to attempt tracking through the hummocks. Then Brooks told him the *Hope* was nearly done for.

"Strained her bottom timbers and no wood for repairs."

Bit by bit they had already cut up and burned the runners and crossbars of two sledges. The third must be kept for unavoidable ice crossings.

Taking his First and Second with him, Kane climbed a berg to determine the extent of the ice tongue. At the top all three stood mute. Kane felt as if a hand had closed around his throat. It was an effort to breathe, to maintain an aspect of calm, to raise his glass and study the appalling scene.

The glacier was roughly seven miles across at its *débouché*. Only by its color was the tongue ice distinguishable, since it flowed into a vast *mer de glace,* an unending plain of purple-tinted ice reaching all the way to Cape York far, far to the south. The extreme southern horizon was gemmed with the varied glitter of sun-tipped crystal. It was beyond words beautiful—and deadly. Where the whalers' "North Water" should have rolled was solid ice.

"Summer seems tardy this year," he was finally able to say almost casually. "The floes have not yet broken up."

"Almight tardy," Brooks rumbled. "Winter's due in a month to six weeks."

"Gale seems to a-blown all the birds away," McGary noted. By implication he was asking what they would do for game, while they waited as wait they must, with their stores diminishing. At least they would have time to work on the boats.

"Never in recorded history has this ice failed to break up. Our release must come soon! Meanwhile make nothing of the delay. Tell the men they need to recover more of their strength for our last big push. Is that clear?"

Brooks, looking down at him with steady gray eyes, nodded, and McGary, giving his breeches a resolute hitch, said "Clear, sir." In silence they dropped down the berg and returned to the boats.

38. ON THE TRACK OF DR. KANE

ON A RAW January day, six months earlier, the Senate gallery had been crowded for the debate on the Pacific Railroad Bill. The senators were in no mood to be interrupted, but Senator Brodhead nevertheless rose to try again for consideration of the resolution on the relief of Dr. Kane. Brodhead, as he talked, kept a wary eye on Badger of North Carolina. Badger had insisted that the resolution be held over when Brodhead first introduced it.

"For a couple of days," Badger had said. "It is a very serious question, I think, whether we should engage in a series of these expeditions, each new one to look for the one preceding it!"

Hunter of Virginia had supported him, contending it was hardly humane to risk more lives in search of men perhaps already dead. That had caused a flurry in the gallery. The public generally wanted help sent the gallant Kane.

In fact, the public was deluging the Committee on Naval Affairs with letters, petitions, memorials, and resolutions urging Kane's rescue. Influential gentlemen were forever buttonholing its members. Badger might feel independent of the pressure, but northern senators had to heed the flood of memorials from the New York Chamber of Commerce, the Philadelphia and Boston Boards of Trade; from this academy and that society; and not least from the state legislatures of New York, New Jersey, and Pennsylvania.

Almost daily he himself received telegrams from Mr. Grinnell and Griswold, who had a nephew with Kane. Those two controlled a deal of American shipping and were not men to be denied. Then this morning a petition had come in, headed simply, "James Brown and others." James Brown, however, was no simple citizen, but a Brown of Brown Brothers. So Brodhead knew he must act. Kane had too many influential friends to be ignored. Trouble was they were northerners when one southern senator could kill the measure.

There was Badger on his feet, objecting to the Kane resolution's taking precedence over his own compensation bill. Providing increased salaries for Supreme Court justices, gentlemen in no danger of starving, Brodhead thought irritably, before the Senate sent them relief. Where the devil was Mallory? The senator from Florida had agreed to lead the fight for the Kane resolution to prevent its becoming a sectional matter.

Ah, here he came. The chair recognized him. In his Irish brogue the Senate's naval authority boldly repeated Badger's and Hunter's earlier objections.

"But, gentlemen, the relief of Dr. Kane will be no wild cast, but a careful search of an area already laid down. Because Franklin lamentably failed to leave behind notice of his plans, Dr. Kane took a contrary course. For any who might follow in his tracks, he wrote out instructions clear as water, with maps and sketches of landmarks. His course was for Smith's Sound and along the way he promised to leave all manner of cairns, beacons, and clues. After wintering there and nowhere else at all he planned to explore the Arctic last spring, sailing in the summer for home. By last autumn the brave Doctor should have been here. He has not arrived."

This was hardly news, but Mallory's Irish voice made it sound a fresh sorrow.

"And why is he not home? It's the inference of them that are acquainted with those desolate regions that Smith's Sound is frozen solid after the worst winter known to the Arctic. Only such a winter could have delayed Dr. Kane."

The senator from Florida shook his fist toward the icy north. It was cold enough right in Washington. The ladies in the gallery drew their mantles closer.

"For two years the gallant American explorers were provisioned. By sharp shooting, since the region abounds in game during the summer, those heroes could live another half-year.

"But meanwhile, the Senate must act before it is too late. Not even this Senate, powerful as it is, can send to the frozen north any vessel it chooses any time it pleases. A suitably equipped vessel must reach Greenland early this summer, or the rescue will be delayed an entire year and Dr. Kane's heroic party destroyed altogether."

Mallory bowed his head. Raising it, he said, "If we act now, the rescue will be easy. By following the brave Doctor's instructions, Smith's Sound can be searched in four months. On the edge of the ice there the relief party may well find the Union flag, its Union down in token of distress, with a watch standing by to guide the rescuers to Dr. Kane.

"There will be no risk to the search party! If they fail to find the Doctor in Smith's Sound, they will return at once." With a flick of his coattails, Senator Mallory sat down. The gallery buzzed approval until the chair rapped.

Thereupon Senator Hunter rose to say a trifle sharply that he was glad his objection "elicited this statement. I was not previously aware that Dr. Kane left signals, indeed monuments, by which his track could be discovered. I have no further objection."

Badger, at sixty still strikingly handsome, urbanely stated that he had been in "the same position as my friend from Virginia: entirely ignorant of the forethought with which Dr. Kane made his arrangements. Since we will not be sending an expedition to wander the polar seas without any certain course; and since I understand a large party of the Navy has volunteered to go in search of this noble, generous-hearted, and sagacious young man, I have no objection to this resolution."

Brodhead exhaled a sigh of relief. The resolution was read a third time and adopted. Shortly thereafter the House approved the Kane measure, and it was then the Navy Secretary's responsibility.

A barque, the *Release,* was finally found at Boston; a steam propeller, renamed the *Arctic,* at Philadelphia. They were fitted out, manned, and ready to sail May 31, two years to the day since Kane's departure.

Mr. Grinnell, his lean face a little leaner, accompanied the vessels to Quarantine. With him went Judge Kane and his sons and his only daughter. John Kane was sailing as surgeon on the *Arctic.*

The Judge, sprightly as ever, was confident they would find Elisha. "Boy's indestructible, or he'd have been dead long ago. You'll find him, Hartstene," he assured the expedition's commander.

Captain Hartstene, his face noncommittal, said he was happy to hear it. His wife's lips trembled occasionally as they pushed down the stormy bay. She did not appear confident of his return, let alone Dr. Kane's.

Mrs. Hartstene felt quite surrounded by Kanes, one of them, Tom Kane, an active Abolitionist who had also taken a peculiar interest in those dreadful Mormons. And Dr. John Kane had been just wished on her husband. He wasn't even a Navy man. And Judge Kane was so cheerful about it all! Only the girl, Bessie, seemed disturbed, blowing her nose into a lacy handkerchief.

Mrs. Hartstene heard her say to her brother, "Bring him back to us, Jack, bring him back!" As if one of the surgeons, rather than Captain Hartstene, were in command!

What struck her even odder was another remark of Bessie's that she overheard. "Don't be cross with Lish, John, no matter *what's* happened." Mrs. Hartstene wondered, too, at Mrs. Kane's absence, and inquired after her.

Bessie blew her small nose again. "Poor Mama is much too upset!"

At that Mr. Cornelius Grinnell looked upset himself and moved uneasily over to talk to Mr. Lovell to whom he gave a packet of letters that should, properly, have been given to the Captain.

When bad weather detained the vessels at Quarantine overnight, and her husband came ashore to wait out the storm, Mrs. Hartstene had an opportunity to tell him how strange she found all this. "His sister told the young man who's sailing with you—I can't call him Dr. Kane since it's Dr. Kane you will rescue—"

" 'Mr. Kane' will do."

"Well, she told him not to reprove the Doctor as if he got lost out of mischief. Isn't that absurd?"

"You misunderstood her, my dear."

"No, indeed! The adieus of the whole party seemed quite *outré* to me. Did I tell you young Grinnell slipped letters to Mr. Lovell behind his father's back?"

"My dear, you're overwrought at my going."

"Dearest, don't take the slightest risk, promise me, for a man we've never seen! Endangering your life when he'll be the hero!"

"Now, love—"

She did not realize that young Kane had been sent along, not for his knowledge of medicine or the Arctic or sailoring, but to identify any possessions of his brother's the Eskimos might have. Not so easy to do as with Franklin's gear, all monogrammed and crested. He could not tell his wife he doubted Elisha Kane was still alive to play the hero.

The *Release,* towing the *Arctic* to save coal, did not get off until June 3. Aboard the little steamer, wallowing at the end of her tow-line, Mr. Kane continued seasick for days. The *Arctic's* officers and men were all polite about it. During a storm off the Banks, Newell, the engineer, took time to calk the port over John's bunk to keep out further inruptions of salt water.

John, lying there starving himself well, wanted to tell Newell that Elisha Kane, the great explorer, was always seasick, too. Newell and no one would believe it. Every man of them had volunteered for this duty out of admiration for *the* Dr. Kane.

"Heavy fog we're in. Not too good, when we're smack in the path of the Liverpool packets. Any moment the *Baltic* or the *Pacific* may come down on us at twelve knots and we not able to see a ship's length." Chuckling at the grisly prospect, he left John struggling to his feet.

He might as well die up on deck. Once there he leaned glumly on the rail, noting everyone's suppressed amusement at his bedraggled state, and that the watch carefully called him "Mr. Kane." If Lish lived to return, Dr. John Kane would forever have to explain he was not *that* Dr. Kane, not the famous Dr. Kane, not the notorious Dr. Kane, should Lish's connection with the little rapper get out.

The family knew now. Aunt Lieper had let slip her part in Elisha's conspiracy. At tea the Sunday before he sailed. Tom's wife Elizabeth and the Pattersons had been there, too.

They came to bid him farewell, but every time the relief expedition was mentioned, they wailed over Elisha. To hear them, Lish was the only one facing danger. His mother had been so full of self-reproach that the Judge withdrew to his study. More than once she said, "His father would never try to influence him, but I should."

"Now, dear," Aunt Lieper finally put in, "no use crying over spilt milk, water over dams or what-might-have-been. You're very fortunate. You have your dear family to comfort you. Not like that poor child at Crooksville—"

His mother gave a puzzled frown. "What child?"

Behind his mother's back Mrs. Patterson had frantically waved for Aunt Lieper's attention and put a silencing finger to her own lips. She was in the "secret," too. And how many others?

Aunt Lieper blandly continued, "Elisha's dear little Margaretta. He left her with the Turners to be educated while he's away. She has a piano and her pets, but they're small comfort to a stranger in a strange land. Such a romantic story—" The plume on her antique turban waved. "Giving up her family—disreputable people, perhaps, though *she* appears well bred—her fame as a rapper, her large acquaintance in New York society—not that it equals Philadelphia's—to be schooled in the country. Very brave of the young chit."

"A rapper!" His mother fastened on that essential bit.

"Margaretta, the pretty Fox. You must have heard he was constantly at their séances."

A look of confused suffering distorted his mother's lovely face. "I thought him interested in the knockings."

"Elisha?" Aunt Lieper laughed down the idea. "Nonsense. It was the girl."

"No. He would have told me." That was the severest blow for her. Not the scandalous situation, but Ly's keeping it from her. "No, it isn't true," she said in a steady voice, convincing herself.

Aunt Lieper folded her hands in her lap. "Yes, dear, it is. Elisha himself asked me to keep an eye on her."

Bessie asked fiercely, "He told you and none of us?"

Worse, John thought, he perjured himself to me.

"Apparently." Aunt Lieper's plume gave a satisfied swoop.

Bessie turned to them all, her glance searching for allies. "A party of us attended a séance once in fun and I saw her, a common little fraud who couldn't fool Elisha!"

"I suppose I'm no judge of breeding, Miss," Aunt Lieper said. "Better see her for yourself, Jeannie. Few girls judge a prettier girl fairly. Meeting you would make Maggie so happy."

"No." His mother rose to her feet and moving like a sleepwalker was halfway to the door when she slumped to her knees. Bessie ran to her, screaming, "Father! Father!"

His mother had not fainted. "Dizzy. Such a shock," she whispered. John got her to the sofa, where she lay, eyes closed.

"Jeannie, I thought you knew." Aunt Lieper bridled uneasily.

"No. Not this secret. Everything else—he confided in me. This one disastrous time Elisha did not tell me. Or I could have warned him—so young and innocent—for his years."

His father, hurrying in, bent over his wife. "Jeannie, dearest, what's wrong?"

She answered as if he had heard the whole tea-table talk. "Get him out of this—entanglement! Before it's public knowledge."

"Oh, everyone knows it," Aunt Lieper declared impatiently. "There have been worse stories about the Kanes. I've heard Tom joined the Mormon Church."

Tom's wife flushed. "He never told me so."

"Perhaps he doesn't confide in his nearest and dearest either."

The Judge, bewildered, asked, "Is Tom in another scrape?"

"Indeed he isn't!" Tom's wife got very red then.

His mother plucked the Judge's sleeve. "It's Elisha, dear. In terrible danger. You must help him."

"What in God's name have I been doing, Jeannie? Prodding the Congress, prodding the mechanics to get the rescue ships fitted out in time—"

"No, no. This is something else. A scheming girl has him in her clutches, my poor innocent!"

The Judge had looked at her, then at them all, as if they had gone stark crazy. "In the Arctic? How in blazes could you know?" Suddenly his face lighted. "He's been heard from! Why wasn't I told immediately? Eskimo wench or no, he's alive. That's all that matters."

Played by any other family, the scene would have been highly comic. Remembering it, John cringed. What other family would get itself into such a situation?

The women all began talking at once, but the Judge was used to order in his court, and obtained it; he was used to sorting out testimony, and did so. Facts in hand, he turned on Aunt Lieper.

"You can swear only to the fact that Elisha removed this young woman from her dubious profession and provided for her education."

"It was perfectly understood between us that his interest in the girl was romantic. And honorable."

"A woman always 'understands' a man's interest to be romantic. In this case the man is an idealistic fool, ready to risk his life at Lady Franklin's bequest, without your thinking his sympathy for that beldame romantic. This is just another piece of knight errantry."

"She has letters." Aunt Lieper sat back. "A casket of them."

"Now I know I'm at the play: here's a casket of letters." But the Judge for the first time had appeared worried. "In due time we'll see if Lish has written anything actionable. Meanwhile, all of you, if anyone mentions Ly's educating the little piece, say it was a sailor's largesse to a hapless child."

"John Kane"—the Judge's turbaned sister-in-law rose to her full height—"your son has made certain vows to Maggie Fox. If he lets his family talk him out of his honorable intentions, he'll never set foot in my house again, hero or no hero."

"Better a cad than a fool!" the Judge shouted.

Bessie broke down then. "The way you're talking when he may—be dead. I can't bear it!" She ran out of the room, her brother John on her heels, past bearing another word himself.

His mother had been too distraught to travel to New York when he had sailed for the Arctic, perhaps to his death. She always had loved Elisha best. His father—

Knowing the Judge's bump of curiosity, John had warned him: "Don't go out there to see her for yourself. It would aggravate the gossip if it were known. When we find Elisha, I'll get this—this unfortunate association formally broken off. In writing."

The Judge had cocked a wise eye. "Do what you can, boy. But remember Lish must be handled right. Skittish as a blood horse." His voice reflected affectionate admiration for his difficult son.

John, slumped over the *Arctic's* rail, watched the fog lift, only to be succeeded by a cold, drizzling rain. The rain stopped just as they entered another fog bank. He could barely make out the *Release* as a darker gray shape towing them steadily along, when out of the fog slid not the big *Baltic* but a little fishing smack, her captain angrily shaking his fist after the barque that had nearly run him down. From the bow of the *Arctic* John yelled at the wretch who swung around to see the propeller ship coming at him. He barely managed to sheer off, and, shaken by the experience, the frightened wight snatched up a long tin horn to blow shrill warning.

For a half-hour he could be heard tooting. Obviously he had not seen the towrope. For him, John felt a gloomy sympathy. He, too, was threatened by dangers seen and unseen. If the *Baltic* did not run them down and he lived to reach the Arctic, he might never escape it. Or if he did, and Elisha did not, Mama would forever blame *him*. But Elisha, saved, would not be entirely so in her eyes, unless he returned free of the little rapper. How could he talk Lish out of that wretched business if both of them were seasick on the voyage home? A miserable comedy that would be! He went below to bury his face in his pillow. There he lay, arguing endlessly with the distant Elisha. He could not truly picture Elisha dead, his perjuring brother had such life in him.

39. LEND AN EAR

THEY PUSHED well north without encountering one berg. "A late season," Lieutenant Simms, the *Arctic's* captain, complained. "Ice hasn't begun to break up yet, and we may never get into Smith's Sound."

For all the woes John had imagined, the total failure of the relief expedition had never occurred to him.

Next morning he was awakened by the roar of surf. But they were miles out to sea! He reached deck just as a convoy of icebergs glided by, the sea breaking around them as if they were a cluster of islands. He was not prepared for their size nor their fantastic forms. At one, shaped like a female figure posed for a dive, lewdly the men whistled and yowled.

Thereafter bergs were encountered most of their way along a coast bleaker, Watson Smith, the master, said, than Tierra del Fuego. "And I thought that the most barren spot on earth."

But aboard ship they were comfortable. The Navy did well by its officers. On the Fourth of July they "spliced the main brace" with champagne punch and dined on mock-turtle soup, stuffed turkey, roast ham, and strawberry tarts. "Not a bad *carte de diner* for Davis Straits," Simms said. John was recovered enough to enjoy the meal and a pipe afterward.

They were so far north that it was light around the clock, and too bright for fireworks. They had a notable salute for the Fourth all the same. A gale rose, and the driving wind wrecked a berg on shore. It smashed with the roar of a hundred cannon.

On the fifth they chugged into Disco harbor. Three days they stayed in that miserable hole, as guests of the Inspector General. Elisha always spoke of Mr. Orlik as if he were a personage, but he lived in less dignity and comfort than the lighthouse keeper on Nantucket south shoal.

Oh, he had a library with books in three languages, a billiard table, and the Broberg girls to entertain him. Those misses were Disco's chief charms in the eyes of the other officers. When Orlik brought the girls out to sing for them, Lovell, Hartstene's First Officer, and Lever, his clerk, became absolutely enamored of the little half-castes.

"Hear how quick they were to pick up a new tune and harmonize on it? The lovely Sophie was schooled in Denmark. That's where she learned French *and* English. Lever begged a picture of her that the Inspector took, but it fails to show her tiny feet. Personally, I'd prefer to beg a slipper." Lovell winked suggestively.

When they finally sailed, the girls kissed all the officers farewell. "They're so proper it was a great honor!" Lever said. John would have foregone the favor if he could, without looking too priggish. Those girls reminded him of the Fox Sisters.

From Disco they spent days in a nearly vain hunt for coal. Then Hartstene located some inferior stuff on Havoc Island. Loading it, their commander injured his arm. The steamer, John decided, was more bother than it was worth.

That Sunday both vessels were aroused by the cry, "Ships on the port bow!" There were two. Seeing the Navy pair, they tacked toward them. Simms said, "They have news! News of your brother."

The ships came on slowly. While still three miles off, their captains, impatient with the light and baffling winds, each lowered a boat.

"They must have news!" Simms said. "Dr. Kane may even be aboard. You'd better join the *Release*. Kane will go direct to our flagship."

On board the barque, Hartstene was almost cordial. "Our search may come to a happy end before it starts."

John nodded absently. He was trying to frame his greeting for Elisha; warm yet dignified, with no hint of the trouble at home for strange ears to catch.

Standing at the rail or on the spars, officers and crew waited for the small boats to pull near. When the first was close enough, a distinct Scots voice called, "Ahoy! We be the *Lord Gambier* out of Kircaldy, Simpson, captain. Any news, lads?"

"United States Navy barque, *Release,* Hartstene commanding. Have you word of Dr. Kane?"

"Who, now?"

"Kaa-ne! American explorer in search of Franklin."

Before an answer was given the boat's men began rowing. At the foot of the barque's ladder they swung round while the whaling captain lifted a bony Scots face to Hartstene. "No, Captain, nae word of auld Sir John. My brother and me come to look at a Christian face forby and news of the Crimea. Hae we beat them, lads?"

His brother hailed from the second boat. "*Messenger* out of Dundee, J. Simpson, captain."

For some minutes the disappointed Americans failed to acknowledge his hail. So listless a reception in polar waters startled him until he came aboard and it was explained. Then both brothers were sympathetic, but could give little encouragement.

"Captain, ye canna gae into Smith's Sound," the elder argued earnestly. "The ice in Melville Bay is turning back every whaler in de-spair, and Smith's is beyond Melville as ye ken."

"A Scot isn't driven off lightly, but we gie it up," his brother added.

"You're your own men." Hartstene's face was stiff with worry. "We sail under orders to search Smith's Sound."

"Not the Admiralty itself would be so onreasonable as to order ye where the ice wilna gie ye room!"

But Hartstene could hardly abandon the search on the word of two Scots whalers. He pushed on to the Upernavik whose inhabitants lived in burrows John took for dog kennels. There they had a difficult scene with Mrs. Petersen, the wife of Elisha's interpreter. When she saw ships flying the American flag she believed her husband was at last returning, and met them on shore, surrounded by all her children. Her only boy she pushed forward. "Let him see his fader! Paul, go to Papa."

Learning they came not from the Pole but Disco, she moaned in grief, and young Paul said, "Papa is dead, I think. Mama says this a month. Papa is dead, or he comes home now."

"The vorse ice in forty years," Mrs. Petersen denounced it bitterly. "And my Carl Christian is dead in it because the little American captain talks him to go!"

Hartstene attended only her remark about the ice. With Lever and John he went up to view it from the highest hill. As far as the eye could see with a good Chevalier glass stretched a prairie of ice, sparsely veined with black water.

"Well, how do you like the look of Melville, gentlemen? And Smith's Sound is beyond that."

"Just as the whalers said, you can't get to it," John said.

"Our orders are for Smith's Sound." Concisely he explained the various techniques of ice navigation. "If we are beset, as Kane probably was, I have this day requested the Navy Department not to send an expedition after *us.*"

With prideful step Hartstene marched down the hill, his arm in its sling as straight across his coat as if posed with a level. Lever could keep pace with him, but John on short legs had to hurry. You'd think it was his fault Elisha was in trouble, due to his old foolhardiness.

That night, with other officers from the *Arctic,* John was invited to dinner on board the *Release,* a farewell dinner to the civilized world, before they entered the ice. Lovell, Hartstene's First, spent most of the meal reminiscing about Elisha, with whom he had sailed on the First Grinnell Expedition. John, having just written his dear family perhaps the last letter they would ever receive from him, listened resentfully.

Over the soup Surgeon Laws complained of the cold.

"Where we're going, it's so cold you'll find no bugs in your blanket, nits in your hair, nor maggots in the cheese," Lovell said. "So the cold has compensations, but not the Arctic night. That's unrelieved hell. Worse, when you spend it as we did that first trip, with our two ships stuck in a blasted island of ice riding all over the polar seas."

"How big was your island?" Midshipman Phyffe asked.

"Dr. Kane measured it at three miles long by three wide. When the floe started moving, thank God it was light again, so we could at least see where we were being carried. Hard on Captain De Haven, our situation." He smiled at Hartstene. "You know him. Determined man. He was down with scurvy and it didn't help his state any to have no say where his ships went."

"Aggravating," Hartstene agreed.

"He'd have died of it, I do think, except for Dr. Kane. Others, too. But Kane drove us out on the ice, making us stir our stumps and keep alive. Made us run races, hunt bear and seal, though we shot precious little. Seals are sly. Bears will take a bullet and keep going. My first got away. The second, an enormous brute, Kane and I shot at so simultaneously we had to weigh the ball when we stripped the carcass."

"Whose was he?" Phyffe asked.

"It was Kane's ball. Took the skin home, I think."

"Stuffed, that bear is in the Academy of Natural Science at Philadelphia," John acknowledged. Everything Lish did became a public show in the end.

"Killed our second bear, too, with an old Navy flintlock that hung fire half the time. I'll wager he didn't take Navy issue guns this voyage." He looked at John.

"Borrowed some Sharpe's rifles and a couple of Marstons."

Hartstene said a little sharply, "A Navy expedition doesn't borrow, so you gentlemen will have to settle for smoothbores."

Lovell politely changed the subject. "Never forget the time he had me rig up a swing."

"A swing?" Hartstene thought he hadn't heard aright.

"Hung it on the main studding sail boom. Cold work, pumping a swing near the Pole, but first-rate exercise. Pulls on every muscle you own. Original mind, Kane's."

"Equal to anything, wasn't he?" Phyffe sounded reverent.

Lovell frowned. "No. He hated the dark months. Really suffered from them. The day the sun was due to return, the Doctor was so wrought up he went off alone to view the sunrise.

"Said to me when he came back, 'Never again will I forswear the light of day, Lovell. Not until the grave sod or the ice covers me.' I believed him. For a while." Lovell ate energetically.

"What changed your mind?" Laws led him on.

Lovell laid down his knife. "It was the day he went off on one of his long walks with old Blinn at his heels."

"Not the Blinn in my crew?" Simms asked, astonished. "Phlegmatic old Dutchman?"

"Noticed he was along." Lovell smiled. "Didn't surprise me he had volunteered. Kane fascinated him, just as he did our other wooden Indians, Brooks and Morton. They used to follow Kane around, too. Still with him, wherever he is, and Blinn's with us." Then Lovell added with a half-embarrassed laugh, "So am I."

"What happened on that walk with Blinn?" Simms covered an over-long pause.

"Peculiar light that day. The sun, low on the horizon, cast a purplish glow. Around our floe there was open water, of course, so he walked to a point where a high block of ice thrust out like a glass spearhead over the water. Sat there all day sketching the astonishing life you find in polar seas. Showed me his drawings."

"Which lot were they out of the hundreds I've seen?" And what was so remarkable about them, John wanted to ask.

"Sketches of seals, breast high, treading water with their horizontal tails; of narwhals sporting like porpoises, their spiraled horns clashing like the lances of jousting knights. At rest, their horns stood up out of the water like the masts of sunken ships. I remember there was a lovely sketch of a white whale blowing purple sprays into the sunshine. Kane and I were on the late watch that night, and heard a white whale sing as he swam back and forth, deep under our ship and the floe, too."

"Cetaceans have no voice," John said flatly.

Simms raised his eyebrows at his surgeon's rudeness, but Lovell only smiled.

"So you scientists say. I only know what I heard over and over. A peculiar note between a whistle and a yodel. Blinn allowed it sounded like a jew's-harp. Your brother"—his eyes on John's face seemed to be trying to trace a resemblance—"hung over the side, listening. I knew then he'd return to the Arctic. He's lived through two winters—"

"We hope and trust," Hartstene said.

"If he isn't rescued, he faces a third. I don't think he'd survive it. That's why I asked for this duty." He pushed his plate away. "With your permission, sir—"

Hartstene nodded, and Lovell left.

"A very sound man," Hartstene said, almost defensively. "The best British captains catch the Arctic fever."

The region had no charms for John. He found it both monotonous and, after their first nip, terrifying. He and Watson Smith were walking the deck when they heard a noise like the humming of bees. "What the devil?" They stared at the empty ice plain.

The hum rose to a howl, followed by a crashing and roaring

quite supernatural, since it seemed to have no cause. Then they saw the ice was closing on their little steamer. She creaked and groaned as the vise shut tighter and tighter. The pressure became so fierce that the pitch between the planking was squeezed out like mud through a child's fingers. A companionway door swung on its hinges, and when John tried to close it, it would not shut. Its very framework was pushed askew.

"She's going, isn't she?" he screamed.

At that instant the steamer sprang right out of the water to rest on the ice. John was thrown to the deck and lay stunned. He never knew when the reverse action of the tides let her down into the lead again. Smith thought Mr. Kane's fright very funny, particularly after the nips became commonplace.

By grinding labor the ships crawled on, every man taking his turn at the capstan or rue raddy. John's muscles throbbed and his very bones ached, but Lieutenant Simms thought he scamped.

"Put your shoulder into it, Mr. Kane!" Lieutenant Simms yelled at him once, when John was near collapse. Only the steamer's coming into an open lead which gave her a clear run for miles saved him that time. He detested Simms.

The *Arctic* traveled in the van now, ready to butt a passage. Hartstene stayed aboard her, perched in the crow's-nest, deciding when to ram. At his command she would back, build up a head of steam, and then rush forward, smacking the ice hard while Hartstene's lofty tub yawed wildly.

One stretch he stayed up there thirty-six hours, subsisting on the soup hoisted to him. When he came down, he was so stiff that he fell on the companionway and sprained his ankle.

John, acting as ship's surgeon for once, said, "Better stay off that, sir."

Hartstene only looked at him. Next morning he had himself hoisted in a rope sling as his soup had been the day before.

At last they steamed out of the Great Pack into open water, the *Release* in tow, officers and men jubilant. Simms recklessly sent the *Arctic* coasting in so close they almost grounded. "Can't miss a cairn."

It was Hartstene, however, who spied the first "monument," rude stones piled atop a rocky eminence. The landing party, Lovell in command, included John. The sailors, excited, rowed with a will, and ashore, ran up to the cairn. Quickly dismantled, it contained—

John's fists clenched at the meaningless array. A tale told by an idiot. Elisha could not have left this, but there was the letter "K." Perhaps two Arctic winters had overthrown a mind already delicately balanced. Perhaps his infatuation for the little rapper had been not a fault but a symptom. Genius was close to madness and everyone thought Elisha a genius.

Lovell squatted to study the items: Four lucifer matches, two laid crosswise, two pointing north; a Sharpe's rifle bullet; and a specimen bottle with "K" cut in its cork, wrapped in cotton flannel. In the bottle, wrapped in a smaller piece of flannel covered with a folded cartridge paper, lay a dead mosquito. Lovell looked at the paper. "Writing on it." He handed it to John.

In coarse characters was written, "Dr. Kane—'53."

"That's not Elisha's writing."

"Of course not! He never set this up. D'you think your brother's crazy? This is sailor's horseplay. Whoever did it had better left it undone. Misleads us."

Hartstene, insisting they had not uncovered everything, had himself rowed ashore. Despite his bad ankle, he climbed to the cairn. Sailors with pickaxes dug up for him the spot where it stood. They found nothing, nor did the search parties he ordered out.

Disappointed, the ships pushed north. Hartstene was not made happier when the lookout called early next morning, "Ice ahead."

It lay solidly athwart Smith's Sound. "That"—he shook his fist at it—"obviously prevented your brother's bringing the *Advance* out, just as it prevents our going in. It's impenetrable."

"Yes, sir."

"Kane must by now have abandoned ship and started southward. We can only look for him on Beechy. If he's not there—" He turned a challenging eye on John. "That's the best I can do, orders or no orders."

"No one could expect more," John said. This, then, was the end. The relief expedition had failed.

"Lieutenant Simms, we'll run to the south and have a fair wind for it. Bank your fires to save coal. The barque will tow you."

The *Arctic's* fires were hardly banked when the wind failed. Between capes they took for Alexander and Hatherton both ships lay becalmed in open water.

In the silence of the windless, late afternoon the watch on the *Arctic's* fo'c'sle heard a howl on shore. A wolf? No wolves up here, the lieutenant said, and a bear didn't make that kind of noise, did it? He ran to Watson Smith.

"Heard something queerlike. Will you listen, sir? There it goes again!"

Smith, who had a musical ear, heard a long-drawn D flat, with a fall dying upon A. There it came again, swelled by a slight puff of wind. It was clearly an English or American halloo.

40. HAIL AND FAREWELL

WHILE Watson Smith yelled across to the *Release,* the *Arctic's* boat, already manned by volunteers, hit the water. They rowed over to get Hartstene, who took the tiller. As they swung toward the point whence the sounds had come, there was no fresh hail.

"Lie on your oars."

They listened, hardly breathing.

"Ha-a-loo!" It came again.

The men cheered wildly, throwing their caps in the air. "We've found them! We've found them!"

Even Hartstene appeared moved that they had, at the very instant of turning back, achieved their goal. John's own eyes misted over, and, his resentment thawed, he wanted only to put his arms around Elisha and welcome him back to life.

"There they are!"

Silhouetted against a wall of white, two black figures danced and hugged each other. Hartstene started to raise his glass.

"Doctor"—it was the first time he had so addressed the *Arctic's* surgeon—"you are even more interested here than I." He handed the Chevalier glass to John.

His hand unsteady, John had trouble adjusting it. The instant he had a sight on them, one of the men whirled in an exuberant somersault while the other leaped up and down in the peculiar "jump" with which Eskimos showed pleasure. Had Elisha's men been here so long they had adopted Eskimo ways? Or were the men actually Eskimos? Their faces looked dark and Mongolian.

"Captain"—he had to clear his throat to get the disappointing words out—"they appear to be Eskimos."

The oars faltered as if a cannon ball had struck the boat, the men stock-still while Hartstene took a view. "I'm afraid you're right." Then in a hearty tone, "But let's talk to them. They wouldn't be so bold if they had never seen a ship before."

Thus encouraged, the sailors rowed pretty well again. They no sooner pulled onto the shore than the Eskimos bounded down, and leaping right into the boat, made themselves comfortable. Babbling brutish sounds, they fingered everything, smelling and tasting handkerchiefs and tobacco pouches. They were the filthiest, most repellent humans John had ever seen.

They began to rock backward and forward, looking hard at Hartstene.

"They seem to want us to row on."

Now the savages pointed inland. When Hartstene made signs indicating they should pilot the boat, they nodded and laughed. "Eiss! Eiss!" That sibilance was the way southern Eskimos also said "yes."

"There's no doubt they've been with white men." Hartstene was now convinced.

Along a narrow channel between the ice and the shore their skin-clad pilots directed them. Rounding a grim crag, they found themselves in an enchanted bay. No ice intruded here. Sheltered by high cliffs, the water lay smooth and clear as a mirror the wind had never breathed upon. The cliffs themselves were variegated in color and covered with moss. Blue sky and mossy cliffs were reflected in the bay's glassy surface while in the watery stillness far below weird plantations of seaweed waved gently over the great white pebbles that paved the bay floor. Overhead, auks flew, their cries like the whirr of locusts.

They pulled up on a pebbled beach, crossed by a rivulet of fresh water. Their guides followed this stream to a meadow encircling a hidden lake. In the soft and pale green grass, poppies and other wild flowers made patterns in the carpet.

"I would never have believed it," Hartstene said softly, as if by speaking overloud he might wake them from this dream.

For three miles they followed the lake's edge to its source: a pinnacled glacier from whose silver rim a cataract fell two hundred feet in an unbroken sheet of water. At the glacier's foot, in disgusting contrast to all this beauty, stood seven small tents, black with crusted grease and dirt. Through the flaps they saw naked babies and puppies lying together on piles of birdskins. A vat for tanning skins, heaps of dead birds, and piles of putrid seal combined in a stench like a blow in the face. On a green mound beside this "village" twoscore of dirty, hideous creatures waited.

With one voice they cried, "Hullo! Hullo!" Then, in measured accents, "Doc-to Kay-en."

Startled, the white men turned bewilderedly toward "Docto Kayen's" brother.

John said, "He must be here or near here!" He ran toward the natives, yelling as if they were deaf, "Is Dr. Kane here?"

"Eiss!" They laughed uproariously, and pointing straight at him, said again, "Doc-to Ka-yen."

Not Elisha, but the world was mad. Or did he so resemble his lost brother the creatures recognized him? But now they pointed at each American in turn, chanting, "Doc-to Ka-yen, Doc-to Ka-yen—"

Hartstene brought returning sense. "They seem to call all white men 'Dr. Kane.' So they know him and may know where he is."

"He could be lying sick in one of those tents, and with their shrieking, we wouldn't hear him call!"

The men plunged toward the tents, but only found more litters of babies and pups and an Eskimo woman, naked to the waist, to whom Midshipman Phyffe said, red-faced, "Beg pardon, ma'am."

Botsford, one of the seamen, pointed out to Hartstene. "Sir, them tents ain't skins, they're canvas, there's tin cups aplenty around, and one of the pups is bedded on a india-rubber coat."

The sailor was right. "Sharp of you, Botsford."

Among the Eskimos now crowding round one big fellow wore a Guernsey shirt. "Docto Kayen geef," he declared proudly.

The Americans really turned the place out then, finding all manner of objects alien to these savages. Whenever they touched such an article and asked, "Dr. Kane?" the Eskimos said, "Eiss!" To a bone-handled spear or anything of obvious Eskimo origin, they said "Nahmee." "Means 'no,' apparently," Hartstene said.

Nothing found bore any personal marks, however. Then the half-naked woman emerged from her tent to display to Midshipman Phyffe a large white shirt.

"Why don't she put it on?" he asked plaintively.

"Let me see that!" Hartstene examined it carefully. "A big man's shirt and fine linen. Ah!" He showed where it was embroidered at the neck in fancy stitching, "H. B."

"Henry Brooks!"

"Minorcan work. Bought some for my missus once," Botsford identified it.

"Dr. Kane said Brooks's wife was a native of Port Mahon," John remembered. Elisha had seemed pleased at the stolid Brooks having so exotic a wife, his own tastes being similar! "But where are they?"

They could get no sense out of the brutes, though Hartstene persisted so long that they were late returning. Lovell, alarmed, had organized an armed party to rescue them. Their news so excited him, he wanted to set right off, though it was nearly midnight. "I know a little of the lingo, sir. Let me try."

His try was postponed until morning. The Eskimo pair again waited ashore. "Hullo! Docto Kayen, *naligak.*" Their grins were wide.

"*Naligak* means chief," Lovell explained. "They think we are all Kane's men. In the village, let me pick a bright one to talk to apart from the others. With them all jabbering, we'll never learn anything." It sounded feasible.

At the tents they were saluted royally. A cocky young fellow came up to announce, "Me My-ouk." After one glance at him Lovell led him away.

"You come along," he told John. "You can draw, can't you? Your brother could draw anything."

"A little." They all assumed that he possessed Elisha's every talent and blamed him if he fell short. When they were settled by the lake, he sketched a hermaphrodite brig in Lovell's notebook.

"Docto Kayen," My-ouk said instantly, and pointed north.

John reversed the drawing so that the brig was headed south.

My-ouk shook his head. "Nahmee." He jabbed north again.

"Brig's still north of here, that's clear," Lovell said. "Now draw your brother with a beard. He'd grow one up here."

My-ouk watched him. "Docto Kayen," he said before John was done. But when Lovell pointed to the picture and then north, the boy shook his head.

He began to rock in the Eskimo's gesture for rowing, at the same time nodding emphatically southward.

Lovell gripped John's shoulder. "They have abandoned ship and taken to the boats. Heading for Beechy. Draw several boats."

John hastily sketched a small fleet of rowboats. My-ouk examined them critically. Finally he grabbed the pencil, altering the sterns of two, making them pointed, and then held up two fingers.

"Two whaleboats! Let's make sure of that. Draw two."

Over these My-ouk displayed extravagant pleasure, laughing and nodding and pointing south, only to throw the Americans into confusion by immediately squatting on the ground to give a vivid imitation of a man driving a dog team. "Hup-hup-hup!"

"What the hell does that mean?"

Seeing their puzzlement, My-ouk re-enacted the whole performance. So John drew a dog team. "Eiss! Eiss!"

"Now, see here," Lovell said as if the young savage understood every word, "you've got it turned around. When Kane used a dog team, it was on his searches to the north. Maybe he used whaleboats, too, leaving the brig to the south. That's it, boy."

My-ouk listened bright-eyed but uncomprehending. So Lovell, using the drawings, indicated the brig had been left to the south while the dog team and the whaleboats went north. This threw My-ouk into a rage of frustration.

"Nahmee!" he yelled, and put his hands to his ears to shut out such lies. Abruptly, he ran to the water and picking up two large white stones, laid these on the ground at their feet. Snatching Lovell's clay pipe, he set it between them.

"Vomiak sooak, Docto Kayen." He pointed to the pipe.

"Dr. Kane's big ship," Lovell translated, watching.

Graphically My-ouk pressed the two flat stones together until the pipe shattered. Then he looked intently into their faces.

"That does it," Lovell said. "The *Advance* was nipped. Somewhere north of here."

My-ouk was now busily rowing and driving a dog team by turns, always, whatever he pantomimed, southward.

"For some reason, Kane used a dog team, too, after they left the *Advance,* that is plain. Ask how many men."

John did not draw enough matchstick men to satisfy My-ouk. He demanded three more. When there were eighteen he said, "Eiss."

"They're all alive!" John said. "Seventeen in the crew and Elisha makes eighteen."

But Lovell was frowning. "Plus the interpreter, Petersen, and an Eskimo hunter Kane signed on. Draw two more."

My-ouk rejected them. He would accept only eighteen.

"Two gone," Lovell said thoughtfully. Which two? If every white man was "Docto Kayen," Dr. Kane himself need not be one of the survivors. Lovell leaned over to point to the first figure in the row of matchstick men. *"Naligak?"*

"Eiss."

"I think that means Kane is leading the party. Hope to God it does. How long since they left?"

He and John tried to think how to picture the passage of time to this child of nature. "Eats when he's hungry and sleeps when he's tired, and does nothing by the clock or the calendar."

So Lovell tried pantomime. Pointing to the sun, he traced its path across the sky to the west. "Damn sun doesn't sink for long in this unnatural land," he muttered as he settled himself on the ground and pretended to sleep. Rising, he stretched elaborately, and pointing to the east, started the sun on another day.

My-ouk, nodding, ran to the water where he pretended to wash his face, never letting a drop touch his greasily shining countenance. He did this solemnly as a religious rite. "Docto Kayens."

"God knows they're the only ones would wash."

That ritual proved little help. The most they could extract from My-ouk was the information that the Kayens had spent some time at the village. None of the older men could help either. Then, a native poked Lovell's arm. The fellow clutched his stomach as if in agony.

"Docto Kayen, *angekok,*" the crowd yelled, nodding,

John stared at them, his face tight. "Elisha was ill. Does that word mean 'dead'?"

"Don't know what it means."

"He should never have gone. His heart was bound to give out under strain."

"You don't know it was the Doctor! Don't inflict your ideas on Hartstene. We were ordered to find Kane."

When Hartstene made a second visit to the village, that bit of acting was fortunately not repeated. "South they say Kane's boats were headed, but how long did he stay on that tack?" With My-ouk, John, and Lovell, he stood on a promontory overlooking the bay. A headland far to the south cut off the view. "Below there, they may have swung west for Beechy, and the Eskimos here would never know."

My-ouk suddenly spoke to the captain. "My-ouk, me," he said, pointing to himself. Then he began to pantomime a sad farewell, waving and waving after the departing Kayens, weeping real tears as he did so. "Gone!" he said distinctly.

41. SEA CHANGE

AT MESS Hartstene discussed their course with the officers of both vessels. "If Kane's party continued south, they're either lost in Melville Bay or safe at Upernavik and, either way, beyond help from us. If, however, they went, as Kane planned in an emergency, to Beechy, ignorant of Belcher's abandoning his fleet in Lancaster Sound, they may be starving."

"They may not," Lovell said. "How d'you think Belcher's captains took all their supplies off? No room in the store ships that had to carry five crews to England. Be damned funny if Kane worked one of the English vessels loose and sailed her home."

How could Lovell talk so absurdly when he had seen that Eskimo pantomime Elisha's sad departure?

"A delightful daydream, Mr. Lovell," Hartstene said, "but we may find Lancaster as tight as Smith's Sound. We must try for Beechy, even so."

Through fog and drizzle, ice and sleet, they bent course for Lancaster. The ice there was vastly heavier than in Melville, and two hundred miles from Beechy the floes closed on both ships. They were held like flies in amber. With her power built up until John thought she would burst, the *Arctic* could not break loose. Black smoke pouring from her funnel only dirtied her consort's sails. He thought how helpless, how fragile and exposed, Elisha's whaleboat would be, caught this way.

Lovell tramped cheerfully across on the ice. He called up to John brooding at the bow, "A gale will blow us loose soon. Don't take it so hard!"

But they were held there until a peculiar numbness began to grip John as firmly as the floes the steamer. He moved through a grayness permeated with the conviction that he would never escape this spot, as Elisha, too, had failed to escape. The very look on his face began to annoy Simms.

When a gale finally justified Lovell's optimism, John was fathoms deep in sleep. He awoke to an unbelievable fury of movement: the ships fairly flying as they scudded toward Cape Isabella, jostled by uproarious ice plunging along in company.

Watson Smith bellowed to him on deck, "Kane said he'd leave a cairn on Isabella. Now we may really find out something."

But the ice would not allow it. Traveling faster than the ships, it circled ahead to shut them off from that cape. It made them detour perforce into Possession Bay and from there into Pond's Bay in a weary and fruitless search. In vain they fired guns, burned blue lights, sent up rockets. Nothing answered.

When they emerged to try the east coast of Baffin's Bay, the ice had vanished and they had an eight-knot breeze.

"Damnedest waters," Simms said, but he grinned. "We're reckoned two hundred miles from Upernavik and south of the Great Pack. Hartstene will put in there to inquire. Looks like clear sailing."

Within a day, wind and water stilled. It was the ice again, lying in wait. They were not yet south of the Pack but had only been traveling across a great bay in that continent of ice. To circumvent it, they must push still farther south, as Hartstene promptly signaled to Simms.

Again and again the ice deceived them, luring them into one cul-de-sac after another.

They at last reached open water, Simms was sure. He caught a doubting sneer on John's face and flushed. "Take my glass, Mr. Kane. Can you see any ice to the south? Anything like the blink Mr. Lovell described? Can you?"

"No," John said, pushing the glass back at the lieutenant. "We never can. But it's only waiting to close on us, and we stupidly fall into the trap. Every time."

"Take the glass and go to the crow's-nest, Mr. Kane," Simms ordered, "and tell us the instant you see ice."

"I can't climb well enough. I'm no sailor, sir," John protested in a tight voice.

"You're aboard ship, Mr. Kane, and I am ordering you to the crow's-nest." Simms's face set.

Behind him, Watson Smith suppressed a smile, and old Blinn

grinned like the village idiot. His acute dislike of them all enabled John to crawl to that sickening height.

There he stayed, half-frozen, straining to see, the strange light making moving water gray-white as ice, the calm making the surface of the water heavy and sluggish as ice, until finally the floes were on them almost before he detected them. He yelled warning and the *Arctic* quickly put about, the *Release* also tacking hurriedly, but not fast enough. The ice closed with a deadly grip, carrying them along with it exactly as the floe had De Haven's expedition in '51.

The jibes of his fellows grew more insufferable as they drifted. It was Harmon Newell, their engineer, whom John had previously admired, who made the unpardonable observation. "It's my opinion, Mr. Kane," he said thoughtfully, "that ever since Lancaster Sound you've wanted to go south and keep going, away from the ice toward home, whether we find your brother or not." He nodded amiably at the ship's surgeon. "Scared, aren't you?"

Not for himself, but for Elisha. All the more terrified because he had wished Elisha dead! Without a word John went over the side to tramp the ice to the *Release.*

"Captain Hartstene, I must ask to be transferred from the *Arctic.* I find it impossible to get along with her officers."

Hartstene let out an explosive sigh. "Mr. Kane, haven't I had enough difficulties in this effort to relieve your brother?"

"I cannot go back. Not even to get my gear." John stood there, not seeing the Captain, not noticing his nod to Lovell.

"You have been under a strain, I appreciate," Hartstene said, frowning. "Surgeon Laws will go in your place."

Hartstene's luck proved better than De Haven's. For a second time a gale struck loose their shackles, though it nearly wrecked the *Release* doing it.

"Blew in the right direction," Lovell said. "We're handy to Lievely for repairs. May get news there of Kane."

At Lievely the Broberg sisters waited. That was why Lovell, Lever, and company trod the deck with a springy step.

The lookout in the crow's-nest could see over the ugly rocks that hid the port. "Brig in the harbor," he yelled.

"Danish supply ship." Hartstene nodded.

When they had sailed around the obstructing rocks, they saw her plain. "She's Danish." On they went at a good clip before a favoring wind. "She's run up an American flag!"

Hartstene had seen it. "She recognizes us for Americans and is saluting us. Break out a Danish flag, Mr. Lovell."

"She's hoisting another flag, sir," the lookout yelled.

Hartstene used his glass. He sucked in his breath. "Mr. Kane, will you take a look?"

At first John saw only a fluttering rag. Then the wind straightened it and he knew that swallowtail pennant! "It's Mr. Grinnell's personal flag, sir. It went out with the *Advance*." They all, men and officers, stood intent. "What does it mean?"

Hartstene had no ready answer. "Dr. Kane may have brought it in, or," that tense young man might as well be prepared, "or Eskimos who discovered the remains of his party."

Two boats suddenly pulled out from the Danish brig.

"Who are they?"

Again silence ruled the deck as everyone studied the rowers. Finally Botsford said, "Those are Yankees, sir. No Danes ever feathered their oars like that."

The sailors' yells were deafening, as John tried vainly to identify the men in the boats. All were so heavily bearded and weather-beaten! Garbed in such wild costumes! Then a stocky little man in a red flannel shirt stood up in the stern of the first boat. The way his spyglass was slung around his neck was characteristic.

"Elisha!" John cried so loud and high that the word rasped his throat.

Lovell pointed to a big hulking figure. "Must be Brooks!" He kept saying, "Can you count them? Are they all there? I swear to God I can't count!"

When the first boat pulled to the side of the *Release,* Elisha Kane looked straight up into his brother's face. "John! You're not really there! You're only another trick of the polar light." Every word came clear and distinct, and his happy laugh was a shock.

John could only reach toward his brother, an Elisha unfamiliar in almost every respect. Heavier, his skin leathery, his beard coarse and iron gray; years older but with the familiar wild glitter in his eyes. "Alive," John whispered.

Alive and a stranger. Did the Arctic do this to every man? Would he himself appear as alien to his family? He must find another known face, Jeff Baker's. Jeff was near his age, and Jeff's face would tell him how much his own had changed. He could discover no one who even resembled Jeff.

Elisha, smiling, saluted Hartstene. "I am honored, sir, to have you come to my relief. Mr. Orlik said you were in the neighborhood."

"You seem to have done remarkably well without us."

"We came thirteen hundred miles in open boats," Kane said.

"Good God!" That was Mr. Lovell.

Elisha's face lighted. "Lovell! You, too. Yes, it was with the help of a kindly God. But my Second"—he turned toward the heavy-set fellow behind him—"said when you arrived, 'All our trouble for nothing!' May I come aboard, Captain?"

"We are rude from excitement," Hartstene said.

The crew at no one's order ran to the guns. The harbor echoed with the roar. Now the *Arctic* was firing, too, its crew yelling madly. Elisha had tears in his eyes when he stepped on deck.

He shook Hartstene's hand, embraced Lovell, waved to every man of them, before he took John by the shoulders. "Is everyone well at home?"

Only now he asked. John nodded, but muttered, "Mother's upset. She's been disturbed by rumors. Not of your death."

Elisha's hands fell away. "So *you* were sent." His face expressionless, he turned back to Lovell. John's contorted face sobered some of the more boisterous. They nodded to one another in sympathetic understanding, when they understood nothing! However was he to tell the grim, assured adventurer Elisha had become that he must, for Mother's sake, give up that wretched girl? However?

At Anchor

42. THE RETURN OF DR. KANE

EARLY THE MORNING OF OCTOBER 11 THE STEAMER "UNION," OUT of Havre, reached New York with news that sent the *Herald* reporter running for a cab. She had spoken the Kane Relief Expedition and Dr. Kane and all his party were aboard. "Off Sandy Hook by now. In late this afternoon," the *Union's* captain calculated.

On his knee in the rattling vehicle the reporter wrote: "The intrepid young hero for whom all have lately entertained the gloomiest apprehensions is safe!"

A messenger from the wharf ran all the way to Henry Grinnell's house on Bond Street. He was immediately dispatched to the telegraph office with word for Dr. Kane's family in Philadelphia. Only when he was taking his own sweet time returning to the wharf did the middle-aged Mercury give passing cronies the tidings.

"Kane's found. 'sGod's truth. *Union* spoke him. Just told Henry Grinnell myself." He flashed a greenback and they were convinced.

In a Cherry Hill dive sailors off the *Union* also told the tale. Thereafter the news spread like scandal in a country town.

In the saloons that hadn't seen a sailor, topers within the hour were slapping down coins for another round, "To the safe return of Dr. Kane!" Omnibus drivers going up Broadway yelled to omnibus drivers going down. Aboard those lumbering stages quite genteel ladies talked to perfect strangers about "that heroic young man!" In the shops the richest merchants, their dignity forgotten, chatted of Dr. Kane with their very clerks. In the oyster houses, the bowling saloons, on the Exchange, they abandoned the Malakoff and forgot Sebastopol to tell of Kane's rescue.

By the time the newspapers all had extras out, the streets were thronged with people on their way to the Battery for a glimpse of the adventurers. Only the pigs rooting in the gutter by City Hall Park remained indifferent.

Near dusk the crowd at the Battery heard the Navy Yard guns boom in salute. The two ships came into view. "There they are! Dr. Kane! Kane! Kane!" The mob yelled for him to show himself like a star performer, but who could tell if he did or didn't? "Was that him in the bow of the steamer or by the rail on the barque?"

Maggie heard early of Dr. Kane's return. Dr. Bayard, picking up the news on his rounds, had hurried to Mrs. Walter's.

"Take me to the Battery, Dr. Bayard. Dear Dr. Bayard, just let me see him. He's alive! Elisha's alive!"

"No, no, no." Ellen Walter shook her head at Dr. Bayard. "You must be calm and serene, Maggie dearest, when he comes. At the Battery, you might break down publicly."

"Let me go, Ellen! I promise not to get excited."

"A promise no mortal could keep. You've waited this long, you can wait until Dr. Kane calls here."

"Wait!" Maggie made it a word to loathe, but she obeyed.

To pass the hours she dressed with tedious care. Never had Ellen seen her hair so neat. In a blue gown, worn with a hoop-skirt, she was graceful as a bellflower in the breeze. But hoops would be strange to Dr. Kane. The fashion had come in since he sailed, and some men professed to find such an expanse of skirt ridiculous.

"Perhaps I shouldn't wear my hoops, Ellen."

"Nonsense. He'll see a dozen before he reaches here. But that lace is shabby."

Maggie put up a protective hand. "He gave it to me."

"Then you must wear it. You must also eat. It may be very late when he arrives. Officials, journalists, well-wishers—"

"And all his family. I know, Ellen." Maggie tried a bite or two and then laid down her fork. "But how can I eat when I can't swallow?" She gave a tremulous sigh and began to laugh wildly.

"No hysterics. Not that now. Sip your tea."

Like an automaton she sipped. Like an automaton she sat in the parlor waiting, hands folded in her lap, her head turning jerkily when Ellen spoke, or when a carriage rattled by. Still they waited. The room was growing dusky, though it was light enough outside. "I'll light a lamp," Ellen said, and Maggie's eyes in its glow were dark and wide.

She touched a fold of her blue silk. "It spreads around me like the sea around Italy. Where Dr. Kane said we're going on our honeymoon."

"That's a rare pretty thought." Just then they heard the salute guns. "There now," Ellen Walter said, "he's come."

At seven that evening, pursued by a score of reporters, Dr. Kane made a clear run to the Astor House, but was caught before he could reach a private room. A circle of eager questioners he answered as frankly as he could. "Navy regulations, however—"

"The rules of the service to which Dr. Kane is so brilliant an ornament forbid making official reports except to the Secretary of the Navy," the *Herald* reporter wrote. Truth was Henry Grinnell had to hear it first.

Odd how Kane stood out in the crowd around him. It wasn't his red shirt. Short as he was he loomed, somehow. He's aged, the reporter noted. Under that glazed leather cap Kane's hair was iron gray and he was bronzed and stocky. Years older and twice the man he had been. Hardly know him except for his eyes, bright as those of the bird he held. It looked like a silver sea gull.

"Entirely domesticated." Kane stroked its plumage. Yes, he had brought back another pet, their only surviving husky.

"What's his name?"

"Tood-la."

Most of the reporters wrote, "Toodles."

"What happened to the others?"

"We were reduced to the necessity of eating them." Kane's teeth flashed in a smile. Apparently he hadn't yet been told to what necessity Franklin's men had been reduced. "The gun was ready, Tood-la about to be sacrificed to the stew pan, when a seal appeared and he was saved."

"Bring him as a gift for anyone?" There were whispers about Kane and the pretty knocker, but Maggie Fox had not gone down the bay in the small boats that took Kane's family out to meet him.

"Merely as a curiosity."

Yes, they had taken passage on a Danish ship. "For England by way of the Shetland Isles. Fortunately, we encountered the relief expedition. Otherwise, I should not have arrived for another three months. We celebrated that meeting with a gay ball."

"Can Eskimo women dance?"

"Far better than most of us, gentlemen. They tried in vain to teach me the Redowa mazurka—" His expression evoked laughter. One serious-minded soul would not be distracted. "What about the Open Sea? Did you discover it, Doctor?"

His smile flashed again. "The Secretary of the Navy will make any announcement."

They let him escape finally. Only an *Express* reporter was at his heels when he arrived at the Grinnell house. It was lighted from top to bottom and Grinnell himself opened the door.

Kane's voice rang in the darkness. "I have no *Advance* with me."

"Never mind, so long as you are safe, Doctor. That's all we care about. Come into the parlor and let us hear the whole story."

In the lobby of the Astor House "Dr. Kane" was pointed out to a group of latecomers. They went eagerly to shake his hand. Dr. John Kane, disproportionately annoyed, identified himself and shortly pushed his way out to follow his brother.

Coming up the bay, when his family had boarded the *Release,* Simms had sent John across to join them. He drew the Judge aside. "I never could talk to Elisha. At Disco he made sure we were never alone. Then he had Hartstene transfer me back to the *Arctic,* so I wouldn't be with him on the voyage home."

"Back to the *Arctic?* You *were* her surgeon!"

"I managed to get myself aboard the *Release* before we met Lish." John was carefully no more specific. "But Lish told Hartstene that special treatment to any member of his family would reflect on him, so back I went." He would never forgive Lish.

He did not report to the Judge all Lish had said. "Since my brother"—Lish had looked from John to Hartstene—"was brought along on my account, he should have submitted gratefully to Navy discipline. Any difficulty he experienced could only have been due to nerves."

"Understandable," Hartstene had said. "Nervy there once or twice myself." He and Lish had smiled broadly while John stood in mute rage. Lish had deliberately maneuvered him into this position.

"I'm the one should talk to him anyway," the Judge had said this afternoon. But there had been a crowd around Lish the whole way from Quarantine. There was a crowd now at the Grinnells', all old Henry's relations together with almost all the Kanes.

Mrs. Grinnell's beaming face made Ly acutely conscious of his mother's absence and of the constraint he felt in the Judge and his brothers. His mother's health was not the true reason she had not come. But it would, he decided grimly, give him an excuse for hurrying to Philadelphia tomorrow, where he would go at once to Crooksville and Maggie's arms. He was no longer a child to be told what he could and could not do.

He quickly launched into an account of his voyage, with maps to engross the Grinnell men, beautifully beaded women's jackets and his tame bird to enchant the Grinnell ladies, and it was late when Henry's brothers carried the bulk of Ly's audience home.

Ignoring the hour, the Judge took the floor, rambling on about some Abolitionist case before him.

Gripping the back of his chair inlaid with mother-of-pearl, the Judge concluded, "So I am abused in the entire penny press! Week after week Passmore Williamson stands up in my court and refuses to obey a writ of habeas corpus, insisting that those blacks, being freedmen, are not his to deliver up. I say they are! He'll remain in contempt and in jail until he rots, the damned, prim, yellow-legged Quaker, unless he obeys that writ!"

Mrs. Grinnell said gently, "I always find Quakers so restful!"

"Abolitionists these days, too many of them." The Judge glared at Tom, the family's Abolitionist. "My son's friends, ma'am, who are proposing to move my impeachment at the next session of Congress, for 'tyrannical abuse of judicial power.'"

"Dear no," Mrs. Grinnell said, distressed.

A tyrannical little man, the Judge, Ly thought, looking at his father's flushed face. He was showing none of the quirksy humor Elisha remembered so fondly. His whole family appeared curiously unlike his loving recollection. Only the Grinnells were themselves.

"When they know," the Judge thundered, "Passmore Williamson stands in flat defiance of the law."

He might end in making Williamson a martyr as he nearly had Tom.

"This case has plagued us, pillorying me in the newspapers, just when your mother fretted for her lost lamb. Your Aunt Lieper gave her worse cause for anxiety. That worry she must be relieved of at once!"

Mrs. Grinnell said placidly, "With her dear son safely returned, I'm sure Mrs. Kane will dismiss any small worries."

"Yes and no, ma'am, yes and no." The Judge raised the little chair and brought its legs down to the floor with the thump of a gavel. "Women get more worked up over a marriage than a birth or a death. Births and deaths they take in stride."

Did his mother fear a scandalous engagement more than his death, Ly wondered. Was that what the Judge actually meant?

Mr. Grinnell came in from bidding the last of his guests good night. His lean face was alight with Dr. Kane's and his triumph.

"My Jeannie has been in a state since before the relief expedition sailed," the Judge told both the Grinnells. "I haven't discussed the whys of it, thinking it a family matter."

Mr. Grinnell obviously had no idea what the Judge was talking about. "Let's leave it so," he said politely. "I am anxious to read Dr. Kane's report before he dispatches it to the Secretary. If you have it ready, Doctor. I take proud interest in every word," he went into a little speech, "since a Grinnell ship, as I just reminded my brother, stands farther north than any vessel has yet reached, a fitting monument to the Discovery of the Open Sea." He smiled at Ly.

"I've no doubt it's ready," the Judge said sharply. "Elisha is a great hand at writing, unfortunately. He's written a casket of letters I want recovered. Do it myself if I didn't have to be in court tomorrow with that damned Williamson case. How many letters in a casket would you say? Forty? Fifty? Fifty fuses to set off a scandal I promised Jeannie I'd scotch without delay. Elisha, I want those fool letters before the newshounds get them!"

Mr. Grinnell, a little flustered, said, "My wife wishes to retire now, Judge Kane. Will you excuse her?"

She looked across at the Doctor, his face weary as death.

"Nonsense. I'm old enough to be Dr. Kane's mother. I doubt any word he might write would shock me. Since his mother's not here—"

"What he has done sent her to her bed, ma'am!" the Judge said.

"She's his mother," Mrs. Grinnell replied cryptically.

"Stay, then, ma'am, and hear your son's involvement in this—this—conspiracy against my wife's peace of mind!"

When Nealy turned a painful red, his mother said sturdily, "That makes me all the more sure it can be nothing wicked."

"You're *his* mother," the Judge riposted. "Elisha, ma'am, to put it boldly, has been keeping a young girl in the country."

Dr. Kane spoke up then, every word precise, his tone brooking no interruption, not even from the Judge. "With a respectable farm family, Mrs. Grinnell. The daughter, a spinster schoolteacher, has been acting as the girl's governess. My Aunt Lieper has supervised her progress. The young woman is being educated to take her place as my wife. Your son kindly forwarded to her any news of me and encouraged her to continue her studies far from family and friends."

It sounded as romantic as *Jane Eyre*. "Is she an orphan?"

"No." The Doctor turned to Nealy. "Has she kept her promises?"

Nealy wet his lips. "She stayed in New York two or three times because of illness. Otherwise, Mrs. Turner thinks she has done very well. Yes, sir."

"Whose illness?" the Doctor was frowning.

"Hers. Brain fever once, Dr. Bayard said. From anxiety when you didn't return on schedule. Then the details about Franklin's men caused a relapse."

The Doctor had by now heard that tragically ugly story. "My poor overwrought child!" Then he asked sharply, "Where did she stay? Not with that wretched sister?"

"No, sir, never once. With Mrs. Walter usually."

The Judge exploded. "What matters it where she stayed? You heard him say she had a wretched family. Now he wants to make her a member of ours! Make his mother a laughingstock, with a rapper for a daughter-in-law! I won't have it! Once you get those letters safe to hand, you'll break your engagement to Miss Fox, Elisha."

"Miss Fox!" Mrs. Grinnell was utterly astonished. Why ever hadn't she connected the Doctor's protégée with Miss Fox? The two years he had been gone had made her quite forget their rumored romance. "She was here, Mr. Grinnell," she said to her husband. "I *met* her."

"Here!" From the Judge's tone you'd think her parlor had turned into a nest of snakes. She did wish he'd put down that chair.

"She called, when the Doctor was convalescing here, and a pretty, well-bred girl she was, just as Nat Willis said." The journalist had married into the Grinnell family, as Judge Kane knew. "He told me when the Fox Sisters first rapped at Dr. Griswold's that they were very respectable. And my sister-in-law, Mrs. Moses Grinnell, who is Mr. Irving's niece, said Mr. Irving pronounced the girls genteel and as quiet as mice."

Ly could have laughed aloud at this brief for his wicked Maggie. Little mouse indeed! But true to her vows.

"What does it signify that their manners are nice?" the Judge asked angrily. "They're still cheats and frauds who victimize the bereaved, whom all but the most callous would pity!"

He might have been Maggie's own preacher speaking, but Ly said, "She was only a child when it began and has now given it up."

"Her sisters haven't! If you had died up there"—the jerk of his head made the Pole seem not so far off—"they'd have had you rapping messages from eternity, along with Clay, Webster, and Calhoun. With your taste for adventure and your uncertain heart, they may do it yet. Break it off, boy, before your mother reads worse things in the penny press than attacks on me. Before she reads messages from her dead son! You can't inflict such horror on her."

Ly, listening to the Judge, realized bitterly that the threat of his death no longer had power to terrify his parents. They might, in fact, be relieved to lay him at last in the family mausoleum. But the threat of scandal, being new and strange where he was concerned, really shocked them.

Any fame he won would only aggravate their feeling. The celebrated discoverer of the Open Sea, friend of the noble Lady Franklin, their hero son, whom learned societies and even governments and crowned heads might recognize, should have a proper wife.

Almost as he thought this his brother John and Mr. Grinnell were arguing along the same lines. Tom and Patterson kept quiet, for different reasons, but at length good, kind Mrs. Grinnell, stifling her weakness for romance, was saying, "Dear Dr. Kane, when you go to England, you will surely be presented to Queen Victoria, and she might not wish to receive Miss Fox."

Such arguments weighed nothing against Maggie's fidelity. But he faced a grimmer pressure, that might prove as relentless as the closing floes. So far they none of them knew their power over him.

By midnight Maggie's hysterics finally erupted, and Ellen, unable to stop them, sent for Dr. Bayard. When a stiff dose of morphine had put the girl to sleep, Mrs. Walters and the doctor whispered in the hall.

"Why didn't he come? Is he ill, do you think?"

"No. I saw him from a distance at the Astor House looking very hardy." Dr. Bayard considered the matter. "Does he know she's here? Isn't she presumed to be in Crooksville?"

Ellen's jaw dropped. "God forgive my stupidity! But in the excitement she forgot, too, that she never told young Grinnell she was here. We'll send word in the morning. How could we have been so stupid! Making her suffer for no reason. I'll wake her!"

"Let her sleep, but if she rouses, tell the poor child."

43. THE BARGAIN

LY FINALLY PLED weariness to escape them and was grateful to find a key in the door of the room Mrs. Grinnell assigned him. His father and his brothers would sleep in this hospitable house tonight and might attempt to batter again at his defenses.

"I am sorry this trouble had to break out tonight of all nights," Mrs. Grinnell said. "The Judge might have waited a little, but he is so extraordinarily devoted to your mother."

And extraordinarily intolerant of other men's devotions. Aloud Ly said, "My life has never been simple. For me, joys always has some overlay of sorrow. I'm used to it."

She took his hand. "Dear boy, if there's anything we can do— But I'm as bad as Nealy, encouraging you to be unwise—"

He locked the door after her and pulling off his rough clothes, lay rigid as a cataleptic, his mind circling round and round his problems, while first one and then another unknown visitor tried his door.

What he needed as desperately as he ever had food for his starving men was money for them. To half his crew, those not on the Navy rolls, he owed a year's wages. Some of the Navy men had crippled themselves in his cause and could not again go on active duty. His own meager Navy pay was all he had to draw on, and it was hopelessly inadequate to his debt.

The unbearable part of it was the wages owed Godfrey and Blake. To be under obligation to either of them was a torment to his pride. They must be paid at once! Or he would be hobbled as he once had Godfrey.

The others, the loyal and loving ones like poor Tom Hickey, deserved more of him than selfish neglect of their interest. They must have money to stay in New York and be lionized. This was their moment of glory, and their captain could not rob them of it. Ohlsen's widow and orphans must also be provided for. Ly had counted on his father for funds, but now the Judge would drive a hard bargain, demanding his pound of Ly's flesh and Maggie's.

Maggie! Must he, to give his men their due, deny his trusting child hers? But he denied himself most of all when he gave up the one reward he asked, his child and wife. She must understand that, and obey her master, submissive as Griselda to whatever her lord required. If she was the girl he hoped she had become, she would do this for his sake. The thought made him almost eager to try her. But no, she had been tried enough.

Perhaps Mr. Grinnell would help. But he doubted that upright man would encourage any son to defy his father. Morning would tell.

After breakfast his father, leaving for the cars, said, "Elisha, I want those letters. That unsavory connection must be broken off at once!"

"Will you wait while I have a private word with Mr. Grinnell? Sir, could I see you in the library?"

As the slightly surprised merchant led his young friend across the hall, a servant came up with a note for Dr. Kane. Maggie was not at Crooksville! She was here in New York.

Elisha was trembling at the thought of seeing her as he faced Mr. Grinnell. With one of his gentle smiles, Grinnell said, "This personal trouble in your hour of triumph is unfortunate. But perhaps you should not have arranged Miss Fox's future before consulting your parents. I know I would be disturbed if Cornelius took such a course."

It was a clear reproof. As calmly as he could, Ly said, "I was thirty-two and my own man, I thought." Had he really thought so he would have boldly told his parents his intention!

Mr. Grinnell shook his head. "Actually you were not, so long as you depended on your father, and it is my understanding that your own earnings have never met the cost of your adventurous life. Before long, you will have to adopt some—ah—more remunerative career, if you are to keep a wife, establish a home."

There was no asking a loan now, since Mr. Grinnell had just indicated that Elisha Kane was a poor financial risk; had just said that his young friend could not afford to dream of love until he could pay for it. However could he earn enough to buy happiness with Maggie? He was too tired to consider ways and means. His every atom of will and energy he had spent to reach the point where he now stood.

"Your problem will be solved in time," Mr. Grinnell was saying.

How much time had he, who had already outlived all reasonable expectation?

"About your Open Sea," Grinnell was asking, "did others of your party reach its shores later?"

"No, they were all too enfeebled by spring to attempt such a search. No, Hans did not see it, only Morton."

"Not," Mr. Grinnell said, "that the testimony of a savage would mean much. I would be better pleased if you yourself and another officer had viewed your sea, not that Morton isn't a solid man. He may well please the American public more than an officer. I was thinking of the Admiralty. You know the English regard for form."

"You think they may question the discovery?" Unused to command, he had mismanaged everything! But Morton and Hans had been the only men fit for the journey. His own miserable body had been no use then. A shell he would not be sorry to cast off! But first he would have Maggie. He would live that long.

"Meanwhile, Doctor, it might be judicious to accede to your dear mother's wish. Until the Kane Sea is on the Admiralty charts, association in the minds of the Admiralty with any sort of hoax—and many consider the little Fox girls hoaxers—could prove unfortunate."

Ly held onto the desk to stay erect. He looked into Grinnell's long, kindly face and knew the merchant did not realize that he had stabbed Dr. Kane to the heart. But if, after all his effort, he had won not one scrap of fame, one rag of immortality, what had it been worth? Long ago he warned Maggie he was avid for fame. To protect his small claim to it, he would sacrifice even her. Nodding a head that felt too heavy for his neck, he followed Mr. Grinnell out.

His father paced the hall, while Nealy stood uneasily in the parlor doorway.

Elisha told the Judge, "If you will provide the funds I need to pay off my mercantile crewmen, I will break my vows to Miss Fox."

"Agreed," his father said instantly. "The letters?"

"I will not ask for them myself. Spare me that! Send Nealy. He is devoted to my mother." He took a fleeting pleasure in Nealy's look of shock; in his wretchedness striking out at his one friend.

"When he asks for the letters, Miss Fox will know she has been betrayed. If you will excuse me, I'm due on board the *Release.*"

Mr. Grinnell went with him to the door. "Elisha—"

"I always recover," Ly said, as if Grinnell had been solicitous of his health, and moved blindly into the clear, cold morning.

He was meeting Hartstene at the Astor House before going on board. On his way, time and again, he was recognized. He shook hands and nodded and smiled as automatically as a political candidate, though every face was a blur. At St. Paul's churchyard his vision cleared and he saw the trees there, ablaze with autumn. After two years in the Arctic they made a strange and lovely sight, the only aspect of his homecoming that gave him happiness.

All that day Cornelius Grinnell found excuses to put off his appalling errand.

At Clinton Place Mrs. Walter had wakened Maggie early. "Maggie, Maggie! Dr. Kane doesn't know you're here. We forgot you're supposed to be at Crooksville!"

"That's why he never came!" Maggie began to cry in relief. "Oh, Ellen, I was so frightened. I thought he had forgotten me. He may already be on the way to the Turners'! Stop him, Ellen! Send a note!"

With trembling hands but glowing face, Maggie readied herself again to meet her love. If her hair, done in a rush, was not quite so neat as yesterday, her face, Ellen thought, was lovelier. Slowly its light faded as hour after hour no carriage stopped at Mrs. Walter's door. By nightfall, Maggie, sitting in the same chair as yesterday, wearing the same dress, hardly resembled yesterday's Maggie and was a stranger indeed to the Maggie of that happy morning.

Ellen herself fell silent. All day she had rattled on, trying to distract Maggie from the carriages rolling right past. What was there to say now? That he had gone to Crooksville? But her coachman had seen the note put into the Doctor's hand. For long minutes the two weary women neither moved nor spoke.

Then Maggie said listlessly, "I'm going home, Ellen, to Mother and Kate. I should never have left them. Where is my cloak?"

"Let me send for the carriage."

"I'd rather walk." They found her wrap and a bonnet she put on anyway.

"I can't let you go off alone! But what if he comes and there's no one here to tell him where you are?" Ellen felt torn.

"Poor Ellen. He won't come." Maggie brushed a kiss against her friend's cheek and vanished like a wraith in the twilight.

Exasperated, exhausted, Ellen Walter wept. Would to God she had never heard of Dr. Kane! Everywhere she went, people would be talking about nothing else when she was sick of his very name.

When the *Arctic,* towing the *Release* to the Navy Yard, had passed Manhattan's miles of masts and wooden piers that morning, they were crowded with cheering people. Across to Brooklyn the ships had trailed, accompanied by a churning ferry whose passengers howled excitedly. The Navy men Kane had expected to take the expedition's exploits more casually, so he was moved to see the yardarms of every vessel at the Yard swarming with yelling sailors. The commandant seemed as enthusiastic as his men, and Ly, much flattered, shrank from his plaudits even while he enjoyed them. At that very moment Cornelius might be confronting Ly's poor, confused little pet.

Later in the day Ly took refuge for a while in Brooks's room at the Astor House where Nealy knew a message would reach him. None came, though Ly waited long, trying to sleep a little, but too distrait to relax. He went, finally, in response to innumerable notes and cards, down to the perpetual levee in the lobby. His very dinner he ate in the midst of a throng Nealy might have difficulty penetrating. There was no sign he attempted it.

They might know something at Bond Street. Ly hurried there, taking Morton with him. Cornelius had not yet returned.

"He had a dinner invitation," Mrs. Grinnell said. "That may be where he is. I wouldn't be surprised if he never went for the letters. Cornelius detests scenes."

"I had no right to inflict this one on him," the Doctor acknowledged. "By morning I may find courage enough to go myself." Leaning heavily on the limping Morton, as if not Morton but he were the cripple, Dr. Kane went up to bed.

It was nearly eleven, but Dr. Bayard, seeing a light in Mrs. Walter's parlor, stopped by. "How went the romantic reunion? Mrs. Bayard will want to know." Then he saw the widow's eyes were red.

"He never came nor sent any message. So Maggie has gone to her mother's." A second carriage pulled up behind Bayard's. She grabbed at his arm. "It's Dr. Kane at last! Slip out the back way and fetch her. He must never know she went home." She fairly pushed the startled doctor out the kitchen door. "Bring her in this way. Quietly!"

She ran to answer her front door and, opening it, said, "Dr. Kane," before she saw her caller was a tall man.

"I'm sorry, Mrs. Walter, it's Cornelius Grinnell." He followed her uncertainly into the parlor. To get his courage up he had taken too much wine at the dinner that was his last possible excuse.

"Wherever is the Doctor? That child has been waiting two blessed days for him with never a word. She was half-dead from the strain when I put her to bed," Ellen lied without a qualm.

"Just where the Doctor is," her lie inspired Nealy's. "His rheumatism flared up yesterday. Down flat with it."

She reddened with indignation at such a falsehood. "Dr. Bayard saw him at the Astor House looking the picture of health!"

"He did?" He always was a miserable liar. "Probably so," he agreed gloomily. "It's his family that flared up. Raising the devil—beg pardon, ma'am—over Miss Fox. Won't hear of any—ah—engagement. For his mother's sake—beautiful woman, Mrs. Kane—I've come for Dr. Kane's letters to Miss Fox. He wants them returned. If they're here," he concluded lamely. They could be at Crooksville.

"Mr. Grinnell"—the little widow actually shook with fury—"if this scoundrel everyone is hailing as a hero intends to betray an innocent girl, don't you be his cat's-paw!"

"Only doing it for his mother," he mumbled.

"In Maggie's state, I couldn't ask for those letters, and I won't let you do it. Let the little hero come for them!"

"Feel as sorry for him as Miss Fox," Nealy said stoutly. "He took his father's demand very hard. That's really why I came."

"What kind of hero is he if he isn't man enough to stand up to his father?" She heard the kitchen door click. "Wait a moment—" Maggie must not be allowed to run, arms wide, into this trouble.

In the kitchen Maggie, her hair tumbled, her face tear-stained, embraced Ellen. "I should have had more trust. Kate said so. Dear Elisha!"

"No, wait." Ellen hung on to her. "It isn't Dr. Kane. I made a mistake. It's a gentleman on business."

"At this hour?" Maggie twisted suspiciously around.

"It's Cornelius Grinnell. I told him you were in bed so he wouldn't know you left here," she whispered vehemently. "He might tell Dr. Kane."

That halted Maggie.

"The Doctor's been detained but will be here early tomorrow. So here you'll sleep, not at the house he forbade you to enter."

Maggie sank into a kitchen chair, her shawl trailing wearily across the floor. "Always tomorrow."

In the parlor Cornelius Grinnell was studying a steel engraving as though to fix every line in his memory forever.

"Maggie was stirring. She thought you Dr. Kane. I didn't tell her why you came, but that you said the Doctor would be here in the morning. See that he comes!" She held out his hat with a gesture that could have been Rachel's.

44. SWEET SORROW

MR. CORNELIUS'S message prompted Morton to wake the Doctor early.

Struggling up, Kane said, "I am Achitophel."

Someone in the Bible, Morton reckoned.

As if he had been up and talking for hours, the Doctor continued, "Pope's lines describe me exactly.

"Pleased with the danger when the waves went high,
He sought the storms; but, for the calms unfit,
Would steer too nigh the sands to boast his wit."

"Shoal water this morning, Cap'n Ken. Mr. Cornelius never seen Miss Maggie yesterday, he said. Promised you would before we go off to Philadelphia." Morton frowned. "I'd of thought–"

"Don't you reprove me, Morton. Miss Fox's tears will be reproof enough when I tell her my family has forbidden the marriage." His tone impersonal, he said, "In Philadelphia I can raise money for the mercantile half of my crew and for Ohlsen's widow."

"Yes, sir." His family couldn't get a better handle on the Captain. "Have to wear your uniform calling." As he never liked doing.

"What's proper morning dress for a villain? I am a disgrace to that uniform, but put it out." He stared at his bearded face in the mirror. "My appearance may repel Miss Fox. She may gladly give up the weather-worn sailor I have become."

She, too, might have changed in the wearisome time, grown into a buxom, proper miss, unlike his changeling child. He almost hoped so. Parting with the reality, he could hold hard the memory.

Mrs. Walter could not, in the end, let Maggie meet her doctor without warning of the shock to come.

Maggie took it dry-eyed. "It never was any use, was it, Ellen?" She turned her face to the wall. "Don't talk about it any more. Leah will talk enough. She'll talk for years."

She lay there for an hour. When she did get up, she dressed carelessly and would not eat, but sat in a rocker by the window, rocking steadily, her face closed.

"Dearest girl, let me fix your hair."

"Let it be. I'm not going down. But tell him I'm here, that I kept my promise, except at the end. He never thought I could."

"You're the brave one while he's wicked weak!" Ellen said.

"Weaker than I." There was the faintest hint of satisfaction in her voice as she rocked and talked evenly. "He's the one who lied and broke his solemn oath, Preacher did, who used to sermonize at me all the time. I did what he commanded, but it wasn't any use. No use from the first." There had been no knock, but she told Ellen, "He's coming now. You better go down."

Ellen, not at all sure the Doctor would obey the order she had sent, went skeptically downstairs. Her hand was on the newel post when a carriage drew up and a small man in uniform sprang out. He came swiftly to her door. Never having seen him, she was unprepared for the intensity of his eyes.

"You are Mrs. Walter. Where is my poor child? Take me to her." As she backed away from his advancing figure, he threw his cape on the hall seat and turned with an air of command.

"No. No, you can't see her," it took all her courage to say.

With a brooding look he nodded and reached for his cape. "She isn't here."

"She is indeed! She's upstairs praying God she will never lay eyes on you again," she burst out.

"Let her tell me that," he said in an unsteady voice, as if he were the one betrayed. "After two years of such desolation, such despairing effort that death would have brought surcease, I am here and she proposes to send me away without sight of her. I refuse to believe she is so heartless!" His eyes filled.

Confused, Ellen ran up to Maggie. "He's heartbroken! He insists on seeing you."

"No." Maggie rocked on.

"What shall I say? He won't go."

"Give him this ring, tell him the engagement is over, and that I don't have to see him to say so."

The Doctor took the ring, and then thrust it angrily back into Ellen's hand. "You have told her this is the proper course, because you think I have wronged her. But she is young and has the future before her! I have nothing, no hope, no honor left me. She will be happy one day, I never! Who is the sorrier victim in this situation? Tell me!" He held her glance with brilliant eyes.

"All right! I'll ask her again, but it's no use."

The stairs were killing her. In Maggie's room she shook the girl's shoulder. "He's blaming me, and won't leave. You'll have to see him."

"No," Maggie said, but watched her.

"I can't face him again." Ellen twisted her hands. "And you're just as bad. The two of you will drive me crazy!"

"For your sake, then." Maggie walked to the head of the stair, and stood there, Ellen peering around her, looking down at the Doctor pacing the hall below. He raised his really beautiful head to look up at them, his eyes glittering with tears.

"My own Maggie! Dearest pet!" He held out his arms, and Maggie's mask crumpled. With a strange cry she ran down to him, clinging to the miscreant while he kissed her forehead, eyelids, and tumbled hair.

"You have *not* changed! Look, your hair has fallen down as always." He buried his face in it.

Maggie, her voice muffled by his breast, only repeated, "Elisha, Elisha, Elisha!" Clinging together, they moved slowly into the parlor and out of Ellen's sight.

She sank onto the top stair, leaned against the banister, and could make no sense of the scene, nor predict how it would end.

At last, from what seemed a vast distance, she heard their voices, the Doctor's in a flood of words that swamped Maggie's occasional murmur. Once the girl cried out, "It's not right! It's not true, Ly!" Then the Doctor's voice rushed on.

Very soon he was at the door, nodding at Ellen. "Mrs. Walter, will you come down, please." Automatically she obeyed.

In the parlor Maggie sat with bent head at the table farthest from the chair where she had waited two miserable days.

"Miss Fox has written out a statement which she wishes to sign in your presence." Calmly, he handed her a single sheet of paper.

In Maggie's hand but his words and no mistake, Miss Fox stated that she had always considered Dr. Kane her good friend, almost her brother with a brother's interest in her education. At no time had she believed him a suitor for her hand, and no matrimonial engagement existed between them.

"Maggie," Ellen shook the paper at the foolish girl, "look at me and tell me this is true!"

Maggie glanced sidewise first at the Doctor and then at her friend. "No, it isn't true," she said indifferently. "The Doctor proposed to me on a carriage ride in Philadelphia."

"You are not the Maggie I took you to be," the Doctor said sternly, "a brave girl with implicit trust in me whatever I ask of her."

She smiled at him then. "You taught me to speak the truth, Preacher. So I won't lie to Ellen, though I will sign that paper."

"Never do it, you foolish girl!" But Maggie would not look at Ellen again, only steadily at the Doctor.

"Let her make up her own mind," he said. As if he had not already made it up for her! "Give her the paper, Mrs. Walter."

A second time she obeyed automatically. Then angry at herself for doing it, at him for his power over the girl, and at Maggie for her foolishness, she burst out: "Such wickedness I never saw in my life! Taking this child from her mother and sister, letting her endure two lonely winters with a wife's patience because she thought herself as good as married, only to cast her off! Tell me which are you, Dr. Kane, a craven or a villain? Mrs. Fox, poor thing, was no match for your cleverness, but Maggie has friends not so easily taken in. They will know you for what you are, whoever calls you hero!"

Maggie, deaf to this tirade, signed with childish care that lying statement: "Miss Margaretta Fox."

The Doctor took the paper, folded it, and nodded somberly at Ellen. "All Maggie's friends will agree with you. For my mother's sake, however, I must have this, and not for her sake alone. My little sister will never suffer for this gesture." He leaned over to kiss Maggie's cheek tenderly. "I will see you tonight without fail before I go to Philadelphia."

This was the final shock to Ellen Walter. "Maggie, you don't intend to receive him after this? What will people think?"

"That she has in me a loyal friend and loving brother," the Doctor said coolly.

For the first time Maggie looked straight at Ellen. "You wouldn't deprive me of my dearest brother, would you, Ellen?" Such impudence left the widow speechless.

At the door the Doctor turned. "Trust Brother Ly without faltering, little pet, no matter what they say of me." With an absent nod to Mrs. Walter he was gone. Maggie actually ran to the window to wave after him.

"One of us is a great fool, that I'm sure," Ellen said.

Maggie said simply, "I'm sorry you're angry at me, Ellen. I'll pack my trunk now and send a cart around for it later. Tell Dr. Kane I'm at my mother's. He can call on me there." Again Ellen caught a hint of satisfaction in the girl's voice. Maggie picked up the ring where Ellen had laid it, and smiling slid it on her finger.

In a confused silence Ellen helped Maggie pack and saw her tuck that fancy box of letters under a pile of petticoats. She had kept them, at least; in that, displaying the only sense she had evinced so far, the poor girl was so ignorant of this world, however much she knew of the next.

45. OPEN SECRET

DR. KANE, everyone complained jestingly, brought a wild northeast storm with him from the Arctic. It tied up all business in New York and Philadelphia. The chill in the Kane house, however, was not due to the weather.

The document signed for his mother's sake the Doctor at once gave to his father.

"Where are the letters? Damn it all, I want them!"

"This should serve your purpose."

"Not if she's still a minor. A child when you took up with her, I heard. 'An adult,'" he quoted the axiom of common law irritably, "'deals with an infant at his peril.'"

Ly stood withdrawn from the circle of light cast by the reading lamp, and saw the shadows of the library peopled not by a multitude of books, but, as this exact space had been aboard the *Advance,* by his pasty-faced crew. He could almost smell the brig's foul aroma instead of the library's beeswax, fine leather, and tobacco. Across his mind the motto of their little ship's newspaper was suddenly blazoned: *In tenebris fidem. In darkness, sustain your trust.* In his personal night he could not fail his men.

Still grumbling the Judge counted out the sum his son asked. "Thank you, sir." Ly went at once to his room.

At supper his conversation was limited to polite inquiry after friends or impersonal mention of the expedition. When he said good night to his mother, who had kept to her bed to show how his conduct afflicted her, he was most unsympathetic.

"My patients have all been rough men, desperately ill, so I never developed a bedside manner, Mother." His glance was hardly apologetic. "You will forgive the lack. I also had no time to play the invalid, but by exercise of will became strong and fat as a walrus. Will power is the only remedy in many cases."

Hers, he clearly meant! Even his voice was different. He no longer resembled her delicate boy. "You are so changed, Elisha!"

"Time and experience alter anyone, and in me the Arctic compounded the effect. The book I'm writing will explain my aging. With your permission, I'll get back to my writing."

"Can't the book wait until you have had a little time at home?"

"No," he said flatly. "It must be published before people lose interest in Dr. Kane, if it is to earn the money I need—to repay Father."

"He is in no hurry!"

"But I am." Let her make what she could of that. "And there will be many unavoidable interruptions, such as tomorrow's trip to Washington." He bowed politely and left her.

On his return from the capital, he reported only that the Secretary of the Navy had presented him to President Pierce and the entire cabinet.

"No one held a reception for you? Or gave a dinner?"

"I had told the Secretary earlier I could accept no invitations, having to return at once to Philadelphia. To my writing."

The book! The book! It was his escape from them. Hour after hour he bent over his littered desk, covering pages in his flying hand. To stretch legs and back stiff from confinement, late each afternoon he romped in the garden with Tood-la.

"That brute is his only familiar," Bessie complained. She liked dogs but not that shaggy black beast with languid eyes. She distrusted his melting glance, sure he only waited the opportunity to leap at her. Ly never laughed now except at Tood-la.

Far into the night his lamp burned. On the eighteenth he went off to New York. "To pay my mercantile hands," he informed the Judge at breakfast, "the same day the Navy is paying the men on its rolls. Later, we will all pose for Brady, who wants a group picture for his gallery. I'll order one for you, sir, so that you can see where your money went."

Henry Goodfellow rode up from Philadelphia with the Doctor. "Small boys, I hear, consider you another Robinson Crusoe," he told Kane. "In your furs, you will look the part. Morton in blackface can pose as Friday!"

"I miss him desperately. He nursed me like an old woman." With Morton to care for his stiff body and Maggie to stimulate his soul, he could endure cheerfully the labor of writing, which he had always hated. But the Navy denied him the one and his family the other. No one, however, could prevent his seeing his dear pet occasionally; tonight, for instance.

He liked being cast as Crusoe, he admitted to Henry. "Someday I may write an account of our adventures for boys to read. Such a boy as I was."

At Brady's studio his crew greeted him as warmly as if he had returned from a perilous search, and cheered his invitation to dinner. "To the dinner we dreamed of last Christmas, with Sillery that has a taste to it."

When the tedious posing was over, and hot and thirsty, they all reached the Astor House, his men, their pockets ajingle, insisted on buying several bottles themselves. "To toast Cap'n Ken."

As they stood to drink it, he felt deeply touched, though in honesty he could be glad to see the last of Godfrey and Blake. Nor would he suffer at parting from the rest of his non-Navy men. They had bid him farewell once without a qualm. All except Tom Hickey. For that faithful, clumsy boy he wished he could provide, but he had already come to grief over educating one child. Better for Tom to let him go.

Dr. Hayes, he noticed, kept his distance. That young man had, doubtless in the name of science, told a reporter no one could be certain the water Morton saw was really the Open Sea. Kane had read Hayes's statement, but this reunion was not the place to discuss it. Besides, the book would settle the matter.

His faithful few he would see from time to time. Brooks and Morton were so crippled that the Navy would doubtless retire them, when he hoped he could secure Morton for his service. McGary had retired himself. "Back to New London. Set me up as a chandler and stay ashore."

They lined up to shake his hand off at parting, aware they would never be together again though they said the survivors of the Second Grinnell Expedition ought to form a society. They had cost him so much, Kane did not think he would enjoy being a member.

At Tenth Street Mrs. Fox was fretful and allowed him only a few minutes alone with Maggie. "It don't make no sense, I declare. It's your 'sister' Mag says she now is, since your family won't allow no marriage, account of us being farmers."

"No, Mrs. Fox. In fairness, I must say they would not object if she were an ordinary farm girl, instead of an extraordinary rapper."

"Bygones," Mrs. Fox said. "She don't rap no more."

"Unfortunately her sisters ply their trade."

"My land, Doctor, the whole family can't turn themselves inside out so's you can marry Maggie!" Her worn hands beat the air. "Kate's rapping keeps this house, and feeds Mag and me, too."

"Dear Kate. I know." It was an insoluble problem.

"What I can't figure," the good woman advanced timidly, "is why you don't set up for a doctor. Folks is talking about how you saved all those men from dying. They'd clamor to have you treat 'em, and keep you and Mag in comfort."

He wanted to cry out to that practical soul, "But I have a chance now to establish not a practice but my claim to fame; to be honored by principalities and powers, not use my heroism for an office shingle!"

Instead, deliberately imposing on her sympathy, he said, "My health doesn't allow it. I look hardier than when I left, but it's not a genuine improvement. A physician's daily routine would destroy me."

To his surprise, she nodded. "Kate says the spirits warned her the eagle must not be caged. That's you, she declares."

He must accept those doubtful allies. "Until I am on my own terms able to afford a wife, let Maggie receive me as a brother." *But her kiss had not been a sister's!* "Trust me to make good my promises one day!"

"My mind's all turned around," she confessed. "I used to think my Margaret wasn't right for you. Now I ain't sure you're good enough for her! An' you so famous. It ain't just Leah speaks hard of you now, but people you'd admire to know!"

"If our engagement had been kept secret, as I wished, they would not have this chance to leap to false conclusions."

"Secret, for the Lord's sakes! We tried, but you was seen together everywheres, Washington especially, and that's a gossipy place. Then she quits the circles, and people that followed her faithful was upset. Next she goes off to the country to stay, and Mr. Greeley for one has to be told *why*. A girl can't disappear without no questions. Likely she wrote some of her friends. That Bouton girl in Troy. Told a few yourself, didn't you?" Angrily, she ticked them off, "Your aunt, your cousin, the Turners, Morton, young Grinnell, they all in it. So how was it a secret?"

Within a fortnight an infinity of people heard of Dr. Kane's strange love. The sides were instantly drawn up. The combatants fought lustily, though they only knew, most of them, what they read in the newspapers. The Troy *Whig* set the small war off, Miss Bouton having talked. Thereafter every journal in New York and Philadelphia and points north and south printed paragraphs on the romance. A variable approximation of the facts was proclaimed absolute truth or complete falsehood, depending on the editor's attitude toward the rappers in most cases. In others, the use of the Judge's phrase, "sailor's largesse," indicated the Kane family, too, had talked.

The Judge did his talking at home. Every reference to the romance sent him into a rage his eldest son watched in stormy silence. In this matter, Elisha made clear, he had done all he intended. He would make no public statement. The Judge continuing to demand one, a contest of wills raged between them, very like the Judge's long struggle with Passmore Williamson. Her husband aged so perceptibly and her son thinned down so sharply that Mrs. Kane took alarm, and, forgetting her own grievance, endeavored to act as peacemaker. To small effect. The Judge sat hours in his study, glowering over every clipping, while Elisha, turning his back on the bitter conflict, would catch the cars for New York. Where he probably saw that girl.

But no reporter caught him entering the house on Tenth Street. No reporter, seeing him elsewhere, had the temerity to question him. "The commanding little hero is *wrapped* in a cloak of reserve! You ask him!"

The only journalists in a position to learn anything from either of the principals were Greeley and George Ripley. "Friends of the Foxes from the start. What does the *Tribune* say?"

The *Tribune* only protested editorially at this prying into a personal matter. Whether an engagement did or did not exist was of concern to no one but Dr. Kane and Miss Fox.

This satisfied neither side. "Beating the *Herald* with the same old stick because Bennett spotted that paragraph in the *Whig*. You notice he didn't flatly deny it! Where there's smoke—"

Was there, in fact, any fire? Greeley could not truthfully say. He had gone to Tenth Street to advise the Foxes and had come away troubled. Mother Fox and his dear Kate had appeared anxious, but Maggie Fox had been composed, if pale. Looking at her, white eyelids modestly lowered, ladylike little white hands folded across her lace undersleeves, he was at a loss to begin.

"You were under age, Margaret, when this fellow carried you off—to be educated. If he took advantage of your innocence—"

Her brilliant blue eyes glanced off his almost furtively. "How do you mean, Uncle Horace?"

His moon face reddening, he continued vaguely, "Led you to believe he would marry you on his return—"

"Oh, no!" Her laugh trilled easily. "Dr. Kane always had a brother's interest in my welfare, though I used to call him 'Cousin.' If I had called him 'Uncle,' perhaps people wouldn't be gossiping and mean now. He's almost as old as you, Uncle Horace, but you're married and not a hero, so they don't make a fuss over your educating Kate, do they?"

That fairly winded him. Flummoxed, he turned to the minx's mother. "That the truth of it, Mrs. Fox?"

"Who's to know if Mag don't?" She didn't face him. "If she says he was brotherly—" She wiped her neck with her fichu.

"He never told you his intentions?"

Flushing a dull, painful red, she said, "I wouldn't say he did or he didn't."

"I gather you wish no help from me," he said, peering through crooked spectacles.

Kate, who had been drooping in a corner, flew to him. Shaking his sleeve, she said, "You can so help, Uncle Horace! Make them stop talking! If they stop it, things may come out all right."

It was at Kate's behest that he wrote that editorial, he tried to tell himself. But when he had been leaving the Fox house, he had caught his reflection in the glass of the front door and noted again how much he did resemble the bumbling Mr. Pickwick. The likeness had amused even Dickens. Then in the glass he saw another face reflected, a mask of dreadful sorrow. Startled, he swung around, and it was Maggie. That was her expression when unobserved! She had fled up the stairs before he could say anything.

The editorial stopped not a tongue. Nor did Bennett's astonishing performance. Bennett, who never retracted, shortly apologized for not one but two stories in the *Herald,* saying his informants were in error and the rumors about Dr. Kane utterly unfounded. If, Nealy thought glumly, his father and the Judge believed that would put an end to it, they would be utterly confounded. It only set off a new set of speculations. Who put the clamps on Bennett? No one, however, dared speak of it to Kane himself, in town with his brother at the very time.

They had come to see George Curtis, the editor, who was publishing an article John had written about the relief expedition. "Because Lish's book is tied up and he wants something about Dr. Kane, *the* Dr. Kane," John said. "What I wrote is nothing like Lish's Arctic fairy tales, so he probably wants to ask Lish if the place can be as stupid as I make it appear."

"Probably just using it as an excuse to meet the Doctor. Don't be so touchy." Nealy wished John would get that chip off his shoulder.

Curtis, "Howadji" to his friends because of his book, *Nile Notes of an Howadji,* which he would never live down, found the younger Kane a dull dog and the elder a coiled spring. Of burnished metal, Elisha Kane had such a glitter. When the editor had extracted from John enough additional data to enable someone (himself, usually) to liven up that search article, John Kane left, but the famed explorer lingered.

"I heard," he said with a surprisingly shy smile, "that Thackeray has taken to dropping in here. I hoped to meet him."

That would be an encounter! Curtis sprang to his feet. "When he doesn't stop by, I usually find him at the Century Club. Dr. Kane, I would consider it a great honor to present you to him there. The club members would also be delighted to see you, if you feel up to another reception!"

"To meet Thackeray I can endure a surfeit of kindness."

In the Century Club the visiting novelist, his giant bulk balanced on the small of his spine, was gossiping as happily as if it were the Garrick Club at home. Cozzens, wine merchant and fellow humorist, was telling how he had unloaded several of his mistakes on a newly rich customer. "I warned him not to tell where he got them, saying my regular customers would resent it."

"A Yankee trick. Y'know, Cozzens, in New York you could fool my palate. Wines don't taste themselves here. May be the climate, may be New York's infernal haste. A good wine demanding leisure, you all gulp spirits instead."

"Not all of us." Cozzens craned across the room. "That's a champagne man who just came in with Curtis. Sold Dr. Kane a couple of cases of a vintage year that he took to the Arctic."

"Kane here?" If Curtis knew he was in the club, he wouldn't fail to introduce him. Howadji was consistently kind.

Thackeray stood up, sure no one could miss the landmark thus presented and there—Howadji was waving and guiding his guest toward them.

Very slight figure of a man, Kane, to have lived through two winters of howling horrors and brought his crew out alive. But then, big men always pictured heroes as being tall as themselves when from Alexander on most were undersized. More astonishing was the Doctor's dandified turnout. Dickens aimed at such elegance but overshot the mark. Watching Kane's quick movements, noting his coin-cut profile as he greeted this man and that on his way, the tall, hoary-headed novelist was again reminded of Boz, and rubbed his own broken nose a little ruefully.

Howadji did the presentation handsomely, flattering both parties. Thackeray as he loomed over the little lion felt ungainly. "Kane, any Englishman would be damned honored to meet you!"

Kane's smile did not reach his eyes. They had light in them but little warmth; shone with the cold sublimity of his icy north. Curious.

"Anyone who reads English must regard mine as the greater honor. Sir, I am pleased to tell you in person that a towering Arctic cliff is marked 'Thackeray Headland' on charts I have sent to the Admiralty."

"Its sheer bulk suggested me?"

"Its magnitude, rather, and there was another reason for our feeling you should have a monument in the Arctic."

"What was that?"

Kane's smile flashed again. "I forced you to ask, because I want to tell you an extraordinary episode."

"My curiosity is notorious. What the devil happened?"

"First let me say that during the polar night brute needs—a morsel of food, a breath of warmth—absorb a man's whole being. The simplest idea takes effort to comprehend, and dreams, ambitions, emotions are lost in darkness. A man gropes his way through each twenty-four hours—not each day—there is no day—like an animal that only half hibernates." He spoke rapidly, eloquently, yet with overtones of weariness. "That was our state."

He hasn't entirely recovered from it, Thackeray decided, nodding.

"One morning—by the clock at least—I was surprised to see one of the crew crouching in the hold, reading. Passing him again, hours later, I saw he still read by a feeble lamp. My curiosity being equal to yours, sir, I had to know what book could absorb a man's attention under such conditions. It was *Pendennis.*"

Dear Pen! His very self, whose history had been written so painfully and laboriously. For Pen to win such praise made Thackeray's eyes fill up. He blinked owlishly. "I have never been paid a finer compliment."

They shook hands, and Kane turned quickly away, without another word. Cozzens had the tact to be quiet, too, until Thackeray himself finally spoke.

The bleak isolation in Kane's eyes troubled him. "Is he ill or only heartsick?"

"Semi-invalid since boyhood, but he's survived adventures that would have killed either of us. Heartsick? Why should he be, in his hour of glory?"

"Isn't there gossip of an unhappy love affair?"

"Oh, that. Nothing to it. The penny press distorted a simple kindness of the Doctor's into a titillating romance. With his fame and the little Fox's notoriety, it made a tidbit the public snapped up."

"What kindness?" *For beauty dwells with kindness—*

"You understand, she's a little humbug, but pretty and ladylike. Someone thought her deserving of a better fate than performing in her sister's troupe. So a fund to educate her was started just before Kane sailed. He contributed with a sailor's largesse—"

He didn't appear the hearty tar to Thackeray.

"—and that's how the story started. After all, she's a schoolgirl, half his age, with whom he would hardly fall in love!"

A schoolgirl! Cozzens would be shocked to know how often the aging heart of W. M. Thackeray had been captured by the flower-fresh face of some girl child! Was even now in bondage to a young chit who had married another. When, if ever, he was free of his own sad shackles, he would marry the youngest, most wholesome miss he could find, still in pinafores and with a taste for barley sugar. Not Sally. Never Sally Baxter, his *Beatrix* but never to be his. Sally Baxter Hampton to whom he must send a wedding present when he had girded himself to the task of choosing it.

He felt one of his headaches coming on. At forty-four he was old, many times Sally's age, in bitter truth; nothing like the Regency buck his lecture audiences expected, confusing him with one of his characters. But Kane had a boyish mien, except fôr his eyes; he had no impediment, no mad wife, like a certain Rochester-Thackeray. As the Englishman left his companion and the club, he was muttering irritably to himself. "Why don't they let him have his little rapper? Better a sweet humbug than no love at all!"

46. HAVEN

LEAVING the Century Club, Elisha felt meeting Thackeray on equal terms set the seal on his own fame. But in the great man's eyes he thought he had seen solicitude, almost pity. Or had he imagined it, sure the novelist, with his insight into the human heart, must instantly recognize a star-crossed lover? How would Thackeray judge him, given the whole story?

How he judged himself he hardly knew from day to day. *The fault, dear Brutus, lies not in our stars—*

He stared up at them glimmering dimly in the New York sky. Even Morton's confidence in him had been somewhat shaken, he thought, though the dear fellow had gladly accepted service with him. Of all the world, Maggie, whose fidelity he had first doubted, then abused, alone trusted Elisha Kane blindly. He must see her, though he had no chance all day to send round a note and it was late.

At the kitchen door on Tenth Street he tapped softly, and Mary, the Irish housemaid, dozing by the stove, roused to let him in. Miss Maggie was in her room, and slipping a coin into his fellow conspirator's hand, he went softly up the back stairs.

Maggie, prettily disheveled in an old gray woollen dress open at the throat, was ransacking a closet. At sight of him she dropped an armload of petticoats on the bed. "Oh, Ly, in all this mess! And Leah's downstairs! She brought a party to Kate's circle. You'll have to leave before it breaks up."

Tommy coming out from under the bed to snap at his old enemy, she muzzled him with a fold of her skirt and said grandly, "I'm getting my gowns ready for ever so many engagements. Tuesday Kate and I go with a party to Greenwood—"

"Cemetery? Does a funeral offer any real opportunity for a display of finery?"

She ignored this gibe. "Saturday we go off to a wedding and will be away for days!"

"Since I am neither a corpse nor a bride, when can I see you?" He and his picture on the wall smiled together at his little pet.

"I don't really know, because then we go to visit Mrs. Van Warts at her country seat."

"All the way to England! Over here we call them country homes or, more commonly, farms. Is she really afflicted with such a name?"

She let go of Tommy to slap at her tormentor whom Tommy promptly bit. At that, Maggie burst into tears. "Both of you behaving so badly when it may be weeks before I see my dearest brother again! They've arranged all these engagements, Mrs. Walter, Mrs. Bayard, and the rest, to keep me away from you."

Picking up Tommy by the scruff and shutting him out of the room, he took his trembling Maggie into his arms. "Dear one, they can't separate us forever. I'll be here when you return from your bridal party, providing you aren't the bride, and bring a husband with you."

"Don't laugh at me any more, Ly! And tend your hand!"

While he bled and wrapped it in a clean handkerchief, she stood with bent head. "Maybe I am bewitched—"

"Bewitching!" He caught her face in his good hand and kissed her most unfraternally.

She did not twist away for minutes. "They're right, aren't they? I don't receive you as a brother, or ever think of you so! If my music teacher understood English, he could tell them."

"Music teacher?"

"A kind and gentle Italian. Kate planned it all, knowing I wanted to keep on with piano and singing lessons. He came for the first time today, and all through the lesson I called him 'Doctor.' If he knew a word of English, he would think me desperately in love with some medical gentleman!" Wiping her tears with the back of her hand, she laughed at her infatuated self.

He was deeply touched that she continued, in the face of every discouragement, to mold herself into the shape of his dream. "You are my dear good girl!" He touched her delicate white throat as if to feel a clear pure note pulsing forth. "Keep up your music while I labor at my book. In the end we'll be together."

Leah's voice echoed through the hall. They tiptoed out to listen.

"Bolt and bar the house day and night if you don't want him slipping in behind your back. And keep an eye on that piece in the kitchen. She ain't above bribes, and if she's listening, then she knows I'm onto her!"

She stomped out, and Mrs. Fox slid the rasping bolt.

Ly drew Maggie back into her room. "Write me when you return," he whispered, "and I'll come at once. But be at home the day you set. I am your obedient brother, your faithful slave," he continued in a low voice, "but too busy to ride a hundred miles only to ride back again."

"Ly." Her little face drawn with distress, she clung to him. "This could be the last time! They're bearing down hard on Ma, and she can't stand up to them, Dr. Gray least of all."

New York's leading homeopathist, though he disagreed with him in matters of science, was, Ly admitted, an impressive figure.

"He's been lecturing her and Judge Edmonds, too. They say if she hasn't the will power to turn you away, she should send me off to live with my father or my brother David."

Far away from "Brother Ly." Never! "Your mother has given me her word I may pay brotherly calls on you. She won't break it."

"She gave her word out of weakness. She could take it back for the same reason when I'm not here to wheedle her round." Gently she pushed back his forelock, looking at him sadly. "I think we would have been very happy, Elisha, if they had only let us be."

"Believe me, little pet, everything will all come out all right." He could not leave her like this, oddly resigned to sorrow, almost cherishing it. He had caught that expression on Kate's face, but never before on Maggie's.

"Maggie," Mrs. Fox called up, "who are you talking to?"

As he slipped toward the back stairs, Maggie leaned over the railing to say with instant deceit, "Myself, Ma. To keep myself company, it's so lonesome. Send Kate up."

No word of her return ever came, but he did not, somehow, think she was lapsing into her old carelessness about correspondence. So he wrote to her. His letter came back unopened. Bessie, with raised eyebrows, handed it to him.

Mrs. Fox had weakened before the combined forces of Gray, Edmonds, the Bayards, and perhaps Wainwright. "Miss Fox's family," he gravely told his sister, "on the advice of a judge, two eminent physicians, and, I believe, an Episcopal bishop, have decided I am not a fit person for an innocent young woman to receive."

"All the better for you!"

"But not my reputation. Aunt Lieper, too, has forbidden me her house. So I go out very little socially, not knowing what doors may be closed to me."

"Aunt Lieper is doing it to spite Mother."

"On the contrary, she is doing it because of her own motherly feelings—toward Miss Fox." He dismissed her with a nod, and, picking up his pen, finished another sentence. Mentally, he chalked each off, as a prisoner each day of confinement.

When he next visited New York, he went directly to Tenth Street. "Miss Fox," Mary said, rubbing her empty palm on her apron, "ain't to be home to you."

"It's Mrs. Fox I'm calling to see."

That good woman came forward, her manner not at all defensive, but truculent. "You can come in this time, Doctor, so's I can have my say. Got my dander up, your family has. I knew your father was a regular tyrant—our friends says he's a wicked judge—"

There would, of course, be many Abolitionists among the spiritualists. Such people were drawn to all cults and causes.

"—so I wasn't surprised he set his face agin us. But he shouldn't of give out those lies they printed in the Philadelphia paper and lands know where else."

"I don't think I saw the statement you mean."

"About some fund for educating Maggie which you was supposed to have contributed to, over and above. It went on about the Kane family being noted for their charities, as if Mag was a public charity you took pity on. The Foxes ain't never been objects of charity! You didn't give Mag as much money as you took away when you made her quit rapping. You and your notions! You done us enough hurt. Now, you just stay away! Margaret's behaving herself and I won't have you upsetting her." Her face set mulishly.

Had Maggie's injured pride brought her, too, around to their way of thinking? "Is she rapping?"

"No, she ain't." She conceded the truth reluctantly, but could not lie. "But she'll come to it!"

"Not against her sworn oath, if she's the girl I think she is." He smiled at the piano, piled with music. "What days does her music master come?"

"Mondays and Fridays. No one's agin her improving herself."

Kate stood in the doorway. She ran to him and leaned over to kiss him, her long braids falling around his shoulders. "I don't care what they say, dearest Ly, I love you dearly, and I've missed you so!"

"None of that, Miss." Mrs. Fox tried to re-establish the parlor's hostile atmosphere, but Kate beamed at him. His arm around her, he moved toward the hall. In the shadows of the third floor he was certain Maggie eavesdropped. "Tell my dear little sister that one Monday or Friday I'll be under the window listening to her sing."

"Catch your death for your *sister,* if you want," Mrs. Fox said, "but I ain't letting you in."

At Christmas he dispatched bonbons to Maggie and Kate and Mrs. Fox, too, but was himself chained to his desk at Philadelphia, laboring as hard to pay off his modest debt as Sir Walter Scott his greater one. The book progressed so slowly! The pages he wrote at night he tore up next morning. He seemed to shrink from the truth of each episode, and glossed over the ugliness, error, and pain of many days. He hardly took time out for the holiday, and came down haggard to dinner. Bessie saw him in the late afternoon standing motionless in the snow, staring down at Tood-la, who had burrowed so deeply into a drift that only his paws and muzzle showed.

Holiday week Mr. Grinnell telegraphed news that sent Kane hurriedly to New York. Further word would eventually be published in Philadelphia, but not in sufficient detail to satisfy him. He wanted all the facts and Grinnell would know. He would have liked to go on to New London, where McGary must be now strutting the water front, talking very knowledgeably about this seagoing miracle.

Incredibly, one of the vessels Belcher had so cravenly abandoned in the ice more than a year ago had put into New London this Christmas Eve. She was the *Resolute.* During the breakup this spring she had worked free of her imprisonment and drifted, with the curious purpose the inanimate sometimes displays, through Barrow's Strait and Lancaster Sound into Baffin's Bay and out Davis Straits, Mr. Grinnell reported.

"A thousand miles she had journeyed when those astonished whalers found her." The Doctor had never seen Grinnell so purely delighted. That a ship could behave with seeming intelligence had a special charm for him. "She seems to have suffered few mishaps. Tops'ils and topgallants'ils gone and her rigging disordered, but otherwise sound. Left with sails close reefed, and her stores intact. But not a soul on board."

He laughed at the sight he could imagine: the whalers treading her decks gingerly, expecting *someone* to accost them. Even the *Flying Dutchman* has a spectral crew.

"Who found her?"

"The *George Henry* out of New London, J. M. Buddington, Captain. Quite a Christmas present for him to bring home, wasn't it?"

"The *Resolute* was Austin's flagship when I went aboard her during the first expedition," Kane told the merchant. He did not say that he had at the time eyed her admiringly, noting how perfectly she was organized and equipped for the polar winter in contrast to the poor little *Advance*. "What course will the British Government take?"

"The consul was here this afternoon." Mr. Grinnell frowned at being brought back to hard reality. "He thinks Her Majesty will waive all claim. It's clear case of salvage. I myself"—he paused, smiling again—"have rather a romantic notion in mind."

"I suspect you are an incurable romanticist."

"No, no. But in this instance, it strikes me our government has opportunity for a handsome gesture. Recompense the whalers, and return Her Majesty's ship to Queen Victoria!"

"Congress will think you an incurable royalist if you propose it."

"I think not. It would set us up in the world as a generous, open-handed nation, a republic able to give royally."

With a sailor's largesse, Kane thought wryly.

"I haven't told you the whole of my plan," Grinnell said.

The Doctor looked questioningly at him.

"If Congress can be persuaded to take this action, the Secretary of the Navy might be persuaded, in turn, to send the *Resolute* home under the command of Captain Elisha Kane." He beamed to see the Doctor actually start at his words. "You, who were thought lost, returning with a ship believed lost!"

"No. Don't even suggest it to me. I would like to use my small influence with Congress to save a ship of Her Majesty's Royal Navy from becoming what? A whaler? But I would not like to think I was doing it to win further acclaim for Dr. Kane!"

"I'll not mention it again." Grinnell twinkled. "Lady Franklin, mark my word, may have a similar dream, once the Congress has acted, but I will discourage her."

"If you will," the Doctor said soberly. "You may remember, sir, once pointing out to me my need to earn money. So I must finish my book. Such a command would bring me only glory." But the small boy in him yearned to make so romantic a voyage. As captain of the *Resolute* he might well be remembered when his discoveries, his writing, his very suffering were forgotten; and his appearance in that role might influence the Admiralty to deal kindly with his charts.

Resolute: the name suddenly struck him. How often he had used the word to urge his little pet to hold to her promises. *Be resolute,* little sister, while your base brother wavers at every temptation!

"Complete your book, by all means, Doctor. This proposal will take time. Congress is hard to hurry. So you have time."

Did he, indeed?

"Stay over to see the New Year in with us. We really must celebrate the *Resolute's* rising from the deep, and I have some Heidsick you will find just the thing. Besides, it has begun to snow heavily."

It continued to snow. The morning saw New York buried under the heaviest snow in twenty years. It muffled the church bells when they rang the New Year in. It muffled the footfalls of the few who ventured on streets that were like Jordan, "hard roads to travel."

One venturer was that experienced traveler, Dr. Kane. "This is my element," he told Mrs. Grinnell, "in which I must have a long tramp, not the eighty miles to Etah I have walked in such snow, but for a mile or two. The exercise will do me good."

Through the glittering isolation he moved straight to Tenth Street to pay a New Year's call on Mrs. Fox, cut off today from her meddling friends. They could have a long talk, and perhaps she would let him see Maggie. Only see her.

Not their solitude, but her motherly heart made Mrs. Fox greet him warmly. "Dr. Kane, in this weather! Come right in for a warm. Kate! Maggie! Where in the world have those girls got to?"

Unused to physical effort for weeks, he had perhaps overtaxed himself. His heart pounded with its old noisiness. Then it pounded in jubilation when Maggie ran in to hover over him, making him lie back on the couch, and rubbing his hands warm while her mother bustled out to make hot tea.

"What have they done to you, dearest brother?" Maggie's cry was so piteous he nearly smiled.

"Nothing at all. They only watch me with long, anxious faces, as if I were just recovering from a dreadful disease and might suffer a relapse. Like this!" He kissed and nuzzled her sweet face until she pulled back in confusion. Then soberly he continued, "But not my father. With him I wage a struggle exhausting to us both, though we never say a word. We are like men who must wrestle fiercely without making any sound that might wake the sleepers around us."

She crooned over him, caressed him, stroking his hair, his forehead, his eyelids, holding his face to her breast while every tension in his body eased and love and warmth together were mandragora to make him drowse. He half-dreamed Francis would appear with a chafing dish, but it was Mrs. Fox with a tea tray so laden she staggered under it.

Before he left a thaw had set in, not in the weather, but in Mrs. Fox's dudgeon. They banished the girls while they had a long talk.

The separation, he told her, had gone harder on him than Maggie. It also made his book more difficult to write, since he labored joylessly. If only he could see Maggie occasionally, he would progress by leaps and happy bounds. "I have done her no real injury, Mrs. Fox, and will one day make up to you both for any slight to your pride."

"I been thinking some." She nodded to herself. "Take Leah now. Fish deserted her without hurtin' her chances none. Got herself our good Caleb for a husband after, and now they's a president of an assurance company courtin' her. She takes him, she'll be wealthy."

He did not enjoy the comparison to Fish but submitted for his purpose. "Let me see her here privately. As for that, an occasional public appearance with Kate might do much to quiet the rumors. Now I imagine they are saying Maggie must have been betrayed since the Fox family has forbidden Dr. Kane the house. Seeing us all together, their tune would change. 'You see,' they'd say, 'he's just a friend of the family.' I do believe you have been ill-advised by Maggie's self-appointed protectors."

"Self-anointed," she said with surprising sophistication.

When he came up again in February for a long conference with Mr. Grinnell over plans for the *Resolute,* he was able to take Maggie and Kate sleighing, since the winter continued snowy. Holding his little pet's hand contentedly under cover of the lap robe, he seemed to renew his very energies. That night he told Grinnell that his book would be done in a month. "Or six weeks, at most."

But April found him still buried in manuscript, in notes, and maps, and Butler's dozens of proofs of the engravings for his book, and the end nowhere in sight. He fled again to Maggie, and the soft April evening, fragrant with approaching spring, tempted him to take her and Kate to the opera at Niblo's. Maggie's blue-and-white satin opera cloak set off white skin and blue eyes too effectively. She became the object of general admiration, and at Bond Street next day Mrs. Grinnell told him kindly she thought Niblo's a reckless choice. "Everyone noticed her in that blue opera cloak."

The Foxes were moving uptown to Twenty-second Street, and a third-floor room there, he decided after that, should be Maggie's sitting room and a retreat for them both from mischievous eyes and tongues. A sanctuary where, like wounded deer, they could escape the hunters. "With her piano up there, Mother Fox, and books to occupy her while Kate is having a circle." He sent Morton to lend a hand.

To use in preparing little suppers for them, Ly searched days for the right sort of alcohol stove, and finding it at last in an out-of-the-way shop, bore it in triumph to Maggie.

"The gentleman who had it was no gentleman. He was an old maid. This stove, he said, he kept in his curiosity shop to cook his own dinners. 'Never saw the like nowheres else in the country,' he said, 'and I ain't parting with it for love nor money.'

" 'Bright eyes will glow over its mysterious blue flames, if you let me have it,' I pled with him, 'sweet lips will close with a kiss over each delectable bite cooked in this pan.' "

"Ly, you didn't say it!"

"In vain I said it. 'No,' the wretch persisted. He began to eye me suspiciously, as if I wanted this oddity to lay at the feet of my mistress. So I confessed the truth. 'I want it for my little sister, my dear little sister. She is delicate and we are trying to tempt her appetite.' Instantly the wretch relented. So you see, if I did not consider you my sister, we would have no stove!"

He cooked the supper himself, served it with extravagant elegance, and was altogether happy. It was so late when he left that Maggie smuggled him down the back way and told her mother next morning that he had gone while the circle still met. Several times that May and June he was reported to have left equally "early," although Mrs. Fox would have sworn she heard the stairs creak long after midnight.

Watching Maggie wash the china and glasses from her third-floor cupboard, Mrs. Fox said drily, "He must of et and run."

She had let the Doctor talk her too easy into that third-floor sitting room. "Away from prying eyes," he wanted to see Maggie, but maybe that third floor was just too far away.

47. THE SINGLE REWARD

"A BODY'S GOT to sleep, Cap'n Ken. You know it's struck five bells?"

"Go to bed, then! All you do is distract me." This was manifestly unkind and untrue.

Morton's patience did not falter. "You git up sudden, you'll find yourself too cramped to walk. Without a rub you won't sleep. Your face is swole agin. Means your legs is, too."

And his hands. With eyes as sandy as if snow blindness threatened him, he conned Morton's long, anxious face. The good fellow was right. Flinging down his pen, Ly struggled to rise up out of his sea of papers. They stuck to his puffed and sweaty hands.

"A sweltering night! Or am I feverish?"

"Onseasonable hot for June, and I reckon you got some fever."

When it wasn't fever it was chills that shook him until his bones rattled. Twice Morton ordered him to keep his bed. But he in turn ordered Morton to prop him up there, so he could at least read proofs. Back at his desk at last, he found it almost impossible in such weather to recapture the aching cold of their long retreat from the north.

"Like Napoleon on St. Helena trying to remember Moscow!"

"Ain't likely he ever forgot," Morton said dourly.

For no reason his swelling subsided, leaving him weak but able to get around, and he hurried to New York. Full summer had raised a sulphurous stench in the streets, but Maggie's top-floor room stayed cool and dusky. It should be fragrant as well, a bower for his beloved sister. He sent Morton to fetch all the white roses he could buy.

His faithful steward returned laden, the delicately furled buds so framing his face that he resembled a horse strayed into a rose garden. The sight roused Ly to happy laughter, but Mrs. Fox, overcome by numbers, said, "Where we gonna get vases for all them?"

Water pitchers, spoon holders, celery vases, and spill vases were commandeered by Kate and Maggie. When the pair had done arranging the flowers, Ly would allow no lamp lighted in the little room. "It would snuff out the roses. In this twilight they shine whiter than snow."

While Kate and her mother performed for the evening "circle," he lay with his head in Maggie's lap, finally falling into his deepest sleep in weeks. He awoke half-drunk on the scented air, Maggie's flowerlike face glimmering in the shadows.

Abruptly he tumbled her onto the floor beside him, her hoops yawing wildly. He pressed her down, down, his legs lapped in a foam of petticoats, her hair spread in a halo on the carpet.

"A halo of darkness for a witch! They used to crush witches to death in Salem. Like this!"

"Ly! I can't breathe! Ly!" But she was not really frightened.

It was he who shortly took alarm, they rolled so near the precipice that could destroy them. "Maggie! Maggie! You must not let me behave so badly. You must resist me with all your strength, with all your will!"

She lay passive, her wrists as limp as if they were broken. Laughing, she said, "See? I can't lift a hand against you. You are my dear master!"

"No." Not yet, not yet. "For a little while, your—" he could not say "brother"; her amorous, incestuous brother! "—your loving friend who sometimes forgets he can be only a friend."

He crawled to his knees, to his feet, and lighted both lamps. He gently raised his disheveled little pet. She brushed her hair and dressed it carefully. Then they sat well apart, talking in subdued tones. At parting she extended her hand politely, and not meeting his glance, whispered, "Good night, Brother Ly," before she quickly shut the door.

Walking back to his hotel, he noticed, as somehow he never had before, several couples embracing half-concealed by bushes or brazenly out in an open churchyard. He tried to denounce himself for a fellow lecher, but his heart soared with the knowledge that he was truly Maggie's master whenever he chose to exercise his powers!

In his next letter to her, however, he promised, "When we see each other, I will be very good and you will treat me with the respect due a much older brother."

It was easy to promise this, he was so ill again, his legs crippled with rheumatism and dropsical swelling. Could it be scurvy when he drank milk by the quart, ate his meat rare, his greens in profusion, and sunned himself daily? But the book was finished; that ominously pleasant word, *finis,* was at last written.

The incubus was off his back, but there was a kind of moral in the fact that now the holy day was at hand he had not the capacity to enjoy it. And he knew that in making it readable he had destroyed its permanent value. It would injure rather than enhance his reputation.

After he had done nothing for two weeks but sleep, he would go off to the shore. Sea bathing should prove a suitable remedy for an Ancient Mariner.

Morton carted him to Long Island; he did so literally, lifting him off the cars and onto the boat and into the carriage. "You're skun down to the bone, Cap'n."

He was indeed a skeleton of Dr. Kane, too weak to breast the mildest surf. The first wave bowled him over, and he dragged himself to the sand and lay limp. If Maggie were cast up beside him, her soft hair trailing like fronds of seaweed, they would appear another Paul and Virginia, freed at last of every distress. He had a momentary illusion she was there, bending over him.

But it was Morton. "Cap'n, you all right?"

After giving Morton a fright, he did not again bathe, but stretched on the sand while his faithful attendant dashed sea water over him and the sun burned him dry. Salt and sun, he hoped, would draw out his body's poisons. But the beneficial effect was canceled by hot, humid nights.

Swabbing down his fever late, Morton said, "If you was living by a glacier now, you'd likely be yourself agin, Cap'n."

"Morton, you are my guardian angel!" And a homely comic angel he made. "I can live by a glacier—in Switzerland. A month of quiet in the chill, thin mountain air will cure me."

From there they could go directly to England, where Nealy already was, conspiring with influential English friends concerning the honors to be paid Dr. Kane during his visit.

If only he could take Maggie with him, see his dream-child with eidelweiss in her hair, the blue of the lakes in her eyes! But this would be their last separation. Once the British officially recognized him—presented him to the Queen, voted him medals, set his discoveries down on Admiralty charts—they would never undo what they had done, no matter whom Dr. Kane married.

Morton was surprised when the Cap'n fell at once into healing sleep. Perhaps he was not actually better in the morning, but Ly felt so, and the day after he took the ferry to New York to tell Mr. Grinnell his plan and to see how his love endured the hot blasts.

Mr. Grinnell approved, with certain provisions. "Let Cornelius meet you at Havre and accompany you to the high Alps. And of course you will take Morton."

Did he appear to need a nursemaid? A little irritably he said, "In common with other members of the expedition, including myself, the American summer bears hard on Morton. I'll take him for his own sake and Cornelius for company."

Only then did Mr. Grinnell produce Lady Franklin's latest letter. "She is deeply distressed by your poor health, she so looked forward to your early arrival—in command of the *Resolute*."

"I never entertained the idea," Ly said quite untruthfully. But it was true that he had nearly forgotten the resurrected ship, symbol to him once of his own eventual escape.

"About the *Resolute* there have been difficulties. Congress will hand her back to the Queen all right. But we wished the *Resolute* returned with the stipulation that she be used in one last great search. For Sir John's logbook and other records."

Cached in some area not yet probed, Lady Franklin and her niece, Miss Cracroft, passionately insisted. Sir John would not have allowed himself to die before his papers were properly disposed.

"Such a stipulation, together with the excitement over your visit, would influence the Admiralty, she believes. Several congressmen, however, strongly oppose any further search, as a useless risk of brave men."

"Useless! Because they see no possibility of trade with the Eskimos, or of discovering gold. More men have died trying to reach California than the North Pole!"

"Don't waste your energies on me, Doctor." Grinnell smiled affectionately. "Beard those political lions. With your eloquence and your authority overwhelm their arguments! But that's out of the question. The oppressive heat of the capital might be fatal."

The very thought of that quagmire on the Potomac made Ly uneasy, but he said, "Not at all. I can endure anything. Since I failed Lady Franklin in the Arctic, the least I can do is help her here."

Reluctantly, Mr. Grinnell pointed out, "Until you are much better, your condition might allow the opposition to say, 'Look what the Arctic did to the heroic Dr. Kane!' No, it won't do, my young friend! We must get you better first."

Once again his puny body hindered Elisha Kane! But in an even tone he asked, "Where can I find Alpine weather nearer than Switzerland?"

The Yankee merchant drummed thoughtfully on his desk. In a nostalgic voice he said after a little, "In my New England boyhood, the summers were always pleasant. Clear and cool in the shade. In Vermont or perhaps the Berkshires—"

Dr. Kane had friends in Brattleboro, Mr. Grinnell several in Stockbridge, who would be happy to entertain the celebrated explorer. When they had sketched out Kane's New England stay, Mr. Grinnell remembered, "There was a year early this century that my elders called 'Eighteen-Hundred-and-Froze-to-Death.' Spring and summer never came. There were blizzards in July and August. The crops failed and people went hungry. Except for that, I wish for your sake this were such a year."

Kane, climbing into Grinnell's carriage, its leathery upholstery blistering to the touch, stared at the dusty street before him. The very leaves on the trees hung limp. "It sounds delightful, though, as usual, cold and starvation went hand in hand."

When the carriage had pulled away, Ly directed the coachman to Twenty-second Street. Perhaps his dear witch could conjure up a little coolness. He had sent no word, but his Griselda was lately always patiently waiting. This time he found her gone.

"For a carriage ride." Mary, the maid, said, "A lady come by, to take the girls for a breath of air. You heard they're going to Canada to visit their pa's folks? French, they are, and spells the name foreign: V-a-u-x." Mary smiled at the outlandishness of it.

He was momentarily amused to learn Fox's real name was the same as that of Philadelphia's highly distinguished mayor. He would enjoy presenting Maggie to his mother as "Marguerite Vaux."

For two hours he waited, resting on her bed, his cheek against her pillow, her scent in his nostrils. Grinnell had telegraphed the Judge his invalid son's time of arrival. "So I must leave," he wrote in a note he laid in the hollow his head had made. "If you love me, write and comfort your attached friend, brother, everything!"

They were apart most of August. When he returned from New England, "much improved," he told all inquirers, he went again to Twenty-second Street, to the third-floor room that was his heart's home. The house, as he knew it would be, was dark and solitary; their sitting room as desolate as Mrs. Sullivan's parlor long ago. Tommy, fat and strangely amiable, licked his hand.

"We should be friends, since we both have the same mistress!" Ly told the little beast. "Lonely for her, you will settle for me, will you?" Rumpling Tommy's ears, he called to Mary, "He's disgracefully fat. The butcher's boy must have an eye on you!"

Giggling, she acknowledged, "It's the butcher himself that's smitten! Thinks the way to my heart is through Tommy's stomach. The more fool he. I never liked the little beast."

"Nor I," Ly said, "until now."

For a long time he sat like an old man, the dog in his lap, and both of them wheezing. That his life's span would be brief he had realized since he was sixteen, but not that he might pass from youth into old age, without enjoying full manhood. Oh, he had experienced a man's responsibilities and anguish, but never his freedom and pleasures. He had never had carnal knowledge of a woman. How the lusty males who admired the "heroic Dr. Kane" would laugh to hear it!

The respectable misses were too strait-laced, while the trollops repelled him. Only Maggie was at once an innocent and a minx. His hands closed so hard on poor sleeping Tommy that the lethargic creature was at last moved to nip his old enemy. Pushing the dog away, Ly stood up.

"Your company is a sad substitute for hers. But she will be here soon, our little mistress."

Tommy, looking up at him, began to bark frantically, as though some danger threatened. The menace lay in this little man.

"You always sensed it," Ly acknowledged, "and you were right!

Now stop barking!" Tommy instantly stilled, and peered anxiously up at Ly through the hair that veiled his silly face. "Good dog." Ly gave him an affectionate pat. "Remember, from now on I'm your master, too."

His secret resolve giving new life to the blood in Ly's veins, he stood his visit to Washington very well, though he accomplished nothing.

Congress would return the *Resolute* all shipshape to the Queen. But not an additional penny would it spend equipping the ship with a propeller to make her an ideal search vessel. Nor would it stipulate her use by the Admiralty. Nothing he said could alter their disinclination toward further polar exploration.

"What's the good of it?"

No answer of his could satisfy them, since the question really meant, "What's the going market price on pure knowledge?"

They were practical men, but they were also fair. Their sense of fairness prompted another query. "If we say she's got to be used in another search, in fairness, shouldn't we man her, too, not ask Englishmen to risk their lives on our say-so?"

He had to admit the good sense of this. Not the strength of an expedition's ship, but the courage of the crew determined the outcome. Belcher's original abandonment of the *Resolute* proved that.

At the Navy Department, the Secretary, Dobbin, furtively eying Kane, said, "Well, now, Doctor, proud as we would be to return the *Resolute* under your command, we can't impose such a responsibility on you before you have regained your strength. Your health is our first concern."

Against his protests, he was detached on the special duty of recovering it. As for the *Resolute,* Hartstene would return her. "In an unostentatious manner," which would be the height of ostentation. "He's just the man," the Secretary pointed out, "since the public considers him your rescuer."

"We rescued ourselves, Mr. Secretary."

"Not a fact we want to stress, is it, Doctor? Might make the voters consider the $150,000 spent on the Kane Relief Expedition utter extravagance! Might set them against a recommendation I intend sending to Congress: the purchase and distribution of several thousand copies of your book to Navy men, to libraries, colleges, and other worthy institutions." This from the man who had refused Dr. Kane the little help he needed when it would have been worth more than vast sums later!

Dr. Kane only smiled and said, "Very good of you." But the Secretary, if he ever read it, and the public, too, would find the truth of the "rescue" made sufficiently clear in his book.

In his own opinion, the book was a poor thing, except for its scores of handsome engravings. Perhaps they would make it a popular "parlor album" and with the help of official purchases, it would prove financially successful. (Congress had shown no disposition to vote him a medal or pay him any other honor.) Abroad, he must fare better, but on that expectation alone he would no longer deny himself happiness of a sort with Maggie. She would be his own dear wife, mistress, whatever the world chose to call her but his *own,* before he sailed. The single reward he was sure of he would claim.

48. A SPELL OF HAPPINESS

HIS EXISTENCE had a curious impersonality those last August days that he waited for Maggie. He lived altogether in hotels, hardly seeing a woman he knew, and few men.

His mother and Bessie were at the shore, and when the Judge joined them, Ly left their sheet-shrouded home for the Girard House. He was not sorry to escape the Judge's company. The Judge, aging, silent, had won, in his opinion, his long struggles with, first, his own son, and, second, the Quaker Williamson, but appeared to take no joy in his victories. There was such a barrier between him and Elisha, they had little to say to each other.

Cousin Patterson was away, and his Aunt Lieper would give him no welcome. No woman's smile warmed him in Philadelphia.

In New York Mrs. Grinnell had gone to the mountains. While he could have shared Mr. Grinnell's bachelor hall on Bond Street, Ly's uncertain health made it wiser to live at the Brevoort House with Morton. Faithful Morton and the Foxes' maid, Irish Mary, were often the only people Ly spoke to round the clock, though Curtis did drop into the hotel more than once and Wilson came for a long, sad talk that made Ly know that young man better.

Kane welcomed the first hints of autumn, fall asters and dahlias blooming in Battery Park, though they heightened his elegiac mood. He was on his way to the Navy Yard where the *Faith,* together with the Fair Augusta, occupied a place of honor. The smile on their little wooden girl's mutilated face had such a pitiable fixity that he turned away from her, somehow stricken. When, when would Maggie return? What if she were delayed beyond the *Baltic's* sailing? That liner was due to leave in a fortnight, but Ly evaded booking passage until he had seen Maggie.

Improved as a correspondent, she wrote him the day, though she could hardly predict the hour, of their arrival. That day he went a half-dozen times to Twenty-second Street.

"Wear yourself out with all this to-ing and fro-ing, Doctor." The busy Irish girl found time for concern. "It's a cup of tea you're needing. Them grapes is too fine to be real."

The luscious hothouse cluster of them he had seen in a fashionable victualer's window. Dreaming of Maggie with vine leaves in her hair, her mouth purple as a bacchante's, he bought the basket, though he was already loaded with two magnums of champagne.

"Look at the size of them now!" Mary said as she put the bottles to chill. When he began to twist leaves and stems into a wreath, she asked, "What in the name of the Lord is that you're doing?"

"Making a wreath."

"Is it a touch of the heat?" She looked so pitying he burst into laughter.

"Here he is! In the kitchen having a cozy tea with Mary," Kate announced from the doorway. Maggie pushed past her.

"Dearest, dearest Ly! Keep Mother away, Kate," the minx ordered, and kissed him until he trembled violently in reaction to such love after so much loneliness. "You must have the ague!" Maggie said archly.

"That's why Mary is giving me hot tea—until the champagne's cold enough."

"Dear, silly Doctor—"

Then he stopped her tongue for so long that Mary muttered it wasn't decent. Kate hissed warning and Mother Fox came beaming in, fussed at his thinness, shook her head over the wine bottles, peered into Mary's oven to see what was for dinner, and Ly felt, fantastically, at home.

Later he deceived the poor matron, exhausted from the cars, into thinking Morton would call for him soon. She went heavily up to bed, and Kate, too, vanished. When Ly and Maggie, bottle in hand, tiptoed up to the third floor, that Mrs. Fox was securely down her snores testified. Where Kate was he had no idea.

At her mirror Maggie laughed at her wreath's tilt but left it becomingly askew while she patted pearl powder on skin whiter than pearl. In the glass she saw him moving blindly toward her. His expression made her turn quickly, puff held high.

"A feeble weapon for your defense!" His voice sounding very strange in his own ears, he reached for her.

She tried to swirl out of his grasp, but not quite soon enough. His hand closing on her skirt tore it partly away at the waist.

"My new traveling dress," she said crossly, and not to tear it further, let him, still clutching her skirt, reel her into his arms by the very clothes that covered her.

"If I scream—" She tilted back from the waist.

"—they would never let me see you again. If you were so heartless, knowing my desperate need of you, I shouldn't care." He caught her close. "But sail for England to forget forever a little prig who resisted her master. Do you want that? Or shall I return to my own loving child?"

"Let me think."

She rested her head against his chest. He waited, his heart so loud that she said in a compassionate voice, "Dearest Ly, don't upset yourself so. I always obey you. But first pour me some champagne and don't *tear* my dress off! It hooks up the back."

She fed him sips from her glass while he unfastened at least a hundred hooks. When her dress slid off ivory shoulders down past a waist his hands could span, he saw her stays were laced so tight there would be ugly welts on her white flesh.

"I forbid such lacing absolutely!"

Then his eyes fell for the first time on the igloo-shaped framework of a hoopskirt, and he laughed until he had to stifle himself with a pillow.

"They're not that ridiculous," she said, indignant.

He lay laughing on the bed. "My little bird has caged herself for me. But where's the door to that contraption?"

The ties that held it around her waist were tangled into such a knot that he had a time with it. But there was an almost painful pleasure in the protracted removal of layer on fluffy layer of clothing. No Eastern or Eskimo woman, naked to the loins, was half so enticing as his little pet under muslin and whalebone, lace and ribbons, absurd but enchanting armor for fragility.

"If women in Byron's day had worn all that he would never have had time for so many conquests, dying young as he did. I'm dying, too. Faster, faster, little bird!"

"Mr. Fagnani painted one of his—his—"

"Paramours."

"I thought they were only in the Bible. Well, Mrs. Fagnani said nice people never mention Byron," Maggie, down to her last petticoat, pronounced critically.

She looked too prim to be endured, so he swung her onto the bed beside him. One of her slippers flew through the air. It landed on the floor with a thump. They lay quiet, waiting to see if the noise had roused anyone.

"Who sleeps below?" he whispered in her ear. A tendril of dark hair tickled his nose.

"Kate." She twisted around and raising herself on an elbow, said, "I told her not to come up, no matter what!" and with a chuckle deep in her throat, put her mouth to his.

When he called next day Kate opened the door and drew him to a corner of the hall. Her gray eyes shone with tears, but her voice was calm. "You *will* marry Maggie, won't you, Elisha?"

"I swore to long ago, Kate."

"Mind you don't wait too long now!" Her schoolgirl's face became an old woman's, her straight young back was almost bent as she turned away.

Momentarily he was chilled into a sense of responsibility. At the very sight of Maggie, however, the fever flared up that only she could dispel. Employing every ruse, they were constantly together, usually in their little sitting room, but once drawn up in a little rural glade and once along a deserted stretch of Long Island shore. She had never heard of Paul and Virginia.

That day he told her the fright he had the night before. A slender little woman, deeply veiled but with a figure like Maggie's and wearing a sprigged cotton—

"Like mine?"

"As near as any male could tell, walked boldly into the Brevoort. I was terrified. But when the clerk nodded to her, I realized she must be staying there."

She thought it a great joke on poor Ly.

They could not meet next day, he had so much neglected business to attend. With Mr. Grinnell, he finally went to sign up for his and Morton's passage. From there they rode over to the Navy Yard to inspect progress on the *Resolute*. Her refitting was proceeding handsomely, though Dr. Kane's surprise visit did delay the mechanics some minutes.

"She should be ready by the twentieth, but I doubt she'll get off before the first of November," Mr. Grinnell said.

Ly, making his farewells to the Fair Augusta, was startled to discover she no longer resembled Maggie! His living pet had fattened on the food of love. The oval of Maggie's face was softer, the curve of her neck more tender, her lips fuller, and her eyes more languorous. At times he thought the richness in her whole aspect must disclose everything to good, stupid Mother Fox. He must have a picture of his love in the transformation that was his doing.

In case his rush of work before sailing prevented his taking her to Brady himself, late that night Ly jotted down instructions: "Ambrotype—large plate—figure erect—full profile with eyelids drooping and head bent."

This pose would catch only two aspects of his protean mistress: the compassionate woman and the mysterious enchantress. But what of the depraved schoolgirl whose knowledgeability could shock him? Who then turned without warning into a passive wraith with tear-stained cheeks? Or the earthy, laughing peasant who rose up a meek and modest wife? Were all women capable of such variety and he in his abysmal ignorance unaware of it?

The quiet tap at his door would not have waked him if he really slept. "Morton?"

His knob turned. A shadowy figure slipped in, closing the door softly. He lighted his lamp as Maggie, in sprigged cotton, threw back her veil and perched smiling on his bed.

"Don't scold! The clerk greeted me most amiably. The lady's name is Renshaw. I shall walk out as calmly as I walked in, and Mother thinks I'm staying at Mrs. Keymes, who is entertaining with a late supper. So you see!"

"Maggie, Maggie!"

She had only to twine her arms around him to stop all argument.

He kept Morton out next morning by being up, dressed, and at the door when his faithful steward arrived. "Will you go order breakfast, Morton? I'm due at the Foxes' in an hour to take Miss Maggie to the daguerrean gallery. Or is it overcast?"

"Looks to be a bright day. Hot later."

"Good. Then don't delay." When Morton had left, he turned to his composed child. "Hurry home, saying you have just remembered this appointment with me, and no one will suspect us of parting within the hour! Wear a dress that exposes your neck and shoulders, an evening toilette. I want you to look the Circe who has changed me into a wild boar." He gave a rough demonstration.

"How you talk!" she said when he let her go, and settling her bonnet and veil, drifted gracefully along the empty passage to the stairs. He watched her, devoid of all emotion but pleasure in her movement. From the beginning he had known she was Circe whose love would alter him irrevocably.

Just when he felt most alive, though he acknowledged something febrile in his vigor, he suffered a severe lapse, and was for several days bed-bound.

"Been a mite too cocky, ain't you, Cap'n?" Morton knew a mite too much. "Out till all hours. A little sleep won't hurt none."

Exhaustion did not account for all his symptoms. Brooding on them brought him to a sober realization that Maggie must be provided for. In any eventuality.

What, exactly, could he do? To marry her publicly would raise a disastrous furore before he reached England. To ask that she be given a widow's dower in his will would bring the Judge to a stroke. His father had drawn up that document and held it in his charge. If his son superseded it with a later will he knew nothing of, the Judge would be mortally insulted. Ly could not do that either.

Providentially, he had named Tom and Pat as his executors. Between them they could quietly arrange for Maggie to receive her share of the book's earnings. Tom since his marriage had become a regular *pater familias,* but Pat he could rely on to respect his wishes.

Money was not the sole protection Maggie needed. Suppose there should be a child, a son whom he, like Ohlsen, might never see? His first day up, he searched Mr. Grinnell's library for a handbook on Common Law. He found it wedged between two volumes on Marine Law and a fat tome on Torts. That shrewd businessman did not, as Ly suspected, rely wholly on his lawyer. The information he sought, Ly read carefully.

That evening at the Fox house he and Maggie stayed in the parlor, since she had a guest, Miss Bouton of Troy, in town for a visit. That miss regarded the famous Dr. Kane, reclining on the sofa, with such awed interest that Ly was tempted to play the hero. But Kate's behavior sobered him.

She pleaded in a low voice, "Marry Maggie before you go!"

A little startled, he asked, "Has she confided some secret in you that she has not told me?"

"No." Her jaw set.

"Who else, then? The spirits?" he teased.

"I cannot tell you!" She ran stumbling from the room.

Maggie, sitting by her friend, called across to him, "Whatever did you say to disturb Kate?"

"The spirits upset her, not I." He must put his plan into effect at once. It would ease Kate's mind and his own. "Maggie—" He let a half-spoken request for privacy hang in the air.

Miss Bouton's ears were sharp, and she excused herself.

"Maggie, I remembered last night a near relative's being privately married for some years before the fact was made public." He had also remembered his mother's distress over the situation. "He and his—love simply acknowledged before witnesses that they were in truth man and wife. Under Common Law such a declaration is a legal and binding marriage. You have been my wife, truly my little wife, for many happy days."

She snuggled against him, playing with his hair.

"Would you be willing tonight to enter into such a bond? For your protection, whatever happens?"

At that she sat bolt upright. "What did Kate tell you?"

"That she wants to see us married, naturally. Now run and fetch your mother, Kate, Mary and Miss Bouton, too."

The quartet assembled, puzzled. He explained to them the declaration he and Maggie wished to make. With Mary and Miss Bouton to witness it, "this will be as binding, Mrs. Fox, as if made before a magistrate."

"Well, I declare!" that good woman said, surprised.

"No, we declare!" Smiling, he stood, Maggie's hand in his, his left arm encircling her slender waist. Then he told the little congregation firmly, "Maggie is my wife, and I am her husband. Wherever we are, I am hers and she is mine. Do you understand and consent to this, Margaretta?"

"I do, Elisha. You are my dear husband."

He kissed her gently, and then patted Mrs. Fox's shoulder.

"There, now, Maggie is my legal wife. As I swore she would be."

"You sure?" Her round face was troubled. "No veil or nothing. I never thought to see as pretty a girl as Mag married so poorly. She'd of made a lovely bride."

"We can go through another ceremony when I return," he comforted her. "Meanwhile, Maggie is my legal wife. You have witnesses to that."

Kate kissed him and her sister. "Now Maggie's safe." From what? He raised an eyebrow at Kate, but she was hugging Mother Fox and did not notice.

His departure on October 11 was as confused as Maggie's for Crooksville long ago. He went early in the morning to Twenty-second Street. Maggie, pale and nervous, clung to him.

"I wish you weren't going, Ly! Kate's behaving so odd. She's been talking to Mrs. Collins but she won't say what about."

"Who, in heaven's name, is Mrs. Collins?"

"Her husband owns the *Baltic.* You know that! They used to attend our séances together before she went down with the *Arctic.* They made an agreement that if they were ever parted, they'd try to reach each other."

He could hardly believe it of E. K. Collins, a man whose standing nearly equaled Mr. Grinnell's.

"So he had private séances until the *Pacific* disappeared," she continued.

Hartstene, as a matter of fact, had been sent in search of that second lost Collins liner.

"He was very angry that the spirits didn't tell him the danger, and for a while he stayed away. But he's back now."

"And you think his dead wife has warned him about the *Baltic?*" Kane's tone mocked her fears. "If so, Collins won't let the ship sail. It's as simple as that, if he really believes this nonsense."

"Maybe it wasn't about the *Baltic,* but whatever it was, it upset Kate."

"Think of me now, not Kate's moods. Look, here are some envelopes, lined with muslin and addressed to me, for you to use when you write. This one has a private mark. See those stars on the inside corners? They mean you want me to return immediately. You need say nothing specific in your letter."

"About what, Ly?" she asked in all innocence.

"Any emergency that might arise." He could not add fear of pregnancy to her more formless fears. "My dearest child!" And wife. How could he have been so selfish, never thinking of the consequences to her? Shaken by sudden concern, he buried his face in her neck. "We cannot part in this state. I'll do other errands and return to make my farewells over again, with both of us smiling."

Smiling they were on his second visit, even gay when he found he had left without the ambrotype and had to go back for it. "This time I forgot *my* little bird."

Maggie went with him to the carriage where Morton waited. She put her hand on the good fellow's arm. "Take care of the Doctor, Morton, and bring him safely home!"

"Done it twice." Morton smiled thinly. "Third time's a charm."

49. NIGHTFALL

WITH AN impatience he knew was childish, Ly turned away from his view of the gloom-shrouded Southampton street. What the devil delayed Cornelius? But he must control his nearly desperate anxiety to escape this island of blasted hopes. Away from England, the sun might shine. In England, it had not shown its face since his arrival three dank, miserable weeks ago, and the sun of his aspirations had been as clouded.

"Mr. Nealy 'ull be back right soon, Cap'n," Morton soothed him. He tucked the blanket around Kane's knees. "You stood the trip right well, considering."

Considering— Considering his presence was a blight, everyone had treated him remarkably well, except possibly Miss Sophia Cracroft. Thinking of that admirable female's barely contained irritation at Dr. Elisha Kane, Ly smiled mischievously. Poor Miss Cracroft!

Poor Cornelius, snatched from Paris to accompany his ailing friend to the West Indies, since, had Nealy not gone, Lady Franklin most certainly would! The very possibility threw Miss Cracroft into tremors, and she had no doubt written anxious pages to Mr. Grinnell. Harassed Henry Grinnell!

What a mess the celebrated Dr. Kane had made of everything! Ly began to laugh helplessly.

"Here now! Bit of brandy's what you need." Morton poured him a tot and Kane savored its warmth. Until this English visit, wine, not spirits, had been his tipple, but here only brandy dispelled, even momentarily, the foggy damp.

It seeped in his window now as it had from the moment he landed. That had been at Liverpool and the hotel the Adelphi, but the view was the same and both very like his view from Morley's Hotel in London: thick oily fog parting now and then to show wet pavement with shadowy figures carrying flambeaux before the few carriages that ventured out, since at midday the fog was so thick that the street lamps could not be seen. From the first these little processions made him think of Renaissance funerals, of catafalques winding by torchlight through Florentine streets: a strange impression to form of bustling, modern Britain.

His voyage over had begun too well. He and Morton had been astounded that he was not seasick, not at all, not once. It had worried him, seeming to indicate a change in his constitution, for good or ill he could not tell. Before Liverpool, however, utter lassitude had overtaken him, and his first encounter with an English fog set him coughing. Hacking like a consumptive, he had dragged himself to meet one disappointment after another.

To his shock, Lady Franklin was not in London but off in Lincolnshire with her sister, Mrs. Majendie. Could he meet her in Cambridge and go with her to the Majendies' place, Hedingham Castle, in Essex? He had not been equal to the effort, and could only await her return to London. Mr. Barrow, Colonel Sabine, and others of the Arctic coterie had kindly called, and Dr. Kane himself had gone with Morton to the Admiralty.

He was received warmly by several of his erstwhile heroes. They had none of them committed themselves to his Open Sea, though Morton gave them an excellent description of it in homely, realistic terms. Their faces a blur to Kane, they had hemmed and hawed and gently made several devastating points.

"The extensive—haw—body of water Mr. Morton viewed from one shore might—haw—prove on further examination to be a considerable—haw—sound or straits as important—haw—as Davis Straits. That this water was a sea in the—haw—strictest sense could only be determined by—haw—traveling across it and from one of its western outlets into the Pacific or—haw—by circumnavigating it, taking bearings at several points around its boundaries."

Several voices contributed qualifying phrases to this summing-up. Listening, he could think only that it was to this anti-climactic end he had betrayed his sworn promises to Maggie! He trusted they took his pallor for a symptom of physical not soul sickness. Before his call was ended, however, old Sir John Ross burst out: "Damned important discovery, your Kane Basin, Doctor. May lead directly into your Open Sea as you'll discover next voyage."

He had always loved Sir John, but the old sailor's opinions carried little weight with the Admiralty's careful scientists. As a scientist, Elisha Kane admitted this was just. In his eagerness to prove his theory, Dr. Kane had leaped to unscientific conclusions.

Sir John's "next voyage" had been tactful. The others, before he left, were recommending to him the waters at this and that continental spa. Immediately he had traveled no farther than Camberwell, staying two weeks at a pretty villa, driving out once to view through a mist Camberwell Green with its pleached lines and the Meeting House on High Street where William Penn had preached before he was taken to the Tower. As a Philadephian, Dr. Kane was presumed interested in this relic.

Lady Franklin's presumptions were vaster. That wonderful, warmhearted matron swooped down on Dr. Kane and took him to her heart. His letters had apparently won him her unreserved friendship. Accompanied by the stiff Miss Cracroft, she called at Camberwell.

"My dear Doctor, I have been so distressed by reports of your illness! It is on my account you committed the imprudence of coming over before you were completely recovered. You were prompted by my anxiety over the business so near to both our hearts!"

"Blame my incurable impatience, Lady Franklin."

"No, no. Don't attempt to relieve me of responsibility! For my sake, you felt you must be here when the *Resolute* arrived, to give me full and timely assistance. If only we had known when you were coming! We were at Ilkley Wells near Harrogate, and would have persuaded you instantly to join us in taking the waters, providing, of course, that was the thing for you to do. What does your physician say?"

"Dr. Watson tells me I have a cold."

"A cold! It's apparent even to me you are more seriously afflicted. We must consult the best physicians at once! And then get you away from our English winter."

"Indeed we must." Miss Cracroft watched her aunt, dark brows frowning to see Lady Franklin hold Dr. Kane's hand, adjust his coverlet, harken sadly to his cough. "The season is too advanced for Ilkley Wells. The south of France or Madeira perhaps." The farther the better.

"Madeira!" Lady Franklin tapped the edge of the tea table so emphatically that the kangaroo on her handsome gold bracelet (gift of admiring New Zealanders) jumped. "Madeira is ideal. It has a most healthful atmosphere, as I know from experience. Your devoted mother in a charming note entrusted her eldest and dearest to me, so I shall accompany you to Madeira and myself nurse you back to health. There! It's all arranged."

"Lady Franklin, I could not allow it." She took his breath away.

"Aunt Jane, with the *Resolute* arriving next month, you cannot leave!" She horrified her niece.

"Exactly. So we must see that Dr. Kane is recovered by then. His health is my first consideration, dear Sophia. For his own dear sake and because he is the key to my entire plan! With him willing *and* able to assume heroic leadership, and the *Resolute* returned to us from its icy grave, the government *must* resume the search. Until the gentlemen at the Admiralty observed his poor health, it was understood between us that, providing I obtained the *Resolute,* Dr. Kane would be tendered the command."

"An American?" Ly asked, amazed. Had she dreamed this?

"—who stands in splendid contrast to the latest Admiralty commander in Baffin's Bay. Belcher behaved shamefully! Now his adherents excuse him by saying all Arctic exploration entails dreadful privations. Dr. Kane's very person will give them the lie."

"Not as he now appears," Miss Cracroft argued warily. "They will say such privations broke him down."

Smiling, he had baited her. "Dear Miss Cracroft, Dr. Kane, a semi-invalid since he was sixteen, has survived two polar expeditions. England, not the Arctic, has laid him low."

"Well taken!" Lady Franklin flashed him a gleeful smile. They were fellow conspirators. "Sir John *always* felt much less healthy at home than in Greenland. Now we must plan your transport to Madeira. Once you have recovered, I will arrange an audience with the Prince Consort. A most intelligent man, he is deeply interested in new discoveries and can influence Her Majesty. You will be presented to the Queen a little later and receive her medal for polar exploration. Meanwhile, there is no time to be lost!"

When she had swept her despairing niece out with her, he had lain back to dream that all that wonderful old woman envisaged might come true: that Dr. Elisha Kane, an American Navy Passed Assistant Surgeon merely, on the resurrected *Resolute* would sail for the Arctic in command of an Admiralty expedition. It would be unprecedented! So much so, it was plainly impossible, with his poor health the chief hindrance. He had presumed a rapid recovery when he sailed on the *Baltic* and had been wrong. Madeira could provide no surer, speedier cure, and Lady Franklin could not undertake a long-drawn-out nursing of him.

She must be here to make representations to her government *before* the *Resolute* was returned. Where would Elisha Kane be then?

When Miss Cracroft, well chaperoned, called the next day to plead with him, she found Dr. Kane calmly of her mind. He fully appreciated how unfortunate it was at this juncture for his illness to distract her aunt.

"I cannot tell you how unhappy it has made her and how absorbed she is in her plans for your recovery," Miss Cracroft said. "It may jeopardize all our hopes! Other arrangements must be worked out at once to relieve her mind of worry over you. At once, Dr. Kane!"

He realized this, but resented that strong-minded female's regarding Dr. Kane as a nuisance. "Perhaps Cornelius Grinnell could accompany me—"

"To Madeira without delay!"

"—to some tropical island."

Madeira having no charms for him without Lady Franklin, he decided on the West Indies. Cuba was only a week out of New York. Someway, his little pet might be able to join him there. His happiest times since his return from the Arctic had been with her. This morning he had written her a note hinting of his hope. It was brief, but even so the effort exhausted him, and Nealy had to address it.

Sir John's last letter to Lady Jane had been sixteen quarto pages; his own latest to Maggie not sixteen lines. But what value were words on paper? In his portmanteau, strapped and ready, was a stack of letters and testimonials, from the whole body of savants with Humboldt at their head, from the governments of a dozen nations with England in the van, all paying him flattering tribute. They did not alter the fact that he was, in the end, a sickly man who had failed in his major purposes.

There were medals there, too, the newest presented him—*in absentia*—by the Royal Geographic Society the day before yesterday, together with expressions of sympathy and admiration for Dr. Kane's "heroism and endurance." It was not sympathy he wanted!

Nealy came in to report their passage set. He had also picked up a bundle of mail. Childs sent reviews of Kane's book. Ly skimmed through them. Here his *Arctic Explorations* was pronounced "singularly irresistible." There a critic found "good sense as the mainspring of his genius." The Judge's lip would curl to read that of the author of a casket of "actionable" letters. Ah, here his book was described as "exquisitely illustrated" and "the most beautiful ever issued by the American press." So perhaps it would sell and words on paper finally provide happiness for him and Maggie.

Their ship went only to St. Thomas, where they would await the Havana packet. Again he was not seasick. Instead, his rheumatism became acute, shifting to every part of him. As the guest of Grinnell's friend, Swift, Ly believed himself improved during his stay on the picturesque, somnolent island.

On December 20 they sailed for Cuba, due to reach there before Christmas. The sea was boisterous and for the first time in months Ly yelled for a basin. Though he retched frightfully, he was pleased at the return of his old malady. Morton, clucking, settled him in the bunk. He rested quietly, watching his faithful steward unpack their luggage.

Suddenly their ship, the earth itself lurched, as the most excruciating pain he had ever endured cleft his brain. Unless he could cry out he was a dead man. In agony, he raised up and in a thick voice said, "Morton!"

"Cap'n Ken, what is it?"

"Ship's doctor." He clung to consciousness until the doctor came. Then the fearful ax struck again. "Give me anodyne!" To show where the pain was, Ly touched his forehead, no more than touched it, and agony rent him. "Anodyne!" Were those moans his?

Mercifully, the morphine acted quickly. The pain dulled, though he remained conscious. When the doctor had left, Morton, meeting his eyes, said, "You know more'n him. Is it bad, Cap'n?" Through all the terrors they had faced together, he never saw Morton so frightened.

So loyal a friend deserved warning. "You'll not have me to trouble you long."

"Don't talk so, sir!"

The ship rolled hard to starboard and to avoid jolting his tortured head, Ly tried to brace himself. His right hand did not move. He was thrown sidewise before Morton caught him.

"Turn back the blanket," he ordered in a thick, unfamiliar voice. With all his will he strove to raise his right hand, his right leg. They lay inert.

"Cap'n Ken, sir, what does it mean?"

Ly heard him, but could not answer.

By Christmas Eve he had revived surprisingly, could sit up in his bunk, and with effort move his semi-paralyzed leg, though his right arm hung limp and his utterance continued difficult. Morton spoon-fed, massaged, bathed, and encouraged him. The ship's doctor did little more than worry, not liking responsibility for so celebrated a patient. Cornelius wavered in and out of the cabin, solicitous but helpless.

"I'll recover, Nealy. Always do." Ly intended to sound reassuring, but on his sick tongue it came out drunken. "Port soon?"

"Late tonight or early tomorrow."

Merry Christmas to all: to Morton and Cornelius, burdened far from home with a sick man; to the Judge and Jeannie, upset by news of Elisha's latest seizure; to his child-wife, left desolate, with no gift, no Christmas-morning kiss from her love; to all whose friendship for Elisha Kane had disrupted their lives.

When they dropped anchor next day, his brother Tom came aboard to relieve Nealy at last of his charge. When the Kanes were settled comfortably at Mrs. Almy's Hotel, Nealy came to say good-by. "Understand your mother and John are coming down after the New Year. Won't be needing me. Be in the way, in fact."

The parlor of their suite would be crowded with Kanes, lovingly barricading Ly from the world. He must get a message out before it was too late. "Let Maggie know that I'm better." The newspapers had reported him dying. "Mr. Wilson can call on her. Don't fail me, Nealy!"

The newspapers would also report his mother's sailing for Cuba. Reading that, Maggie would never dare come. If he was ever to see her camellia face again, he must go to her; recover at least partially; enough to stand another voyage.

Dr. Ainsworth, who attended him, was shortly amazed by the success of his patient's struggle to regain the use of his limbs. Kane could stand up while being dressed, walk with a little support to a chair. He scorned to stay in bed, and for hours every day concentrated on moving first his fingers, then his wrist. Soon he would be able to hold a pen and write Maggie. He had received no letter from her, but then, Tom collected the mail, and she might have written without his learning of it. The barricade was nearly up. When his devoted mother was finally beside him, the gates would swing gently to.

She was actually in Havana, here at Mrs. Almy's, though he had not spoken to her. There had been another of the serio-comic developments that so infuriated John. A woman at their table aboard ship had come down with the smallpox, so they dared not approach Elisha. His beautiful mother, in subdued clothing that was not exactly mourning, walked every day past his window, waving to her afflicted son.

When at last she had access to him, she broke down. "My poor, poor boy! Your face"—he realized his smile was permanently askew but she swerved away to finish—"so pale and your hair white! But Mother's here to care for her precious one."

Slowly rotating his wrist, he studied her still notable loveliness. She had hardly a gray hair. "Morton does that, Mother. You will read to me and we can drive out together. I am so much better. Very soon we'll go home."

"Not yet, dearest. Not until the horrid winter is over. Besides, Mother is right here with her boy and so are Johnny and Tom."

To her ears, his confused speech sounded like baby talk! Then and thereafter she spoke as if to a toddler. It made him cringe. To escape it at least part of each day, he suggested she read the Bible aloud to him. Its majestic phrases could not be prattled.

He dreaded Morton's absence on some errand. When Ly asked for a drink of water or a fresh handkerchief, invariably she said, "Mother will get it right away, dearest," and when he had gulped awkwardly, "There, now! Wasn't that good?" Always, she wiped his mouth, though he had the full use of his left hand.

How she felt, he overheard when they thought he slept. "But I love to run and fetch for him, John! It's my delight. Then he is my child again, come back after the long voyage of a lifetime to his mother's knee. Only the trivial troubles of the nursery bother him now, hurts his mother can kiss away."

On his thirty-seventh birthday there was an elaborately frosted pink cake and his mother proposed the toast, her face alight. "To my dear son Elisha, whom heroism has not hardened nor the world weaned away from his dependence on his loved ones."

With Maggie he had been a man. When Tom came in late to see how he rested, he caught at his brother with his good left hand. "Have there been any letters I was not told about?" Perhaps a birthday greeting from his dear one.

"Any that might have disturbed your progress I believe John destroyed."

"Any from Miss Fox?"

"I don't really know."

"She is not named in my will, but I told Pat she must be provided for. Swear you'll see she gets her dower rights!"

"Dower?" Even in the shaded light Ly could see Tom was startled. "You didn't marry her?" he whispered.

"I acknowledged her as my common-law wife before witnesses." His words came out so garbled that he could not be sure Tom understood.

When he tried to repeat what he had said, Tom put a soothing hand on his. "Don't talk of wills now, when you're improving so markedly. Excitement could bring on another attack, Ainsworth says."

A week later Kane suffered a second seizure when Dr. Ainsworth was fortunately present. Morton, limping frantically around his prostrate hero, kept crying out, "Like the dogs! Like the dogs the first winter!" which made no sense at all to Dr. Ainsworth.

He had been dosing Kane with nux vomica and quinine. In view of his patient's rheumatic heart, however, in this crisis he could risk no drugs. When Kane fell into a coma, Ainsworth simply applied a few leeches and cold cloths to the head. Kane's pulse was extremely feeble, his skin cool and moist. Later in the day the iris of his eyes responded to light and he swallowed liquids put into his mouth. Otherwise, he was completely paralyzed.

He did not die that night nor the next. Ainsworth had never seen such tenacity for life. Kane actually regained full consciousness and could indicate "yes" or "no" by moving his eyes. Five days he hung on. Then, while his mother read the Bible to him, without her knowing the instant, darkness profounder than the polar night closed over Elisha Kane.

50. THE LONGEST JOURNEY

EARLY THE morning of February 20 the street outside Mrs. Almy's was crowded with Europeans and Americans living in Havana, and many Cubans, too, Miss Maria Wharton noted. The funeral of Dr. Kane, dead so young, at the height of his fame, naturally appealed to them.

Though herself a Philadelphian, she had never met the Doctor in life. She had, however, gone several times to the room at Mrs. Almy's where his body lay in state. He looked exactly like his picture in *Arctic Explorations,* though of course much emaciated. Nearby stood the outer box in which the coffin would be shipped. Reading the direction on it—HON. JUDGE KANE, PHILADELPHIA, U. S. A.—she thought, thus does an idolized son return to his father's house!

She had not known the Kanes at home. Here, however, she felt she must write a letter of condolence to Mrs. Kane, whose serene courage during her son's illness deeply impressed Mrs. Almy's guests. In reply, Mrs. Kane had copied out a lengthy poem, "Dr. Kane in Cuba," sent by an admirer of the Doctor's. Perhaps Miss Wharton would like this souvenir of the mournful occasion? Was ever a bereaved mother as thoughtful?

At seven-thirty the coffin, wrapped in the Stars and Stripes, was borne out by six white bearers, the Committee on Arrangements walking alongside. (Miss Wharton heard much criticism that no sea captain had been named to the Committee.) Quietly the procession formed: a military band behind the coffin; then the American and British consuls on foot, the Englishman in full uniform; then everyone else, walking two by two, Miss Wharton on her papa's arm. The Kanes and their servant, the man with the limp, had gone on board the *Catawba* earlier, Mrs. Almy said.

At the Plaza de Armas the procession was met by Colonel Echabarria, Governor of Havana, with his staff and the aide-decamp of the Captain General of Cuba, the morning sun glittering on their epaulets, the morning breeze tossing the plumes on their helmets. With them stood more soberly garbed members of Cuban learned societies, and a military band playing a dead march. Two by two this assemblage joined the procession.

At the government landing the Captain General's barge of state, draped in black, waited to receive the coffin. Two more government boats carried the Cubans out to the *Catawba*. Rowing in admirable unison, they led a parade of boats from every American ship in port besides two flying the Union Jack and one the Bremen flag. Miss Wharton had never seen a prettier sight than this little fleet following the dark barge up the harbor, while the morning light danced on the waves. All around the ships' flags were at half-mast, the ships' crews, heads bared, standing at attention. How suitable, for the brave discoverer of the Open Sea this water-borne funeral was!

On board the *Catawba* Colonel Echabarria made an eloquent address in Spanish, Colonel Blythe, the American consul, replying in English, and everyone agreed later never had a foreigner in Cuba been so honored.

In New Orleans Lieutenant Todd thought that Monday before Shrove Tuesday one of the loveliest days that ever dawned. " 'The soft'ning air was balm,' " he quoted as his Continentals fell into parade formation. In honor of General Washington's Birthday and the Continentals' own anniversary, the day had been ushered in by a salvo of artillery. He raised his sword and the Continentals stepped out smartly, holding high their handsome new colors. Even with halts for refreshments in both the upper and lower towns, the Lieutenant calculated that the parade would be over by two, giving everyone time to finish preparations for the troop's anniversary ball tonight.

It was close on two when Mayor Waterman's messenger caught up with the Lieutenant. "Don't disband, sir! Dr. Kane's dead! The *Catawba's* due in now with his body. Died in Havana last week and the coffin goes north by river steamer tomorrow. The Mayor's arranged for Kane to lie in state at the City Hall, and you're requested to escort the body."

"Where will she anchor?"

"Foot of St. Joseph Street."

The Mayor was already on board the *Catawba* condoling Kane's heavily veiled mother when the Continentals reached the landing. Waterman had acted with dispatch. A band with muffled drums and a gun carriage borrowed from the Washington Artillery were already at hand. A file of Todd's men bore the body to the gun carriage on their muskets and in slow step, the band playing dirges, the Continentals marched to Camp Street, from Camp to Canal, turning on Charles toward the City Hall, past gaping revelers in carnival costume.

The rest of Monday and until four Tuesday afternoon Captain Hunting's Washington Artillery saluted Kane at fifteen-minute intervals. That repeated "boom" cast a pall on the bright closing of New Orleans' most successful carnival week. People said, "In the midst of life we are in death," or perhaps "*Telle est la vie,*" and fell silent. Flags at half-mast on all ships in port, on river steamers, public buildings, foreign consulates, and some private dwellings were another reminder of man's mortality in the midst of the fatiguing round of parties and balls.

In Lieutenant Todd's opinion, Kane's funeral procession Tuesday was the finest parade that week. The military were out in strength. Besides his own troop, there was General Tracy's First Brigade and General Palfrey's Legion. The foreign consuls marched in uniform and the Grand Lodge of Masons in full regalia. On a caisson drawn by four perfectly matched grays the coffin was carried through the Old French Quarter to Poydras Street and along Poydras to the levee.

Every steamer tied up there was crowded with spectators, though it was dark when the procession reached the *Woodford.* Captain Mather was already an hour past his announced sailing time. All the steamer bells tolled, the church bells and the fire bells. With the muffled drums of several bands and Captain Hunting firing minute salutes in the square, the air was filled with a "damned mournful and beautiful sound," Todd said to his first sergeant. The glare of the flambeaux on the *Woodford* shone through the gloom as a platoon of Continentals carried the coffin onto the river steamer.

When his men at last came down the gangplank and the bands struck up a lively tune, Lieutenant Todd felt some relief from the sorrow that strangely gripped him, when he had never met Kane! At home, he had a stiff drink while he freshened up for the night's entertainment. A very secret society of eighty gentlemen calling themselves "The Mystick Krewe of Comus" had taken over Crisp's Gaiety, and at their first Mardi Gras ball were presenting a series of elaborate tableaus illustrating Milton's *Paradise Lost.*

The man listed on the *Woodford's* passenger list as "and servant," standing at the rail at dawn next morning, cringed to see that the river, eating at the bank before one of the finest plantations, had torn away part of an old burying ground. A coffin stuck straight out of the earth, and, worse, through its rotted boards he could see a a pile of whitened bones. They hadn't ought to let such a thing stay like that! Blindly William Morton stumbled to his cabin and for the first time in his life was seasick.

In Louisville, where freight and passengers were transferred from Mississippi to Ohio River steamers, early March changed from tolerable "sugar weather" to nearly Arctic winter. There were heavy snows. When the clouds cleared, it continued bitter cold, with a hard gale blowing.

In anticipation of the arrival of the *Woodford* some time March 4, the schools were closed to allow the children to see the parade for the great hero of peace, the dauntless warrior of science, Dr. Elisha Kane. But the *Woodford,* delayed at every stop—at Evansville, Indiana, for more than two hours—by crowds coming aboard to view Kane's coffin, did not reach Portland, the end of the line for Mississippi River boats, until nearly midnight. So the reception committee installed the coffin temporarily in the parlor of the St. Charles Hotel there, and Louisville children had another holiday March 5.

At eight in the morning fire bells tolled the signal for assembly. While the Grand Lodge of Masons, together with the New Albany (Indiana) Cornet Band and the Oceola Fire Company conducted the coffin from Portland, Louisville marchers surged on Mozart Hall. They lined up in jig time: local and visiting fire companies, city officers, police, the entire medical profession, the legal profession in a body, the civic societies and plain citizens, many from New Albany and Jeffersonville across the river. Captain Flato's Band joined the Cornets in playing solemn marches for the thousands on foot, in carriages, and on horseback. At Mozart Hall the reception committee turned the body over to the escort committee (though the Adams Express Company would have actual charge *in transitu*) and the cortege got under way.

A minute gun fired steadily as the marchers flowed through the business section, the leading establishments closed and draped in black. At the mail-boat landing the knowledgeable noted the river was low, only four feet in the chute on the Indiana side, but the *Telegraph No. 3* got off nicely. From the shore women waved black-bordered handkerchiefs in farewell, and the children cried in sympathy with their elders. A New Albany poetess was moved to write:

> The North Pole is thy flagstaff, and unfurled,
> Thy banner lords it o'er the frozen world.
> But best of all, thy nobly acted part
> Has writ thy name upon a nation's heart.

The only flaw in the solemn proceedings was the damage to Peter Weber's house, considerably injured by reverberations from the heavy cannon fired close by during the ceremony.

The Cincinnati reception committee took the steamer, *Jacob Strader* to Vevay, Indiana, where they boarded the *Telegraph No. 3*. In the mail-boat's cabin they were impressed to meet not only Dr. Kane's brothers, but also his faithful friend and companion at the Pole, Lieutenant Martin they understood his name was.

The mail boat reached Cincinnati too late at night for Dr. Kane's body to be accorded due honor. So the remains were transferred to the steamer *Champion,* which dropped down stream to anchor, while the Kanes retired to their suite at the Burnet House. (At the Madison House, the Hon. E. W. McComas, Lieutenant Governor of Virginia, had arrived to tender Old Dominion's respects to Dr. Kane.)

At nine next morning a gun was fired to signal all was ready, and the *Champion* started slowly upstream, her bell tolling mournfully, her flag at half-mast. At Fifth Street wharf the coffin was loaded into a magnificent black hearse, drawn by four black horses, and the procession moved slowly forward on its winding route to the Little Miami railroad depot. As in Louisville, stores and many private houses were closed and shrouded. Here, however, Tom Kane was pleased to see, arches draped with American flags intertwined with black crepe had been thrown across the streets.

The array of carriages carrying state and local authorities, including the mayors of Newport and Covington, Kentucky, as well as Cincinnati, was more imposing, too. More carriages had been provided for Ohio and Cincinnati pioneers, and besides the usual volunteer companies, United States troops, under Major Heintzelman, were in the line of march. Mexican War veterans paraded in force, among them the Duquesne Greys from Pittsburgh, who had fought with such gallantry at the siege of Puebla. Cincinnati's very considerable German population was represented by the German Turners Association, marching in a stiff martial style.

The whole pageant was grandly solemn, but Tom Kane was bitter cold. The temperature was twenty above zero. Neither he nor John relished, either, being displayed in their sorrow to the thousands who thronged the streets. They had known the ordeal would be too hard on Mother, and were relieved when the Judge arrived to escort her to Philadelphia by the early train. Tom and John would find a way to escape, too. The newspaper reporters were more interested in Morton anyway.

In Columbus a member of the General Assembly called that body's attention to the arrival there late Saturday of the Kane funeral train. There was, of course, no train out until Monday. Where should the coffin lie in state on Sunday?

"Where else but here in our magnificent new capitol? No other edifice is large enough to hold the great heart of Elisha Kane!"

A resolution duly adopted, a joint Committee on Arrangements named, the committee members hustled to catch the one o'clock for Xenia, the best point to meet the funeral train. At Xenia they had to shove through the crowd at the station.

"Farmers," one of the Cincinnati escort committee said, "in town of a Saturday night and bound they're going to see Kane's coffin. Pa and Ma and every last one of the children."

By the hundreds they pushed through the funeral car. In vain the conductor tried to stem the tide. The train was two hours late leaving Xenia, and it was nearly midnight when the engineer whistled shrill warning to the chilled men waiting at Columbus Depot. The oldest of them shivered more at the engine's lonely whistling across Ohio farmland than at the cold, but his neighbor said cheerfully, "Almighty late, but she's still making up time."

Whispering, the men fell into line, the bayonets of the State Fencibles glistening in the moonlight. Other listening men had heard the whistle. Almost with one voice church bells all over town began to toll, and people long abed got up to light lamps or lean out darkened windows to watch men marching past to the beat of muffled drums.

"Funny to be seeing a parade in the middle of the night, ain't it, Pa?" young Orlando Smith said.

"Help thee to remember thee saw Dr. Kane's body. He died in the cause of humanity and knowledge, not in a bloody war," his Quaker father pointed out.

Seemed to Morton like there was as many Quakers in Ohio as Philadelphia, as he heard them thee-ing and thou-ing in the river of people that flowed past the coffin all that Sunday. Not that it was even a fourth Quakers. They was every sort of folks, and more of 'em than Columbus could hold. "Where they coming from?" he asked the captain of the Honor Guard.

"Every town and crossroads and county around here. That man with the gawky boy just up to the dais happens I know him. Will Smith, a Quaker farmer come over from Union County. You see the Governor at the memorial service this morning?"

The Governor was also in the cortege that conducted the coffin to the station Monday morning. The State Fencibles and the Columbus Cadets, headed by the Continental Pioneers, had the hearse in charge. Will Smith didn't like such a military display at the funeral of a hero of peace, he told young Orlando.

Except for the Quakers, everyone else considered Kane's funeral one of the grandest processions ever seen in Columbus. Mrs. McCrary, a great reader of novels, described it eloquently to her invalid mother-in-law.

"The wailing march for the dead, floating on the wintry blast, the gay plumes and glancing bayonets of the soldiery, the sable ensigns of mourning, thrown over the entire array, gave a most picturesque appearance to the slowly advancing column."

The elder woman, relishing every word, said, "It must have been a fine sight." What she hated most about being so poorly now was never getting out to a good funeral. "How was the train draped?"

"The car which carried the bier was tastefully festooned with black while the locomotive bore the Stars and Stripes, creped, and black streamers, Death's own pennons, floated from every part of the engine. Mother McCrary, the very smoke the locomotive emitted appeared another mourning streamer!"

"Black enough," the old lady agreed. "I can't get used, though, to a railway car serving for a hearse and hauling a body, jolting and thumping, clear across the country. But, then, the brave Doctor was an adventurous lad."

At Zanesville and other principal stations of the Central Ohio Railroad crowds stood uncovered while the train passed. Depots were draped in black. In Martinsburg, at six-thirty in the morning, a throng of Virginians waited, the committee from Baltimore with them, and two extra cars had to be put on for the accommodation of the many committees.

Baltimore's Camden Station was crowded, largely with women and children, waiting patiently for the train. The stationmaster couldn't get over how orderly they were. For so many children to wait without creating a din seemed unnatural, but then the noisiest were always the boys, and Kane was the boys' own hero. People kept saying how young Kane was and how small, so they probably took him to be their own age and size.

The Independent Greys were given the honor of escorting the coffin to the Maryland Institute. The Doctor had lectured there, and Baltimore people were proud to have known him in life—as others hadn't. When the Greys marched out of the station, that was the signal for the First Hose Company to begin swinging its bell, the other fire companies taking it up, all the fire bells in town clanging steadily from eleven to four. On Federal Hill the Eagle Artillery fired salutes the whole day, but the people, watching from sidewalks, windows, balconies, and rooftops as the procession passed, were profoundly quiet.

So was the endless line that filed through the West Hall of the institute, the shuffling feet the only sound. They were so mournful mute they affected Morton more than the crowds elsewhere.

On the Doctor's bier, the sword the Wistar Society gave him lay across its scabbard on a lambskin apron with a sprig of evergreen alongside, symbols of Masonry. There was no other decoration until an old gentleman tottered up to lay a wreath of white camellias on the coffin. Morton would have liked to tell the old gentleman they were the Doctor's favorite flower that he always sent Miss Maggie. In the big procession to the station, Morton, walking in his now established place right behind the coffin, carried that wreath carefully. It reminded him of happier days.

This time the streets were jam packed but the crowd was as quiet as before, though the Flying Artillery from Fort McHenry caused a little stir. Morton blew his nose hard when the seamen from the *Allegheny,* very smart in their uniforms, paraded by. Up to now the Army had everything its way, but here was a bit of the Navy.

At Elkton, the Wilmington committee entered the cars, but the train reached Wilmington too late to permit the public to come aboard. The crowd was so disgruntled that someone thought to pacify them by introducing Morton, "the only living man who has viewed the Open Sea, Lieutenant Morton, Dr. Kane's second in command." In one sentence the fellow got so many things wrong, Morton was thunderstruck, and bobbing jerkily at the cheering throng, declined to make any remarks. Still holding the camellias, he went to sit behind the coffin. He'd be crowded out of his place by the Doctor once they reached Philadelphia.

All along the way the crowds had grown bigger and bigger, but even so, Philadelphia surprised Morton. In Broad Street Station the Washington Greys and the First City Troop could hardly get the coffin through, and outside, Broad Street from Prime to Walnut was a living mass. Morton's heel throbbed, and the mob had made a muck of the street, but he walked again behind the hearse, ahead of all the notables, the mayor, the members of the select and common councils, the committeemen from a half-dozen cities (a new one from New York wore silver badges and carried batons of office), the heads of the Philadelphia city departments, members of the Corn Exchange, clerks of the councils, the police—except for those trying to handle the crowds—and the firemen. This lot was just escorting the body to Independence Hall. The real funeral procession would march tomorrow.

On the sidewalk a cluster of men and women were singing a hymn. Must be some church choir or singing society.

> "From Greenland's icy mountains
>   From India's coral strand
> Where Afric's sunny fountains
>   Roll down their golden sand–"

The Doctor certainly had been all them places.

In the Hall, when the body had been solemnly turned over to the honor guard and the officials were disbanding, Morton stood trying to think what to do. He'd no mind to go to the Kane house and be treated as a servant again. The chairman of the committee on arrangements was busy introducing the Baltimore committee to the New York committee. When those gentleman had shaken hands all around and gone off together to their quarters at the Girard House, Morton got his ear.

"The Kane Expedition survivors? Staying at Webb's Union Hotel, I believe. Yes, that's right, Lieutenant Morton." He was still promoted, Morton grinned to note, as he limped along to Arch Street.

Not all of them were there, but enough of those who mattered to make it a real reunion. Just as Morton arrived, Henry Goodfellow called to see how his old messmates fared, and they drank to the Doctor's memory. With the scarred crew of them Morton wasn't ashamed to choke up. Even Brooks cried when he heard the Captain had spasms like the dogs and could only move his eyes at the end.

"Must of drove him near crazy, with him always up and doing."

Bonsall asked about Tood-la, thinking he ought to be in the parade the way they usually had a dead general's horse. Goodfellow said he'd read in the paper some lumberman in the Allegheny Mountains had him.

"Got rid of him in a hurry, didn't they?" Morton said.

A note from Tom Kane–"a dispatch, really, Tom is marshaling his forces so efficiently," Helen Patterson said–informed Elisha's cousins that Independence Hall would be closed at eleven in the morning to allow the family time to pay their respects to the body before the cortege started. They would not have to brave the dense throng that since yesterday had been pouring through the old hall.

"Go down Chestnut Street, dear," Helen urged Dr. Patterson. "Arch is in the line of march and will be draped in that horrid cheap black."

So was Chestnut. Orleans House was conspicuous with broad bands of stuff, relieved by white rosettes, across its front. Its balcony covered in black flaunted in white letters the legend

PHILADELPHIA MOURNS AN ILLUSTRIOUS SON
AND THE WORLD
A MARTYR TO SCIENCE AND HUMANITY

More white rosettes bordered this. Along the lower floor of another building gigantic mourning female figures illustrated the theme:

SCIENCE WEEPS, HUMANITY WEEPS, THE WORLD WEEPS.

"Really!" Mrs. Patterson cringed at this vulgar display.

The scene on Walnut Street so shocked and frightened her that she did not cry. There the mob, angered when the doors of Independence Hall were closed in their faces, broke through a cordon of straining police. She saw women with children in arms in the struggling, screaming mass. Some fell and had their clothes torn, others were trampled. The Pattersons' carriage was nearly overturned, and it took her some minutes to compose herself.

Drawn up on the main avenue of Independence Square, waiting to receive Elisha's coffin, was the most enormous and elaborate catafalque she had ever seen. "Ly was such a little man," she whispered sadly as they inspected the car. It was at least twelve feet long by five wide, so big for Elisha. " 'A fiery soul which, working out its way, Fretted the pigmy body to decay.' "

Rich drapery concealed its low wheels. On its four corners upright spears with gold heads were entwined with the American, British, Spanish, and Danish flags creped.

"Greenland is a Danish possession," Dr. Patterson explained.

Above the center of the car was a dome of black with white stripes, ornamented with white stars and cording and lined with white silk. Its team of six glistening black horses was in charge of a groom all in black. Only the handsome team, snorting and stamping, seemed fitting. Before Elisha became so weak, he used to relieve the tedium of desk work with a hard gallop.

In the Hall, Aunt Jeannie, heavily veiled and carrying a nosegay of white flowers, leaned hard on the Judge's arm. Poor Uncle John had aged so this last year. Bessie's face was red and swollen, and young Pat appeared stricken, but Tom and John conducted themselves with an aplomb Helen resented. Aunt Lieper was wearing a monumental black turban topped with a white plume. Though they had been allies in the campaign to win Elisha some happiness, Helen did not go to speak to Mrs. Lieper. Instead, she wondered, where she stood to one side, what Maggie Fox was doing this sad March day.

The State House bell struck noon, the signal for the military, drawn up on the south side of Walnut, to receive the coffin, borne by a detachment of the United States sailors and attended by the pallbearers. Henry Grinnell, George Peabody, Major Biddle, James Brown, Esquire, and Bishop Potter, a connection of Mrs. Walter's, were among them. Amid the tolling of all the bells in Philadelphia the cortege moved forward, the survivors of Dr. Kane's expedition walking alongside his coffin with the flag of the *Advance*.

Up Walnut to Seventeenth, Seventeenth to Arch, Arch to the Second Presbyterian Church on Seventh. There they halted briefly, while the bier was arranged on an elevation in front of the church, the survivors standing beside it, the pallbearers in a semicircle at the rear. Then the vast procession moved past the body: dignitaries (governors or lieutenant governors of five states), military and naval men, city, state, and federal officers, representatives of foreign governments, faculties and students of several colleges, Sons of St. George and the Albion Society bearing the Union Jack creped, the Scots' Thistle Society, the Hibernians, the St. Andrews Society, on and on they came.

Morton had never been so tired. After the rescue of Brooks's party, was he so tuckered?

Still they came, walking slowly to the dead march beating on the winter air: the members of the American Philosophical Society, of the Academy of Natural Sciences, the Wardens of the Port, the Scott Legion, officers and workmen from the United States Mint, the Philadelphia County Medical Society, members and ex-members of Congress, the Music Fund Society, and the Ancient Order of Druids.

The sixth division of the parade consisted of simple citizens in charge of an assistant marshal named Lafayette Baker.

They were still filing past long after one-thirty when the body was taken into the church, where none but ticket holders could enter. The church music was so fine, the Judge, a charter member of the Music Fund Society, must have arranged the program. It opened with Mozart's "I Heard a Voice from Heaven" and closed with Handel's "Unveil Thy Bosom, Faithful Tomb."

When the coffin at last reached Laurel Hill and the Kanes' Egyptian mausoleum, very like Moyamensing Prison in style, Mrs. Patterson noticed Tom, with a puzzled frown, remove from the bier the lovely wreath of camellias which had lain on it the whole time. Curious, she read the attached card. It was no official wreath nor from any of the family. Liking it, one of Ly's crew must have put it there. The card said simply:

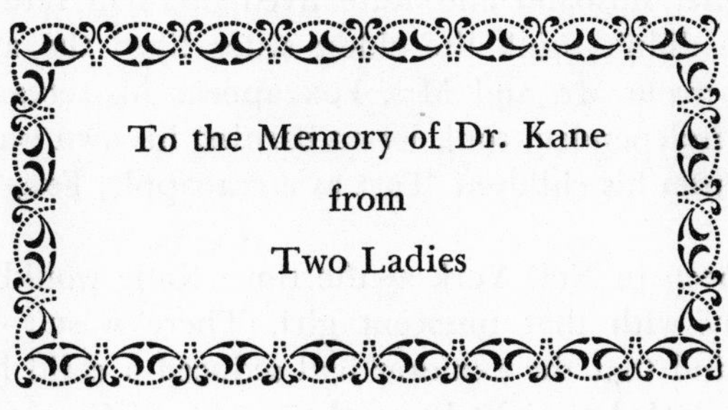
To the Memory of Dr. Kane
from
Two Ladies

EPILOGUE

THE ODD THING was that Greeley had been thinking about Kane just a few minutes before, though the fellow was seldom mentioned nowadays, the War had created so many new heroes. Perhaps it was the snow draping New York in an Arctic mantle that had reminded him of the explorer. The blizzard was such that he couldn't hope to reach Chappaqua after being kept so late at the office. On foot he set out for his house in town where Mrs. Fox would have his room ready and prepare a simple breakfast for him.

She and her husband and Kate lived there in return for such services. He didn't think the eldest sister liked the arrangement, thinking it made Mr. and Mrs. Fox appear his servants, but old Fox was an independent soul, set on earning his own way, accepting no charity from his children. Tart as a crabapple, Fox, but Greeley liked him.

Had he been in New York at the time, Kane would never have had his way with that innocent girl. There wasn't a doubt in Greeley's mind that the explorer had seduced a child half his age, and hero though he might be to the world, to Greeley and a few others he was a cad and a scoundrel, and no *nil nisi bonum* nonsense about it.

As a sop to Mother Fox, Kane had gone through some common law hugger-mugger that some friends of the Foxes believed did give Maggie a legal claim on Kane's estate. (It was considerable enough. He heard Kane's book made $65,000 the first year after publication.) They had encouraged her to file a suit in the Philadelphia Orphans' Court for dower on the widow's part.

But it was Kane's scandalous letters that, in Greeley's opinion, forced his family to settle out of court. The threat of their being published had persuaded Brigadier General Thomas Kane, commander of the famed Bucktails, to pay the girl a little money. Blackmail, if you like, but with a legal and respectable cast to it.

Dr. Bayard, for instance, had been named trustee to hold the letters under seal.

In return, Kate told him, the Kanes agreed to pay Maggie the interest on an annuity equal to her dower, though they weren't always regular in their payments. (Old Judge Kane was dead or he would have seen they behaved as legally bound. Always a stickler for the letter of the law, Judge Kane.)

"She has a hard time, Uncle Horace, but she won't rap. Because of her vow to Elisha. She just lives for his memory," Kate had said.

Styling herself "Margaret Fox Kane," the few times Greeley had seen her the waiflike young woman wore full mourning, though Kane had been dead for years. Her tiny flat, Kate described as crowded with mementoes of the explorer, a regular shrine to him. Morbid, Greeley felt, and wished Kate wouldn't stay there so often. But he could hardly speak out against such natural kindness.

As he turned onto East Nineteenth Street, head down into the wind, he almost collided with a woman. Muttering apologies, he plodded on, thinking New York's poor lived by entirely different standards than her middle class or her rich. No well-to-do woman would be allowed out unescorted at this hour in the best weather, while in such a storm—

There had been something familiar about that slight, veiled figure. Greeley stopped in his tracks. Then, swinging around, he lumbered back to the corner. A block ahead, the woman struggled on, stopping once or twice to peer through the snow as if she had lost her way. Sure as he lived that was Maggie Fox!

"Maggie! Maggie!" he bellowed above the wind.

The little figure wavered, almost fell against a wall, but catching herself, turned slowly, stood motionless a minute, and then darted toward him, only to stop halfway and bury her face in her arms. When he came up she was sobbing desperately.

"Maggie, it's all right. I'll take you home."

"I thought you were—someone I knew!"

"You do know me. It's Horace Greeley, child. Whatever are you doing on the streets at this hour?"

"Searching—searching—" She swung her head back and forth. Angrily she pulled her arm out of his grasp. "You let me go! Don't stop me! I can't stop now— The snow might stop!" She ran, not in the direction of her little flat.

"Maggie!" Puffing, he ran after. "You must go home!"

She ran faster and fell. When he caught up, and raised her to her feet, he thought her out of her head, delirious with fever. Living alone, there was no one to prevent her wandering out if she fell ill. Where, in heaven's name, were all the cabs? Never around when they were needed, and he must get this girl home. It wasn't healthy for him, either, a man his age, to be roaming around in a storm.

Maggie stood there crying, her skirt all over snow to her knees, her veil, wet with tears, sticking to her face in front while in back it streamed into the wind. They were near a street lamp, and he pulled her firmly toward it, to wipe her face and tie her veil under her chin before the wind blew her bonnet away.

"Let me go, please, please! I may miss him."

"Maggie, you are not meeting a man at this hour?" Had she fallen on really evil ways, a young woman living unprotected?

She wavered, this time toward him, lurching against Greeley's breast, and the reek of alcohol on her was strong enough to smell in spite of the wind. She was not delirious. She was drunk.

"Miss Fox, you have been drinking!"

"I'm Mrs. Kane," she corrected with attempted dignity, "and all I drank was a little champagne, a harmless bever—bever—"

"Beverage," he concluded impatiently. "Drinking in solitude," he accused. The most dangerous type of tippling!

"Oh, no! With Kate. A little champagne with my sister Kate. When it began to snow, I had to go. Have to go now. Before the snow stops."

So Kate was drinking with her, a pair of children in their cups! Did Mr. and Mrs. Fox know what their daughters did? "You're going with me. Your mother can find a spare bed in my house for you until you're warm. And sober."

"No! No! I have to search, you stupid man!" She jerked frantically.

"What are you looking for in such a storm?" He would humor her. "Perhaps I can help." Pretending to help, he might get her home before they both caught their death of cold.

"You can't help me!" She raised really beautiful eyes to smile scornfully at him. "Don't you understand? I'm looking for Elisha. I always find him in the snow!"

DATE DUE

GAYLORD

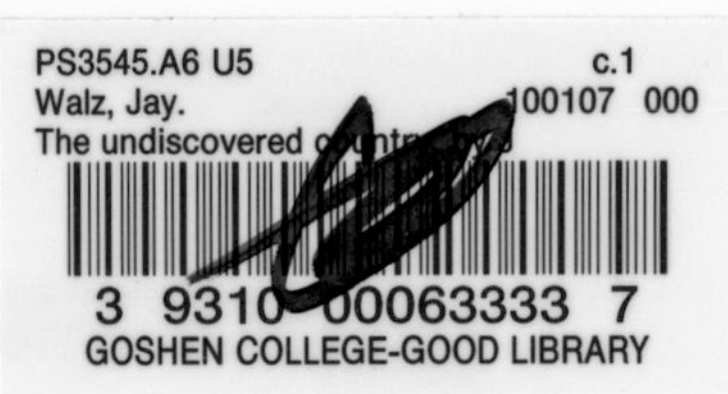